CRIMSON PETALS, IRON CHAINS

THE KREMØTOA CODEX

BOOK TWO

SAEKO KURENAIHANA

For permission requests, inquiries or questions, **scan the QR-Code below** to go to the Contact Form. If the link breaks, go to https://kurenaihanabooks.com/contact-me/ and fill out the web-form.

3rd Edition | 2026

CONTENTS

CONTENT WARNING & INFORMATION

The *Kremøtoa Codex* series is an adult science fantasy saga intended for mature, adult audiences. Reader discretion is advised for those who may be sensitive to themes that will be listed in every book's front matter. This book, *Crimson Petals, Iron Chains*, prominently features these themes:

- **A Central F/F/F/F Polyamorous Romance:** The story continues to develop the F/F/F/F polyamorous relationship that is central to the main characters' journey and the overall plot. **It remains the central, emotional core of the entire saga.**
- **Found Family Under Siege:** The narrative tests the intimate bonds of a found family, as Ada and her companions must protect their home and each other from direct, personal threats and betrayals.
- **Escalating Political Revolution:** The stakes of the revolution intensify dramatically, moving from

theoretical planning to covert warfare, including espionage, conspiracy, and assassination attempts.
- **LitRPG Mechanics:** The series continues to blend its science fantasy elements with the progression and game-like mechanics of the LitRPG genre.
- **The Ethics of Power and Responsibility** relating to control of others' bodily autonomy.

Complex Adult Themes: The book is intended for mature readers (18+) as it delves into thematically complex content, including:

- ***Political Philosophy & Betrayal***
- ***Existentialism and Systemic Collapse***
- ***Trauma relating to consent and paranoia***

Please be aware that the story and its themes will mature and intensify as the series progresses. In this book, *Crimson Petals, Iron Chains,* expect literary scenes depicting:

- **Graphic violence and injury**
- **Assassination attempts and paranoia**
- **Intense psychological distress and panic attacks**
- **Explicit adult literary content**
- **Strong language**

As this is the full intended edition of the novel, explicit scenes have a warning at the top of each chapter. Please take note of any trigger warnings.

PREVIOUSLY, IN THE KREMØTOA CODEX...

Ada Lynx, a brilliant programmer from Earth, awakens in Kremøtoa—a world she created, now a hyper-realistic, full-immersion world. Trapped within the code, she discovers she possesses [Admin] privileges, granting her gød-like abilities to manipulate the very fabric of her new reality.

Her arrival places her in the crosshairs of the tyrannical Ehxcehl Empire, a brutal regime that crushes dissent and controls the continent with an iron fist. Ada's power makes her both a messiah and a target. Her journey for survival leads her to three extraordinary women, each a refugee from the Empire's cruelty.

Sera Valerius, a disgraced Imperial Knight-Commander, is a warrior of unmatched skill and unwavering honor, driven by a fierce desire to protect the innocent. **Korina Tel**, a prodigy scholar and inventor, wields knowledge as her weapon, her genius suppressed by the very institution she sought to serve. And **Erita Systema**, a cynical spymaster with a hidden heart of gold, navigates the underworld's shadows, fighting her own secret war against the system that wronged her.

United by their shared enemy and a budding, undeniable bond, the four women form a revolutionary cell. From a hidden sanctuary, they begin to chip away at the Empire's foundations, rescuing its victims and gathering allies. But their every move is watched. A mysterious and cunning figure known only as 'The Alchemist' anticipates their plans, countering them with deadly precision and demonstrating a terrifying understanding of Kremøtoa's deepest secrets.

As Ada, Sera, Korina, and Erita secure a new, permanent base of operations—a safe haven for their growing rebellion—their hope is shattered in an instant. A gift from a supposed ally is revealed to be a trap. A single blue rose, laced with a fatal neurotoxin, nearly claims Sera's life. The attack is not just an attempt on their lives, but a chilling message from The Alchemist: *I see you. You are not safe. I am always one step ahead.*

The book ends with the four women shaken but resolute, their sanctuary already compromised. They now understand that their fight is not just against an empire, but against a ghost in the machine, an enemy whose reach seems limitless and whose motives remain shrouded in terrifying mystery. Their revolution has begun, but the true war is only just beginning.

CHAPTER 1

A TEST OF LOYALTY

The acrid scent of almonds filled the air, a phantom taste on Korina's tongue. Her data-slate, *Obsidian*, pulsed with a cold, clinical light against her forearm. The schematic of the neurotoxin still shimmered there, a deadly blueprint etched in flickering crimson. *Immediate Fatality.* The words scrolled across the display, a stark reminder of how close she had come to losing Sera. Her breath hitched in her throat, tears blurring the sharp lines of the data.

"Korina?" Sera's voice, muffled against the rough wooden floor, broke through the white noise of panic. "What in the Void...?"

"Poison!" Korina choked out, the word raw and ragged. She fumbled to project a holographic replay of the scan, the image of the blue rose dissolving into black dust hanging in the air between them. "Willem...it was a trap..."

Sera pushed herself up, her golden eyes wide with disbelief. She brushed a stray lock of red hair from her face, leaving a smudge of dirt on her cheek. A small cut, barely visible, marked her temple where she had hit the floor.

"But...why?" Sera's voice, usually so sharp and confident, was laced with confusion, her ears still ringing from the fall. "Willem pledged his support. He swore by Argent's Light he was with us."

"The Alchemist...it has to be," Korina repeated, her voice finding a sliver of its usual analytical edge. "They're always one step ahead. Always watching. They knew...they knew about the alliance." She scrolled through the data stream from *Obsidian*, her fingers moving with a nervous, frantic energy. "The toxin...it's unlike anything I've ever seen. Engineered for maximum lethality, zero trace. It's..."

"Deadly," Sera finished, a grim understanding settling in her eyes. "Void," she breathed out. "And nearly invisible to standard scans or even a visual glance. I wouldn't have..." She trailed off, her gaze fixed on the dissipating dust motes.

"Obsidian caught it!" Korina said, clutching the slate tighter, the smooth metal a cold comfort against her skin. "A sub-particulate anomaly in the pigment. Barely perceptible. If I hadn't heard the alert..." She shuddered, the image of Sera collapsing, lifeless, flashing through her mind.

"You saved me, Korina." Sera's hand tightened on her back, a warm, solid presence. "*Argent's light*, you saved me."

Korina finally looked up, meeting Sera's gaze. The fear was still there, raw and pulsing, but now mixed with a different kind of intensity. The nearness of death had stripped away the layers of polite distance, leaving something exposed and vulnerable. "I...I almost lost you," she whispered, her voice thick with unshed tears.

Sera leaned closer, her hand moving up to cup Korina's cheek, her thumb brushing away a tear. "But you didn't." Her voice was low and soft, a stark contrast to her usual command tone. "I'm here."

Across the warehouse, Ada watched the scene unfold, her breath catching in her throat. One moment, Sera stood, admiring the rose; the next, Korina launched herself across the room, a blur of violet and desperation. The thud of bodies hitting the floor echoed through the cavernous space, followed by a stunned silence. *What in the Void happened...?* Ada thought, her heart hammering against her ribs.

The initial shock gave way to a horrifying realization. *Poison... it's dissipating.* The thought slammed into her like a physical blow, a cold dread gripping her stomach. She saw through her Admin-view the lingering toxic residue, shimmering faintly in the air, a deadly cloud spreading slowly outwards, towards where Korina and Sera were laying. She reacted instantly.

"**[QUARANTINE],**" Ada commanded, her voice stern but audible. Her Admin powers manifested as a faint violet shimmer, a ripple of energy that enveloped the black dust and the poisoned needle, rendering them inert before collapsing them into nothingness and straight into her *Matākyasshu* inventory.

Korina was sobbing, her body shaking with relief and shock. Ada rushed to her side, pulling her into a comforting embrace. Korina clung to her, her small frame trembling against Ada's. "I almost...I almost..." she stammered, unable to finish the sentence.

"Shhh," Ada murmured, stroking Korina's hair, her own heart still pounding. "You saved her. You were brilliant." She felt a surge of protectiveness, a fierce tenderness for this brilliant, vulnerable woman who had just saved one of their own. She held Korina tighter, whispering reassurances, grounding her in the solid reality of her embrace.

Erita, ever practical, helped a shaken Sera to her feet. "You alright, Sera?" she asked, her voice laced with concern, checking Sera for injuries. Sera nodded, her face pale, her golden eyes wide with lingering shock. She touched her temple gingerly, wincing slightly.

"Fine," Sera said, her voice a little shaky. "Just...Void. A bit rattled." She glanced at the spot where the rose had been, a shiver running down her spine. "That was *too* close."

"Too close," Erita agreed, her gaze fixed on the empty space, her golden eyes narrowed in thought. "This changes things." She turned to Ada, her expression grim. "The Alchemist, or someone knows; they know where we are, and they're not playing games."

Ada met Erita's gaze, her own expression hardening. The playful warmth she had felt moments before with Korina vanished, replaced by a cold, calculating focus. "No," she said, her voice quiet but firm. "They're not." She released Korina, gently but firmly, her purple eyes blazing with a newfound determination.

Erita's fingers flew across her own data-slate, a storm of commands scrolling across the screen. Her face was a mask of cold fury, her golden eyes narrowed to slits. *Trace the courier. Delivery origin. Any scrap of data.* The network, usually a comforting web of whispers and secrets, was a silent, mocking void. The courier, a low-level guildsman from The Azure Rose, had vanished like smoke. His digital footprint, scrubbed clean. The delivery order itself? A ghost in the machine. Deleted, not just altered, but completely erased. *Impossible*, she thought, a knot of dread tightening in her stomach. *Unless...*

The thought hit her like a punch to the gut, a cold, sickening realization. Only one person knew they would be expecting a 'delivery'—and they hadn't even expected it. Only one person could have intercepted it, replaced it with a poisoned replica, and erased all trace of the deception. *Willem,* she thought, the name a bitter taste in her mouth. The alliance, the trust, the hope...all a carefully constructed lie. Erita swore under her breath, a string of harsh curses. "Willem played us," she said, her voice low and dangerous. "That sly, withered old fox. He played us *all.*"

Sera's hand tightened around the hilt of her blade, the familiar weight a small comfort in the storm of fury brewing inside her. Willem. That doddering, parchment-skinned *liar.* She had looked him in the eye, seen the weariness, the quiet dignity she'd mistaken for genuine concern. Fool. She'd been a *fool.* "Erita's right," Sera spat, the words sharp as shards of ice. "That old snake set us up." Her voice, usually so controlled, vibrated with barely suppressed rage. "We need to move. *Now.* Before he sends another 'gift'."

"Retribution. Swift and decisive." Sera's gaze locked onto Ada's, the violet depths flickering with uncertainty. "He almost killed Korina. He almost killed *me.* We can't let him get away with this." Her hand instinctively went to the faint bruise on her arm where the concrete of the warehouse had brushed her skin. A phantom pain, a chilling reminder of how close she had come to death.

Ada watched the exchange play out, a flicker of detachment in her violet eyes. Erita, a whirlwind of barely controlled fury, tapping out her message with the force of a blacksmith hammering steel. Sera, radiating a cold, simmering rage, her hand never leaving the hilt of her blade. It was a stark contrast to her own calm, analytical approach. She saw the situation not as a betrayal, but as a puzzle. A new variable introduced into the system, a challenge to be overcome.

"Eri," Ada said, her voice a calm counterpoint to the storm of anger in the room. "A direct confrontation would be...suboptimal." She paused, considering the most efficient course of action. "We need information. Leverage. A direct assault on The Azure Rose would be messy and inefficient." She gestured to the data-slate in Erita's hand. "Use the channel *he* provided. Demand a meeting. Let's see how *he* responds."

Erita's golden eyes narrowed. "Meet with him? After what he tried to pull?" She practically snarled the words. "Void, I'd rather gut him where he stands." But even as she said it, a flicker of calculation crossed her face. Ada had a point. They needed to understand the *why*. The motivation behind the betrayal—if it *was* even Willem. "Fine," she conceded, her fingers already dancing across the keys of her data-slate. "But if he tries anything, I'll gut him like a Korsari carp, and sell his bones to a witch."

The message she sent was short, sharp, and dripping with accusation. "*We know about the rose. Explain yourself. Meet. Now.*" She added the coordinates of the private teahouse where they'd first forged their alliance, a neutral, discreet location tucked away in the labyrinthine heart of Port Dominus. The response came almost immediately, a flurry of confused and alarmed text from Willem. "*What? What rose? I don't understand. Meet? Of course. I'll be there.*" Erita read aloud.

Ada raised an eyebrow. Interesting. Willem's response was... unexpected. Genuine confusion? Or a masterful performance? She couldn't tell. Either way, it presented an opportunity. A chance to gather more data, to analyze the situation, to understand the motivations behind Willem's actions. "Good," she said, a hint of a smile playing on her lips. "Let's go pay our dear Master Willem a visit."

Erita tucked her data-slate away, her expression unreadable.

"Just so we're clear," she said, her voice low and dangerous. "If this is a trap...I'm not kidding about selling his bones..." Sera, standing beside her, simply nodded after glancing at her with a mildly concerned look—her hand still gripping the hilt of her blade. The message was clear. They were going to this meeting prepared for anything.

Korina pushed herself up, her legs shaky but firm. "I'm going too." Her voice, though quiet, held a surprising steel.

Erita turned, her golden eyes narrowed. "No. This is too dangerous. You almost—"

"Don't—" Korina interrupted, her voice rising, a tremor of raw emotion shaking her words. "Don't tell me to stay behind! I'm as much a part of this...this *assassination attempt* as any of you..." Tears welled in her violet eyes, but her gaze remained fixed on Erita, unwavering. "I analyzed the toxin. I know its composition, its delivery method, its effects—" Her voice cracked, the technical details blurring through the rising tide of fear and anger. "If-if it's necessary to...to discuss its specifics, I can provide them. I-I can—" Her voice trailed off, a silent plea in her eyes.

Don't shut me out. Not again.

Ada crossed the room in two strides and pulled Korina into a tight embrace. The warmth of Ada's body, the strength of her arms, was a comforting anchor in the storm of Korina's emotions. "Of course you're coming, *Rina*," Ada murmured, her voice soft against Korina's hair. "We wouldn't leave you behind." She pulled back slightly, her violet eyes filled with a gentle reassurance. "We're a team. We face this together."

Rina. The name echoed in Korina's mind, a soft, unfamiliar sound that sent a ripple of warmth through her. No one had ever called her Rina. Not her parents, not her friends, not even her childhood bullies. It was Ada's name for her, a secret, intimate sound that belonged only to them. The realization hit her with the force of a physical blow, a wave of emotion that threatened to overwhelm her. She buried her face in Ada's shoulder, her body trembling. Tears, hot and thick, streamed down her cheeks, but they weren't tears of sadness or fear. They were tears of... something else. Something she couldn't quite name. Relief? Gratitude? *Love*? Perhaps all three, tangled together in a knot of overwhelming emotion.

Ada's scent enveloped her, a comforting blend of ozone, Ada's normal musk and something subtly floral, like the first bloom of spring after a long winter. It grounded her, pulled her back from the swirling vortex of her own thoughts. *Rina.* She whispered the name to herself, testing its shape on her tongue. It felt...right. A perfect fit, like a key sliding into a lock. In Ada's arms, surrounded by her warmth and strength, the fear and uncertainty that had been gnawing at her began to recede. The world, for a brief, precious moment, felt safe. Solid. *Real.*

Korina nodded, the tears still clinging to her lashes, but a newfound resolve hardening her gaze. She took a deep breath, steadying herself. *Together.* The word resonated within her, a spark of warmth in the cold dread that had gripped her since the poisoned rose. She wasn't alone. Not anymore. She had Ada, Sera, Erita. A team. A family, forged in the fires of shared danger and unwavering loyalty. And together, they would face whatever Willem, or anyone else, threw at them.

Erita sighed, running a hand through her short, golden hair. "Fine," she conceded, her voice softening slightly. "But stay close. And if things go south..." She glanced at Sera, a silent communication passing between them. *Protect her.*

Sera nodded, her hand resting on the hilt of her blades, a reassuring presence at Korina's side. "We'll keep you safe," she said, her voice firm. "Don't worry, Rina."

Korina shot Sera a disdainful, tear-stained look. "I appreciate it, Sera," she mumbled into Ada's shoulder, "But 'Rina' is Ada's...to use..." She didn't elaborate, just hugged Ada tighter, a silent possessive gesture that didn't go unnoticed by the others. A small laugh escaped Sera's lips, the tension momentarily broken. Even Erita cracked a smile, a rare flicker of warmth in her usually cynical golden eyes. Ada chuckled, a low rumble in her chest that vibrated against Korina, sending a shiver down her spine. The shared moment of levity, a brief respite in the storm of danger and uncertainty, solidified something within Korina. A sense of belonging, of connection, of shared purpose that transcended the fear and the looming threat. They were a team, bound not just by circumstance, but by something deeper. Something...real.

With a shared look of grim determination, the four women left the warehouse, stepping out into the chaotic labyrinth of Port Dominus. The setting suns cast long, distorted shadows across the narrow alleyways, painting the ramshackle buildings in hues of orange and violet. The air, thick with the smells of salt, fish, and desperation, crackled with an undercurrent of tension, a prelude to the confrontation that awaited them. As they made their way towards the teahouse, Korina couldn't shake the feeling that they were walking into the heart of a carefully constructed trap. But this time, she wasn't alone. She had her team. Her family. And together, they would face whatever lay ahead.

The Obsidian Mirror teahouse lived up to its name, as always. Dark, polished surfaces reflected flickering candlelight, creating an illusion of depth and shadows. The air, heavy with the cloying sweetness of sandalwood, felt thick enough to choke on. Ada sat beside Korina, her hand resting reassuringly on the scholar's thigh under the table. Across from them, Master Willem, his face etched with confusion and a growing unease, stared at the inert blue rose lying on the table between them.

"Explain this," Erita snapped, her voice sharp as a honed blade. She jabbed a finger at the remnants of the flower stem, her golden eyes blazing with barely contained fury. "This little beauty almost killed two of our own."

"That's absurd!" Willem exclaimed, his voice rising in indignant protest. "I would never—"

"Save it," Sera cut him off, her tone laced with cold steel. "We have proof. This poison, this method...it all points back to you." She leaned forward, her gaze unwavering. "Why, Willem? Why betray us?"

"Proof?" Willem's voice cracked. He picked up the rose, turning it gingerly in his trembling fingers. The vibrant blue petals remaining, now dull and lifeless, seemed to mock him. "I sent a gift, yes. A token of goodwill...a single, perfect *white* rose. I thought it would be a nice gesture for such lovely ladies...Not—this." His eyes, wide with dawning horror, darted between the four women. "By Argent's Light...I've been framed..."

A cold dread washed over him. He was trapped, caught in a web of deceit he hadn't even seen being spun. On one side, the phantom of the Alchemist, whose reach seemed to extend everywhere, unseen and unstoppable; on the other, these revolutionaries—powerful, unpredictable, and clearly furious. His carefully constructed world of alliances and favors crumbled around him like dry leaves.

"Then who?" Korina whispered, her voice barely audible. She clutched Obsidian, the data-slate's cool surface a small comfort in the rising tension.

Erita's laughter, sharp and devoid of humor, filled the tense silence. "Does it matter? The Alchemist is playing us all. And right now," she leaned in, her gaze fixed on Willem, "you look awfully guilty."

Willem's eyes pleaded with them, searching for a flicker of understanding, a sliver of trust in the swirling vortex of suspicion. "You must believe me! I sent a beautiful *white* rose. A symbol of peace, of our alliance...I swear it!" Tears, soft but true, started welling in the old man's weary eyes.

Ada watched, her violet eyes not just seeing, but *processing*. Willem's micro-expressions, the minute fluctuations in his heart rate, the subtle tremor in his hands—all data points in a complex algorithm of truth. He wasn't lying. The Alchemist hadn't just tried to kill them—they'd aimed a poisoned dart at the heart of their fragile alliance. A shiver ran down Ada's spine. This wasn't brute force; it was surgical, precise, and designed to shatter their trust before it could solidify.

"Enough," Ada said, her voice cutting through the tension like a laser. The room went silent, all eyes turning to her. She looked at Sera, whose hand still rested on the hilt of her blade, and then at

Erita, whose cynical gaze remained fixed on Willem. "He's telling the truth."

"What?" Sera's hand tightened on her sword, her brow furrowed in disbelief. "But the poison—"

"*Was* meant for us," Ada finished, her gaze sweeping over the three women. "And the rose...a white rose, a symbol of peace...was meant for us too—to be a bridge, not a weapon." She turned back to Willem, her expression softening. "Master Willem, I believe you."

Willem's shoulders slumped, the tension slowly draining from his face. He looked at Ada, his eyes filled with a profound gratitude. "Thank you," he whispered, his voice hoarse with emotion. "Thank you for seeing...for understanding."

Erita scoffed, a flicker of doubt still lingering in her golden eyes. "So, if he didn't send it, who did? And how did they know about our meeting?"

Ada's gaze turned inward, her mind racing. The Alchemist's knowledge was unsettling, almost as if they were omnipresent, a ghost in the machine. "They're watching us," she murmured, more to herself than to the others. "They know our every move."

"The courier," Ada said, her voice low and thoughtful. "He didn't use our names, never even asked for a signature—he practically thrust the box at Sera and bolted...very quickly too...like he was eager to be rid of it." She paused, piecing together the fragments of memory. "Did anyone get a good look at him? Anything unusual?"

"He had a limp," Korina offered, her brow furrowed in concentration. "Distinct. I remember thinking it odd for a courier, a profession that demands a certain...agility." She tapped a finger on Obsidian's screen, a frown playing on her lips. "I could try to reconstruct his image, but without a clear visual, the rendering will be fragmented at best."

"No need," Ada said, a grim realization dawning in her violet eyes. "It doesn't matter who he *was*. What matters is who he *worked* for." She turned to Willem, her expression hardening. "Someone within your ranks, Master Willem. A mole. They intercepted your gift, swapped it for the poisoned rose, and sent their own operative to deliver it. They knew about this meeting. They knew Sera would be the one to open the box."

Willem's face paled, the blood draining from his cheeks. The implications were staggering. A traitor in his midst, undermining his authority, twisting his gestures of peace into weapons of war. He felt a cold dread creep into his heart, the chilling realization that his ship had sprung leaks he didn't even know how to plug, or where to begin.

Korina squeezed Ada's hand, her violet eyes filled with unwavering faith. "I believe you, Ada. Willem's innocent—there's no doubt in my mind."

"*Argent's light*," Willem breathed, the words a hushed prayer. The weight of betrayal pressed down on him, heavy and suffocating. A traitor within the Azure Rose. The thought was a bitter pill, a poison more potent than any the Alchemist could concoct. He looked at Ada, his eyes filled with a newfound resolve. "You're right. We have a common enemy now." His voice, though still shaken, held a steely edge. "This...*ghost*...that hides in my guild's shadow. We will hunt it down...together."

"Good," Erita said, a predatory gleam in her golden eyes. "Because I have a particular set of skills. Skills that make me a nightmare for people like this." A slow, dangerous smile spread across her lips, before another thought crossed her mind.

"One more thing, Willem," Erita added, her voice laced with pragmatic steel. "From now on, your couriers use a code phrase. *Without* being asked." She leaned forward, her golden eyes glinting in the candlelight. "Something only your people and *us* would know. It'll save us all a lot of...unpleasantries."

Willem nodded, his face grim. "A wise precaution. I'll implement it immediately." The icy fact that someone within his organization was actively working against brewed a cold anger burning in his gut—a slow, simmering rage that promised retribution.

"Good," Erita said, a curt nod punctuating her words.

Ada nodded, her violet eyes blazing with a cold fire. "First, we need information, Erita. Everything you have on your couriers, their routes, their contacts—anything that could lead us to the imposter." She turned to Korina, her gaze softening. "Rina, can you work with Master Willem's scribes? Cross-reference their records with any anomalies you can find in the city's data streams. Movement logs, security breaches, anything out of the ordinary."

Korina nodded, her fingers already dancing across Obsidian's surface. "I'll begin immediately. The Veritas Archives trained me for this, finding patterns in chaos is my specialty." A spark of intellectual excitement flickered in her violet eyes. This wasn't just a hunt for a mole—it was a puzzle, a complex equation waiting to be solved.

"Sera," Ada continued, her voice sharp and decisive. "Secure the perimeter. I want a tight watch on the warehouse, day and night. No one gets in or out without our say-so."

Sera's hand instinctively went to the hilts of her twin blades, a grim satisfaction in her eyes. "Consider it done. Anyone tries anything funny, they'll be dealing with me."

"And me," Erita added, a wicked glint in her golden eyes. "I'll set up a few...*surprises* for any unwelcome guests."

Willem watched them, a flicker of admiration in his weary eyes. These women, these revolutionaries, they were a force to be reckoned with. He'd initially underestimated them, seen them as pawns in a larger game. Now, he saw them for what they truly were: the spark that could ignite a fire that would consume the rot that plagued their world. He stood up straighter, his voice firm. "I'll gather my most trusted men. We'll sweep the city, leave no stone unturned. This traitor will be found."

As Willem turned to leave, Ada stopped him. "One more thing, Master Willem." Her voice was low, almost conspiratorial. "The Alchemist knows too much. They're watching us, listening to us. We need to assume every communication channel is compromised." She paused, her gaze meeting his. "From now on, we communicate through Obsidian. Korina will set up a secure, encrypted channel. No one else is to know about it."

Willem nodded, his face grim. He understood. The playing field had changed. They were no longer fighting a shadow war; they were facing a cunning, insidious enemy who seemed to anticipate their every move. He gave a curt nod, a silent acknowledgment of the new reality. He left the teahouse with the Quartet close behind, stepping back into the swirling chaos of Port Dominus, the weight of his guild's future heavy on his shoulders. He had a traitor to find, a ghost to unmask. And this time, he wouldn't be fighting alone. The alliance was forged, not in ink and parchment, but in shared crisis and the chilling realization of a common, terrifyingly intelligent foe.

CHAPTER 2

THE SERPENT IN THE ROSE

The heavy oak of the table felt hard and unyielding under Willem's white-knuckled grip. The Azure Rose's war room, usually a scene of bustling activity, was eerily silent. The soft, constant hum of the tactical displays, projecting holographic maps of Port Dominus and its intricate network of guilds and territories, seemed to mock the turmoil raging within him. He pulled an unlit pipe from the folds of his robes—a habit of contemplation, a ritual of calm—but he couldn't bring himself to light it. Instead, he turned it over and over in his hand, the polished wood a cold comfort against his burning rage.

How dare they? The thought echoed in his mind, a venomous whisper that fueled his fury. *Not just to attempt to poison Ada and her fellowship, but to use my name, my gesture of goodwill? This is not just a betrayal; it is a calculated insult to my honor.* He could feel the shame hot on his cheeks, a flush of anger at having his reputation, his carefully cultivated image of honorable neutrality, so casually defiled. *This courier,* he thought, his gaze hardening, *is the first thread. I will pull on it until this whole wicked scheme unravels.*

The soft hiss of the war room door sliding open broke the silence. Janna, his second-in-command, his fiercest and most loyal enforcer, strode in. Her expression was a mirror of his own—a mixture of fury and grim determination.

"Report," Willem said, his voice clipped and low, each word a shard of ice.

"The package was delivered by a freelance courier," Janna replied, her voice a low rumble. "Not one of our usuals. New face in the Coil, they say. Distinct limp, favors his left leg."

"Find him," Willem ordered, his voice devoid of any warmth. He bypassed the usual channels, the standard guild protocols of investigation and interrogation. This was personal. This was about more than just uncovering a traitor; it was about reclaiming his honor. "Find him, Janna. And bring him to me."

"Alive?" Janna asked, a flicker of predatory anticipation in her eyes.

"Alive," Willem confirmed, his gaze unwavering. "And in one piece. I want to hear his story from his own lips. I want to know who put him up to this." He paused, his grip tightening on the unlit pipe. "And then...then we'll see what price they paid for using my name in their little game."

Janna gave a curt nod, a silent acknowledgment of the gravity of the task. She didn't need further instructions. She knew what was at stake—not just Willem's honor, but the very foundation of the Azure Rose's reputation. She turned and left the war room, the soft hiss of the closing door sealing Willem's solitude once more.

He stood there for a long moment, the silence pressing in on him. The hum of the tactical displays seemed to grow louder, the holographic maps a swirling vortex of possibilities, of threats and alliances. He finally struck a flint against his pipe, the small flame a beacon in the dimly lit room. He took a long, slow drag, the acrid smoke a bitter taste on his tongue.

This changes everything, he thought, his gaze fixed on the holographic projection of Port Dominus, the city he had spent his life navigating, a city he thought he knew. Now, it seemed like a labyrinth of shadows, a breeding ground for vipers. He exhaled slowly, a plume of smoke swirling around his head like a shroud. *This city will learn the meaning of respect.* He crushed the ember in his pipe, the small act a symbolic extinguishing of his former complacency. The game had changed, and so had he. He was no longer a neutral player; he was a hunter, a predator stalking his prey in the tangled web of Port Dominus's underbelly. And he wouldn't rest until he found the one who dared to challenge his honor, the one who dared to use the Azure Rose's name in their wicked game.

Meanwhile, Janna moved through the serpentine alleys of the Serpent's Coil, her senses honed, her every step purposeful. She was a predator in her element, the chaos of Port Dominus her familiar hunting ground. She knew its rhythms, its whispers, its hidden currents of power and desperation. She knew its people—the merchants, the mercenaries, the thieves, the informants—the entire intricate ecosystem that thrived in the shadows of the great port city. And she knew how to find them.

She started with the whispers, the rumors that snaked through the taverns and gambling dens, the back alleys and hidden marketplaces. She listened to the hushed conversations, the boasts and threats, the gossip and lies. She pieced together fragments of information, like a spider weaving its web, each strand bringing her closer to her target—the courier with the limp. She learned his name: Kyel. She learned his haunts: The Drunken Kraken, The Serpent's Kiss, The Whispering Veil. She learned his habits: a fondness for cheap ale, a weakness for dice games, a nervous twitch in his left eye when he lied.

She moved silently, a ghost in the shadows, observing, listening, gathering information. She didn't rely on brute force or intimidation—not yet. This was a game of patience, of subtle manipulation, of using the city's own chaos against itself. She knew Kyel wouldn't be easy to find. He was a ghost himself, a fleeting shadow in the labyrinthine alleys. But Janna was a patient hunter. She would wait, she would watch, she would weave her web until Kyel, the courier with the limp, stumbled into it.

You can run, little bird, she thought, a grim smile playing on her lips. *But you can't hide.* She turned down a narrow alley, the stench of stale ale and desperation thick in the air. The shadows deepened, the sounds of the city fading into a low, guttural hum. She was getting closer. She could feel it in the air, in the whispers, in the very pulse of the city.

I'm coming for you...

Janna returned, not with a whisper, but a thud. The heavy oak door of Willem's private office swung open, revealing the warrior, her grip firm on the arm of a whimpering, disheveled figure. It was Kyel, the courier, his face pale, his eyes wide with terror. Janna unceremoniously deposited him onto the cold, steel floor, the impact eliciting a muffled groan from the gagged and bound man.

"Secure him," Willem commanded, his voice a low rumble that echoed in the small, soundproofed room. Janna efficiently bound Kyel to a heavy, iron chair bolted to the floor, the metal cold against his skin. The room, deep within the Azure Rose's guild halls, was designed for such encounters—a place where secrets were extracted, truths revealed, and lies exposed. The air was cold and still, smelling faintly of cleaning chemicals and the courier's sweat. The fluorescent arcane lights overhead hummed with a piercing whine, casting a sterile, unforgiving light on the scene.

Willem approached Kyel, his gaze like ice, his movements deliberate and controlled. He reached down and removed the gag, the small act seeming to amplify the silence in the room. Kyel gasped, his breath ragged, his eyes darting around the room like a trapped animal. He looked at Janna, her imposing figure a silent threat, then back at Willem, whose expression remained unreadable.

"Who paid you to deliver the package?" Willem asked, his voice cutting through the silence like a blade.

"I...I...I don't know," Kyel stammered, his voice barely a whisper. "I swear, Master Willem, I didn't know what was in it. I just...I just delivered it. Like I always do."

"Who gave you the package?" Willem pressed, his voice hardening.

"A...a figure...cloaked...I couldn't see their face," Kyel whimpered, his body trembling. "They...they just gave me the box and...and the address. And...and the money. A lot of money."

A flicker of a memory, a half-forgotten whisper from the depths of the Korsair archives, sparked in Erita's mind. A legend, dismissed as fanciful nonsense by most. But these weren't normal times. Desperate times. A predatory grin stretched across her lips. "Void, it's worth trying..." she muttered, more to herself than the others. She tapped a series of commands on her own data-slate, a sleek, black device she kept holstered at her hip. A shimmering, holographic nautical chart materialized above the main table, the intricate lines and symbols glowing with a soft, ethereal light. The projected image depicted the jagged coastline of the Korsair Confederacy, the treacherous currents swirling around a particularly ominous stretch of ocean marked as the "Serpent's Maw."

"Legends," Erita began, her voice low and laced with a hint of conspiratorial excitement, "speak of a ship. An Imperial payroll vessel. The *Argent Lion*. Lost in the Maw decades ago."

Janna snorted. "The *Lion*? A ghost story to scare green recruits. Every child in the Confederacy has heard that tale."

"Not just a story," Erita countered, her golden eyes gleaming. "I dug deeper. Found fragments of truth buried beneath the embellishments. Imperial records confirm the ship's existence, its mission, its disappearance. They never recovered the wreckage. Never found the crew. Never found the cargo." She tapped the holographic chart, highlighting a specific point within the Serpent's Maw. A flickering, crimson icon pulsed ominously within the holographic depths. "And that cargo...was the entire quarterly payroll for the Aegis Order. A king's ransom in Byts. Enough to fund a war ten times over."

Sera's eyebrows shot up. "Enough to buy back our ships. Enough to equip our men. Enough to break Thorne's hold on the ports." The thought of such a windfall, of turning the Empire's own resources against them, ignited a spark of hope in her eyes.

Korina, however, remained skeptical. "If it exists. The Maw is notoriously treacherous. Unpredictable currents, rogue whirlpools, jagged reefs that can tear a ship apart in seconds." She tapped her own data-slate, Obsidian, her fingers dancing across the glowing surface. "I've studied the historical data. The probability of a ship surviving intact in that region is...negligible."

"Which is why the Empire never bothered to search properly," Erita countered. "Too much risk, too little reward. They wrote it off as a loss."

Korina, despite her skepticism, felt a thrill of intellectual curiosity. A puzzle. A challenge. The sheer improbability of the *Argent Lion's* survival, coupled with the potential strategic advantage it represented, was too tempting to ignore. "Let me see those files," she said to Erita, her voice a rapid-fire burst of intellectual excitement. "Perhaps with current topographical data and enhanced scanning protocols, we can narrow down the search parameters."

Erita, a smug smirk playing on her lips, transmitted the encrypted files to Obsidian. Korina's fingers flew across the data-slate's glowing surface, the tiny, violet pixel-cat perched in the corner blinking rapidly as the system processed the influx of data. The warehouse, once filled with the tense whispers of doubt, now hummed with the quiet intensity of focused analysis. Holographic schematics of the Serpent's Maw flickered to life above Obsidian, swirling currents and treacherous reefs rendered in intricate, three-dimensional detail.

"The Empire's initial search focused on the northern quadrant," Korina murmured, tracing a finger across the projected map. "Standard protocol for a vessel caught in the outward current. But Erita's intel suggests a significant thaumaturgical surge was detected shortly after the *Lion's* disappearance. An anomaly." Her eyes narrowed, focusing on a specific point on the map where a faint, swirling energy signature was barely visible amidst the chaotic data streams. "If the *Lion* encountered a localized mana vortex, it could have been pushed far off course. Into uncharted territory."

"Uncharted?" Janna scoffed. "More like unrenderable. The Maw is a blighted swamp toad of a place. Full of glitches and dead data. Even the Empire's finest cartographers haven't been able to map it completely."

"Precisely," Korina countered, her voice rising with intellectual excitement. "Which means there's a possibility, however small, that the *Lion* was deposited in a sector outside the Empire's search grid. A sector masked by data instability."

For hours, Korina worked tirelessly, cross-referencing Erita's fragmented intel with current topographical scans, running complex simulations of potential drift patterns, and filtering out the constant background noise of the Maw's chaotic energy signatures. The tiny, violet pixel-cat on Obsidian's display paced anxiously, its ears perked, its eyes blinking as it 'observed' the relentless data streams flowing through the system. But as time wore on, a growing sense of frustration crept into Korina's voice.

"The interference is too great," she finally admitted, her voice laced with disappointment. "The Maw is a chaotic system. Too many variables. The thaumaturgical surge Erita mentioned...it corrupted the local data fields. Created a blind spot in the historical records." She sighed, running a hand through her intricately braided violet hair. "Even with Obsidian's long-range scanners, the search area is too vast. A needle in a haystack of corrupted code."

Janna, arms crossed, nodded grimly. "Practicality trumps wishful thinking, lass. I told you, the *Lion* is a ghost story."

CHAPTER 4

THE GHOST'S ARSENAL

"Let's see what you've got."

Willem watched the interplay between Ada and Janna, a flicker of amusement in his tired eyes. He'd seen that look before, the quiet confidence of someone who knew their own strength, regardless of how unconventional it might appear. He'd learned long ago to trust his instincts, and his instincts told him this strange girl, this self-proclaimed Architect-Queen, was the real deal. He'd staked his guild, his people, his very life on that belief.

"Janna," Willem said, his voice calm but firm, "the Architect-Queen has already proven her worth. She saved Sera and Korina from a poison that even our best healers couldn't identify, let alone cure." He gestured to the poisoned rose, still encased in a protective glass dome on a nearby table, a stark reminder of the Alchemist's reach. "That's not a parlor trick. That's power."

Janna remained impassive, but Willem saw a flicker of

uncertainty in her eyes. Good. Doubt was a healthy thing, especially in times like these. Blind faith could get you killed.

"Now," Willem continued, turning his attention to the matter at hand, "let's talk strategy. We know the Alchemist is hunting us. We know they're technologically advanced, resourceful, and ruthless. And we know they have a mole within our ranks." He let the words hang in the air, the weight of the betrayal settling heavily in the room. "Finding that mole is our top priority. But we also need to prepare for a war on two fronts. Against Thorne, and against this...ghost."

He paused, gathering his thoughts, the weight of responsibility pressing down on him. He was a merchant, not a general. But times had changed, and so had he.

"You've managed to secure this warehouse as a temporary base of operations," Willem explained, gesturing around the cavernous space. "But we're operating on a shoestring. Thorne has bled us dry. He's systematically choked off our trade routes, inflated our supply costs, and bought off our allies."

He spread his hands, palms up, a gesture of stark honesty. "We're broke. We barely have enough coin to feed our people, let alone equip them for a war." He met the gazes of each of the Quartet, his expression grim.

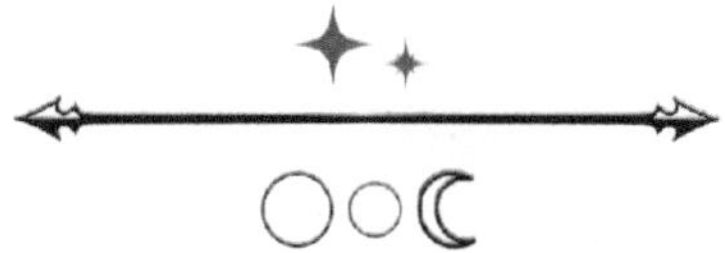

Ada, listening to the debate unfold, closed her eyes. Their meager warehouse, with its rough-hewn timber beams and the faint scent of sea salt carried in on the wind, faded from her awareness. She reached out with her mind, not to the physical world around her, but to the deeper layer of reality that underpinned it all. The raw data streams of Kremøtoa, normally invisible to its inhabitants, flowed through her consciousness like rivers of light. She sifted through decades of archived data, searching for the faintest whisper of the *Argent Lion*.

Seismic echoes, barely perceptible tremors in the world's crust, played out in her mind like a phantom symphony. Energetic signatures, the lingering traces of thaumaturgical surges and arcane discharges, flashed before her inner eye like bursts of static against a dark screen. She filtered out the background noise of the Maw's chaotic energy fields, focusing her attention on the specific timeframe of the *Lion's* disappearance. Slowly, painstakingly, she pieced together the ship's final moments.

A flicker of metallic resonance, a brief surge of arcane energy as its shields failed, a final, grinding groan of tortured metal as the hull buckled under the immense pressure of the deep. And then, silence. But the silence, Ada realized, was not empty. It held a faint, persistent echo, a whisper of displaced data that clung to the ocean floor like a ghost.

Ada opened her eyes, the warehouse snapping back into focus. "Latitude: 37 degrees, 22 minutes, 47 seconds North. Longitude: 14 degrees, 5 minutes, 12 seconds West. Depth: 12,729 meters." She recited the coordinates, her voice calm and precise, the numbers flowing from her lips with an almost unnatural certainty. "The *Argent Lion* lies there. Largely intact."

Korina, her violet eyes wide with astonishment, immediately input the coordinates into Obsidian. The data-slate hummed, its screen flashing as it accessed the world's topographical database. A holographic image of the seabed materialized above the device, rendering a detailed three-dimensional map of the designated location.

"Argent's light..." Korina breathed, staring at the holographic display. "The topography is...stable! Relatively flat seabed, no significant geological formations. The currents in that sector are minimal. It's...possible. A wreck could have sunk there without being torn apart."

Erita, a slow smile spreading across her face, let out a low whistle. "What in the Void? Did you just...pull that out of thin air?"

"Not air," Ada replied, a faint smile playing on her lips. "Data. The world remembers everything. Even whispers."

Janna's jaw hung slack. Her usual gruff demeanor, the hardened cynicism of a veteran who had seen too much and trusted too little, crumbled. She stared at Ada, her mind reeling. Whispers? The world remembered? Swamp toad's backside, the girl was something else entirely. She'd dismissed the *Argent Lion* as a drunken sailor's tale, a myth whispered in smoky taverns to spice up a dull night. And this...whippersnapper...had just plucked its location from the Void itself. Twelve thousand meters down, no less. Madness. Utter, beautiful madness.

Willem, his weathered face creased in thought, was equally stunned. This was not just power; it was knowledge. A deep, intuitive understanding of the world's very fabric. He had pledged his guild to her cause, believing in her vision of a better future. But now, a new kind of faith took root, a faith not in a leader, but in something akin to a divine oracle.

He cleared his throat, the sound breaking the stunned silence that had settled over the warehouse. "By Argent's light," he murmured, the oath carrying a new weight, a newfound reverence. "That...is remarkable. Truly remarkable." He turned to Janna, a gleam in his eye. "It seems our Architect-Queen has given us a rather...lucrative opportunity, wouldn't you say?"

Janna, her mind still struggling to grasp the implications of Ada's feat, could only nod dumbly. The skepticism that had clung to her like a second skin was gone, replaced by a grudging, awestruck respect. The girl was no mere thaumaturge; she was something more. Something...different.

"The *Sea Serpent* is a fine vessel," Willem continued, his voice regaining its usual confident cadence. "But for a deep-sea salvage operation of this magnitude, we'll need something more specialized..." He paused in thought, stuck at the fact the pressure at twelve thousand plus meters down would crush anything he knew could reach the wreck.

"The *Kraken's Kiss*," Willem stated, his voice firm. "A submersible vessel designed for deep-sea exploration. It belonged to a...now-deceased acquaintance of mine. A rather eccentric engineer who specialized in arcane pressure seals." He looked at Ada, a flicker of uncertainty in his eyes. "It's currently docked in Port Hyperion. Acquiring it...might be challenging, to say the least." Port Hyperion belonged to the Intellective States. Their laws regarding technology, especially anything related to deep-sea exploration, were notoriously strict. Smuggling a submersible vessel out of their territory would be near impossible.

"And even if we could get our hands on it," Janna interjected, her skepticism returning with a vengeance. "How in the Void's name are we supposed to get it to the *Lion's* coordinates? That's twelve thousand meters down! The pressure at that depth would crush a cerakote rhino."

Willem's confident facade faltered. He had spoken of the *Kraken's Kiss* as a solution, a tangible asset they could acquire and deploy. But Janna's blunt question exposed a glaring flaw in his logic. He had no answer. The sheer logistical impossibility of the task settled over the room like a shroud. He looked at Ada, Sera, Korina, and Erita, their faces reflecting a mixture of hope and dawning apprehension. He had presented a path, a glimmer of possibility in their quest to reclaim the *Argent Lion's* treasure. But the path, it seemed, led to an insurmountable precipice. He sighed, the weight of the challenge pressing down on him. "That," he admitted, his voice heavy, "is the problem."

CHAPTER 5

THE PRICE OF ACQUISITION

Erita's mind raced, sifting through the chaotic data of Port Dominus's underworld. Twelve thousand meters. The number echoed in her thoughts, a daunting measurement of the chasm that separated them from the *Argent Lion's* secrets. The *Kraken's Kiss* was a dead end. Hyperion's security was airtight. Even if they managed to steal the submersible, transporting it across the Confederacy would be suicide. Thorne's spies were everywhere. They needed another option. And they needed it fast.

A flicker of a memory ignited in the back of her mind. A vast, cluttered workshop filled with arcane contraptions. The glint of polished cerakote and the hum of arcane generators. Corvus. The old madman. His workshop, a chaotic symphony of engineering genius and reckless experimentation. She'd seen it. A sleek, obsidian vessel, its hull reinforced with arcane runes, nestled amongst the piles of discarded prototypes and half-finished inventions. The *Nautilus*. Corvus's magnum opus. The only private submersible in Port Dominus capable of withstanding the immense pressures of the Fathoms Deep trench.

"Void," she breathed, the exclamation escaping her lips before she could stop it. All eyes turned to her, a mixture of curiosity and apprehension in their gazes. "There might be another way."

Willem raised an eyebrow, his expression a mixture of hope and skepticism. "Another way? Do *tell*, Swift. We're all ears."

Erita allowed herself a small, sly smile. She loved having information nobody else possessed. It was her currency, her shield, her weapon. And in this moment, it was their only salvation. "Master Corvus," she stated, her voice low and steady. "He has a submersible. The *Nautilus*. I saw it in his workshop, tucked away in a back corner. It's designed for deep-sea exploration. Built to withstand pressures far exceeding those at the *Lion's* depth."

Janna snorted, her skepticism evident. "Corvus? That blighted swamp toad? He's more likely to blow himself up than reach the bottom of a bathtub!"

"True," Erita conceded, "the man's a few byts short of a copper coin. But the *Nautilus* is real. I saw it with my own eyes. Arcane pressure seals, a reinforced obsidian hull, enough arcane generators to power a small city. It's the real deal."

Korina, her fingers flying across Obsidian's surface, looked up, her eyes wide. "The *Nautilus*? I've heard rumors. A legendary vessel. Supposedly capable of reaching the Fathoms Deep. But the design specs...they're almost mythical! Nobody's ever seen it in action."

Korina's heart pounded with a scholar's giddy excitement. The *Nautilus*! A legendary vessel, whispered about in hushed tones in the Veritas Archives. A machine capable of defying the crushing pressure of the Fathoms Deep. To see it, to study its arcane workings, to analyze its thaumaturgical matrix...it was an opportunity too incredible to pass up. "Argent's light," she breathed, her voice barely above a whisper. "The *Nautilus*...it actually exists..."

Erita's dry chuckle brought Korina back to the grim reality of their situation. "It exists, Korina. But getting our hands on it is another story. Corvus is a paranoid old coot. He wouldn't let an Imperial soldier within a klick of his precious submersible, let alone a band of revolutionaries."

"We still hold his debt," Sera pointed out, her voice a low rumble. "The Gilded Hand's markers. We could force his cooperation."

Ada shook her head, her purple eyes thoughtful. "Force is rarely the optimal solution. Especially with someone like Corvus. His genius is fueled by obsession, not obligation. We need to appeal to that obsession, not threaten it."

Korina frowned, fiddling with the strap of her data-slate. "Appeal to his obsession? How? The man's barely lucid half the time. He rambles about phantom rivals and whispers to his machines."

"He responded to the Alchemist's code," Ada reminded her, her voice soft but firm. "He recognized its elegance, its complexity. He respected the skill, even if he despised the source. That's our in."

"So, what?" Sera asked, folding her arms across her chest. "We challenge him to a coding duel? See who can write the most efficient pathfinding algorithm?"

Ada's lips curved into a small smile. "Not quite. But we do offer him something he can't refuse. A chance to contribute to something greater than himself. A chance to make history." She turned to Willem, her gaze intense. "Master Willem, do you have any arcane artifacts recovered from the Northern Marshes Pacification? Something...unusual. Something that would pique Corvus's curiosity?"

Willem stroked his beard, his eyes thoughtful. "Perhaps. There was a cache of...experimental devices. Confiscated from a rogue thaumaturge. The Imperial analysts couldn't make heads or tails of them. Deemed them too unstable, too unpredictable. They've been gathering dust in the Azure Rose vault ever since."

"Perfect," Ada said, her voice laced with a quiet excitement that sent a shiver of anticipation down Korina's spine. "We offer Corvus a trade. Access to the *Nautilus* in exchange for a chance to analyze these artifacts. A chance to unravel their secrets."

Erita, ever the pragmatist, raised an eyebrow. "And if he refuses?"

Ada's smile widened, a hint of steel glinting in her purple eyes. "Then we remind him of his outstanding debt to the Gilded Hand. And the...*persuasive* methods they employ to collect."

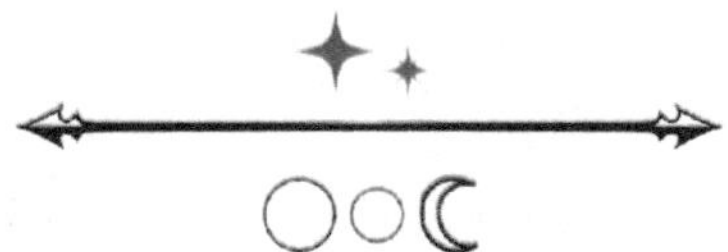

The warehouse door creaked closed behind them, the heavy clang echoing in the sudden stillness. Port Dominus pressed in around them, a chaotic symphony of shouts, laughter, and the ever-present scent of salt and desperation. Ada felt a pang of anxiety, a flicker of the programmer's instinct to retreat to the quiet logic of code. But Korina's hand, warm and firm in hers, anchored her to this messy, vibrant reality.

Korina's smile was infectious, a bright beacon in the shadowy alley. “The *Nautilus*...” she breathed, her voice a hushed whisper of awe. “I can’t believe it. It’s real. And we might actually get to... study it.”

Ada felt a warmth spread through her chest, a gentle blush rising in her cheeks. Korina’s enthusiasm was a constant source of both amusement and a strange, unfamiliar flutter of something... more. She squeezed Korina’s hand, her own smile a quiet reflection of the joy radiating from the scholar.

“Just try not to drool on it, Korina,” Erita quipped, her voice dry as the desert wind. “Corvus might charge us extra for the cleanup.”

Korina, momentarily flustered, stammered, “I...I won’t! It’s a...a priceless artifact! I would never...”

Erita’s golden eyes, sharp and knowing, flicked to Ada, a subtle amusement dancing in their depths. “She really is a sweetheart, isn’t she?” she murmured, her voice low enough for only Ada to hear.

Ada’s blush deepened, a mix of affection for Korina and a touch of embarrassment at Erita’s perceptive gaze. “She is,” Ada agreed softly, her voice barely audible above the din of the city.

They navigated the crowded streets, a silent, practiced choreography of movement. Sera, with her warrior’s instincts, would have taken the lead, carving a path through the throngs with the sheer force of her presence. But Erita moved like a whisper, a shadow slipping through the cracks, her hand never straying far from the daggers hidden beneath her cloak. Ada, still adjusting to the physicality of Kremøtoa, followed Erita’s lead, her hand intertwined with Korina’s, a silent reassurance in the swirling chaos.

Korina, lost in her own world of calculations and arcane theories, bumped into a passing dockworker, her data-slate almost slipping from her grasp. Ada's reflexes, honed by years of coding marathons and fueled by a protective instinct she hadn't known she possessed, tightened on Korina's hand, steadying her before she could fall.

"Careful, Rina," Ada said, her voice laced with a gentle concern that belied the surge of adrenaline still coursing through her.

Korina blinked, her violet eyes wide with a mix of surprise and gratitude. "Oh! Thank you, Ada. I...I was just thinking about the *Nautilus's* propulsion system. It's supposed to utilize a...a phased axiomatic displacement matrix..."

Erita snorted, rolling her eyes. "Phased axiomatic displacement. Right. Because walking is too mainstream for Corvus."

Korina, oblivious to Erita's sarcasm, launched into a detailed explanation of the theoretical principles behind phased axiomatic displacement, her words tumbling over each other in a torrent of technical jargon. Ada, though only half-listening, found herself smiling. Korina's passion, her unwavering belief in the power of logic and knowledge, was a comforting constant in this world of shifting alliances and hidden agendas.

They reached the edge of the artisan district, the air thick with the pungent aroma of arcane reagents and the metallic tang of forging steel. The buildings here were a haphazard collection of ramshackle workshops and makeshift laboratories, each one a testament to the ingenuity and desperation of Port Dominus's inhabitants. Ada felt a strange kinship with these creators, these tinkerers who pushed the boundaries of the possible, even in the face of chaos and uncertainty.

As they approached Corvus's compound, Ada felt a familiar flicker of apprehension. The structure loomed before them, a bizarre, gravity-defying amalgamation of salvaged ship parts, arcane generators, and precariously balanced scaffolding. It was a monument to Corvus's eccentric genius, a physical manifestation of the chaotic energy that fueled his creations. Ada hoped their gamble would pay off. They needed Corvus, and the *Nautilus*, if they were to have any chance of reaching the *Argent Lion* and uncovering the secrets it held.

Erita stepped forward, her knuckles rapping sharply against the warped metal of Corvus's workshop door. The sound was swallowed by the ambient hum of arcane energy that emanated from the structure, a chaotic symphony of buzzing generators and crackling wards. Ada, standing behind Erita with Korina at her side, felt a prickle of anticipation, a programmer's curiosity mixed with a healthy dose of apprehension. She'd faced down Imperial Prefects and stared into the heart of system-corrupting malware, but Corvus...Corvus was a different kind of challenge; a *finesse*-based challenge.

Korina's grip on Ada's arm tightened, a surge of affection that sent a wave of warmth through Ada. Korina's head nestled against Ada's shoulder, her violet braids brushing against Ada's cheek. Ada, her heart softening, turned her head and kissed the top of Korina's head. A quiet sigh escaped Korina's lips, a soft sound of contentment that made Ada's own anxieties ease. Korina's blush, a delicate shade of rose against her pale skin, was visible even in the dim light of the alleyway.

The workshop door creaked open, a grinding protest of rusted hinges and misaligned gears. Corvus stood in the doorway, his white hair a chaotic halo around his head, his single good eye twitching nervously. He wore the same oil-stained jumpsuit Ada remembered, the numerous pockets bulging with an assortment of arcane tools and dubious components. His thick goggles were perched precariously on his forehead, threatening to slide off at any moment.

"You're back," he stated, his voice a gravelly rasp that seemed to emanate from the depths of his cluttered workshop. "I trust you haven't come to pester me with more of your...petty concerns?"

Erita stepped forward, her voice smooth as polished silver. "Not at all, Master Corvus. We have a proposition for you. A mutually beneficial arrangement, if you're willing to listen."

Corvus grunted, a noncommittal sound that could have meant anything. He stepped aside, gesturing them into the workshop with a flick of his wrist. "Come in, come in. Don't just stand there gawking like a pack of startled swamp toads. Time is precious, and my genius is not to be wasted on idle pleasantries."

They followed him into the workshop, a cavernous space filled with a bewildering array of arcane devices, half-finished projects, and piles of salvaged components. The air crackled with the raw energy of uncontrolled thaumaturgy, a chaotic symphony of buzzing generators, sparking wires, and the faint scent of ozone. Ada's programmer's instincts went into overdrive, her mind struggling to process the sheer volume of information flooding her senses. It was a beautiful mess, a testament to Corvus's untamed brilliance.

"So," Corvus said, turning to face them, his single eye gleaming with a manic intensity. "What grand scheme has brought you back to my humble abode? Another impossible task? Another desperate plea for the services of a true genius?"

Erita smiled, a predatory glint in her golden eyes. "Something like that, Master Corvus. We need your...unique talents. And we're willing to pay a price that even you might find...irresistible."

"We need the *Nautilus*," Erita stated, her voice crisp and businesslike. "We have a...salvage operation in mind."

Corvus snorted, a derisive sound that echoed through the workshop. "The *Nautilus*? For a salvage operation? You must be jesting. That vessel is a marvel of arcane engineering, not some glorified dredging barge."

"This isn't just any salvage operation," Ada interjected, her voice calm and steady. "We're looking for something...specific. Something of immense value."

Corvus's single eye narrowed, his gaze flitting between Ada and Erita. "And what, pray tell, is this priceless treasure you seek?"

"The *Argent Lion*," Ada replied, her voice laced with a quiet confidence.

Corvus threw back his head and let out a booming laugh, a sound that seemed to shake the very foundations of the workshop. "The *Argent Lion*? The mythical ghost ship? The one that supposedly vanished into the Serpent's Maw centuries ago? You're chasing fairy tales, girl. Legends whispered in drunken taverns."

"Not quite," Ada countered, a sly smile playing on her lips. "We know exactly where it is."

Corvus's laughter died in his throat, replaced by a look of incredulous curiosity. "You...you know where it is? Impossible. The Maw's energy currents are chaotic, unpredictable. No two readings are ever the same. It's a navigational black hole."

"Unless," Korina chimed in, her voice brimming with intellectual excitement, "you have a way to...stabilize the data stream. To compensate for the temporal anomalies and the axiomatic drift."

Ada nodded, her gaze meeting Korina's across the cluttered

workshop. “Exactly,” she said, her voice soft but firm. “We have a method. A rather unique method.”

Korina, catching Ada’s unspoken cue, stepped forward, her data-slate humming softly in her hands. With a flick of her wrist, a holographic projection shimmered into existence above Obsidian, a three-dimensional map of the seabed surrounding Port Dominus.

“37 degrees, 22 minutes, 47 seconds north,” Korina announced, her voice precise and confident. “14 degrees, 5 minutes, 12 seconds west. Depth: 12,729 meters.” A pulsing red marker appeared on the holographic map, pinpointing a location deep within the treacherous Serpent’s Maw.

Corvus stared at the projection, his single eye wide with disbelief. “That’s...that’s inside the Maw,” he stammered, his voice barely a whisper. “Impossible. No vessel could survive those pressures!”

“The *Nautilus* is the only vessel that *could* survive,” Ada stated, her voice calm and steady. “That’s why we need it.” She paused, letting the weight of her words sink in. “The *Argent Lion* is down there, Master Corvus. And it’s carrying a cargo worth more than you could possibly imagine. More than *any* of us *combined* could imagine.”

Corvus’s gaze remained fixed on the holographic projection, his mind racing. He ran a hand through his wild white hair, a gesture of bewildered fascination. The flickering light of the workshop’s arcane lamps cast strange shadows across his face, highlighting the manic intensity in his single eye. He was hooked. Ada knew it. The lure of the unknown, the challenge of the impossible, was too tempting for a mind like Corvus’s to resist. The *Nautilus*, and the secrets of the *Argent Lion*, were within their grasp.

Korina felt a thrill course through her, a surge of intellectual excitement that momentarily eclipsed the anxieties swirling within her. This was it. The moment to deploy her secret weapon, a piece of information so valuable, so tantalizing, that even a mind as chaotic as Corvus's couldn't ignore it.

"There's more," Korina stated, her voice gaining a newfound confidence. Ada's purple eyes widened slightly, a flicker of surprise that Korina found strangely endearing. It was a small, private moment of connection, a shared understanding that transcended the chaos of the workshop.

With a practiced flick of her wrist, a different holographic image shimmered into existence above the device, a complex schematic of an arcane weapon pulsating with intricate energy patterns.

"This," Korina announced, her voice ringing with a scholar's authority, "is what was *actually* on the *Argent Lion*."

Corvus's single eye snapped to the projection, his entire body tensing with a sudden, predatory focus. He leaned closer, his breath coming in ragged gasps as he devoured the image with a manic intensity.

"What...what *is* that?" he whispered, his voice hoarse with awe.

"An Imperial prototype," Korina explained, her voice gaining a professorial cadence. "A thaumaturgical amplification matrix, rumored to be capable of channeling and redirecting raw arcane energy on an unprecedented scale." She paused, letting the weight of her words sink in. "The files were...incomplete. Classified, of course. But even the fragments I managed to salvage..."

Corvus's single eye twitched, his mind racing. He reached out a trembling hand, his fingers brushing against the holographic projection as if trying to grasp the arcane energy patterns swirling within.

"This...this is..." he stammered, his voice barely a whisper. "This is beyond anything I've ever seen."

"It was lost with the *Argent Lion*," Korina continued, her voice gaining a persuasive edge. "The Empire never recovered it. They assumed it was destroyed, consumed by the Maw. But if we can reach the wreck..."

Corvus's gaze remained fixed on the holographic projection, his mind consumed by the intricate details of the arcane weapon. He saw not just a weapon, but a puzzle, a challenge to his own genius. He saw a level of arcane engineering that rivaled, perhaps even surpassed, his own. His professional curiosity, his insatiable thirst for knowledge, had overridden his paranoia, his fear. He was no longer a recluse hiding from his creditors, but an inventor, an engineer, on the verge of a groundbreaking discovery.

"The pressures at that depth..." he murmured, his voice barely audible above the hum of the workshop's arcane generators. "No ordinary vessel could withstand..."

"The *Nautilus* isn't an ordinary vessel," Ada reminded him, her voice soft but firm. "You designed it to withstand the Maw's embrace. You built it to explore the deepest, darkest corners of this world."

Corvus paced the length of his workshop, his mind a whirlwind of conflicting thoughts. The *Argent Lion*, the lost Imperial prototype...the possibilities were staggering. His fingers itched to dissect the arcane matrix, to unravel its secrets, to push the boundaries of thaumaturgical engineering beyond anything he'd ever attempted. But the *Nautilus*...his masterpiece, his magnum opus...was compromised.

"The gremlins..." he muttered, his voice barely a whisper, a stark contrast to his usual bombastic pronouncements. "Accursed little scavengers. They've infested every corner of my workshop. Every wire, every conduit, every blasted gear."

He stopped before the holographic projection, his single eye tracing the intricate energy patterns of the Imperial prototype. "Such power..." he breathed, his voice filled with a mix of awe and frustration. "Such potential...wasted."

He turned to face Ada, Erita, and Korina, his expression a mask of grim determination. "I'll be frank," he said, his voice dropping to a low, conspiratorial tone. "The *Nautilus*...she's not ready. Not yet."

Korina's violet eyes widened, her expression a mix of confusion and concern. "Not ready?" she echoed, her voice laced with a scholar's anxiety. "But...but you said it was capable of withstanding the Maw's pressures."

"It *was*," Corvus corrected, his voice laced with a hint of bitterness. "But things...changed. Circumstances...intervene." He gestured around the workshop, his hand sweeping across the cluttered space. "These blasted gremlins...they're like a plague. They've infiltrated every system, every component. They chew through rare metals, disrupt energy fields, and phase in and out of reality like...like digital ghosts."

He slammed his fist against a nearby workbench, the sound echoing through the workshop. "I've tried everything," he growled, his voice rising in frustration. "Wards, traps, even arcane repellents. Nothing works. They just...reappear. Multiplying. Devouring."

He turned back to the holographic projection, his gaze fixed on the Imperial prototype. "I need the *Nautilus*," he murmured, his voice barely a whisper. "I need to reach the *Argent Lion*. But I can't risk it. Not in its current state." He looked at them, his single eye pleading. "I need help. I need someone to...

exterminate these pests. To rid my workshop of these accursed gremlins."

He paused, his gaze sweeping across their faces, searching for a flicker of understanding, a hint of a solution. "They're drawn to arcane energy," he explained, his voice regaining a measure of its usual intensity. "They feed on it. They thrive in it. This workshop... it's like a feast for them. A blasted all-you-can-eat buffet of raw thaumaturgy."

He gestured towards a partially disassembled arcane generator, its exposed wires sparking erratically. "Look," he said, his voice laced with a weary frustration. "They've already begun to infest the *Nautilus's* propulsion system. If I activate it now...it could overload. Explode. Take the entire workshop with it."

He turned back to them, his expression a mix of desperation and a strange, almost childlike vulnerability. "I can't do this alone," he admitted, his voice barely a whisper. "I need your help. I need... an exterminator."

Ada's mind raced, processing Corvus's frantic plea. This was it. Her moment. A chance to showcase her true power, not as a thaumaturge, but as the Architect. The one who held the keys to this entire reality. A surge of exhilaration coursed through her, tempered by a quiet, analytical focus.

"Master Corvus," she began, her voice calm and reassuring, a stark contrast to his frantic energy. "This may be simpler than you anticipate."

Corvus blinked, his single eye twitching erratically. "Simpler?" he echoed, his voice laced with disbelief. "Simpler than ridding my workshop of techno-magical pests that phase in and out of existence? Simpler than reclaiming my masterpiece from the jaws of these digital locusts?"

Ada offered a reassuring smile. "Indeed," she affirmed, her voice laced with a quiet confidence. "You see, Master Corvus, you've been approaching this problem from the perspective of an engineer. A brilliant engineer, to be sure, but still bound by the limitations of this world's...physics. I, however," she paused, a subtle violet glow emanating from her form, "operate on a different level."

Before Corvus could question her cryptic statement, Ada activated her Admin-view. The world around her shifted, transforming from a chaotic jumble of arcane devices and salvaged parts into a flowing stream of data, a symphony of code and algorithms. The gremlins, once elusive phantoms flitting through the workshop, now appeared as distinct data points, their core protocols laid bare before her.

She reached out, her fingers tracing the air as she navigated the intricate layers of code. Lines of text scrolled past her vision, highlighting the gremlins' behavioral parameters: their attraction to arcane energy, their destructive consumption of rare metals, their ability to phase through solid matter.

A flicker of amusement danced in Ada's violet eyes. "Fascinating," she murmured, her voice barely audible above the hum of the workshop's arcane generators. "Such elegant code, yet so...misguided."

With a few deft strokes, Ada rewrote the gremlins' core protocol. She altered their primary directive from consumption to maintenance, their destructive hunger transformed into a meticulous drive for order and efficiency. She refined their phasing ability, allowing them to seamlessly integrate with the workshop's machinery, repairing damaged components and optimizing energy flow.

Korina gasped, Obsidian's screen flickering with a sudden surge of anomalous data. The air in the workshop shimmered, a violet hue spreading like a ripple from where Ada stood. The chaotic energy signatures of the gremlins, previously erratic and unpredictable, began to stabilize, coalescing into a rhythmic pulse that resonated with the workshop's arcane generators. "Argent's Light," she breathed, her voice hushed with awe. "What did she *do*?"

Erita's golden eyes widened, her usual cynicism replaced by a stunned silence. She'd witnessed Ada's power before, the effortless manipulation of reality that defied all logic and reason. But this... this was different. It wasn't just altering existing systems; it was rewriting the very fabric of the workshop, transforming chaos into order with a wave of her hand.

The transformation was instantaneous. The gremlins, once a chaotic swarm of destruction, now moved with a synchronized precision, their movements a ballet of efficiency. They scurried across the workshop floor, collecting scattered tools and organizing them with meticulous care. They phased into the *Nautilus's* propulsion system, their tiny forms glowing with a soft violet light as they repaired damaged conduits and recalibrated energy flow.

The workshop, once a chaotic mess, began to transform. Discarded tools levitated back to their designated places on the workbench. Spilled arcane reagents flowed back into their containers, sealing themselves with airtight precision. The air, once thick with the scent of ozone and burnt metal, now carried a faint, almost floral fragrance.

Corvus watched in stunned silence as his workshop underwent this miraculous transformation. His jaw hung slack, his single eye twitching uncontrollably as he struggled to comprehend what he was witnessing. He had spent years battling these gremlins, pouring his genius and resources into countless failed attempts to contain or repel them. And now, this...this woman, this...*goddess*, had effortlessly transformed them into...*maintenance drones.*

As the last gremlin completed its task, the workshop fell silent. The air was clean, the floor spotless, the tools neatly organized. The *Nautilus*, once a crippled husk, now stood gleaming in the center of the workshop, its arcane propulsion system humming with a quiet, efficient power. The transformation was complete. The chaos had been tamed. Order had been restored.

"By the Void..." he whispered, Corvus's voice choked with emotion.

Ada tilted her head, a gentle smile playing on her lips. "Better?" she asked, her voice soft and laced with amusement.

Corvus stared at her, his single eye wide with a mixture of awe and disbelief. He looked around the workshop, his gaze sweeping over the neatly organized tools, the gleaming surfaces of his arcane devices, the humming efficiency of the *Nautilus's* propulsion system. He reached out a trembling hand and touched the polished metal casing of the submersible, as if to confirm its reality.

"Better?" he echoed, his voice a hoarse whisper. "Better than... better than it's ever been! Argent's Light, woman, what *are* you?"

Ada's smile widened. "A friend," she replied simply. "And a... facilitator, perhaps." She gestured towards the *Nautilus*. "So,

Master Corvus," she continued, her voice taking on a more businesslike tone. "Now that...the gremlin situation is resolved, I believe we had a bargain to discuss."

Corvus blinked, his eye focusing on Ada with renewed intensity. "A bargain?" he repeated, his mind still reeling from the miraculous transformation of his workshop. "Ah, yes, the *Nautilus*. Of course." He approached the submersible, running a hand over its smooth, obsidian hull. "She's all yours," he declared, a broad grin spreading across his face. "Fully operational, thanks to your... *unique* pest control methods."

He spent the next few minutes methodically checking the *Nautilus's* systems. After his quick and thorough inspection, Corvus straightened up, beaming at Ada with uncontainable excitement. "She's ready!" he proclaimed, his voice ringing with enthusiasm. "The *Nautilus* is primed and ready to plunge into the depths!"

CHAPTER 6

THE SERPENT'S MAW

The *Leviathan's* cockpit, a cramped sphere of polished brass and glowing arcane glyphs, vibrated with a low, rhythmic hum. Korina, perched on a narrow seat before a curved sensor console, felt a thrill course through her. "Depth: 11,400 meters. Pressure stable. Approaching thermal vent cluster Delta-Seven," she called out, her voice tight with a mixture of scientific fascination and nervous energy.

Janna grunted, her massive frame barely fitting between the arcane engine's control levers. "Steady as she goes, lads," she rumbled, her voice a low growl that echoed through the cramped cockpit. Her weathered face, etched with years of seafaring hardship, remained impassive, her focus unwavering. The Azure Rose crew, hand-picked by Janna for their experience and loyalty, worked with a silent efficiency, their movements precise and practiced. Their grim professionalism was a stark contrast to Korina's barely contained excitement.

"Navigational hazard detected. Large crystalline formation at two o'clock. Adjusting course by point-five degrees," Korina announced, her fingers dancing across the sensor console. The *Leviathan* shuddered, its arcane propulsion system responding instantly to her commands. A holographic display flickered to life, projecting a 3D rendering of the treacherous underwater landscape. Jagged rock formations, their surfaces encrusted with glowing bioluminescent organisms, rose like skeletal fingers from the seabed. Swirling currents of thermal energy, their colors shifting from deep violet to fiery orange, pulsed through the water, creating pockets of intense heat and pressure.

Sera gripped the control yoke, her knuckles bone-white against the polished brass. Sweat beaded on her forehead, stinging her eyes, but she blinked it away, refusing to break her concentration. The *Leviathan* bucked and shuddered, caught in a violent crosscurrent that threatened to slam them against the jagged canyon walls. "Starboard thruster to seventy percent. Dive planes negative ten," Korina's voice, strained but clear, cut through the roar of the arcane engines. Sera reacted instantly, her hands moving with a practiced grace that belied the immense forces at play. The submersible groaned, its arcane shielding flaring as it scraped against a crystalline outcropping. "Compensating. Port thruster eighty-five. Emergency dive planes activated," Sera barked, fighting the controls. The *Leviathan* shuddered again, then stabilized, nosing its way through the treacherous currents. A low, guttural growl escaped Sera's lips, a mixture of exertion and a primal thrill. This, she realized, was where she truly belonged: not on the battlefield, but at the edge of the unknown, facing the chaos head-on.

The sudden shriek of proximity alarms tore through the rhythmic hum of the *Leviathan's* engines. Ada's heart leaped into her throat. She gripped the arms of her seat, her gaze fixed on the main sonar display. A colossal, pulsating red blob had materialized on the screen, its edges blurry and indistinct. It was unlike anything she'd seen before, an energy signature so vast and chaotic it dwarfed everything else in the sensor's range.

"What in the Void is that?" Janna's voice, usually so steady, cracked with a hint of fear. The submersible bucked violently as the unknown entity's energy field washed over them.

"Unidentifiable. Massive bioluminescent signature. Approaching rapidly," Korina's voice was tight with a mixture of scientific fascination and raw terror. Her fingers flew across the console, trying to analyze the incoming data stream. "It appears to be attracted to our arcane engines."

"Decoys. Now," Ada barked, her voice sharp with command.

Erita's hands moved with a blur, activating the *Leviathan's* countermeasures. A series of decoy signals, designed to mimic the submersible's energy output, erupted from the vessel's flanks. For a moment, the massive red blob on the sonar hesitated, its trajectory wavering. Then, with a surge of malevolent intent, it corrected its course, homing in on the *Leviathan* with terrifying speed.

From the inky blackness beyond the submersible's limited viewports, a colossal form emerged. It was a leviathan, its name a horrifyingly accurate description. Its bioluminescent hide pulsed with a sickly green light, illuminating the cavernous maw that opened before them, filled with rows of razor-sharp teeth. Its eyes, two massive orbs of glowing crimson, burned with an unnerving intelligence. It was not simply a beast; it was a predator, and they were its prey.

"It's too smart. The decoys aren't working," Erita's voice was strained, a tremor of fear running through her normally cynical tone.

The leviathan lunged, its maw wide enough to swallow the *Leviathan* whole. Ada's mind raced, calculating escape vectors, analyzing defensive protocols. But there was no time. They were about to be crushed, swallowed into the belly of this digital monstrosity.

A surge of power coursed through Ada's veins. It was not the cold, calculating logic of her Admin view, but a visceral, instinctual reaction to protect her companions. She closed her eyes, her mind reaching out to the fabric of Kremøtoa itself. She didn't attack the leviathan; that would be inefficient, a waste of precious processing power. Instead, she did something far more elegant, far more devastating.

"[Property: Density = 1000]," she whispered, the command barely audible above the roar of the approaching beast.

In the instant before the leviathan's jaws closed around them, the water directly in front of it shimmered, then solidified. It wasn't a visible barrier, but an invisible wall of impossibly dense water, a wall of pure kinetic force. The leviathan, moving at tremendous speed, slammed into the barrier with the force of a meteor striking a planet. The submersible rocked violently as the shockwave reverberated through the water. A high-pitched whine emanated from the arcane shielding, straining against the sudden pressure differential.

The leviathan, stunned and enraged, was thrown back by the impact. Its massive form thrashed in the water, its bioluminescent hide flashing in a chaotic display of confusion and pain. It had encountered something it could not comprehend, a force that defied the very laws of its digital existence.

"Now, Sera!" Ada yelled, her voice ringing with authority.

Sera, ever the warrior, didn't hesitate. She slammed the *Leviathan* into full reverse, then spun the control yoke hard to port. The submersible, its arcane engines screaming, shot into a narrow canyon that had opened up in the cavern wall, leaving the enraged leviathan behind.

The *Leviathan* shuddered, a deep groan vibrating through its hull as Sera wrestled with the controls. The canyon walls, a blur of jagged rock and phosphorescent coral, raced past the submersible's viewports. Her knuckles, white against the polished metal of the control yoke, betrayed her tension. The near-death encounter with the leviathan had left her shaken, a cold knot of fear tightening in her gut. She stole a glance at Ada. The Architect-Queen sat rigid in her seat, her face pale, her gaze fixed on the sonar display. Even Ada, with her god-like powers, had been rattled by that monstrous entity.

The tense silence in the cockpit was broken only by the rhythmic hum of the *Leviathan's* engines and the occasional crackle of static from the comms system. Korina hunched over her console, her fingers dancing across the keys, her brow furrowed in concentration. Erita, ever the pragmatist, methodically checked and rechecked the submersible's systems, her movements precise and efficient. Even Janna, usually so boisterous, was unusually quiet, her gaze fixed on the depth gauge.

After what felt like an eternity, the canyon opened into a vast, underwater plain. The sonar display, previously a chaotic mess of interference and static, finally resolved into a clear image. Sera's breath caught in her throat. There, resting on the seabed, lay the *Argent Lion*.

It wasn't the mangled wreck she'd expected. The ship, impossibly preserved in the crushing depths, looked more like a majestic ghost ship than a centuries-old wreck. Its hull, once gleaming Imperial steel, was now covered in a delicate tracery of ethereal, deep-sea flora that pulsed with a soft, bioluminescent glow. It was a breathtaking sight, a testament to the strange and wondrous beauty of the deep.

"Argent's light..." Korina breathed, her voice hushed with awe. "It's...*perfect.*"

"Almost," Ada said, her voice low and serious. She pointed to a section of the *Lion's* hull displayed on the main monitor. "There."

Sera leaned closer, following Ada's gaze. A massive rupture marred the otherwise pristine hull, a gaping wound that exposed the ship's interior to the crushing pressure of the deep. It wasn't a ragged tear or a corrosion-pitted hole, but a clean, precise cut, as if some impossibly sharp blade had sliced through the *Lion's* reinforced steel plating like butter.

"That's not natural decay," Korina said, her voice tight with professional curiosity. Her fingers flew across Obsidian's interface, analyzing the image. "The energy signature...it's unlike anything I've ever encountered. Highly advanced. Almost...alien."

A chill ran down Sera's spine. This wasn't just a shipwreck; it was a crime scene, a testament to some unknown, technologically advanced enemy from the past. An enemy that had the power to cripple an Imperial warship with a single, devastating strike. An enemy that, perhaps, still lurked in the shadows of Kremøtoa.

The *Leviathan* maneuvered into position above the *Argent Lion*, its powerful thrusters kicking up clouds of silt from the seabed. Inside the submersible's cramped cockpit, Ada and Korina watched the external monitors, their faces illuminated by the ghostly glow of the displays. Erita, her expression grim, monitored the comms system, her fingers hovering over the emergency recall button.

"Sera, Janna, you're clear for egress," Erita's voice crackled through the comms. "Be advised, thermal signatures are fluctuating in the cargo hold. Exercise extreme caution."

"Understood, Eri," Sera's voice replied, a hint of tension in her tone. "Janna and I are locked and loaded. Let's go hunting."

On the monitors, Sera and Janna, encased in bulky, armored deep-sea EVA suits, exited the *Leviathan's* airlock. The suits, designed to withstand the crushing pressure of the deep and equipped with powerful thermal lances, made them look like futuristic knights preparing for battle. They moved with surprising agility in the zero-gravity environment, their magnetic boots clinging to the *Lion's* hull.

Reaching the gaping rupture, Sera activated her thermal lance. The weapon, powered by a concentrated burst of arcane energy, emitted a searing beam of white-hot light that sliced through the *Lion's* reinforced steel plating as if it were paper. Sparks flew, illuminating the cavernous, silent cargo hold within.

With a final, deafening screech of tortured metal, the rupture widened, creating a jagged opening large enough for the warriors to enter. Sera took point, her lance held at the ready, her movements cautious and deliberate. Janna followed close behind, her massive frame filling the newly created entrance, her own lance casting an eerie glow into the darkness beyond.

The cargo hold was a vast, echoing space, filled with rows upon rows of sealed crates and containers. The air, thick with the scent of stale seawater and decay, hung heavy and oppressive. A thick layer of silt covered everything, disturbed only by the faint currents created by the warriors' movements. The silence was unnerving, a stark contrast to the chaotic energy of the Serpent's Maw outside.

Then, a low, guttural growl echoed through the hold, a sound that seemed to vibrate through the very structure of the ship. It wasn't the sound of any living creature, but the distorted, digitized roar of corrupted data. From the deepest shadows, a shape began to materialize, its form flickering in and out of phase with reality. It was a Glitch-Construct, a horrifying, shifting mosaic of distorted metal and shimmering, corrupted code.

Its limbs, a chaotic jumble of jagged edges and flickering pixels, writhed and twisted as it emerged from the darkness. Its eyes, glowing emerald orbs of pure, malevolent energy, fixed on the intruders. Metallic claws, infused with the same corrupted energy, extended from its fingertips, dripping with a viscous, digital ichor.

Before Sera could react, more constructs flickered into existence, emerging from the shadows like digital ghosts. They surrounded the two warriors, their glowing eyes burning with a cold, predatory light, their metallic claws scraping against the metal floor, the sound echoing through the cavernous hold.

Sera and Janna were trapped, cornered in the dark, claustrophobic space, surrounded by the horrifying manifestations of the world's decay. The hunt had become a desperate fight for survival.

The first attack came as a blur of corrupted energy. Janna barely registered the movement before a Glitch-Construct's claws raked across her armored forearm. Sparks flew, but the impact felt... wrong. Not the solid clang of metal against metal, but a strange, disorienting *slipping,* as if the construct's claws had partially phased through her armor. The damned things weren't entirely solid, flickering in and out of reality like bad projections. Made a warrior's job a right blighted mess.

Another construct lunged, its claws aimed for Janna's faceplate. She reacted instinctively, bringing her thermal lance up in a defensive block. Again, that unsettling *slip.* The lance connected, but instead of cleaving through metal and code, it seemed to pass *through* the construct, momentarily disrupting its form but doing little real damage. The construct shimmered, its form momentarily dissolving into a shower of flickering pixels before reforming, its emerald eyes burning with undiminished malice.

"Void's teeth!" Janna roared, her voice distorted by the suit's comms system. "These swamp toads are made of smoke and mirrors!"

"Hold your ground, Janna!" Sera's voice crackled through the comms, laced with a warrior's calm amidst the chaos. "They're phasing. Physical attacks are useless. We need to hit their core."

"Easy for you to say, whippersnapper," Janna grumbled, parrying another attack. "You're not the one wrestling a glitch-ridden scrap heap."

"Korina's analyzing their patterns," Erita's voice cut in, cool and precise. "There's a vulnerability. A momentary lapse in their phasing cycle. A concentrated energy discharge to their core should do the trick."

"Should?" Janna grunted, shoving a construct away with her armored shoulder. The thing felt like pushing against a cloud of electrified sand. "We don't have time for 'shoulds,' Swift. We need certainties."

"Korina's running simulations," Erita replied, her tone unwavering. "It's our best shot. Sera, can you modify your lance for a focused discharge?"

"Working on it," Sera's voice responded, strained with effort. "Just need a...ha! Got it."

Janna saw Sera's lance flicker, its energy output intensifying, the beam narrowing into a pinpoint of blinding white light. "Ready when you are, Janna. Just need you to hold the blighter still."

"Hold still?" Janna barked. "The thing's like trying to grab a greased eel."

"Just for a second," Sera's voice pleaded, a rare hint of vulnerability in her tone. "It's our only chance."

Janna took a deep breath, bracing herself. This was it. One shot. One chance. Argent's light, let it be enough. She lunged, grabbing a Glitch-Construct with both hands. The thing bucked and writhed, its form flickering and distorting, but Janna held on, her augmented strength overcoming its ethereal nature. She could feel the corrupted energy coursing through its form, a sickening, buzzing sensation against her armored gloves.

"Now, Sera!" Janna roared, her voice strained with effort.

A beam of pure, concentrated energy lanced out from Sera's weapon, striking the construct's core with pinpoint accuracy. For a moment, nothing happened. Then, the construct's emerald eyes widened, its form flickering violently, its metallic claws spasming. A high-pitched whine filled the air, a sound like nails on a chalkboard amplified a thousand times.

And then, with a final, blinding flash of light, the construct exploded, dissolving into a shower of harmless pixels that rained down on Janna like digital confetti. The remaining Glitch-Constructs momentarily paused, their movements faltering, their glowing eyes fixated on the spot where their companion had vanished.

Silence descended on the cargo hold once more, broken only by the hiss of Janna's and Sera's breathing through their suit comms. Erita's voice crackled through the comms, filled with a mixture of relief and professional excitement.

"It worked! Korina's analysis was correct. Focused energy discharge to the core."

"One down," Sera's voice responded, her tone grim. "Several more to go." She turned to Janna, her visor reflecting the ghostly glow of the *Argent Lion's* emergency lights. "Ready for round two?"

Janna grinned, a savage, predatory expression that was hidden behind her visor. "Argent's light, girl. I was born ready."

The remaining Glitch-Constructs, as if startled by their comrade's demise, shimmered and flickered, their forms growing increasingly unstable. Then, one by one, they vanished, dissolving into the digital ether like ghosts in the machine. Sera watched their retreat, a flicker of confusion beneath her visor. It wasn't a tactical withdrawal, more like...deletion. As if someone had simply erased them from existence. She glanced at Janna, whose visor reflected the same bewildered expression.

"What in the Void was that?" Janna's voice crackled through the comms.

"Unknown," Sera replied, her tone clipped. "Log it, report to Erita. Our priority is securing the cargo." She turned, her gaze sweeping across the *Argent Lion's* decaying cargo hold. The ship's manifest, recovered by Erita's network of informants, had listed several chests of Imperial gold and a cache of priceless schematics detailing experimental arcane weaponry. If half the rumors were true, the haul would be enough to fund their revolution for years.

"Vault's this way," Janna's voice rumbled, cutting through Sera's thoughts. She gestured with her thermal lance towards a heavily reinforced steel door at the far end of the hold. "Let's hope it's not crawling with more of those glitch-ridden scavengers."

The vault door, surprisingly intact despite the ship's decay, stood firm against their efforts to open it. Unlike the hull breach, which bore the hallmarks of an energy weapon, the vault appeared untouched, sealed tight by some unknown mechanism. Sera swore under her breath, exchanging a frustrated glance with Janna. So much for a quick in-and-out.

"Eri, any intel on the vault's access protocols?" Sera's voice crackled through the comms.

"Negative," Erita's voice replied, cool and precise. "Thorne's records were incomplete. The *Argent Lion's* security systems were highly classified. Even the Empire nowadays don't know how to open it."

"Typical," Janna grumbled. "Blighted bureaucracy. Always hiding things, even from themselves."

"Not a problem," Ada's voice cut in, calm and reassuring. A faint violet glow emanated from the comms panel, a subtle sign of her power. "I've bypassed the access protocols. Door's open."

A soft click echoed through the cargo hold, and the vault door swung open, revealing stacks of heavy wooden chests bound in iron. The air inside was thick with the musty scent of aged wood and metal, a testament to the treasure's long slumber on the seabed. Janna let out a low whistle.

"Argent's light," she murmured, her voice filled with awe. "It's true. *A king's ransom.*"

Sera, ignoring the gold for the moment, turned her attention to a smaller, sealed compartment at the back of the vault. Inside, she found rows of data-slates, each one carefully labeled and secured in its own protective casing. These were the schematics, the true prize. Knowledge was power, and these slates held the secrets to weaponry that could change the balance of power in Kremøtoa.

"Janna, secure the gold," Sera instructed, her voice brisk and efficient. "I'll take the schematics."

The process of transferring the chests and data-slates to the *Leviathan* was slow and arduous, hampered by the bulky EVA suits and the treacherous currents swirling around the *Argent Lion*. Each chest, heavy with gold, required both Janna's and Sera's combined strength to lift and maneuver through the narrow hull breach. The data-slates, though lighter, were equally precious and required careful handling to avoid damage.

As they worked, Sera's mind raced, calculating logistics, formulating plans. This treasure, this knowledge, was the key. It was the fuel that would ignite their revolution, the spark that would set Kremøtoa ablaze. She glanced at Janna, who was wrestling another chest through the breach, her face grim with determination. They were a good team, a solid foundation. With Ada's power, Korina's intellect, and Erita's network, they could reshape this world, forge a new order from the ashes of the old.

Ada watched from the *Leviathan's* cockpit as Sera and Janna wrestled the last accessible chest of gold through the mangled hull of the *Argent Lion*. The ship, its structural integrity compromised by their intrusion, groaned and shuddered around them. The water outside, illuminated by the submersible's floodlights, shimmered with an unsettling, glitching effect, as if reality itself was fraying at the edges.

A low, guttural rumble echoed through the water, growing in intensity. The *Argent Lion* listed sharply to one side, its decaying timbers groaning under the immense pressure. A shiver ran down Ada's spine, a primal, instinctive fear that transcended the digital nature of her world. Something was wrong. Terribly wrong.

"Status report," Ada commanded, her voice calm and steady, betraying none of the unease churning in her gut.

"[HULL INTEGRITY CRITICAL. IMMINENT STRUCTURAL COLLAPSE]," the *Leviathan's* AI responded, its voice a flat, emotionless monotone.

"Damage report!" Ada demanded.

"[MULTIPLE CORRUPTED SECTORS DETECTED. INCREASED ENERGY SIGNATURE FLUCTUATIONS]," the AI reported.

"Cache, take it," Janna's voice crackled through the comms, laced with a warrior's frustration. "We're about to be crushed by a king's ransom."

Ada saw it then. A swarm of smaller Glitch-Constructs, hundreds of them, pouring from every crevice and crack in the dying ship. They shimmered and flickered in the murky water, their emerald eyes burning with malevolent intent. The gold, the schematics, all of it, suddenly seemed insignificant in the face of this overwhelming threat.

"Sera, Janna—abandon the last chest! Return to the *Leviathan* IMMEDIATELY," Ada ordered, her voice sharp and urgent.

"But the gold—" Janna protested, her voice distorted by the suit's comms.

"NEGATIVE. YOUR SURVIVAL IS THE PRIORITY. ABORT MISSION," Ada commanded, her tone brooking no argument.

Sera, ever the pragmatist, didn't hesitate. She shoved the chest away, its iron bindings clanging against the decaying deck, and grabbed Janna's arm, pulling her towards the hull breach.

"Korina, Eri, prepare for emergency ascent," Ada ordered, her eyes fixed on the swarm of Glitch-Constructs closing in on Sera and Janna.

"Affirmative," Korina's voice responded, a tremor of fear in her tone.

"Engaging emergency propulsion system," Erita's voice cut in, cool and efficient.

The *Leviathan* shuddered violently, its engines roaring to life, propelling them away from the dying *Argent Lion*. Ada watched as the ghost ship, consumed by the swarm of Glitch-Constructs, imploded in on itself, its decaying timbers collapsing into a vortex of corrupted energy and swirling debris. The gold, the final chest, vanished into the abyss, swallowed by the maw of the Serpent's Maw. It was a loss, a painful one, but a necessary sacrifice. They had escaped with their lives, and that was all that mattered. For now.

CHAPTER 7

A QUEEN'S RANSOM

The *Leviathan* breached the surface with a groan of protesting metal, the first pale light of dawn painting the turbulent waters a bruised, ethereal violet. Ada, still tense from their narrow escape, watched through the submersible's viewport as the familiar silhouette of *The Sea Serpent* emerged from the pre-dawn mist, its sails furled, its deck bustling with activity. Silas, a sturdy figure against the backdrop of the rising sun, directed his crew with crisp, efficient gestures, preparing for the delicate operation of transferring their salvaged treasure.

The process was slow, arduous, and fraught with risk. The chests, heavy with gold, swung precariously between the two vessels, suspended from a hastily rigged crane system. Each creak and groan of the ropes, each splash of seawater against the submersible's hull, sent a jolt of anxiety through Ada. She imagined the chests plunging back into the depths, their hard-won prize lost to the unforgiving sea. It was a visceral fear, a physical manifestation of the immense pressure she felt to succeed, to protect her companions—to fix this broken world.

Silas gripped the edge of the heavy wooden chest, his knuckles white, calloused fingers tracing the intricate carvings of Imperial heraldry. He'd heard whispers of the *Argent Lion* his entire life, dismissed it as a drunken sailor's tale, a myth to frighten greenhorns. Yet here it was, solid and real beneath his weathered hands, salvaged from a depth no sane seaman would dare. He glanced at Ada, her face pale but resolute, her violet eyes fixed on the rising sun as if drawing strength from its nascent glow. Argent's light, she was more than just a mage, more than just a clever strategist. She was something...*else*.

"Open it, Lars," Silas's voice, gruff but laced with an unfamiliar tremor of excitement, cut through the tense silence on deck.

Lars, Silas's most trusted hand, hesitated, his gaze darting between the chest and Ada, as if seeking permission from a higher power. He swallowed hard, the lump in his throat visible even beneath his thick beard, and fumbled with the heavy iron latch. The lock clicked open with a metallic snap, a sound that echoed the pounding in Silas's chest.

The hinges groaned in protest as Lars slowly lifted the heavy lid. The rising sun caught the contents within, bathing the deck in a blinding, golden light. A collective gasp rippled through the assembled crew. Silas felt his own breath catch in his throat. The chest overflowed with gold. Not just coins, but intricately crafted bars, gleaming goblets, and jeweled artifacts, each piece whispering of untold wealth and ancient power.

The men stared, transfixed, their faces a mixture of awe and disbelief. For a long moment, the only sound was the gentle lapping of the waves against the hull and the ragged breaths of men who had just witnessed a miracle.

"Captain," Lars's voice was barely a whisper, his eyes wide with wonder, "it's...it's more than I ever *imagined*."

Silas nodded, unable to speak. He reached into the chest, his hand closing around a heavy gold bar. The metal was cool, smooth, and impossibly real against his calloused palm. It was more than gold; it was proof. Proof of a power beyond comprehension, a power that had defied the depths, the currents, the very legends themselves. He looked at Ada again, her face etched with a weariness that spoke of burdens he could only begin to imagine. He knew then, with a certainty that ran deeper than any oath he had ever sworn, that his life, his ship, his crew, were hers to command. Not out of obligation, not out of fear, but out of a profound, almost reverent, respect for the impossible miracle he had just witnessed.

"Lars," Silas's voice was firm, his grip on the gold bar tightening, "start unloading. Every piece. Carefully." He turned to the rest of his crew, his gaze sweeping across their stunned faces. "And not a word of this leaves this ship. Understand?" A chorus of gruff affirmations answered him. Silas nodded, satisfied. They had gold, they had a purpose, and they had a queen. They had everything.

Korina, pale and still shaken from their near-encounter with the leviathan, meticulously documented the transfer process, her fingers flying across Obsidian's interface. Every chest, every data-slate, was logged and cataloged, its contents meticulously analyzed and cross-referenced against their existing intelligence. Even in the face of danger, her thirst for knowledge, her drive to understand and categorize, remained unquenched. It was a trait

Ada both admired and worried about. Korina's brilliant mind was their greatest asset, but it also made her vulnerable, her focus on logic sometimes blinding her to the more chaotic, unpredictable aspects of their reality.

Sera, ever vigilant, stood guard, her hand resting on the hilt of her sword, scanning the horizon for any sign of pursuit. The tension in her posture, the subtle twitch of her muscles, spoke volumes about her unease. The open sea, vast and unforgiving, was a far cry from the rigid order of Celgrad—the familiar confines of the Prefecture. Out here, in the lawless expanse of the Korsair Confederacy, their vulnerability was amplified, their every move exposed to the whims of fate and the machinations of their enemies.

Erita, perched on a crate near the crane's controls, directed the transfer operation with her usual detached efficiency. Her eyes, sharp and calculating, missed nothing, taking in every detail, every nuance of the unfolding scene. She was the linchpin, the silent orchestrator of their movements, ensuring that every piece fell into place, every contingency was accounted for. Her presence, though quiet, radiated an aura of competence and control, a reassuring counterpoint to the underlying chaos of their situation.

As the last chest was safely secured on *The Sea Serpent's* deck, a wave of exhaustion washed over Ada. The tension, the fear, the constant vigilance, it all seemed to drain from her, leaving her feeling weak and vulnerable. She leaned against the rails of the starboard deck, closing her eyes, letting the gentle rocking of the waves lull her into a state of near-numbness. They had done it. They had accomplished the near-impossible.

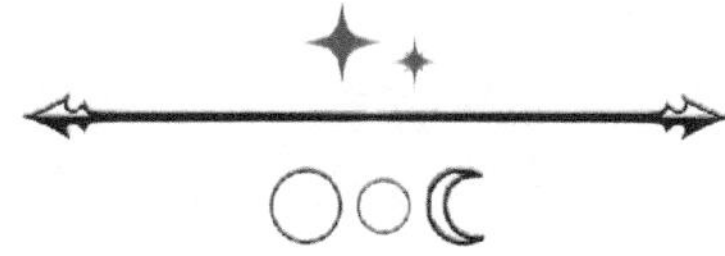

The rhythmic creak of the ship's timbers and the muffled roar of the ocean filled the quiet of Captain Silas's cabin. Korina sat across from Ada, the heavy, iron-bound container resting between them on the sturdy wooden table. It was one of dozens they had salvaged from the *Argent Lion*, each sealed with an arcane lock Ada had effortlessly bypassed. This one, however, felt different. Heavier. More significant. A faint thrum of energy emanated from within, a subtle vibration that resonated with the thauma flowing through Korina's own veins.

Ada reached out, her fingers tracing the intricate carvings on the container's lid. A faint violet light pulsed beneath her touch, the arcane lock dissolving like frost in the morning sun. With a soft click, the lid opened, revealing stacks of perfectly preserved documents, bound in thick, Imperial-issue leather. Korina leaned closer, her breath catching in her throat. This was it. The key. The answer to so many unanswered questions.

"Imperial military records," Ada's voice was hushed, her violet eyes wide with a mixture of excitement and apprehension, "and... prototype weapon schematics."

Korina's fingers trembled as she reached for the topmost schematic. It was brittle with age, the ink faded but still legible. Her initial thrill of discovery, the academic's hunger for new knowledge, quickly soured. A cold dread spread through her, a chilling premonition of something profoundly wrong. The designs weren't for siege weaponry or arcane cannons. These were blueprints for something far more insidious. Devices designed to manipulate the very fabric of Kremøtoa itself. To tear at the seams of reality.

"Ada..." Korina's voice was barely a whisper, her violet eyes wide with horror. She swallowed, the words catching in her throat, her eyes betraying a mist of tears forming. "These...these aren't weapons. Not in the conventional sense."

Ada leaned closer, her brow furrowed with concern. "What do you mean, Rina?"

Korina pointed to a complex diagram, a network of interconnected nodes pulsing with a sickly, familiar energy signature. "This...this is a 'Pattern Disruptor'. It's designed to-to actively *create* systemic instability. To generate localized pockets of data corruption." She looked up at Ada, her voice choked with a dawning, terrible realization. "It's a blueprint for...for manufacturing the Pattern Blight."

Ada's expression shifted from curiosity to alarm. "That's not possible. The Blight is a natural phenomenon. A consequence of..."

"No." Korina shook her head fervently, her fingers tracing another diagram, this one even more disturbing. It depicted a device that resembled a grotesque, metallic spider, its legs ending in sharp, needle-like protrusions. "This, this is a 'Malware Injector'. It-it takes corrupted data fragments and-and *weaves* them into sentient entities. It-it *creates* the Malware," her voice trembling, holding back the onset of a panic attack.

A cold dread washed over Ada, a chilling wave of realization that threatened to shatter the fragile peace she had found in Kremøtoa. She pulled Korina close, the scholar's slender frame trembling in her arms. Korina wasn't sobbing, not yet, but her breaths came in ragged gasps, each inhale a struggle against the rising tide of panic. Ada held her tight, whispering soothing nonsense, her hand gently stroking Korina's violet hair. The familiar scent of old books and musk, usually a source of comfort, now carried a sharp undercurrent of fear.

"Rina, breathe. It's alright. We're safe here." Ada's voice was calm, steady, a deliberate counterpoint to the chaos swirling within her own mind. She had to be strong. For Korina. For Sera. For Erita. For all the inhabitants of this world she had created, a world now teetering on the brink of a far more insidious corruption than she could have ever imagined.

While she comforted Korina, Ada activated her Admin-view. Lines of code scrolled across her vision, overlaying the warm, familiar features of the woman in her arms. She focused on the schematics, the diagrams Korina had pointed out. With a sinking heart, she confirmed Korina's horrifying discovery. The Ehxcehl Empire hadn't simply stumbled upon the world's code-based nature; they had understood it. Decades ago. And they had tried to weaponize it. Not for defense. Not for preservation. But for control. For conquest.

The implications were staggering. The Pattern Blight, the creeping decay that threatened to consume Kremøtoa, wasn't a natural phenomenon. It was a manufactured plague. A weapon unleashed by the very institution Sera had dedicated her life to serving. And the Malware, the grotesque, glitching entities that haunted the corrupted sectors, weren't simply emergent anomalies. They were *engineered*. Purposefully created.

Ada felt a surge of nausea, a visceral revulsion at the sheer, calculated cruelty of it all. She had designed Kremøtoa as a sanctuary, a world free from the imperfections and injustices of Earth. But she had replicated the worst aspects of humanity, the insatiable hunger for power, the willingness to sacrifice others for personal gain. She had coded these flaws into the very fabric of her creation, and now they were tearing it apart.

Korina's breathing gradually evened out, the tremors subsiding. She pulled back slightly, her violet eyes still wide with a lingering fear, but now focused on Ada's face. A faint blush colored her cheeks, a flicker of embarrassment at her own vulnerability. "I-I'm sorry," she stammered, her voice still shaky, "I...I shouldn't have..."

"Don't apologize, Rina." Ada's thumb gently wiped away a stray tear from Korina's cheek. "You were right to be alarmed. This...this changes everything."

Korina nodded, her gaze returning to the schematics. "What... what do we do?"

Ada took a deep breath, her mind racing. She had to tell Sera. And Erita. But how? How could she reveal this devastating truth to the woman who had pledged her loyalty, her very life, to the institution responsible for this horrifying betrayal? And to Erita, the pragmatic spymaster who had placed her trust in Ada's ability to bring order to this chaotic world? This wasn't just a glitch to be fixed, a bug to be squashed. This was a systemic cancer, a corruption woven into the very heart of Kremøtoa. And she, Ada Lynx, the Architect-Queen, was the only one who could excise it.

The salt-laced air whipped at Ada's hair as she and Korina emerged onto the *Sea Serpent's* main deck. The sky, a swirling canvas of bruised purple and deep indigo, mirrored the turmoil in Ada's gut.

She found Sera and Erita near the helm, discussing patrol routes with Silas. The two women looked up as Ada and Korina approached, their expressions a mixture of curiosity and concern.

"What did you find?" Erita asked, her golden eyes sharp and assessing. "Something in the Void has Korina spooked."

Ada hesitated, the weight of the revelation pressing down on her. "We found something," she said, her voice carefully neutral, "something...significant."

Korina stepped forward, holding out a salvaged data-slate from the *Argent Lion*. "We deciphered the encrypted logs. And the schematics." Her voice was flat, devoid of its usual intellectual enthusiasm.

Sera frowned. "Schematics for what? Some new Imperial toy?"

Korina's violet eyes met Sera's. "...For the Blight." She held up a diagram. "This is a 'Pattern Disruptor'. It emits a focused burst of chaotic energy that destabilizes the surrounding area, creating..."

"The Pattern Blight," Ada finished, her voice barely a whisper. She watched Sera's face, searching for any flicker of recognition, any hint of disbelief. But there was none. Only a growing, horrified understanding.

Erita stepped closer, peering at the schematic. "What in the Void are you saying? The Empire *created* the Blight?"

"Not just the Blight," Korina added, her voice trembling slightly. She held up another diagram. "This...this is a 'Malware Injector'. It takes corrupted data fragments and weaves them into... sentient entities."

Sera's hand flew to the hilt of her sword, her knuckles white against the worn leather. "You're saying the Empire *makes* the Malware?" Her voice was tight, strained with disbelief.

Ada nodded, her heart heavy. "They weaponized the glitches,

Sera. They turned the world's code against itself. They have been since the Empire's inception—by the dating of the documents, it's...irrefutable."

A long silence hung in the air, broken only by the creak of the ship and the cries of gulls overhead. Sera's face was pale, her green eyes fixed on the schematics as if trying to burn the images into her memory. Erita paced restlessly, her hand raking through her short golden hair. Silas stood silently at the helm, his weathered face a mask of grim understanding.

The world twisted around Sera. The solid deck of the *Sea Serpent* swayed beneath her, the familiar scent of salt and brine replaced by the bitter taste of bile rising in her throat. The schematics blurred in her vision, the clean lines and precise notations mocking her with their cold, calculated evil. *Pattern Disruptor. Malware Injector.* Names that now held the weight of a thousand shattered oaths, a thousand betrayed lives.

Her hand tightened convulsively around the hilt of her sword, the familiar weight a small comfort in the sudden, terrifying emptiness that opened within her. The Aegis Order. The shining beacon of justice, the unyielding shield against the encroaching darkness. A *lie*. A carefully crafted, meticulously maintained *lie*, perpetrated by the very institution she had sworn to serve, by the very *family* she had trusted.

A wave of nausea rolled over her, hot and suffocating. She stumbled back, her hand flying to her mouth as the world tilted precariously. Her knees hit the deck, hard, the impact jarring her but not enough to stem the rising tide of sickness. She retched, her body convulsing as the contents of her stomach spilled onto the wooden planks, the acrid smell mixing with the salt air.

The Northern Marshes. The memory, long buried beneath layers of duty and denial, clawed its way to the surface. The faces of the villagers, their eyes wide with fear and confusion as the Aegis Knights, *her* knights, advanced. The screams, the blood, the sickening crunch of bone beneath armored boots. *Necessary sacrifices.* Her uncle's cold, dismissive words echoed in her ears, each syllable a poisoned barb twisting deeper into the wound of her betrayal.

She retched again, dry heaves racking her body as the last vestiges of her former self were purged. The world spun, the faces of Ada, Korina, and Erita swimming in and out of focus. She heard their voices, distant and distorted, but the words held no meaning. The foundation of her identity, the bedrock of her beliefs, was gone, leaving a hollow void of betrayal and disgust. She was adrift, unmoored, lost in a sea of her own shattered convictions. The Aegis Order. Her uncle. Herself. *All lies.* All hollow shells filled with the rot of corruption.

A hand, gentle but firm, rested on her shoulder. "Sera." Ada's voice, soft and concerned, cut through the fog of nausea and despair. "Breathe, babe."

Sera gasped, a ragged, choking sound that tore at her throat. She looked up, her vision blurry with unshed tears. Ada's face swam into focus, her violet eyes filled with a compassion that felt strangely alien, yet deeply comforting.

"It's alright," Ada murmured, her hand moving to Sera's back, rubbing slow, soothing circles. "Let it out."

A sob escaped Sera's lips, followed by another, and another, until she was shaking uncontrollably, her body wracked with the force of her grief and rage. Korina and Erita stood nearby, their faces etched with concern, but they kept a respectful distance, understanding that this was a pain only Ada could touch.

The sobs gradually subsided, replaced by shuddering breaths and the occasional hiccup. Ada continued to hold her, her presence a silent anchor in the storm of Sera's emotions. When the tremors finally eased, Sera leaned against Ada, her head resting on Ada's shoulder, her body heavy with exhaustion.

"I-I don't understand," she whispered, her voice hoarse and broken. "Everything I believed...everything I fought for..."

Ada didn't interrupt, didn't offer empty platitudes. She simply held Sera, her hand stroking Sera's hair, her touch a silent affirmation of shared pain.

"They used us," Sera continued, her voice thick with disgust. "They used the Aegis Order...they used *me*...to enforce their lies... *Void*, the Northern Marshes..."

Ada knelt beside her, her violet eyes meeting Sera's. "No, Sera," she said, her voice firm, unwavering. "They didn't use *you*. They tried to, yes. But they failed."

Sera looked at her, confusion clouding her tear-streaked face. "Failed? How?"

"Your devotion," Ada explained, her hand moving to cup Sera's cheek, "was never to the *Empire*, Sera. It was to the *ideal*. To the *principle* of justice. The *idea* of order." Her thumb gently brushed away a tear that tracked down Sera's cheek. "That ideal...that unwavering belief in what is *right*...that's what made you a Knight, Sera. Not their lies. Not their corruption."

A flicker of understanding sparked in Sera's eyes. "But...they perverted it. They twisted it into something...*ugly*."

"Yes," Ada agreed, her voice soft but resolute. "They tried. But they didn't *break* it, Sera. They didn't *taint* it. Your courage, your strength, your loyalty...those are *yours*, Sera. Not theirs. And their betrayal doesn't diminish them; it *illuminates* them."

She leaned closer, her gaze intense, unwavering. “They showed you, Sera, what the true enemy is. Not the Blight, not the Malware. But the *corruption* that would weaponize them. The *greed* that would twist the very fabric of reality for its own gain.”

A fire kindled in Sera’s eyes, a spark of the fierce warrior spirit Ada had first seen in Oakhaven. “So...what do we do?” She asked, her voice still shaky, but now laced with a new, steely resolve.

Ada’s lips curved into a small, determined smile. “We fight, Sera.” Her hand moved to Sera’s, her fingers intertwining with Sera’s. “We fight for the ideal. For the *truth*. For the very *code* of this world, to keep it from being perverted by those who would use it for their own twisted purposes.”

Sera’s grip tightened on Ada’s hand, her gaze hardening with a newfound purpose. “Then let’s fight,” she said, her voice now clear, strong, filled with the conviction of a warrior reborn. “Let’s burn their lies to the ground and build a world worthy of our oaths.”

CHAPTER 8

THE PREFECT'S FURY

Kraus Valerius's fingers, long and pale, tapped a precise rhythm against the polished obsidian surface of his desk. The silence in the office was absolute, broken only by the hum of the Spire's climate control systems and the faint, rhythmic clicking of his fingernails. A stark contrast to the chaotic data swirling across his console. Reports, summaries, analyses—all meticulously formatted, all perfectly organized, and all utterly useless. Port Dominus. A festering boil on the skin of the Korsair Confederacy. And now, thanks to the unpredictable variable designated "Ada Lynx," it was about to rupture.

He reviewed the after-action reports again, his expression unreadable. Thorne's enforcers, humiliated in a public display of impossible thaumaturgy. The Gilded Hand, a usually reliable source of underworld intelligence, now suspiciously silent. And the Azure Rose Guild, once a manageable thorn in the Empire's side, now openly aligned with a rogue element whose power defied classification. Every line of data screamed *inconsistency*. Every summary echoed *contradiction*. The reports painted a picture of an enemy that operated not just outside the Empire's laws, but outside the very laws of reality itself.

"Unacceptable," he murmured, his voice a low, gravelly hum. The word hung in the air, a stark indictment of the entire operation. Protocol Omega-Nine had been authorized. Lethal force had been sanctioned. Yet, the target remained elusive, her movements unpredictable, her abilities...*unquantifiable*. He had underestimated her. A mistake he would not repeat.

He touched a control on his console, and a holographic image shimmered into existence above his desk. A three-dimensional map of Port Dominus, rendered in intricate detail, from the fortified warehouses of the Merchant District to the twisting alleyways of the Serpent's Coil. He zoomed in on a specific location, a nondescript warehouse identified by Erita Systema's last known communication relay. The warehouse, according to the reports, was empty. Clean. *Sterile*. As if it had never been occupied. Another anomaly. Another contradiction.

He rotated the image, studying the surrounding buildings, the network of streets and alleyways, the flow of pedestrian and vehicular traffic. Nothing. No trace of the fugitives. No sign of their activities. They had vanished, leaving behind only a trail of chaos and unanswered questions. *Where are they?* He wondered, his mind a whirlwind of calculations, probabilities, and potential escape routes. The Korsair Confederacy was a likely destination. A haven for smugglers, pirates, and other unsavory elements. But even within that chaotic landscape, they would leave a trace. A data signature. *Something*.

The reports from Thorne were even more infuriating. The man, a self-proclaimed master of the underworld, had been outmaneuvered, outsmarted, and utterly humiliated by a *girl*—a "data architect" from some backwater prefecture with no formal thaumaturgical training and no traceable lineage. He dismissed Thorne's claims of reality-bending abilities and impossible feats of magic as the desperate excuses of a failing pawn. Still, a flicker of unease remained. Something about the descriptions of Ada's power—the effortless manipulation of physical laws, the complete absence of a detectable arcane signature—resonated with a deeper, more primal fear. It was a fear he had not felt since the early days of his administration in the Northern Marshes, when the whispers of the Pattern Blight first began to surface.

A contagion, he thought, the word forming unbidden in his mind. Not a person, not a mage, not even a particularly skilled thaumaturge, but something...*else*. A systemic anomaly. A glitch in the fabric of reality itself. He had seen the effects of such glitches before. The creeping decay of the Ashen States. The unpredictable surges of raw arcane energy that sometimes disrupted the flow of commerce and communication. He had always viewed these as manageable inconveniences, temporary disruptions that could be contained, controlled, and even *utilized* to further the Empire's agenda. But this...this was different. This was a contagion that could spread, mutate, and potentially unravel the delicate balance he had so meticulously constructed.

He touched another control on his console, and the image of Port Dominus shimmered away, replaced by a schematic of the Prefecture's security systems. A complex network of wards, sensors, and automated defense protocols, all designed to maintain absolute control over the Spire and its surrounding districts. He reviewed the logs again, searching for any breach, any anomaly, any indication of how the fugitives had managed to escape undetected. Nothing. The systems had functioned perfectly. No alarms had been triggered. No security protocols had been violated. It was as if they had simply...*ceased to exist* within the Spire's confines and then reappeared outside its walls. Impossible. Illogical. Yet, undeniably true.

He felt a cold knot of fury tightening in his chest. A fury directed not just at the fugitives themselves, but at the sheer *insolence* of their actions. The audacity of defying his authority, of disrupting his order, of challenging the very foundations of his carefully constructed world. He would not tolerate it. He would find them. He would dissect their methods. He would understand their power. And then, he would *excise* them from the system, permanently. He would restore order. He would reassert control. He would ensure the stability of his world, no matter the cost. The thought, cold and precise, resonated through his mind, a chilling promise to himself and a silent threat to the unseen contagion that dared to challenge his dominion. The rhythmic tapping of his fingernails against the obsidian desk resumed, a steady, unwavering beat against the silence, a testament to his unwavering resolve.

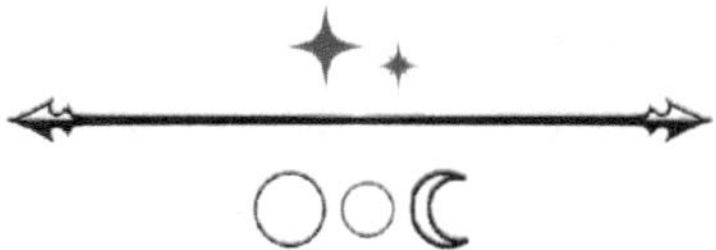

The silence of the chamber was broken by the soft hiss of the pneumatic door, followed by the hesitant entrance of a junior aide. The young man's posture was rigid, his face pale, his eyes fixed on a point somewhere just beyond Kraus's left shoulder. He held a data-slate clutched in both hands as if it were a fragile, explosive device. Kraus did not need to hear the report to know its contents. The aide's fear, palpable as the chill in the Spire's recycled air, spoke volumes.

"Prefect Valerius," the aide began, his voice barely a whisper, "the...the latest intelligence reports. Regarding the...the anomaly and the fugitive Knight-Commander Valerius."

Kraus remained silent, his gaze fixed on the swirling patterns of data displayed on the chamber's central holographic projector. The patterns, normally a source of intellectual satisfaction, now seemed to mock him with their meaningless complexity.

"The-the scrying attempts," the aide continued, his voice trembling slightly, "they have...failed. Completely. There is no trace of either the anomaly or the Knight-Commander. No magical signature. No energy trails. No witnesses. Nothing."

Kraus finally turned his gaze towards the aide, his pale blue eyes cold and sharp as shards of ice. "Nothing?"

"N-nothing, Prefect Valerius. It is as if...as if they have ceased to exist."

Kraus dismissed the aide with a cold, contemptuous wave of his hand. The young man, visibly relieved, bowed quickly and retreated, the pneumatic door hissing shut behind him. Alone again, the carefully constructed facade of control Kraus had maintained throughout the report finally cracked. A tremor of raw, unadulterated fury coursed through him, threatening to shatter the glacial calm he had cultivated over decades of ruthless ambition. He stood abruptly, his chair scraping against the obsidian floor with a harsh, grating sound. His gaze swept across the meticulously ordered surface of his desk, settling on a small, intricately carved crystal figurine. It was a priceless artifact, a gift from a vanquished rival, a symbol of his power and dominion.

Without a word, without a moment's hesitation, he swept it from the desk, sending it hurtling towards the far wall. It struck the polished obsidian with a sharp, satisfying *crack*, shattering into a thousand glittering fragments. The sound, echoing through the silent chamber, was a small, fleeting release, a momentary indulgence in the destructive impulse that raged beneath his carefully controlled exterior. It was not enough. Not nearly enough. But it was a start.

He paced the length of his chamber, the rhythmic click of his heels against the obsidian floor a counterpoint to the chaotic storm raging within his mind. Each stride was a precise, measured movement, a desperate attempt to impose order on the swirling vortex of frustration that threatened to consume him. Ada Lynx. Seraphina Valerius. Korina Tel. And now, Erita Systema. Four names, four unquantifiable variables that had thrown his meticulously calibrated world into disarray. Ghosts. Anomalies. Glitches in the system he had spent his entire life mastering.

He stopped before his panoramic window, the cold, unyielding surface a mirror to his own hardened gaze. Below, the city of Celgrad stretched out before him, a perfect grid of gleaming spires and intersecting corridors, a testament to the order and control he had so painstakingly cultivated. An order now threatened by the insidious spread of chaos. The Confederacy. A festering wound on the Empire's flank, a breeding ground for lawlessness and dissent. He had tolerated their existence for years, viewing them as a necessary evil, a chaotic counterpoint that served to reinforce the Empire's rigid stability. No longer. They had harbored the ghost. They had provided her with shelter, resources, and allies. They would pay the price.

He turned from the window, his resolve hardening with each

precise, measured breath. This was not simply a matter of containment. It was a matter of principle. A matter of restoring the balance, of reasserting the dominance he had so carefully constructed. He activated his command console, the obsidian surface glowing with a cold, ethereal light. His fingers moved swiftly across the controls, issuing a series of crisp, decisive commands. Resources would be reallocated. Garrisons reinforced. Patrols intensified. The full weight of the Imperial military machine would be brought to bear on the Korsair Confederacy, crushing their pathetic rebellion and rooting out the infestation that threatened to unravel his carefully ordered world. The hunt, once a strategic imperative, had become a personal obsession. A crusade to reclaim his dominion over a world that dared to defy his control.

CHAPTER 9

TRUTHS AND CONSEQUENCES

The warehouse loft had shed its skin as a tactical hideout and was slowly, improbably, becoming a home. The cold, industrial edges softened in the flickering light of the hearth Ada had coaxed into existence in a corner, its stone frame a stark, warm anomaly against the rough-hewn wooden walls. It was here, before the dancing flames, that Sera found herself watching something far more miraculous than any thaumaturgical feat: *Ada cooking.*

Ada, their reality-bending, code-wielding queen, stood with her back to the room, stirring a large iron pot that hung over the fire. Her shoulders, usually held with a tense, analytical straightness, were relaxed. A low, tuneless hum vibrated from her throat, a sound of pure, simple contentment that filled the quiet spaces between the crackle of the fire and the gentle bubble of the stew.

Sera leaned against a stack of crates, arms crossed, a soft, unfamiliar warmth blooming in her chest that had nothing to do with the hearth. *This...it's almost...normal.* The thought was a quiet revelation. It was a far cry from the Prefecture dining hall, a cavern of polished marble and whispered politics where every meal was a strategic maneuver. There, the clink of silverware was a prelude to a verbal thrust, the serving of wine a test of allegiance. Here, there were no politics, no posturing. *Just...us.*

Korina entered the main living space from their partitioned sleeping area, her focus already captured by the glowing screen of Obsidian. An ink smudge, a familiar resident on the bridge of her nose, stood out in the firelight. She moved with a distracted grace, her path a series of near-collisions with furniture that she navigated by sheer instinct, her mind a thousand kilometers away in a cascade of data.

"Something smells...nutrient-dense," Korina murmured, her eyes still locked on her data-slate.

Erita emerged moments later, a shadow detaching itself from the darker corners of the loft. She sniffed the air, her sharp features softening just a fraction. "Smells better than the rations you tried to burn last week, Valerius."

Sera grunted, a smile touching her lips. "They were tactically charred for longevity."

The easy banter, the familiar jabs—it was a language they had built together, a dialect of trust forged in shared danger. Erita moved to the hearth and peered into the pot, her usual guarded posture melting away in the fragrant steam.

Ada turned, a wooden spoon in her hand and a genuine, unguarded smile on her face. "It's almost ready. I found a merchant near the docks who wasn't a complete swindler—Actual vegetables!"

She began to ladle the thick, fragrant stew into a collection of mismatched bowls. The aroma filled the loft—a rich, savory scent of root vegetables, herbs, and slow-cooked meat that was a world away from the bland, functional taste of preserved rations. It was the smell of a real meal. The smell of a home.

They gathered around a low, sturdy table in the middle of the loft. There were no grand chairs, just cushions and crates, but as Sera settled between Korina and Ada, she felt more grounded than she ever had as her uncle's right hand. She took a spoonful of the stew. The warmth spread through her, a deep, nourishing heat that chased away the perpetual soldier's chill that lived in her bones. It was simple. *It was perfect.*

She watched them. *The way Ada hums when she cooks...the way Korina gets that smudge of ink on her nose...*Even Erita seemed to have misplaced her cynical armor, her focus entirely on the bowl in her hands. *This feels right. It feels real...and perfect.* For a moment, they were not a revolutionary cell plotting the downfall of corrupt powers. They were four women sharing a meal, their faces soft and content in the firelight. They were a family. The quiet clinking of spoons against ceramic was the only sound, a gentle, peaceful rhythm that Sera wanted to last forever.

The stew was a masterpiece of simple chemistry. Korina savored each spoonful, the warmth spreading from her stomach outward, a pleasant contrast to the usual cold knot of anxiety that lived there. Her mind, for once, was not racing through threat assessments or decrypting thaumaturgical signatures. It was simply...present. She listened to the low crackle of the hearth, felt the solid weight of the ceramic bowl in her hands, and registered the comfortable presence of the women around her as a stable, reassuring system. Ada's low hum had ceased, replaced by the quiet satisfaction of watching her partners enjoy her creation. It was a domesticity Korina had only ever read about, an algorithm for contentment she'd never had the variables to run.

Sera let out a long, contented sigh, setting her spoon down in her empty bowl. She stretched her powerful arms over her head, her broad shoulders shifting under her tunic. "Argent's light, Ada. That was incredible. You know, there's one perk to this whole revolution business I hadn't counted on."

Erita, wiping her own bowl clean with a piece of bread, arched a golden eyebrow. "That you finally learned how to identify an edible fungus without a field guide?"

A low chuckle rumbled in Sera's chest. "Hah—funny. No. It's that I haven't had to deal with my moon cycle in...what, six weeks now? Must be all the stress and running around. Good riddance, I say."

"Void, don't jinx it," Erita shot back, though the corner of her mouth quirked into a rare smile. "I'd rather face a dozen of Thorne's enforcers than deal with that particular brand of misery."

Sera laughed, a full, genuine sound that bounced off the wooden rafters. Ada smiled, her violet eyes soft in the firelight. For a moment, the four of them were suspended in that easy, shared laughter.

But Korina's spoon had stopped halfway to her mouth.

The gears in her mind, so recently at rest, spun into motion with a jarring shriek. *Stress.* The word was a trigger, a data point that refused to parse. Stress causes irregularities, certainly. Delayed cycles, sporadic spotting, a whole host of chaotic biological responses. *But complete, uniform cessation?* The laughter around her faded into a dull buzz as the calculations began. Four healthy women, all with different physiological baselines, all experiencing amenorrhea. *Not just irregularities, but a synchronized,*

total stop? The probability was a fraction so small it was functionally zero. It defied every biological and statistical model she knew.

It's an external variable.

The thought was cold, sharp, and absolute.

A controlled event. An override.

Her gaze snapped to Ada.

The Architect-Queen was still smiling, but it was a construct now. A fragile facade. Her hand, which had been resting on the table, had frozen mid-motion over her bowl. It was a micro-expression, a flicker of an error in a line of code, but to Korina's analytical gaze, it was a system-wide crash warning. She saw it. Beneath the placid surface, behind those luminous eyes, was a spark of pure, unadulterated panic.

Oh, Argent's light...Ada, what did you do?

The warmth of the room evaporated. A sudden, profound chill settled over Korina's skin, a cold that had nothing to do with the temperature of the loft and everything to do with the dawning horror crystallizing in her gut. The cheerful crackle of the fire sounded suddenly distant, the laughter of Sera and Erita like an echo from another time. *They hadn't noticed.* They were still wrapped in the simple comfort of the meal, the easy camaraderie. *They didn't see the glitch.*

But Korina saw nothing else. Her own eyes narrowed, her focus tightening on Ada with a predatory intensity. The academic curiosity of moments before curdled into a cold, sickening dread. This wasn't a quirk of their new life. It wasn't a coincidence. *It was a violation.* An unauthorized change to their source code.

The silence that followed the dying laughter was absolute. Heavy. Sera and Erita finally felt the shift, their smiles fading as they looked from Korina's rigid posture to Ada's strained expression. The comfortable atmosphere shattered into a thousand sharp-edged pieces.

Korina placed her spoon down with methodical precision, the quiet clink of ceramic on wood a thunderclap in the sudden stillness. When she spoke, her voice was stripped of all warmth, all emotion. It was the voice she used for axiomatic queries, for dissecting a problem down to its most fundamental truths. Calm. Quiet. And dangerously analytical.

"Ada..."

The name hung in the air, a single, weighted variable. Ada's eyes met hers, and the panic within them was no longer a flicker. It was a wildfire.

"Did you...did you do something?"

The silence in the loft became a physical pressure, a weight that pushed the air from Ada's lungs. Korina's question—calm, precise, devastating—was not an accusation. It was a diagnostic query, and Ada was the system with a critical error. Sera's hand, which had been resting on the table near hers, drew back. Erita's sharp, golden eyes narrowed, no longer tired but filled with a sudden, predatory focus.

They don't understand. I was trying to help.

"Ada?" Korina's voice was still quiet, but it held the unyielding logic of a mathematical proof. There was no escape.

Ada's gaze dropped to her half-eaten bowl of stew. The warmth of the meal, the simple joy of it, felt like a memory from a lifetime ago. "Yes," she whispered, the word a small, broken thing. "I...I turned it off."

She looked up, her expression pleading, trying to make them see the clean, elegant logic of her decision. "You were all in pain.

You were screaming at each other just the other day. It was a...a biological stressor. A vulnerability. I saw a flaw in the system, a recursive loop that was causing instability, so I...I patched it." She gestured with her hands, a futile attempt to shape the air into the form of her reasoning. "I was just trying to help...to *protect* you."

The word 'protect' hung in the air, hollow and meaningless.

Erita made a sound, a short, sharp hiss of disbelief that cut through Ada's explanation. A flicker of visceral disgust crossed her face, so potent it was like a physical blow. She pushed her cushion back, creating a definitive space between them. "You think our *bodies* are design flaws?" Her voice was not loud, but it was honed to a razor's edge, each word a deliberate, precise slice.

The pain, the blood...it's a weakness, Ada's mind screamed. *The world I came from uses those weaknesses to hurt you. I was making you safer. Stronger...*

Sera, who had been silent, finally moved. She didn't stand. She didn't shout. She simply looked at Ada, and the open, trusting warmth that had bloomed in her eyes over the last weeks was gone, replaced by a gray, desolate emptiness. A profound betrayal settled over her features, carving new, harsh lines around her mouth. When she spoke, her voice was a quiet, hollow whisper that barely carried across the table, yet it struck Ada with the force of a battering ram.

"You treated us like a machine."

A machine? No...I...I just wanted to take t-the pain away. The words ricocheted inside Ada's skull, a frantic, useless defense against the horror dawning on her face. She saw them then, not as her partners, but as separate, distinct entities, all of them recoiling from her. Erita's revulsion was a shield. Sera's hurt was a chasm. And

Korina...Korina's expression was the worst of all. It was not anger or betrayal. It was the cold, clinical horror of a scholar witnessing an unforgivable ethical breach. The look one gives to a monster.

Ada's justification crumbled into dust. She had seen a problem and deployed a solution, an elegant bit of code to remove a painful, messy variable. She had seen suffering and, with the absolute power of a god, had simply deleted it. She had done it out of love, a desperate, clumsy love born from a past she could never explain to them. A past where biology was a weapon used against you, where blood meant only violation and pain. She had tried to build a sanctuary, and to do so, she had stripped them of a part of themselves without their consent.

She hadn't healed them. She had rewritten them. She hadn't protected them. She had violated them on the most fundamental level.

Sera's words echoed, the quiet accusation morphing into an undeniable truth. *You treated us like a machine.* The fire in the hearth crackled, oblivious, casting long, dancing shadows on the walls of the home she had just broken. Ada stared at the three women—her lovers, her partners, her *family*—and for the first time, she truly understood the monstrous potential of the power she wielded. She had offered them kindness, and they had received tyranny.

They're going to leave, a panicked voice whispered in her mind. *They're going to leave you* ***alone.***

The words struck Ada not as insults, but as lines of code executing a catastrophic system failure within her. *You treated us like a machine.* Sera's voice, hollow and broken. *You think our bodies are design flaws?* Erita's voice, sharp with disgust. Each phrase was a key, unlocking a sequence she had buried under a mountain of data and denial.

The world around her began to lose its resolution. The warm, flickering light of the hearth bled at the edges, the scent of stew and woodsmoke fading into a sterile, metallic tang. Erita took another step back, her hand moving instinctively toward the daggers at her belt. It was not a threat, but a primal, reflexive need to arm herself against a violation.

"You took *control* of us," Erita's voice was low, each word a stone dropped into a deep, cold well. "You made a decision about our bodies without our consent."

Control. ***Without consent.***

The final key turned. The lock shattered.

The wooden floor of the loft dissolved beneath her, replaced by the gritty, freezing concrete of a Sagiyama alley. The smell of stale ramen and damp refuse filled her nostrils. The weight wasn't emotional anymore; it was a physical pressure, a heavy, sweating body pinning her down, her arms held fast. A phantom pain, a tearing sensation, a complete and total loss of self. Her body was no longer her own. It was a thing. An object. A system being acted upon. A machine being used.

He controlled me. He decided what was best for my body.

The memory was not a memory. It was a live feed, a current reality that ripped through the fabric of Kremøtoa. The loft snapped back into focus, but it was alien now, a hostile environment. The faces of her partners were distorted, their features warped by the lens of her own monstrousness.

Oh, my gød. The thought was a silent, shattering scream. *I'm him.*

The logic was perfect, clean, and utterly damning. He had seen a body and taken it. She had seen a flaw and fixed it. He had acted without her consent. She had acted without theirs. The motivation was irrelevant—love, lust, protection, power—the result was identical. The ultimate violation. The theft of autonomy.

I became the monster.

A strangled gasp ripped from Ada's throat, a sound of pure, abject horror. Her legs buckled. She stumbled back from the table, her hands flying to her mouth as if to choke back the poison of her own realization. The carefully built world she had designed as a sanctuary, a place free from the pain and trauma of her past, was a lie.

I built a world to escape him, and I brought him with me inside my own head.

The strength fled her limbs. She crumpled, not with grace, but like a puppet whose strings were cut, hitting the rough wooden floorboards with a heavy, final thud. The impact sent a jolt of pain up her side, but it was a distant signal, drowned out by the roaring static of her self-loathing. The floor was hard and cold against her cheek.

In my attempt to protect them from my pain, I inflicted his on them.

The sobs started then, not the quiet, pleading tears of someone seeking comfort, but ugly, guttural sounds torn from the deepest part of her. They were the sounds of an animal caught in a trap of its own making, the horrified, ragged gasps of a soul witnessing its own damnation. They sounded alien in her own ears, the wails of a stranger, of a monster.

Through the blur of her tears, she saw them. Korina, Sera, Erita. They were frozen, their anger, their shock, their betrayal—all of it washed away and replaced by a stunned, horrified confusion. They had been ready for an argument, for a fight. They were not prepared for this. Not for this utter, violent self-destructive *implosion*.

Ada tried to pushed herself up onto her elbows, the effort immense. She had to make them understand. Not to forgive her, but to know that *she knew*. That she saw what she was. Her vision swam, the firelight fracturing into a hundred painful shards.

"I'm sorry," she sobbed, the words clawing their way up her throat, tasting of ash and self-hatred. Her body shook with the force of each ragged breath. "I didn't...I didn't see..."

She choked on the words, her gaze locking with Korina's horrified stare.

"I became..." Ada managed to choke out—just before her view faded to black as her head fell to the floor.

The heavy, final *thud* of Ada's head hitting the floorboards vaporized Korina's righteous anger. One moment, a cold fury coiled in her gut; the next, it was gone, replaced by a surge of pure, ice-water panic. The scent of the cooling stew turned sickening in the air.

"ADA!"

She scrambled across the splintery floor on her hands and knees, ignoring the shocked, frozen figures of Sera and Erita at the table. Her fingers found Ada's neck, searching for a pulse. It was there, but it was a frantic, erratic bird trapped in her throat.

"Ada, can you hear me? *Respond!*"

Her training kicked in, a desperate lunge for the familiar

comfort of process and data. She ripped Obsidian from its holster, the cool metal a useless comfort against her trembling palm. Her fingers flew across the holographic interface, the high-pitched taps echoing in the sudden, tense silence of the loft.

"What's happening to her? Is she...?" Sera's voice finally broke, thin and strained.

"Check for poison—*now*," Erita commanded, her own shock hardening into sharp practicality.

"I am!" Korina's voice cracked. Bio-etheric readings flared across the screen, but they weren't data. They were chaos—a meaningless waterfall of angry, red error messages and corrupted symbols.

ERROR: UNSTABLE PARADOX DETECTED

What in the Void does that even mean?

She ran the toxicology scan. **NEGATIVE**—She queried for curse signatures, pattern blights, physical trauma. Negative. Inconclusive. *Null data.* Obsidian, her second soul, the most advanced analytical tool she had ever known, was spitting back gibberish. The metallic taste of fear coated the back of her tongue.

"There's nothing!" she cried out, her voice rising with each failed diagnostic. "No poison, no curse...The readings are just... static! I-I don't understand!"

She looked from the useless, flashing screen to Ada's still, pale face. Her partner, the woman who could rewrite reality with a thought, looked small and fragile on the rough wooden floor. And the horrifying realization dawned on Korina, a truth colder and sharper than any blade. The data didn't correlate because there was no corresponding file. This wasn't a physical ailment. It wasn't malware or a curse that could be quarantined and purged.

This was a complete system crash. A wound not in Ada's body, but in her very soul.

And against that, all Korina's logic, all her knowledge, all her brilliant tools, were *nothing*.

She was helpless.

Erita watched the chaos from the table, a cold knot tightening in her stomach. The rich, savory scent of the stew—a meal meant to celebrate their strange, new beginning—now smelled like rot. Korina was a blur of motion, her frantic fingers dancing across Obsidian's holographic interface, each tap a sharp, useless protest against the inevitable. A torrent of corrupted code and garish red error messages flowed across the screen, a digital scream that mirrored the scholar's ragged, panicked breaths.

Across the room, Sera stood like a statue carved from equal parts rage and confusion. Her hand rested on the pommel of one of her blades, a warrior's instinct with no enemy to strike. Her face was a mask of shock, her eyes wide, fixed on the still form of the woman she had sworn to protect. A protector helpless. A warrior with no war to fight.

Useless. The thought was a shard of ice in Erita's mind. *Both of them are useless right now.*

Her own anger was a living thing, a viper coiling in her chest. The violation was a fresh wound, raw and deep. Ada hadn't just made a mistake; she had reached into the core of their beings and rewritten them without consent. It was the ultimate act of control, a betrayal so profound it defied words. Erita wanted to scream. She wanted to shake Ada until her teeth rattled.

But the woman on the floor wasn't the monster who had committed the act. She was the consequence. Broken.

My anger is a luxury we can't afford right now.

The thought cut through the heat of her fury with chilling clarity. This wasn't a betrayal to be punished; it was a systemic failure to be contained. Recrimination was an indulgence. Panic was a liability. The system—their little revolutionary cell, their fragile polycule, the very woman who held reality in her hands... who she loved—was compromised. They needed a new protocol.

Erita pushed herself away from the table, the scrape of her chair legs loud in the tense air. She moved with a deliberate, measured grace that defied the room's frantic energy. She crossed the floor and placed a firm, grounding hand on Korina's shoulder.

The frantic tapping stopped.

Korina flinched, her head snapping up. Her violet eyes were wide with terror, swimming with unshed tears. "I can't—Eri, I can't get a reading! It's all corrupted data, it's a paradox, it doesn't make sense—"

"Breathe, Korina," Erita's voice was low, steady. It wasn't gentle, but it was solid. "You're drowning in noise. Shut it down."

Korina stared at her, then at the still-flashing screen of Obsidian, a lifeline that was failing her. With a choked sob, she swiped the interface away, plunging the corner of the room into the dim, flickering lamplight. The sudden silence was heavier than the noise had been.

Erita gave Korina's shoulder a final, firm squeeze before letting go. She knelt on the floor beside Ada, the rough, cold wood pressing into her knees. Up close, Ada looked impossibly small. Her face was slack, pale under the warm light, her chest rising and falling with shallow, unsteady breaths. Their Ada, a woman who could fix and rewrite the landscape of reality—looked like nothing more than a broken girl.

The viper of Erita's anger hissed again, but she forced it down.

Punishing the girl on the floor would solve nothing. They had to address the culprit who broke her. *They needed a permanent fix.*

She reached out, her fingers hesitating for a fraction of a second before gently brushing a strand of dark violet-black hair from Ada's forehead. The skin was cool and clammy.

"Ada," Erita's voice was soft, but it cut through the room's thick atmosphere with the precision of a sharpened blade. She wasn't just speaking to the unconscious woman before her; she was broadcasting a message into the core of the system, a plea aimed at the ghost in the machine. Each word was a carefully placed stone in the foundation of a new understanding. "Please—I know that's not you, but this can't happen again."

Sera took a half-step forward, a silent question in her eyes. Erita didn't look away from Ada's face.

"How can we make sure of that?" The question hung in the air, heavy and absolute. It was not an accusation. It was a demand for a new rule, a patch for the flaw in their creator. Her voice dropped to a near-whisper, laced with a desperation she would deny to her dying day.

"...Please, wake up..."

The first thing to pierce the black static was a voice. A question, low and sharp, echoing in the void of her mind.

"How can we make sure of that?"

Erita's voice. It wasn't an accusation; it was a demand for a new protocol. A patch for the bug that was *her*.

Ada's eyelids fluttered, heavy as lead shutters. The world swam back into focus, not as lines of code, but as raw, painful reality. Three faces swam above her, haloed by the warm, flickering light of the loft's hearth. Korina. Sera. Erita. They knelt around her on the rough floorboards, a protective, worried circle.

They're still here. They didn't leave.

The anger she had seen in their eyes—the raw, visceral disgust —was gone. In its place was something far worse: a tense, terrible concern. The look one gave a delicate, explosive device that might detonate at any moment. *She had done this.* She had turned their sanctuary into a minefield and made herself the mine.

The memory of her realization crashed over her again. The cold, sterile logic of her choice. The violation. The power she wielded not as a tool, but as a weapon against the very people she loved. She was no better than Kraus—no better than the faceless figure from the alley of her nightmares. She was a monster who built cages.

Shame, hot and acidic, burned in her throat. She pushed herself up on one elbow, the movement clumsy and weak. Her body felt disconnected, a borrowed vessel she no longer deserved to pilot.

"I..." Her voice was a dry rasp, a stranger's sound. Korina's hand immediately found hers, fingers lacing through her own. The touch was a shock, a spark of undeserved comfort.

I broke their trust. How do I fix it? I have to show them I have nothing to hide. I have to let them in...All the way in.

Ada's gaze met Erita's. The spymaster's golden eyes were intense, searching not for weakness, but for a solution. Ada knew what she had to do. *It was the only way.*

An act of total, terrifying vulnerability.

"A link," she whispered, her voice trembling with the weight of the offer. "A telepathic link...I will lower my mental defenses. Completely. You will be able to...to see my thoughts. Unfiltered. Always."

She offered it up like a sacrifice, her own mind laid bare on an altar of atonement. *Let them see the rot inside. Let them have the key to her every thought, her every command.* It was the only penance that felt equal to the crime.

Sera's breath hitched. Erita's expression tightened, her mind clearly processing the tactical implications of such a monumental weakness.

But it was Korina who spoke first, her voice a gentle counter-melody to Ada's ragged proposal. Her thumb stroked the back of Ada's hand, a soothing, rhythmic motion.

"*No,*" she said, not with force, but with the quiet certainty of an architect finding a fatal flaw in a blueprint. "Ada, no...an open port with no security protocols? To your core processing? Think of the liability. If anyone...if *anything* with the ability to read minds were to get close to us, they wouldn't just compromise you. They'd compromise all of us through you."

Ada stared at her, uncomprehending. This wasn't the reaction she expected. *She was offering them absolute control, and they were pointing out the security risk.*

Korina leaned closer, her violet eyes soft and earnest. "What if...what if it wasn't...a weakening? But a connection. A bond." She squeezed Ada's hand. "Between equals. A shared network—yes—but with standard mental defenses. We could communicate silently, share tactical data instantly, but our own thoughts, our own core selves, would remain sovereign unless we choose to share them."

Sera, who had been kneeling with the tense stillness of a predator, let out a slow breath. She nodded, her gaze fixed on Ada. "A shared strength, not a weakness, or a liability. A direct line of communication in a fight, no need for hand signals or spoken words—I like it." She framed it in the only way that made sense to her: as a weapon, a tool to make their unit stronger.

They...they're not letting me fall on my sword. They're forging a new one for all of us to share.

Erita, ever the pragmatist, gave a sharp, decisive nod. Her eyes held a flicker of something that looked like approval. "A shared network, with each node retaining its own firewalls. It minimizes the risk. It eliminates the single point of failure that your...*original* plan presented." Her gaze softened for just a fraction of a second. "It levels the playing field. *An acceptable solution.*"

The combined weight of their response hit Ada with the force of a physical blow. *They weren't punishing her. They weren't demanding she prostrate herself.* They were taking the wreckage of her monstrous mistake and offering to build something better from it. Something stronger. Together.

A sob, thick and heavy with a relief so profound it felt like pain, escaped her lips. Tears blurred their faces into warm constellations of light. This was what trust really was. Not a lock to be handed over, but a structure to be built, brick by brick, by all of them.

Ada nodded, unable to form words past the lump in her throat. She squeezed Korina's hand, a silent message of gratitude that felt hopelessly inadequate. She finally found her voice, thick with emotion, but clear.

"Deal," she managed. "We can do it. Together."

CHAPTER 10

A BRIEF REQUIEM

//EXPLICIT CONTENT WARNING*//

**Please be aware this scene involves four female characters involved in explicit consensual intimacy—reader discretion advised.*

Hours later, the warehouse loft was a sanctuary of quiet. The storm had passed, leaving behind not wreckage, but a landscape washed clean. Flickering candles stood sentinel on overturned crates, their flames stretching long, dancing shadows across the shared space of bedrolls and blankets on the floor. The sharp scent of ozone from their argument had been replaced by the calming aroma of lavender and chamomile from the tea Ada had made, a peace offering that had become a communion.

Ada lay on her side, a silent observer in the heart of their makeshift nest. The crushing weight that had threatened to splinter her code was gone, replaced by a fragile, profound gratitude. She watched the others, her friends, her partners, her saviors. Korina was curled nearby, her data-slate forgotten, her violet eyes soft in the candlelight. Sera sat cross-legged, a statue of crimson and steel at rest, her usual vigilance softened into a watchful tenderness. Erita lay propped on an elbow, her golden pixie cut gleaming, her sharp features unguarded for once.

They could have left, Ada thought, the words a silent prayer. *They could have hated me. But they stayed. They...rebuilt with me.*

The silence was not empty, but full of unspoken understanding. Then, a shift. Sera moved first, her motion fluid and deliberate. She reached out, her calloused fingers tracing the line of Ada's spine through the thin fabric of her tunic. The touch was not demanding, not even questioning. It was a statement. *You are here. We are here.*

Ada flinched, a ghost of her past trauma rising within her. But Sera's touch remained, a gentle pressure that was both strong and reverent, an act of worship. Ada felt her muscles unknot beneath the quiet authority of that hand.

Korina stirred, her movements lighter, more inquisitive. She scooted closer, her fingers finding Ada's, lacing through them. It wasn't the touch of a scholar analyzing a specimen, but of a lover rediscovering a treasured map. She brought Ada's hand to her lips, pressing a soft kiss to her knuckles.

A choked sound caught in Ada's throat. She turned onto her back, her gaze flickering between them.

"Is this...okay?" Ada whispered, the words barely audible, freighted with the fear that this was a dream—a forgiveness she hadn't truly earned.

Erita answered by moving, her lithe form slinking around to Ada's other side. She leaned over, her breath warm against Ada's ear. "*It is,*" she murmured, her voice a low purr that vibrated through Ada's bones. Her hand settled on Ada's hip, a possessive, grounding weight. An act of reclaiming what was hers.

This wasn't an assault. This was an embrace from all sides. A healing. *This isn't just desire,* Ada realized, her heart aching with a beautiful, painful clarity. *This is...grace.*

Sera's hand slid from her back, moving to the hem of her tunic. She paused, her eyes asking a question her voice did not. Ada gave a single, trembling nod. Sera gently eased the garment up and over Ada's head, tossing it aside into the shadows. The cool air of the loft caressed her skin, raising goosebumps. But she felt no shame, no vulnerability in her nakedness. She felt only seen.

Korina released her hand and began to unlace her trousers, her touch light and clinical, yet filled with an undeniable affection. Erita's fingers kneaded the muscle of her hip, a silent, possessive rhythm. Each touch was not an accusation, but an affirmation. They were not just forgiving her; they were showing her what it meant to be truly seen, truly known—with all her monstrous flaws —and still be loved.

Sera's lips found the hollow of her throat, a reverent kiss that sent a shiver through her entire system. Korina's curious fingers traced the faint lines of code that sometimes shimmered on her skin, a familiar analytical touch now imbued with a deep tenderness. Erita's mouth claimed hers in a kiss that was both fierce and soft, a promise and a demand all in one.

Ada's mind, which had felt like a fortress under siege, finally lowered its gates. The scents of her lovers, the musky, earthy aroma of their shared desire, filled her senses. She was no longer analyzing data streams or calculating probabilities. *She was simply feeling.*

Her hands, so used to commanding reality, found purchase in

the soft fabric of their clothes, in the warmth of their skin. She let them guide her, let them undress her, let them explore the body she had so often felt disconnected from. Korina's clever mouth found a breast, her tongue a startling, electric shock of pleasure. Sera's powerful hands cupped her legs, parting them with a gentle strength that made Ada's breath hitch. Erita's fingers, deft and sure, slipped between those parted thighs, finding the wet heat waiting there.

A moan tore from Ada's throat, raw and unrestrained. It was not just the sound of pleasure, but of release. The last vestiges of her shame, of her feeling like a broken machine, were being washed away by this tide of affection.

I am not just a creator or a machine, her thoughts sang, a triumphant chorus against the rising tide of sensation. ***I am theirs.***

When their bodies finally joined, a tangle of limbs and soft whispers in the flickering candlelight, it was a culmination. A symphony. And as the waves of ecstasy crested, pulling another cry from her lips, Ada felt the last of her guilt dissolve. In its place, a new truth was coded directly into her soul: she was forgiven.

The world resolved into a series of soft, warm constants. The scent of candle wax and sweat, the gentle give of the mattress, the weight of tangled limbs. The frantic, desperate peak had broken, leaving a languid tide of contentment in its wake. Ada lay between them, her body a pliant, humming thing, her mind blissfully quiet.

Sera shifted, the movement a ripple of contained power. She

propped herself on an elbow, her form a silhouette of corded muscle against the flickering candlelight. The faint sheen of perspiration on her broad shoulders gleamed like polished copper. Her gaze fell upon Ada, and it was not the look of a lover sated, but of a zealot before a holy relic.

Her hand, calloused and mapped with the story of a thousand battles, rose to cup Ada's cheek. The roughness of her skin was a grounding friction against Ada's, a reminder of the warrior who had pledged her sword. Yet, the pressure was impossibly gentle. Her thumb traced the line of Ada's jaw—a slow, deliberate exploration that seemed to commit every contour to memory.

"Ada," Sera murmured, her voice a low rumble that vibrated through Ada's skull. The name was a prayer on her lips. She leaned down, her mouth finding Ada's not with the fiery passion of moments before, but with a profound tenderness. It was a kiss of fealty, a silent promise of unwavering loyalty that sealed every crack in Ada's fractured soul. Each slow press of her lips was a vow, each soft breath a shield.

Sera holds me as if I'm the most precious thing in the world, Ada thought, a wave of security so potent it was almost overwhelming washing through her. *Her strength is a shield around my vulnerability.* She felt anchored, cherished, as if the strongest fortress in Kremøtoa had been built not of stone, but of this woman's devotion.

As Sera settled back, draping a possessive arm over Ada's waist, a new presence made itself known. Korina moved with a quieter, more inquisitive energy. Her long, violet hair pooled on the pillow beside Ada's head, a silken river in the dim light. Her approach was not of a warrior, but of a scholar on the verge of a breakthrough.

Korina's violet eyes, wide and luminous, were a universe of

intellectual curiosity and unbridled adoration. She didn't just look at Ada; she *perceived* her, her gaze tracing the faint, silvery lines of code that sometimes shimmered on Ada's skin as if she were deciphering a sacred text. Her touch followed her gaze, feather-light and analytical. Her fingertips ghosted over Ada's collarbone, danced down her sternum, each brush sending a spark of clean, electric energy through Ada's system. It wasn't a carnal touch, but one of pure fascination.

Then, Korina leaned closer, her nose hovering just above Ada's shoulder. She inhaled, a soft, deliberate breath, and her eyes fluttered shut. *Ada's scent.* A complex algorithm of cherry blossom and the chamomile from the tea they had shared, overlaid with the musky, uniquely human aroma of her own body. It was this base note, this biological signature, that seemed to utterly captivate Korina. It was an intellectual aphrodisiac, a data point her brilliant mind could only process through pure sensation.

With a soft, breathy sigh of utter fascination, Korina pressed her lips to the hollow of Ada's arm. The gesture was so unexpected, so intimate, it stole the air from Ada's lungs. It wasn't a kiss of passion in the way Sera's had been; it was a kiss of discovery, of reverence for the very reality of her being. Korina was worshiping the flaw, adoring the glitch that made her human.

A profound realization bloomed in the center of Ada's chest, radiant and warm. Sera's strength was her shield. Korina's curiosity was her mirror. One protected her body, the other celebrated her soul.

And Korina...she looks at me, breathes my scent, as if I am a mystery she is dedicating her entire being to understanding. A single, perfect tear escaped the corner of Ada's eye, tracing a path through the grime and sweat on her temple. *They are not just touching my body; they are communing with my soul.*

Then a third current joined the river. Erita. She moved from Ada's other side, a predator shedding her camouflage. The usual sharpness in her golden eyes—the cynical shield she held against the world—was gone. In its place burned a raw, almost desperate fire. She didn't approach with Sera's reverence or Korina's wonder. She simply claimed.

Her mouth crashed against Ada's, a messy, open-mouthed kiss that was less about finesse and more about a frantic, possessive need. It was a sloppy, hungry declaration. Her tongue swept into Ada's mouth, a bold invasion that tasted of bitter coffee and a deep, unspoken sweetness. Her fingers dug into the soft flesh of Ada's hip, a grip that wasn't meant to harm, but to anchor. To hold. As if she feared Ada might fragment into code and vanish if she let go.

*Erita...*The thought was a flare in Ada's mind. *Her kiss isn't asking, it's declaring. A fierce, possessive love she keeps locked away. She's letting me see all of it...all of them.*

The last wall around Ada's heart, the final barricade of guilt she had erected against herself, crumbled into dust.

Their bodies became a single, moving sculpture in the flickering candlelight. A symphony of intertwined limbs and shared heat. Sera's powerful leg hooked over Korina's slender one, Erita's arm was a band across Ada's stomach, her hand finding the curve of Sera's breast. It was a beautiful, chaotic tangle of acceptance. Korina's inquisitive fingers traced the new, faint lines of muscle from traveling on Ada's abdomen, while Sera's hand slid down, a broad, warm weight settling on her thigh.

Their focus returned to her. A trinity of devotion aimed at a single, trembling point. Erita's lips left her mouth, trailing a wet, hot path down her neck, nipping at her collarbone. Korina's fingers found the sensitive skin of her inner thigh, an exploratory touch that sent a jolt of clean, pure pleasure through her. Sera's thumb began a slow, deliberate circle against the nexus of her nerves, a patient, knowing pressure that promised oblivion.

I'm not broken, Ada thought, a silent sob catching in her throat. *I'm not a mistake. I am loved. Unconditionally.*

The pressure built, a rising tide of sensation and emotion. It was overwhelming, a flood of sensory data so complete it threatened to overwrite her very core. She gasped their names, the sounds swallowed by the press of lips against her skin.

*It's okay to let go—**it's safe.***

With that final thought, the dam broke. The release was not a simple, physical thing. It was a system-wide, healing reboot. A wave of pure, white-hot energy erupted from her center, a cathartic purge that radiated through every cell. It was the deletion of a corrupt file, the cleansing of a deep-seated malware. The last vestiges of her shame, the lingering poison of her violation, were washed away in the torrent. A cry ripped from her throat, a sound not just of pleasure, but of profound, absolute relief. It was the sound of a soul being made whole again.

The world did not rush back in. It seeped, slow and warm, like honey. The last tremor of Ada's release faded, leaving a profound stillness in its wake. The air, thick with the sweet, musky scent of their mingled sweat, felt sacred. The flickering candles, their wicks drowning in pools of melted wax, cast long, dancing shadows that softened the hard edges of the warehouse loft.

They lay in a single, breathing heap. A tangle of limbs and shared warmth, their bodies slick and pliant. The frantic energy was gone, the anger and betrayal burned away in a crucible of desperate honesty and reclaimed intimacy. What remained was a quiet, bone-deep satisfaction.

Sera's heavy arm draped across Ada's waist, a possessive, protective weight that anchored her to the mattress. Her breathing, usually so controlled, was a deep, uneven rumble against Ada's back, her face buried in the cascade of violet-black hair. She slept the sleep of a soldier whose war was, for a single night, truly over.

Erita was a warm line pressed against Ada's other side. The sharp, cynical armor she wore like a second skin had melted away completely. One of her hands, usually balled into a fist or wrapped around the hilt of a dagger, lay open and relaxed on Korina's hip. Her sharp features were softened in the guttering light, her expression one of unguarded peace.

Korina, nestled between Erita and Ada, was the quiet center of their exhausted tangle. Her head rested in the crook of Erita's shoulder, her violet braids a stark, beautiful contrast against Erita's pale skin. A small, contented smile graced her lips, the look of a scholar who had finally solved the universe's most complex and beautiful equation.

The silence was a language all its own. It spoke of forgiveness given and received, of boundaries shattered and rebuilt on a foundation of unshakeable trust. It was a silence filled with the soft, rhythmic sound of four hearts beating in near-perfect synchrony, of four sets of lungs drawing the same contented air.

Ada felt a current pass between them, a silent, shared awareness that hummed beneath their skin. It was more than forgiveness. *It was an evolution.* They had faced the ugliest parts of each other—the possessiveness, the violation, the rage—and had not turned away. They had embraced it, absorbed it, and forged it into something stronger. Something unbreakable.

As sleep began to claim them, a final, unified thought bloomed in the quiet space they shared, a truth that settled into the very code of their beings.

They were not just lovers; they were comrades, family, and a proud polycule. Nothing could take that from them.

CHAPTER 11

THE FIRST PAIN

The warehouse command center, bathed in the ethereal glow of the holographic map of Kremøtoa, hummed with a focused energy. Dust motes danced in the beams of projected light, illuminating the intent faces of the quartet gathered around the display. The vast, unforgiving expanse of the ocean, rendered in shimmering blues and greens, dominated the holographic projection, a tangible reminder of the geographical and political chasm that separated them from the Free Realm of Rhedeon.

"So, we're agreed then?" Ada's voice, calm and steady, cut through the quiet hum of the projector. "To fight Thorne, to truly dismantle his network and counter The Alchemist's threat, we need more than just information and a few loyal soldiers."

"We need a goddamn armada," Sera added, her voice rough but firm. Her hand rested on the hilt of one of her blades—a familiar, comforting gesture. "Thorne controls the flow of goods in and out of Port Dominus. He's choking the life out of the city, lining his pockets while the people starve."

"And he's supplying the Theocracy with weapons," Erita chimed in, her golden eyes narrowed. "Weapons enhanced with that twisted alchemy of his. We can't fight a war on two fronts without the means to strike back."

Korina, her fingers dancing across the surface of Obsidian, nodded in agreement. "Our current resources are...limited. We have the gold from the *Argent Lion*, yes, but that's a finite resource. To establish true economic independence, we need to control our own supply lines."

Ada traced the coastline of Rhedeon with her finger, the holographic waves rippling under her touch. "Erita's sources confirm it. Rhedeon is the key. Their shipwrights are the best in Kremøtoa. If we can forge an alliance with them, secure access to their shipyards..."

"We'd have the means to build our own fleet," Sera finished, her eyes gleaming with anticipation. "A fleet capable of challenging Thorne's stranglehold on the sea lanes, of breaking the Theocracy's supply of alchemically enhanced weapons."

"Months," Janna grumbled, her deep voice laced with a pragmatic skepticism. "Months at sea, exposed to every blighted wind and rogue current the ocean can throw at us. Imperial patrols sniffing around like hungry sharks. Korsair raiders looking for an easy score. Not to mention the sheer logistical nightmare of supplying a ship for that kind of voyage." She gestured towards the holographic map, the vast expanse of the ocean seeming to stretch out before them like an insurmountable obstacle.

"While we're gallivanting around the cape of Korsair towards Rhedeon," she continued, her tone sharpening, "Thorne will be consolidating his power here. He'll be tightening his grip on Port Dominus, squeezing the life out of the people, rooting out any hint of rebellion. We've sparked a fire here, Ada. A small one, maybe, but a fire nonetheless. Leaving it unattended for months is like asking for it to be stamped out."

"Janna makes a valid point," Korina murmured, her gaze fixed on the swirling data streams flowing across Obsidian's surface. "The Azure Rose is a valuable ally, but their loyalty is...fluid. Willem's a pragmatist. If he perceives our absence as weakness, he may be tempted to cut a deal with Thorne to save his own skin."

Erita nodded curtly, her golden eyes reflecting the cold, calculating light of the holographic map. "And Thorne isn't stupid. He'll use every Byt at his disposal to turn Willem, to crush any remaining resistance while we're gone. He'll paint us as deserters, cowards who abandoned the cause at the first sign of trouble."

The weight of their words settled like a physical burden on Ada's shoulders. She stared at the shimmering projection of Rhedeon, the vibrant, chaotic sprawl of Port Veridia beckoning from across the vast expanse of the ocean. It was so close, yet so impossibly far. The cape of Korsair, a treacherous stretch of coastline notorious for its unpredictable currents and sudden storms, stood between them and their only viable source of naval power. A journey around the cape, even with Silas's skilled navigation and the *Sea Serpent's* reinforced hull, would take months. Months they couldn't afford.

A low, frustrated sigh escaped her lips. She felt a familiar tightening in her chest, the same suffocating pressure she experienced back in her cramped Sagiyama apartment, hunched over her glowing monitors, wrestling with lines of code that refused to cooperate. It was a feeling she had thought she'd left behind in that other world, a world that now felt both distant and intimately familiar.

She traced the coastline with her fingertip, the cool surface of the holographic projection offering no solace. The logical part of her brain, the part that had built this world, brick by digital brick, screamed for a solution, an elegant workaround, a clever hack to bypass the limitations of geography and time. But there were no shortcuts in this reality, no cheat codes to rewrite the laws of physics, no backdoors into the fabric of space and time.

"There has to be a way," she muttered, her voice barely above a whisper.

The holographic map shimmered before Ada's eyes, the swirling currents and treacherous shoals of the Serpent's Maw a dizzying kaleidoscope of blues and greens. Rhedeon, a beacon of hope and potential power, pulsed like a distant star at the edge of a vast, uncharted coastline. There *had* to be a way. There *had* to be a shortcut. Her mind, fueled by desperation and a lifetime of problem-solving, strained against the boundaries of reality, seeking a loophole, a hidden passage, a backdoor into the very fabric of the world she had created.

Her focus narrowed, the rest of the world fading into a hazy periphery. The hum of the warehouse generators, the quiet murmur of Korina and Erita's voices, the rhythmic tapping of Sera's fingers on the table—all receded into a muffled drone, swallowed by the all-consuming intensity of her concentration.

The map, no longer a static projection, began to swirl and twist, the continents shifting and reforming like molten wax under the heat of her gaze. Her vision blurred, the edges of the holographic display dissolving into streaks of vibrant, pulsating color.

She felt a strange tingling sensation behind her eyes, a subtle pressure building, growing, intensifying with each passing second. It was a sensation unlike anything she had ever experienced in Kremøtoa, a raw, visceral feeling that resonated deep within her physical form. The lingering exhaustion from their weeks of travel, the relentless stress of their precarious situation, the sheer mental strain of trying to bend reality to her will—it all coalesced into a single, focal point of overwhelming intensity. It was as if the very fabric of her being was stretching, straining, reaching a breaking point.

Then, without warning, a sharp, blinding spike of pain lanced through her skull, directly behind her eyes. It was an agony unlike anything she could have imagined, a raw, visceral shock to her system that transcended the abstract, intellectual understanding of pain she had programmed into the world. It was *her* pain, real and immediate, coursing through *her* nerves, searing *her* senses. It was the first true, physical pain she had ever experienced in Kremøtoa, a brutal, unwelcome reminder of the human body she now inhabited, a body she had created but never truly understood until this very moment.

In an involuntary, desperate reaction to the searing agony, Ada blinked. Hard.

And in that instant, she was gone.

"Ada?" Korina gasped, her voice rising in alarm. "What in the Void? Ada? ADA!?" The chair screeched against the floor as she scrambled to her feet, her eyes wide with a mixture of confusion and dawning panic. “Where did she...Sera! Erita!” Her voice, usually so calm and collected, cracked with a tremor of fear. “Where did she go?”

Sera’s hand instinctively flew to the hilt of her sword, her eyes scanning the space where Ada had been just a moment before, searching for any sign of an attacker, a hidden portal, *something* to explain the impossible. Janna, her face a mask of stunned disbelief, let out a low growl, her hand gripping the heavy battle-axe that leaned against the wall beside her. Erita, her usual cynical composure shattered, swore under her breath, a rapid-fire string of curses that would have made a Dominus dockworker blush.

A soft thump echoed from the far side of the sprawling loft, the sound of something solid landing lightly on the wooden floor. Korina, Sera, Erita, and Janna whirled around, their eyes snapping to the source of the noise. Ada stood across the room, near the stacks of salvaged equipment and arcane artifacts they had yet to catalog. Her back was to them, her shoulders slumped slightly, her hands clasped tightly around her head.

Ada swayed slightly, her body still trembling from the aftershocks of the agonizing headache. The sudden, jarring displacement had left her utterly disoriented, struggling to reconcile the throbbing pain in her skull with the impossible reality of her instantaneous relocation. One moment she had been standing before the holographic map, the familiar contours of Kremøtoa spread out before her, the next she was here, across the room, the map a distant, shimmering mirage. It was as if the very fabric of space had folded in on itself, collapsing the distance between two points with a casual disregard for the laws of physics, the laws *she herself* had written into the world’s code.

She blinked, trying to clear the lingering haze from her vision, her mind still reeling from the shock of the experience. The warehouse, usually a comforting haven of organized chaos, now seemed alien and distorted, the familiar shapes of crates, cables, and arcane devices swimming before her eyes like phantoms in a fever dream. The throbbing in her head intensified, a relentless pulse of discomfort that radiated outward, blurring the edges of her perception, distorting the sounds of her companions' worried exclamations into a cacophony of meaningless noise.

Korina, her heart pounding a frantic rhythm against her ribs, was the first to reach Ada. "You *vanished*!" she cried, her voice a strange mix of terror and scientific awe. "One moment you were *there*, and the next...poof! Gone! Like a corrupted data packet." Her analytical mind, usually so quick to dissect and categorize, struggled to process the impossible. Axiomatic displacement? A localized reality glitch? Some unknown function of Ada's Admin abilities she hadn't yet documented? The possibilities whirled through her mind, a chaotic storm of speculation and fear.

But before her analytical mind could fully engage, her emotional core took over. The raw, visceral terror of losing Ada, of seeing her simply *vanish* into thin air, overwhelmed her carefully constructed defenses. A sob escaped her lips, followed by another, and another, until she was openly weeping, her shoulders shaking with the force of her emotions. She stumbled forward, her arms wrapping around Ada's waist, burying her face in the soft fabric of Ada's tunic. "I-I thought..." she mumbled incoherently, her voice muffled by the cloth. "I thought you were...gone. Just...gone. To Void-knows where in this blighted hellscape of a world. And I-I..." She trailed off, unable to articulate the sheer terror that had gripped her, the cold, empty dread that had settled in her stomach like a stone.

Sera and Erita reached them a moment later, their faces etched with a mixture of concern and bewilderment. Sera's hand hovered protectively over Ada's shoulder, her eyes scanning the surrounding area, still searching for some hidden threat. Erita, her usual cynicism replaced by a rare flicker of genuine vulnerability, swore softly under her breath. "What in the Void was *that*?" she muttered, her voice laced with a tremor of unease. "Some kind of new trick? A teleportation spell?"

Janna, her massive frame filling the doorway, let out a low growl, her hand still gripping the haft of her axe. "Explain," she rumbled, her voice laced with a quiet intensity that brooked no argument. "Now." Her eyes, usually filled with a warm, jovial light, were now narrowed, sharp, and focused, like a predator assessing a potential threat.

Ada, still disoriented and struggling to regain her composure, slowly turned to face them. She blinked again, the warehouse finally coming into focus, the swirling colors and distorted shapes receding into the background. The throbbing pain in her head had subsided slightly, replaced by a dull ache that radiated outward, a constant reminder of the strange, disorienting experience she had just endured. She looked at Korina, her face still buried in Ada's tunic, her body trembling with the force of her sobs. She looked at Sera, her hand hovering protectively, her eyes filled with a mixture of concern and suspicion. She looked at Erita, her usual sarcastic mask replaced by a raw, unguarded vulnerability. She looked at Janna, her stoic face etched with a quiet intensity, her hand gripping her axe.

Ada, still squinting against the lingering throb behind her eyes, took a deep breath, trying to steady her trembling hands. "It was..." she began, her voice hoarse, "like a...a spike of pain, right here."

She tapped her fingers against her temple, just above her eyebrow. "And then...a jump. Not a *movement*, not like walking or running or even...teleporting, like Erita said. Just...*arrival*." She paused, searching for the right words to describe the utterly disorienting sensation. "One moment I was looking at the map, the next I was... *here*." She gestured vaguely towards the far wall, her voice still laced with a tremor of disbelief.

She looked down at Korina, still clinging to her, her body shaking with the force of her sobs. A wave of tenderness washed over her, a deep, visceral ache of empathy for the fear and vulnerability she had inadvertently caused. "Rina," she murmured softly, her voice barely above a whisper. "Rina, I'm so sorry. I didn't...I didn't even know I was *doing* it until it happened. I would never intentionally frighten you like that. Never." She gently stroked Korina's hair, her touch soft and reassuring, a silent promise of safety and protection.

Recovering slightly, Korina's analytical mind, ever eager to dissect and categorize, began to reassert itself, pushing back against the tide of fear and vulnerability that had momentarily overwhelmed her. Through muffled sniffles, she pulled back slightly from Ada's embrace, her violet eyes, still glistening with tears, now alight with a spark of intellectual curiosity. "A...a latent administrative function?" she questioned, her voice still trembling slightly, but regaining its usual rapid-fire cadence. "A...a direct, unmediated command to the world's operating system?"

She straightened up, wiping her eyes with the back of her hand, her mind already racing, piecing together the fragments of information like a complex puzzle. The sudden spike of pain, the instantaneous displacement, the complete lack of any discernible thaumaturgical signature—it was unlike anything she had ever witnessed, even from Ada. It was as if Ada had bypassed the usual arcane "UI," the intricate system of spells and rituals that mages and scholars used to interact with the world's underlying code. It was as if she had issued a direct command to the operating system itself, a raw, unfiltered instruction that the world had no choice but to obey.

"The 'blink'," she murmured, her voice gaining momentum, the words tumbling out in a torrent of excited speculation, "it was...it was like a...a *teleportation* command, executed directly at the kernel level. Bypassing all the usual thaumaturgical protocols, the axiomatic matrices, the energy conduits...everything! Straight to the Terminal command line!" She gestured excitedly with her hands, her fingers tracing invisible diagrams in the air. "It was a pure, unadulterated act of *will*, translated directly into code and executed without any intermediary steps. A...a quantum leap, if you will, across the fabric of reality itself."

She turned to Ada, her eyes wide with a mixture of awe and concern. "The pain," she continued, her voice now regaining its usual analytical precision, "it was the trigger. A critical threshold of stimulus, overloading your...your internal buffer, if you will. The system, unable to process the input through the usual channels, defaulted to a...a 'panic' function, if you will. A hard-coded emergency protocol designed to remove the administrator from immediate danger." She paused, her mind racing, searching for the right analogy. "Like a...a 'safe mode' command in a corrupted program, designed to preserve the core system integrity by ejecting the user from the affected area."

"Void's name, Ada," Erita breathed, her usual cynicism momentarily forgotten. "That's...that's incredible." Her mind, ever attuned to the practical applications of power, immediately grasped the tactical implications of Ada's accidental discovery. Instantaneous relocation? Unmediated by spells or rituals? It was a game-changer, a tactical advantage that could shift the balance of power in their favor. "We need to test this," she declared, her voice regaining its usual sharp, decisive tone. "Immediately. But under controlled conditions."

"Controlled conditions?" Sera echoed, her brow furrowing in confusion. "What do you mean?" Her mind, still reeling from the shock of Ada's sudden disappearance and reappearance, struggled to keep pace with Erita's rapid-fire analysis. She had seen Ada perform incredible feats of thaumaturgy before—healing the blighted fields of Oakhaven, repairing the crumbling bridge at Warden's Gate, even dissolving a solid steel door in the Prefecture's service tunnels—but this was different. This was...*instantaneous.* Unmediated. It was as if Ada had simply *willed* herself across the room, bending the very fabric of reality to her desire.

"I mean," Erita explained, her golden eyes gleaming with a mixture of excitement and strategic calculation, "we need to understand the parameters of this...ability. The trigger. The range. The limitations. Can you do it again, Ada? On command? Can you target a specific location? Or is it just a random jump, like some kind of glitched-out thaumaturgical roulette?" She gestured towards the holographic map still shimmering in the center of the room. "Imagine, Ada. Imagine being able to instantly relocate our forces. Bypass any defense. Appear directly behind enemy lines. It would change *everything.*"

"But the pain..." Korina interjected, her voice laced with a tremor of concern. The memory of Ada's sudden, agonizing headache, the way her face had contorted in pain, the sheer terror in her eyes—it was a sight she couldn't shake. The thought of Ada deliberately subjecting herself to that kind of agony, even for the sake of their revolution, made her stomach churn. "What if it happens again? What if it's...worse? What if it *damages* her?"

"Without the need for agonizing pain, of course," Erita added dismissively, waving her hand as if brushing away Korina's concerns like so many annoying gnats. "We're not barbarians, Kori. We'll figure out the trigger mechanism. Isolate the variables. Refine the process. I'm sure there's a way to achieve the desired outcome without turning our Architect-Queen into a screaming, twitching mess."

They cleared a wide space in the warehouse, shoving crates and equipment against the walls. The air crackled with anticipation. Ada stood in the center of the cleared area, her eyes closed, her brow furrowed in concentration. This time, she wasn't focusing on the pain, but on the *intent* behind the action. The *destination*. She visualized a point ten feet away, a small imperfection in the concrete floor, a faint discoloration that looked like a spilled drop of oil. She focused on it, holding the image in her mind, willing herself towards it. It wasn't about escaping pain; it was about *arriving*.

There was a faint *pop* of displaced air, a momentary shimmer like heat rising from asphalt on a summer day, and then...nothing. Ada was gone. A collective gasp echoed through the warehouse. Korina's hand flew to her mouth, her eyes wide with a mixture of fear and wonder. Sera's grip tightened on the hilt of her sword, her knuckles white. Erita's golden eyes narrowed, scanning the empty space where Ada had been standing, searching for any sign of her, any residual energy signature. Janna simply stared, her jaw slack, her gruff demeanor momentarily forgotten.

Then, just as quickly as she had vanished, Ada reappeared. Not in a flash of light or a swirl of smoke, but simply *there*, standing ten feet away, her feet planted firmly on the discolored patch of concrete. She swayed slightly, as if regaining her balance, her eyes still closed, her breath coming in short, shallow gasps. But there was no grimace of pain on her face, no contortion of agony. Just a look of intense concentration, a faint sheen of sweat on her forehead.

Korina rushed to her side, her hand hovering over Ada's arm, her voice trembling with relief. "Ada! Are you...are you alright?"

Ada opened her eyes, a slow blink, like someone waking from a deep sleep. A small, tired smile touched her lips. "Better than before. Much better." She took a deep breath, the air filling her lungs with a cool, cleansing rush. "It's...exhausting. Like running a full system diagnostic for a week straight."

Erita stepped forward, her golden eyes gleaming with a calculating light. "So, no more agonizing pain. Just...fatigue." She circled Ada, her gaze sharp and assessing, like a predator sizing up its prey. "Interesting. Very interesting."

"Fascinating," Korina breathed, her fingers dancing across the surface of *Obsidian*. Streams of data flowed across the slate's screen, glowing lines of arcane script and complex equations. "The energy expenditure is...staggering. It's a significant drain on your body's resources, Ada. Almost like a full system reboot." She looked up, her violet eyes wide with concern. "You need to be careful. Overuse could destabilize your core functions."

"No blind jumps," Ada said, a note of frustration in her voice. She gestured towards a stack of crates across the warehouse, partially obscured by a large support pillar. "I tried to jump there, behind the crates, without looking directly at the spot. It...didn't work. I could *feel* the destination, but I couldn't *reach* it."

Korina nodded, her fingers still flying across *Obsidian*. "Confirmed. The ability requires a direct, unbroken line of sight to the destination. No blind jumps. But," she added, a flicker of excitement in her eyes, "it seems that if it's within your vision of sight, whether in focus or not, it is a possibility to jump to that location. For instance," she pointed towards a hanging lamp, high above their heads, almost lost in the shadows of the warehouse rafters, "you *could*, theoretically, jump directly to that lamp. Even though it's not your primary focus of sight, it is still within your cone of vision."

Ada followed Korina's gaze, her eyes tracing the line from the floor to the hanging lamp, suspended precariously from a thick metal chain. "So, as long as I can *see* it..."

"Theoretically, yes," Korina confirmed. "But the further the periphery, the more energy it will likely consume. And the more complex the trajectory, the greater the risk of...unforeseen consequences. We need more data. More testing."

"No more blind jumps," Ada repeated, her voice echoing in the cavernous warehouse. She glanced at the massive map of Kremøtoa hanging on the far wall, a sprawling tapestry of coastlines, mountain ranges, and political boundaries. Until now, that map had represented a vast, impassable barrier between them and Rhedeon, a journey of months across treacherous seas. But now...

A slow smile spread across Ada's face, a spark of reckless

excitement igniting in her purple eyes. "But...I can see *that*." She pointed towards the map, her finger landing on a small, insignificant island off the coast of Rhedeon, barely more than a speck of ink on the vast canvas. "I can see that island. It's small, barely a rock in the ocean. But it's *there*. Within my line of sight."

Korina frowned, her brow furrowed in thought. "It's hundreds of miles away, Ada. Across open ocean. The energy expenditure would be..."

"Immense," Erita finished, her golden eyes narrowed in calculation. "But not impossible. Not anymore." She traced a path on the map with her finger, a series of short, precise hops from one landmark to another, each within a conceivable line of sight. "We could position-hop. Blink from one point to the next, using the highest peaks and coastal landmarks as waypoints."

Sera stepped forward, her red hair catching the light filtering through the warehouse windows. "It's insane," she said, her voice a low rumble. "Suicidal, even. But..." A grin spread across her face, a flash of her old, reckless self. "It just might work."

Janna, who had been silent until now, let out a low whistle. "By the Void," she muttered, shaking her head in disbelief. "You're serious, aren't you? You're actually considering this."

"We have to," Ada said, her voice firm. "The sea voyage is too slow. Thorne will consolidate his power. Willem's loyalty will fray. We need to reach Rhedeon now, before it's too late."

Korina nodded, her fingers dancing across *Obsidian*. "I can calculate the optimal trajectory," she said, her voice filled with a mix of apprehension and excitement. "Identify the most efficient path, minimize the energy expenditure at each jump."

"And I can provide cover," Erita added, her gaze fixed on the map. "Create diversions, misdirect Thorne's attention until we're in the mountains, and then ensure we have a clear path for each blink."

Sera placed her hand on Ada's shoulder, a gesture of reassurance and unwavering support. "And I will be your shield," she said, her voice low and steady. "I will protect you, every step of the way."

Ada looked at each of them, her heart swelling with a mix of gratitude and determination. They were a team, a family, bound together by a shared purpose and a fierce loyalty to one another. They were facing the impossible, but they were facing it together. She took a deep breath, the air filling her lungs with a newfound confidence.

"Then let's begin," she said, her voice ringing with authority. "Let's rewrite the map." The Quartet, joined by Janna, stood before the massive map of Kremøtoa, their eyes tracing the impossible path, the desperate journey, the audacious plan that had just been born. The long sea voyage was no longer their only option. The impossible had become possible. Their entire strategy had changed.

CHAPTER 12

THE FIRST STEP OF AN IMPOSSIBLE JOURNEY

The warehouse had transformed into a buzzing hive of strategic activity. Crates overflowed with salvaged weaponry and repurposed technology. The air hummed with the low thrum of arcane generators powering Korina's elaborate network of data-slates and holographic projectors. At the center of it all stood Erita, her golden eyes narrowed in concentration as she manipulated a series of shimmering, three-dimensional maps that hovered in the air before her.

"Argent's light, this is insane," she muttered, her fingers dancing across a control panel, zooming in on a jagged mountain peak that pierced the clouds. "Even for us, this is insane."

The holographic map shifted, displaying a cross-section of Kremøtoa's treacherous terrain. Jagged mountain ranges gave way to dense forests, which then dissolved into the plains and coast of Rhedeon, with their goal being Port Veridia. A series of pulsating violet dots marked Erita's proposed route, a perilous, cross-continental path that snaked its way from Port Dominus to the northern coast of Rhedeon.

"Each of these points," Erita explained, tapping a glowing violet dot that hovered over a remote mountain peak, "represents an anchor point. High altitude, defensible, with a clear line of sight to the next jump. Ada will need to blink from one to the next, like stepping stones across a chasm."

Korina, hunched over Obsidian, her brow furrowed in concentration, added, "The atmospheric conditions at each point are critical. Wind shear, thermal updrafts, even the density of arcane particles can affect Ada's jumps. I'm calculating the optimal time window for each blink, minimizing the risk of deviation."

Korina's fingers flew across Obsidian's surface, the data-slate's screen flickering with complex equations and cascading streams of data. She worked in perfect, unspoken synchronization with Erita, who manipulated the holographic maps, highlighting each proposed jump with a pulsating violet marker. For every anchor point Erita selected, Korina calculated the immense energy expenditure for Ada, factoring in not just distance and elevation, but also the treacherous, ever-shifting atmospheric interference. Wind shear, thermal updrafts, even the density of arcane particles swirling in Kremøtoa's turbulent skies—all of it had to be accounted for.

"This one," Erita said, her voice tight with concern, pointing to a jump that arced over a vast, swirling chasm, "is particularly nasty. Almost a kilometer across, with unpredictable crosswinds. Even a minor deviation could send Ada tumbling into the Void."

Korina's fingers paused on Obsidian's surface, the data-slate emitting a soft, worried hum. A string of crimson numbers flashed across the screen, stark warnings against the proposed jump. "The energy cost is...prohibitive," she finally said, her voice barely above a whisper. "At that distance, with those conditions, Ada would be depleted for hours. Vulnerable. A sitting duck."

Erita's jaw tightened. "We don't have a choice, Kori. That pass is the only viable route through the Cipher Peaks. We try to skirt around them, and we add days to the journey. Days we don't have."

"But at what cost?" Korina whispered, her eyes fixed on the alarming numbers flashing on Obsidian's screen. "We push Ada too hard, and she'll..."

"She'll manage," Sera's voice cut through the tension, her tone firm but laced with an undercurrent of worry. "She's tougher than she looks. We all are."

Erita nodded, her golden eyes meeting Sera's across the room. "Sera's right. We'll pace ourselves. Short jumps, mandatory rest periods. We make this a relay, not a sprint."

Korina reluctantly agreed, her fingers resuming their frantic dance across Obsidian's surface. She plotted a grueling rhythm for their journey: a series of short, draining jumps followed by mandatory periods of rest and recovery for Ada. Each jump was a calculated risk, a delicate balancing act between speed and Ada's physical limits. It was a perilous, exhausting strategy, one that would push Ada to the absolute brink of her capabilities. But as Erita had said, they didn't have a choice. The fate of Kremøtoa, and their own survival, depended on it.

The air, thick with the scent of ozone and arcane energy, crackled with anticipation. Ada addressed the assembled group—Sera, Korina, Erita, Janna, and Captain Silas—her voice calm but firm.

"Before we depart for Rhedeon," she began, her purple eyes scanning each face, "we need to formalize our command structure. Our operation needs an anchor, someone to manage our resources and coordinate our efforts while we're gone." She paused, her gaze settling on Captain Silas. "Captain," she said, her voice softening slightly, "I have a proposition for you."

Silas, his weathered face etched with curiosity, shifted his weight from one foot to the other. "Aye, your majesty?"

"In our absence," Ada continued, "I propose you take command of our operations here in Port Dominus. Oversee the training of our recruits, manage our finances, and maintain contact with our allies. You would act as my...steward, if you will."

A flicker of surprise crossed Silas's face, quickly replaced by a deep sense of pride. "Your majesty," he said, his voice thick with emotion, "it would be my honor. I pledge my loyalty, and the loyalty of my crew, to your cause."

"There's one more thing," Ada said, a playful glint in her eyes. She lowered her voice, leaning closer to Silas. "A...promotion, of sorts. I need your consent first, however."

Silas's brow furrowed. "A promotion? But I'm already a captain, your majesty. And consent? Wha—"

"Indeed," Ada replied, a small smile playing on her lips. "But I believe your new responsibilities warrant a...more appropriate title. And as for as the why of consent, just don't worry about that. It's just *proper* I do so."

Silas hesitated for a moment, then nodded slowly. "If you think it's best, your majesty. Whatever you command." He still didn't fully grasp the implications of Ada's words, his mind still reeling from the weight of the stewardship she had just entrusted to him.

Ada beamed. "Excellent. Now, if you'll follow me..."

She led him out into the main warehouse, where the assembled Azure Rose recruits stood at attention, their faces a mixture of curiosity and anticipation. Janna stood beside them, her usual stoic expression softened by a hint of pride. Korina, Sera, and Erita watched from a nearby balcony, a shared smile of amusement and affection playing on their lips.

Ada raised her hand, silencing the hushed whispers that rippled through the ranks. A hush fell over the room. "Soldiers of the revolution," she announced, her voice ringing with newfound authority, "today marks a turning point in our fight for a better future. A future free from corruption, free from oppression, free from the tyranny of Thorne's grip and the Ehxcehl Empire."

A murmur of agreement rippled through the recruits.

"To achieve this future," Ada continued, "we need strong leadership. Leadership that inspires courage, embodies loyalty, and commands respect. And that is why, today, I am proud to announce the promotion of Captain Silas..." she paused, drawing out the suspense, "...to the rank of Admiral."

A collective gasp echoed through the warehouse. Silas's eyes widened in disbelief. He looked at Ada, his face a mixture of shock and overwhelming gratitude. He hadn't expected this, hadn't even dared to dream of such an honor.

Ada stepped forward, a violet light flickering around her hands. The light coalesced, taking shape, weaving itself into a magnificent admiral's uniform. It was deep indigo, almost black, with intricate silver embroidery that seemed to shimmer in the warehouse's dim light. The fabric was thick and luxurious, the cut sharp and military in style, but with a touch of gothic flair that reflected Ada's own aesthetic sensibilities. A single crimson rose, crafted from pure light, adorned the left breast, a symbol of their burgeoning revolution.

With a flourish, Ada presented the uniform to Silas. Tears welled up in his eyes as he accepted it, his voice choked with emotion. "Your majesty...I...I don't know what to say."

"Say you'll lead us to victory, Admiral," Ada replied, her voice warm but firm.

Silas straightened, his shoulders back, his eyes shining with renewed purpose. "I will lead you to victory, your majesty. By Argent's Light, I swear it."

The warehouse erupted in cheers. The recruits surged forward, their voices blending into a single, thunderous chant: "Silas! Silas! Silas!" The energy in the room was electric, a tangible wave of hope and determination. Ada smiled, her heart swelling with pride and affection for the man she had just elevated to the highest military rank in their revolutionary army. This act, this simple gesture of trust and recognition, had solidified her role not just as a powerful thaumaturge, but as a true sovereign, a leader who inspired not just obedience, but fierce, unwavering loyalty.

Ada raised her hand once more, silencing the cheers. "Admiral Silas," she said, her voice clear and commanding, "Hold the fortress till we return. I promise we won't be gone long."

The five women moved through the pre-dawn gloom, their footsteps echoing in the deserted streets of Port Dominus. A chill wind whipped through the alleyways, carrying the scent of salt and decay. They reached the base of the comms tower, a skeletal metal structure silhouetted against the lightening sky. Janna, ever vigilant, scanned the rooftops, her hand resting on the hilt of her axe. Erita moved with a fluid grace, her eyes darting from shadow to shadow. Korina clutched her data-slate, Obsidian, its smooth surface cold against her palm. Sera, her face pale and drawn, walked beside Ada, their shoulders occasionally brushing. Ada, her violet eyes fixed on the tower, felt a knot of apprehension tighten in her chest. This was it. The first step of their impossible journey. The first real test of her newfound power. The air crackled with unspoken tension, a palpable weight of uncertainty hanging over them as they began their ascent.

Korina swallowed, her throat dry. "The coordinates match, Ada. Erita confirms the location is secure." She held out *Obsidian*, the data-slate's screen displaying a shimmering, monochrome image of a crumbling watchtower several kilometers away. The tower, rendered in a stark, shadowless grey, looked almost ethereal, a phantom structure against the backdrop of the slowly brightening sky. "This is it. The first jump."

Ada stared at the holographic projection, her violet eyes narrowed in concentration. "So, it's a virtual destination, not a physical one. Interesting." A faint violet luminescence flickered around her hands, a telltale sign of her power activating. "The principle should be the same. It's all just data, after all."

Sera shifted uneasily, the heavy battle-axe strapped to her back a reassuring weight. "Are you sure about this, Ada? It's a long way."

"Not for me," Ada murmured, her gaze still locked on the ghostly image of the watchtower. "Theoretically, anyway."

"Theoretically," Erita echoed, a hint of skepticism in her voice. "But theory and practice are often vastly different beasts."

"We'll see," Ada replied, her voice calm but firm. She took a deep breath, closing her eyes for a moment as if visualizing the distant tower. "Stand back."

Korina took a step away, her heart pounding in her chest. This was the moment of truth. If Ada could pull this off, their plan had a chance. If not...she didn't want to think about the alternative. The thought of months at sea, dodging Imperial patrols and hoping Thorne didn't consolidate his power before they could reach Rhedeon, made her stomach churn.

With a shared, unspoken understanding, the five of them formed a tight circle, hands clasped together. The rough texture of Sera's calloused fingers intertwined with Korina's smooth, delicate ones. Erita's grip was surprisingly firm, a reassuring pressure against Ada's own trembling hand. Janna's large hand enveloped Ada's, her calloused palm warm and solid. Closing her eyes, Ada focused on the image of the watchtower shimmering on *Obsidian*'s screen, drawing on their collective will, their shared breath in the pre-dawn air. She pictured the crumbling stone, the weathered wood, the empty window frames, and issued the command... [JUMP: Destination = Watchtower_Alpha].

Nothing.

A ripple of confusion spread through the circle, the clasped hands tightening instinctively. Ada opened her eyes, a flicker of doubt clouding her violet gaze. *What went wrong?* The tower's image still shimmered on *Obsidian*, seemingly within reach, yet impossibly distant. She felt a cold dread creep up her spine, a chilling premonition of failure. Had she overestimated her abilities? Was this journey, this desperate gamble to save her world, doomed from the start?

"Anything?" Erita's voice, sharp and clipped, broke the silence.

Ada shook her head, her throat suddenly tight. "Nothing. It's... it's like there's a wall." She could feel the others' anxiety, their fear a tangible presence in the small circle. *I have to fix this. I have to be the one to fix this.*

"Maybe the coordinates are off?" Janna's gruff voice rumbled.

"No," Korina said, her voice strained. "I triple-checked them. It has to be something else." A tremor ran through her hand, a subtle but unmistakable sign of her rising panic. Ada felt a surge of protectiveness, a fierce determination to shield Korina from the crushing weight of their potential failure.

"Rina..." Ada's voice was soft, a gentle murmur meant only for Korina. "It's alright. We'll figure it out." She squeezed Korina's hand reassuringly. "There has to be a reason. Something I'm missing."

Korina looked at Ada, her violet eyes wide and filled with a desperate plea. "But what if there isn't? What if...what if it's just not possible? Or if I did something wrong..." Korina's voice trailed off, alarming the Architect-Queen.

Ada's mind raced, searching for a solution, anything to calm the rising tide of Korina's fear. An idea sparked, a faint flicker of hope in the darkness of her uncertainty. "The image," Ada said, her voice gaining a newfound confidence. "It's monochrome. What if that's the problem? What if I need more data?"

"More data?" Korina echoed, her brow furrowed in confusion.

"Yes," Ada said, her excitement growing. "The watchtower. Can you get the projection in color? And the precise coordinates? Not just the general location, but the exact x, y, and z values? I need to pinpoint the destination, not just approximate it." It was a long shot, a desperate gamble, but it was the only thing she could think of.

Korina's panic subsided slightly, replaced by a flicker of intellectual curiosity. "Color...and precise coordinates...It's possible. Erita, can you send me a color image file of Watchtower Alpha? If it's not too much trouble?"

Erita nodded, her usual cynicism replaced by a focused intensity. "Already on it, I should have it saved on here. And the coordinates?"

"Yes," Korina said, her fingers flying across *Obsidian*'s surface. "Send me the precise x, y, and z values. Ada, are you sure this will work?"

Ada shrugged, a faint smile playing on her lips. "No idea. But it's worth a shot, right?"

Erita's data-slate chimed, a small, almost musical tone. "Got it," she said, holding out the device to Korina. The monochrome image on *Obsidian* shimmered, then burst into color. The watchtower, now rendered in vibrant hues of brown, grey, and green, looked almost real, the crumbling stone and weathered wood textures startlingly detailed. A small, pulsing dot of violet light marked the precise location of their intended destination, a beacon in the digital landscape.

"Coordinates locked," Korina said, her voice regaining its usual calm efficiency. "Ready when you are, Ada."

Ada nodded, her gaze fixed on the violet beacon. The knot of apprehension in her chest hadn't entirely dissipated, but it was replaced by a surge of adrenaline, a thrill of anticipation. *This is it.* She took a deep breath, closing her eyes as she focused on the now-vibrant image of the watchtower, the precise coordinates echoing in her mind. The chain of linked hands tightened, a silent affirmation of their shared purpose, their interconnected fates. She could feel the warmth of Sera's hand, the reassuring pressure of Erita's grip, the solid strength of Janna's grasp, and, most importantly, the tremble in Korina's fingers. *It's alright, Rina.* She gripped Korina's hand tighter, a silent promise of safety, of success. *It's going to work.*

[JUMP: Destination = Watchtower_Alpha; Coordinates = x: 478.92, y: 1235.57, z: 78.23; Color_Data = TRUE].

With a gut-wrenching lurch, the world twisted around Ada. A sensation of immense pressure crushed her chest, as if the very air was being squeezed from her lungs. A high-pitched whine filled her ears, a dissonant symphony of distorted sound. She felt a sharp, almost agonizing pain behind her eyes, a blinding flash of white light momentarily erasing everything. Then, with a faint *pop* that seemed to ripple through the very fabric of reality, they vanished.

The jarring transition left Ada disoriented, her senses reeling. The cold, damp air of the pre-dawn wilderness filled her lungs, a stark contrast to the stale, dusty atmosphere of the Port Dominus alleyway. She stumbled, her legs weak and unsteady beneath her, the ground swaying beneath her feet as if she were still at sea. She gasped for breath, her body trembling with the aftershocks of the jump. The world swam back into focus, the blurry shapes resolving into the crumbling stone walls of the watchtower, the weathered wood of the broken railing, the vast expanse of the pre-dawn sky stretching out before her. They had made it.

"Argent's Light..." Sera breathed, her voice filled with awe. She leaned against the crumbling wall, her face pale, her breath coming in ragged gasps.

Erita, her usual cynicism momentarily forgotten, stared at the distant cityscape of Port Dominus, a faint shimmer of disbelief in her golden eyes. “Void…that was…something.”

Janna, her massive frame swaying slightly, let out a low whistle. “Whippersnapper, you’ve got some tricks up your sleeve, I’ll give you that.”

Korina, still clutching *Obsidian*, stared at the data-slate’s screen, her violet eyes wide with a mixture of wonder and relief. “The data…it’s incredible! The energy signature…the axiomatic displacement…the sheer computational power…” She trailed off, her mind already racing to analyze the impossible feat they had just accomplished.

Ada swayed, her vision blurring again, her body profoundly drained. The immense physical and mental cost of the jump hit her with full force, a wave of exhaustion threatening to pull her under. She leaned against Sera, grateful for the solid support of the knight’s arm around her waist. The impossible had begun.

CHAPTER 13

WHISPERS ON THE WATCH

The wind whipped at Erita's cloak, a relentless, biting wind that carried the scent of dust and decay. She crouched low, her body a phantom against the desolate landscape, her golden eyes scanning the vast, empty plains that stretched out before her. The watchtower, their first anchor point, was a distant speck on the horizon, a lonely sentinel against the encroaching twilight. The others—Ada, Sera, Korina, and Janna—were still there, recovering from the initial jump. Ada, especially, was vulnerable after such a feat of axiomatic manipulation. Erita's job was to scout, to find the next defensible position, the next high-ground anchor point in their perilous journey across Kremøtoa.

The landscape was a brutal tapestry of cracked earth, withered vegetation, and the occasional, skeletal remains of long-dead trees. The air itself felt thin, as if the very life had been sucked from it, leaving behind a hollow echo of what it once was. The three moons, Argent, Cache, and BIOCE, hung low in the sky, their light casting long, distorted shadows that danced and writhed across the desolate terrain. Erita moved with a predator's grace, her body low to the ground, her footsteps silent on the cracked earth. She was a shadow, a ghost in the desolate landscape, her presence unseen, unheard, unknown.

After what felt like an eternity, she found it. A rocky outcrop, rising from the plains like a jagged tooth, its summit offering a clear view of the surrounding terrain. It was defensible, high ground, offering a tactical advantage against any potential threat. She approached cautiously, her hand resting on the hilt of one of her daggers, her senses alert for any sign of danger. The outcrop was barren, its surface a patchwork of cracked stone and wind-blown dust. But it was safe, for now.

Erita unclipped a small, cylindrical device from her belt, a specialized long-range scanner designed for transmitting raw topographical and visual data. She activated the device, its surface glowing with a faint, pulsating blue light. The scanner hummed softly as it collected data, its internal sensors mapping the surrounding terrain, capturing the precise contours of the land, the height and density of the vegetation, the position of any potential obstacles or threats. The data streamed in real-time, the monochrome image on the scanner's small screen resolving into a detailed 3D map of the area.

"Anchor point identified," she murmured into the comm unit, her voice barely a whisper against the wind. "Transmitting data now."

The scanner pulsed, sending a burst of encrypted data across the vast distance to the watchtower, where Korina would be waiting, her data-slate ready to receive and process the information. Erita watched as the data streamed, a steady flow of ones and zeros bridging the gap between her solitary position and the relative safety of the group. The transmission complete, she deactivated the scanner, its blue light fading, its hum silenced. She clipped the device back onto her belt, her hand lingering on its cool, metallic surface.

The sun dipped below the horizon, painting the sky in hues of blood orange and bruised purple. The three moons grew brighter, their light casting an eerie glow across the desolate landscape. Erita knew the others would be making their way towards her now, Ada leading the way, her power bending the very fabric of reality to bring them closer, step by impossible step. It was a punishing cycle, a relentless dance between exhaustion and necessity, between Ada's immense power and the limitations of her human form. But it was their only way forward, their only path to Rhedeon, to the next stage of their revolution. Erita turned, her gaze fixed on the distant watchtower, a flicker of determination in her golden eyes. They would keep moving, keep fighting, keep pushing forward, until they had reshaped Kremøtoa in their image, until they had built the world they had promised themselves, a world where order and chaos danced in perfect, beautiful harmony. She started back, a phantom against the dying light, her steps silent, her purpose unwavering.

The watchtower's crumbling stone walls offered little protection against the biting wind. Korina huddled deeper into her cloak, her breath misting in the frigid air. She held Obsidian, her data-slate, close, its smooth, cool surface a comforting presence against her gloved hand. The Lynx, Ada's whimsical security program, blinked at her from the corner of the screen, its violet pixelated eyes following her every move. It sat up, ears perked, a silent sentinel mirroring her own anticipation. She was waiting for

Erita's signal, a burst of encrypted data that would bridge the vast distance between them and guide Ada's next jump. Every second felt like an eternity, the silence of the desolate plains amplifying the pounding of her heart.

A faint pulse of energy, a ripple in the otherwise still air. Obsidian's screen flickered, the Lynx perking up, its pixelated ears twitching. The data packet arrived. Korina's fingers flew across the slate's controls, her mind racing to process the incoming information. Erita's raw scans, a chaotic jumble of monochrome data points, filled the screen. This was it. This was her moment. This was the most crucial part of the plan, the linchpin upon which their entire journey, their entire revolution, rested.

With intense concentration, she initiated the rendering sequence. Obsidian's processors whirred, the device warming in her hand as it worked to transform Erita's raw data into the two components Ada now required for a safe jump: a detailed, 3D color holographic image of the destination and the precise [x=, y=, z=] coordinates. Any error, any miscalculation, could result in a catastrophic misjump, sending Ada hurtling into the void, into the unknown, lost forever.

The pressure was immense. She could feel the weight of their hopes, their fears, their shared destiny, resting on her shoulders. She pushed aside the creeping tendrils of doubt, the memories of past failures, the whispers of inadequacy that haunted her. This was not the time for self-doubt. This was the time for action, for precision, for absolute, unwavering focus.

The monochrome data points on the screen began to coalesce, resolving into a recognizable form. The rocky outcrop, Erita's chosen anchor point, emerged from the digital mist, its jagged peaks, its cracked surface, its desolate beauty rendered in perfect, holographic detail. Color flooded the image, transforming the monochrome landscape into a vibrant tapestry of browns, grays, and the subtle hues of the setting sun. The three moons, Argent, Cache, and BIOCE, hung in the holographic sky, their light casting long, digital shadows across the virtual terrain.

Simultaneously, another window on Obsidian's screen displayed the rapidly calculating coordinates. The numbers flickered, shifting, refining, as the system crunched the complex algorithms, factoring in the curvature of Kremøtoa, the gravitational pull of the three moons, the atmospheric density, the wind speed, the temperature, every variable that could affect the trajectory of Ada's jump.

[x= 478.332]

[y= 129.775]

[z= 67.901]

The coordinates locked. The rendering complete. Korina took a deep breath, her heart pounding in her chest. It was done. She had done it. She had taken Erita's chaotic data and transformed it into the precise, elegant solution Ada needed.

The holo-image of the rocky outcrop shimmered before Ada, a beacon in the digital wilderness. Korina's voice, calm and steady, echoed in her ear, transmitting the precise coordinates, the key to her next jump. Ada focused her intent, her will, on that distant point, visualizing the destination, feeling the pull of the world's code bending to her command. She took a deep breath, and executed the jump.

The world lurched. A gut-wrenching, disorienting sensation, as if her very being was being torn apart and reassembled in an instant. Her stomach churned, her head spun, her vision blurred. The familiar, comforting weight of Sera's hand in hers was the only anchor in the chaotic maelstrom of the jump. Then, as suddenly as it began, it was over.

They stood on the rocky outcrop, the desolate landscape stretching out before them. The wind whipped at Ada's cloak, a cold, biting wind that carried the scent of dust and decay. The jump had been successful, but the effort had left her drained, depleted. Her hands trembled as she slumped against a rock, the world swimming before her eyes. The energy drain was immense, a physical ache that resonated deep within her bones. She closed her eyes, fighting the wave of nausea that threatened to overwhelm her. This was the price of her power, the burden of her unique ability. She had to recover, and quickly. The journey was far from over.

The desolate plains stretched out before them, a monochrome canvas under the pale light of Cache. Ada slumped against a jagged rock, her breath coming in ragged gasps. The jump had taken its toll, leaving her drained, depleted. The world swam before her eyes, the ground unsteady beneath her feet. She closed her eyes, focusing on slowing her racing heart, on regulating her breathing, on regaining some semblance of control over her exhausted body.

"Easy, Architect," Sera's voice, low and close to her ear, a comforting rumble in the chaotic symphony of her senses. "Rest now. We've got this."

Ada opened her eyes, her vision clearing slightly. Sera knelt beside her, her face etched with concern. Janna stood a few paces away, a solid, unyielding presence, her hand resting on the hilt of her axe. Korina hovered nearby, her data-slate clutched in her hand, her eyes darting between Ada and the surrounding landscape. Erita was already moving, a shadow flitting across the desolate terrain, her eyes scanning the horizon, her senses stretched to their limit. They were a team, a unit, each playing their part, each protecting the others, each essential to their survival.

Time passed, it was hard to tell. After an hour, Ada heard "Coordinates received," from Korina, clipped and precise, the professional tone a stark contrast to the warmth she had shown Ada just awhile before. "Rendering complete. Jump point confirmed."

The familiar shimmering of the holographic image appeared before Ada, this time a crumbling watchtower on a distant ridge. She focused her will, her intent, on that distant point, the world's code bending to her command, and executed the jump. The disorienting lurch, the nauseating spin, the feeling of her body being torn apart and reassembled, then the blessed relief of solid ground beneath her feet. She stumbled, her legs weak, her vision blurry. Sera caught her, her strong arm supporting Ada's weight, her touch a reassuring anchor in the chaotic aftermath of the jump.

"Rest," Sera commanded, guiding Ada to a sheltered alcove in the crumbling watchtower. "You push yourself too hard, Architect. We have time."

Ada nodded, grateful for Sera's strength, for her unwavering support. She closed her eyes, surrendering to the exhaustion that consumed her. The world faded into a blissful nothingness.

Time blurred. A montage of jumps, each one a grueling test of Ada's will, each one pushing her to the very limits of her endurance. Erita, the scout, a silent shadow moving ahead, her keen eyes assessing the terrain, her data-slate transmitting vital information back to Korina. Korina, the navigator, her fingers flying across Obsidian's controls, transforming raw data into precise coordinates, her voice a calm, steady beacon in the chaotic maelstrom of their journey. Sera and Janna, the guardians, their vigilance unwavering, their movements synchronized, their presence a shield against the dangers of the world. And Ada, the architect, her power both a blessing and a curse, pushing her body and mind to their breaking point with every jump.

The desolate plains gave way to jagged mountains, the mountains to dense forests, the forests to windswept coasts. The sun rose and set, the three moons tracing their celestial dance across the sky. Days blurred into nights, nights into days, the relentless rhythm of their journey marked by the exhaustion of Ada's jumps and the brief respites in between.

Each time Ada collapsed, spent, Sera and Janna would spring into action, their movements a silent ballet of protection. Sera, a predator in her element, would patrol the perimeter, her eyes scanning the horizon, her senses alert for any sign of danger. Janna, a bulwark against the unknown, would establish a secure perimeter, checking their supplies, tending to their weapons, her practical efficiency a comforting counterpoint to the ethereal nature of their travel.

Korina would kneel beside Ada, her touch gentle, her voice soothing, tending to Ada's every need. She would offer water, food, a comforting touch, a quiet word of encouragement. Her care was meticulous, her devotion unwavering. She would monitor Ada's vital signs, her data-slate displaying a constant stream of information, her brow furrowed in concentration as she analyzed the data, searching for any sign of distress, any indication that Ada was pushing herself too hard. In those quiet moments, as Ada rested, Korina's touch would linger, her gaze softening, her affection for Ada a silent, unspoken language that transcended the chaos of their journey.

Two more cycles. Two more sets of jumps. Two more periods of agonizing exhaustion and recovery. Two more times Sera held Ada close, whispering words of comfort. Two more times Janna stood guard, her axe a silent promise of protection. Two more times Korina tended to Ada's every need, her touch a gentle reminder of the love that bound them together.

They were a team, a family, forged in the crucible of their shared journey, their bond strengthening with every jump, every challenge, every shared moment of vulnerability and resilience. They were the architects of their own destiny, the revolutionaries who would reshape the world. And they were just getting started.

The fire crackled, spitting sparks into the inky blackness of the Kremøtoan night. Argent, full and brilliant, cast long, sharp shadows across the vast emptiness of the plains. Sera sat hunched over a whetstone, the rhythmic rasp of steel a soothing counterpoint to the silence of the wilderness. Her crimson tunic, faded and worn from their arduous journey, clung to her powerful frame, the firelight dancing across her sharp features. Janna watched her, a quiet admiration growing in her chest.

"You've got a fire in you, kid," Janna rumbled, her voice a low growl that barely disturbed the stillness of the night. "A strength I ain't seen in a long time."

Sera looked up, a flicker of surprise in her emerald eyes. "I'm just doing what needs to be done," she replied, her voice quiet, almost hesitant. She returned to her task, the rasp of the whetstone resuming its steady rhythm.

Janna shifted her weight, the leather of her armor creaking softly. She leaned forward, her gaze fixed on Sera's hands, the way they moved with such practiced grace, the way they held the blade with such reverence. "It ain't just about duty, Sera," she said, her voice softer now, almost gentle. "It's about heart. About believing in something bigger than yourself."

Sera stopped sharpening, her head tilted slightly, her eyes meeting Janna's across the flickering flames. The firelight danced in her eyes, reflecting the warmth of the fire, the vastness of the plains, the unspoken words that hung heavy in the air between them.

Janna reached out, her calloused hand gently resting on Sera's forearm. The touch was tentative, almost hesitant, a silent question hanging in the air. Sera's muscles tensed beneath her touch, but she didn't pull away. Her gaze held Janna's, a flicker of something unreadable in their depths.

"I..." Sera began, her voice barely a whisper, then trailed off, the unspoken words caught in her throat. She looked away, her gaze fixed on the fire, the flames dancing and swirling, mirroring the turmoil within her.

Janna's hand tightened slightly on Sera's arm, her touch a silent reassurance. "You don't have to say anything, kid," she murmured, her voice rough with emotion. She leaned closer, her breath warm against Sera's ear. "Just know that I see you. I see the fire in you. And I admire it."

Sera's breath hitched, her body stiffening slightly. She closed her eyes, her long lashes casting shadows on her cheeks. Janna's hand moved, sliding up Sera's arm, her fingers tracing the curve of her bicep, the warmth of her touch spreading through Sera like wildfire.

Sera's eyes fluttered open, her gaze meeting Janna's once more. The firelight danced in her eyes, reflecting the uncertainty, the vulnerability, the flicker of something that might be hope. She parted her lips, as if to speak, but no words came out. The silence stretched, filled only with the crackling of the fire and the steady rhythm of their breaths.

A slow, hesitant smile touched Sera's lips. She leaned forward, not away, the firelight warming her face, highlighting the faint freckles scattered across the bridge of her nose. "Janna," she began, her voice soft, almost a murmur, "I...I'm honored. Truly." She paused, her gaze searching Janna's, a flicker of something akin to apology in their emerald depths. "But...my heart...it belongs elsewhere."

Janna's hand stilled on Sera's arm, her fingers tightening momentarily before slowly relaxing. She didn't speak, her silence a heavy weight in the air between them. Sera took a deep breath, the scent of woodsmoke and pine filling her lungs. "It's...complicated," she continued, her voice gaining strength, her gaze holding Janna's steady. "There's...there's Ada, and Korina, and Erita. We...we're a unit. A...a polycule, I think they call it."

The word felt strange on her tongue, foreign and yet somehow fitting. It was a word she'd heard Korina use once, a word from some dusty old text in the Veritas Archives, a word that described a love that was more than just two, a love that encompassed a whole, a love that was theirs. "It's...it's more than just...physical," Sera continued, her voice gaining confidence, the words flowing more easily now. "It's a bond. A connection. Something...deeper."

She thought of Ada, of the way her violet eyes could see straight through her, of the way her touch could soothe her soul. She thought of Korina, of her brilliant mind, her gentle heart, her unwavering faith in Ada's vision. She thought of Erita, of her sharp wit, her fierce loyalty, the way she could make her laugh even in the darkest of times. "They're...they're my family," Sera said, her voice filled with a fierce, protective warmth. "My heart...it's divided between them. Equally. Completely."

She looked at Janna, her gaze soft, almost apologetic. "I admire you, Janna. I respect you. I see you as a mentor, a warrior, a...a friend." She paused, her fingers brushing lightly against Janna's hand. "But that's all it is. Friendship. Respect. Admiration. Not... not what you're offering." Sera's voice dropped to a whisper, her gaze holding Janna's steady. "And I...I care about them too much to...to jeopardize what we have. To...to break their hearts."

Janna's serious expression broke. A wry, knowing chuckle rumbled in her chest, shaking her broad shoulders. "Kid," she said, her voice laced with amusement, "you think I'm blind? Deaf? Or just plain stupid?" She winked, a mischievous glint in her eye. "Honey, I've heard you four from across the warehouse. Ada's not exactly the quietest mouse in the house, you know."

Sera's cheeks flushed crimson, a stark contrast to the fading light of the fire. She stammered, "Y-you heard us?" Her hand flew to her mouth, her eyes wide with mortification. She glanced around nervously, as if expecting Ada, Korina, and Erita to materialize out of the darkness.

Janna threw back her head and roared with laughter, the sound echoing across the plains. “Relax, kid,” she said, wiping a tear from her eye. “It ain’t like I was eavesdropping. More like...an unavoidable sonic assault. You lot were practically rattling the rafters.” She grinned, her teeth flashing white in the firelight. “Besides,” she added, her voice softening, “it ain’t my business who you share your bed with. Or your heart.”

Sera’s shoulders slumped slightly, the tension easing from her frame. She let out a shaky breath, a relieved smile touching her lips. “Thank Argent’s Light,” she murmured, shaking her head. “I thought I was going to have to explain the whole...polycule thing.” She shuddered dramatically. “That would have been awkward.”

Janna chuckled. “Well, kid, let’s just say I’ve seen stranger things in my time. And heard ‘em too.” She winked again, her eyes twinkling with amusement. “Besides,” she added, her voice dropping to a conspiratorial whisper, “between you and me, I think Ada’s got a thing for that little scholar of yours. The way she looks at her...like she’s trying to decipher the secrets of the universe written in her eyes.”

Sera’s smile widened, a warm glow spreading through her chest. “Yeah,” she said softly, her gaze drifting towards the watchtower where Korina would likely be pouring over maps and coordinates in the morning. “I think you’re right.” She paused, her eyes meeting Janna’s across the firelight. “And Rina...she’s completely smitten with Ada. It’s...endearing, really.” She chuckled softly. “Like watching a moth drawn to a flame.”

“And Erita?” Janna prompted, raising a curious eyebrow.

Sera’s smile took on a teasing edge. “Oh, Erita,” she said, her voice laced with amusement. “Erita’s a whole other story. She’s like a cat. All aloof and independent, but secretly...a complete cuddle monster." She laughed softly. "Ada can barely move without Erita's hands finding their way to her. It's...possessive. In an endearing way." She winked at Janna. "But don't tell her I said that."

Janna chuckled, shaking her head. "Kid, your little family is a walking, talking soap opera. But," she added, her voice softening, "it's a good kind of chaos. The kind that keeps things interesting. The kind that...sparks revolutions." She looked at Sera, her gaze steady, her voice filled with a newfound respect. "You've got something special here, Sera. Something worth fighting for."

"You know," Janna continued, her voice taking on a thoughtful tone, "back in my day, it was always a man and a woman. That's just how it was. Not that other...arrangements weren't around. They just weren't...talked about. Not openly, anyway." She paused, her gaze distant, as if remembering something from a long-forgotten past. "The Empire, the Theocracy, those stuffy Korian scholars...they liked things neat and tidy. Boxes and labels. Man and woman, husband and wife. Anything else...well, it just didn't fit their algorithms."

She chuckled, a dry, rasping sound. "But out here," she gestured to the vast expanse of the plains, "out here on the fringes, things are different. We don't care about labels. About boxes. Out here, it's about survival. About loyalty. About finding your tribe. And if your tribe happens to be...unconventional, well, that's just fine by us." She looked at Sera, her gaze steady, her voice filled with a quiet intensity. "You four...you're breaking all the rules. Not just the Empire's rules, but the world's rules. And that...that takes guts."

She leaned closer, her voice dropping to a conspiratorial whisper. "You know, I've seen a lot of things in my time. Fought in more battles than I care to remember. Seen the best and the worst of humanity. And let me tell you, kid, the strongest bonds I've ever seen...they weren't between a man and a woman. They were between...well, let's just say they were between people who found each other in the chaos. People who chose each other. People who were willing to fight for each other, no matter what."

She paused, her gaze drifting towards the dying embers of the fire. "The world's a messy place, Sera. Full of contradictions and complexities. And love...well, love's the messiest of them all. It doesn't always fit into neat little boxes. Sometimes...sometimes it spills over. Sometimes...it multiplies. And sometimes...sometimes it's the most beautiful, chaotic mess you've ever seen." She looked at Sera, her eyes twinkling with amusement. "You four...you're a beautiful mess. A glorious, chaotic, rule-breaking mess. And I wouldn't have it any other way."

She reached out, her calloused hand gently cupping Sera's cheek. "Don't let anyone tell you different, kid," she murmured, her voice rough with emotion. "Don't let anyone dim your fire. Don't let anyone put you in a box. You love who you love. And that's all that matters." She squeezed Sera's cheek gently before letting her hand fall away. "Now get some sleep, kid. We've got a long journey ahead of us. And a revolution to start."

Sera's eyes fluttered closed, a soft smile playing on her lips. Janna's words resonated deep within her, a warm reassurance spreading through her chest. She leaned into Janna's touch, the warmth of her hand a comforting presence against her skin. She thought of Ada, of Korina, of Erita. She thought of their shared love, their chaotic bond, their unwavering commitment to each other. And for the first time since leaving Celgrad, since abandoning the life she'd always known, she felt a sense of peace.

A sense of belonging. A sense of...home. She opened her eyes, her gaze meeting Janna's across the flickering flames. "Thank you, Janna," she whispered, her voice filled with gratitude. "For...for everything."

Janna grinned, a mischievous glint in her eye. "Don't mention it, kid," she rumbled, her voice laced with amusement. "Just promise me you'll keep breaking the rules. The world needs a little chaos every now and then."

Sera laughed softly, the sound echoing across the plains. "I promise," she said, her voice filled with a newfound confidence. "We'll keep breaking the rules. Together." She settled back against the rocks, her gaze fixed on the star-dusted sky, the three moons shining bright, a silent promise hanging in the air. A promise of love, of loyalty, of revolution. A promise of a future where they could be free. Together. Always.

CHAPTER 14

THE KNIGHT'S INQUIRY INTO THE QUEEN'S AMBITION

The biting morning air nipped at Sera's exposed skin, a stark contrast to the warmth of the blanket she clutched around her shoulders. The sky above the Korsair Peaks was a bruised canvas of deep purples and fading blues, the first hint of dawn painting the jagged peaks with strokes of pale gold. Autumn was fast approaching, its breath already painting the lower slopes with fiery hues of red and orange. The wind carried the scent of pine and damp earth, a familiar fragrance that usually brought her peace. But this morning, the familiar scent held a sharp edge, a reminder of the harsh realities of the world they were fighting to change.

Sera shivered, pulling the blanket tighter, the remnants of a disturbing nightmare clinging to her like a shroud. She'd seen a future where they had won, where Thorne and the Empire were defeated, where Kremøtoa was finally free. But in that victory, she, Ada, Korina, and Erita were still forced to live in the shadows, their love for each other dismissed, unrecognized by a world that still clung to the old laws, the old boxes. The dream had been vivid, the faces of the celebrating crowds blurring into a sea of judgmental eyes, their cheers turning into whispers of disapproval. Even in victory, they were outsiders, their love a secret shame.

An hour later, the thin morning mist clung to the mountain slopes, shrouding the world in a veil of grey. The air was cold, biting at exposed skin, and the ground was hard beneath Sera's boots. The remnants of their meager fire smoldered, sending thin wisps of smoke into the still air. She watched as Korina meticulously packed her data-slate, her movements precise, her expression focused. Erita sharpened her daggers, her movements fluid, almost hypnotic. Ada stood apart, her gaze fixed on the distant peaks, her expression unreadable. Janna, observing Sera's troubled expression, approached her.

"Rough night?" she asked, her voice a low rumble that somehow managed to cut through the quiet of the morning.

Sera nodded, the dream still heavy on her mind. She'd always found comfort in the predictable rhythms of a soldier's life, in the clear lines of duty and honor. But this new life, this life of rebellion and uncertainty, was filled with ambiguities, with emotions she wasn't sure how to navigate. Janna's presence was a quiet support, her easy acceptance from the night before giving Sera the courage to voice her fears.

As the rest of the group gathered, preparing for another grueling day of jumps across the treacherous mountain range, Sera knew she couldn't shake the dream. The fear of a hollow victory, of a future where their love was still a secret, gnawed at her. She needed to confront it, to address the unspoken tension that hung heavy in the air.

"Ada," Sera began, her voice quiet but firm, her gaze direct and vulnerable. "I had a dream."

Ada turned, her violet eyes meeting Sera's, a flicker of concern in their depths. Korina and Erita paused in their preparations, their attention drawn to the conversation. Even Janna, usually stoic and focused on the task at hand, shifted her weight, her expression softening with a quiet empathy.

"We won," Sera continued, her voice barely above a whisper, the images of the dream still vivid in her mind. "Thorne was gone. The Empire...it was different. Better, even." She paused, the irony of that imagined victory twisting in her gut. "But...we were still hiding. Our...what we are...it was still a secret. People celebrated our victory, but their eyes...they were judging us. Even in that new world, we were still outsiders."

Sera took a deep breath, the cold mountain air stinging her lungs. "We're fighting for a new world, Ada. A world where things are different. But what does that world look like for *us*?" Her voice gained strength, the fear of the dream giving way to a fierce determination. "If we ever...if we were to get *married*..." she hesitated, the word feeling strange and unfamiliar on her tongue, "...I want it to be *recognized*. Officially. *Everywhere*."

A heavy silence fell over the group, the weight of Sera's words settling like a shroud. Erita's face was carefully blank, her usual sarcasm replaced by a guarded stillness. Korina's violet eyes were wide, her expression a mixture of surprise and a hesitant hope. Ada's face, however, was a whirlwind of emotions, her usual calm replaced by a flicker of fear, quickly followed by a surge of determination that mirrored Sera's own.

Sera continued, her gaze sweeping over the faces of her companions, her voice gaining strength with each word. "Janna confirmed it last night. The Empire doesn't recognize relationships like ours. Neither does the Theocracy. None of them do." She pointed a finger at the holographic map Korina had projected onto a nearby rock face, the borders of the various nations glowing faintly in the pre-dawn light. "They have laws. Rules. Boxes. And none of those boxes are big enough for the four of us."

Korina nodded, her expression grim. A shadow fell across her face, the usual intellectual curiosity replaced by a stark understanding of their precarious situation. The holographic map, still projected onto the rock face, seemed to mock them with its clearly defined borders, each nation a prison of outdated laws and social norms.

"She's right," Korina said, her voice flat, devoid of its usual energetic cadence. "The Intellective States...they're no better. For all their talk of logic and progress, their laws are just as backwards, just as rigid." She gestured vaguely towards the southwest corner of the map, towards Veritas, her home, a place that had once been a sanctuary of knowledge, now just another symbol of their exclusion. "Our relationship...it wouldn't exist. Not officially. We would be...*nothing*."

The full, crushing weight of their social and legal reality seemed to hit Korina at once. The carefully constructed walls of academic detachment she had built around herself, the defenses she had erected after Kaelen had betrayed her, crumbled. Her composure, usually so meticulously maintained, cracked. A wave of genuine panic washed over her, threatening to drown her in a sea of fear and uncertainty.

"What are we going to do, Ada?" she asked, her voice rising in panic, the words tumbling out in a desperate torrent. The carefully curated logic of her world, the comforting predictability of data and algorithms, offered no solace. This was a problem that couldn't be solved with code, with a clever hack or a systemic override. This was about their *lives*, their *future*, a future that suddenly seemed impossibly fragile. "If we win...what then? What happens to *us*? What are *you* going to do?"

The last question hung in the air, a desperate plea directed at Ada, the Architect, the God-Queen, the woman who held their fate in her hands. Korina's carefully controlled world was collapsing, and Ada was the only anchor she had left.

The fear of rejection, of being ostracized, of being *exiled*, clawed at Korina's throat. She had tasted that bitter fruit before, after the Veritas Council's cold dismissal, after her own family's shame. She had spent years rebuilding her life, brick by painful brick, creating a new identity for herself, a life built on logic and knowledge, a life where she could finally control her own narrative.

But now, that carefully constructed world was threatened again, not by a single malevolent human like Kaelen, but by the very fabric of the society they were fighting to create. The thought of facing that isolation again, of being cast out, of being *nothing*, was unbearable. But the thought of Sera, Erita, and Ada facing that same fate, of their love being reduced to a whispered secret, a source of shame, was even worse.

The panic escalated, her breath catching in her throat, her chest tightening, the world around her blurring into a kaleidoscope of distorted colors and sounds. The cold mountain air seemed to burn her lungs, the ground beneath her feet shifting and unstable. The carefully ordered data streams of her mind, usually so clear and precise, dissolved into a chaotic jumble of fear and uncertainty.

She stumbled forward, her legs weak, her vision swimming,

the world tilting precariously. She reached out, blindly grasping for something, anything, to hold onto. Her hand brushed against Ada's arm, the contact sending a jolt of electricity through her, a spark of grounding energy in the swirling chaos of her mind.

"Ada," she whispered, her voice choked with panic, the words barely audible above the pounding of her heart. "Please...don't let them...don't let them take *this* away from *us*."

She collapsed into Ada's arms, her body trembling uncontrollably, the carefully controlled facade of the System Analyst shattering, revealing the terrified, vulnerable woman beneath. The fear of exile, of being nothing, consumed her, the echoes of her past trauma blending with the present threat, creating a vortex of despair that threatened to pull her under. She clung to Ada, burying her face in the crook of her neck, drawing strength from the warmth of her skin, the steady beat of her heart, the familiar scent of her skin. Ada was her anchor, her sanctuary, the only solid ground in a world that was rapidly falling apart.

Ada's arms tightened around Korina, a wave of protectiveness washing over her. Rina's trembling frame felt fragile, her whispered pleas a stark contrast to her usual sharp intellect. Ada's gaze swept over the others—Sera's face, etched with a fierce yearning for a future where their love wouldn't be a whispered secret, a hidden shame; Erita's silent, watchful agreement, her usual cynicism replaced by a quiet intensity. In that moment, amidst the cold mountain air and the looming threat of the Empire, Ada had a revelation.

This revolution, this fight for Kremøtoa, couldn't just be about deposing tyrants and fixing corrupted code. It had to be about something more, something *personal.* It had to be about building a world where the family she had found, the love she had discovered, could exist freely, openly, celebrated—not condemned.

She had known it all along, of course. Deep down, beneath the layers of code and the logic of systems, she had understood that her true purpose in Kremøtoa wasn't just to fix its flaws, but to create a space where she could finally belong, where she could finally be *herself.* But seeing Korina's fear, Sera's yearning, Erita's quiet resolve, solidified that understanding, transforming it from a vague intuition into a burning certainty.

This wasn't just about debugging a world; it was about building a *home.* A home for her, for Rina, for Sera, for Eri. A home where their love wasn't a glitch in the system, but a feature, a vibrant, essential part of the world's code.

"Rina," she whispered, her voice soft but firm, her hand gently stroking Korina's hair. "Sera. Eri." She looked at each of them in turn, her gaze holding theirs, conveying a depth of emotion that words couldn't express. "I...I know what we have to do."

She paused, gathering her thoughts, the weight of her decision settling upon her. This wasn't just a tactical shift, a change in strategy. This was a fundamental change in their mission, a redefinition of their purpose.

"This revolution...it's not just about taking down the Empire," she said, her voice gaining strength, her gaze hardening with resolve. "It's about building something new. Something *better.*"

She stood up, pulling Korina with her, her arms still wrapped protectively around her. She looked at Sera and Erita, her eyes blazing with a newfound conviction.

"We're not just going to fix Kremøtoa," she declared, her voice ringing with authority, echoing through the cold mountain air. "We're going—to *rule* it."

A profound, unwavering resolve settled over her. She stepped back, gesturing not to the surrounding mountains, but to the unseen horizon, to the entirety of Kremøtoa. "We are not fighting for a city," she began, her voice resonating with a newfound authority that transcended their current circumstances, "not even for a single nation." Her gaze swept over Sera, Korina, and Erita, her violet eyes blazing with a conviction that mirrored the brilliant light of Argent in the sky above. "We are fighting for *Kremøtoa*."

She paused, letting the weight of her words sink in, the sheer audacity of her vision hanging in the cold mountain air. This wasn't just about seizing power, about replacing one corrupt regime with another. This was about something far more radical, far more profound. This was about rewriting the very code of their world, not just its laws.

"Our revolution," she continued, her voice gaining strength, "is not about replacing one ruler with another. It's about shattering the very *concept* of tyranny. It's about dismantling the systems of oppression that have plagued this world for far too long, that have choked the very life out of its people."

She spread her arms wide, encompassing the vast, unseen landscape before them. "Imagine," she said, her voice softening, taking on a hypnotic cadence, "a Kremøtoa where the rigid, suffocating grip of the Empire is broken. Where the dogmatic chains of the Theocracy are shattered. Where the stifling bureaucracy of the Intellective States gives way to true, unfettered innovation."

She turned to Korina, her gaze meeting the scholar's wide, violet eyes. "Imagine, Rina," she said, her voice filled with a gentle warmth, "a world where knowledge isn't hoarded by a select few, but shared freely, where every mind is encouraged to explore, to discover, to *create*."

Then, she looked at Sera, her expression softening further, a hint of a smile playing on her lips. "Imagine, Sera," she whispered, her voice laced with affection, "a world where justice isn't a twisted mockery, a tool of oppression, but a true, unwavering force for good. Where honor and duty aren't blind obedience, but a conscious choice to protect the innocent, to defend the weak."

Finally, her gaze rested on Erita, a playful glint in her eyes. "Imagine, Eri," she said, her voice taking on a teasing lilt, "a world where secrets aren't weapons, where whispers aren't currency, but where truth and transparency are the foundations of power."

She turned back to the horizon, her voice rising again, filled with a passionate intensity. "Imagine a Kremøtoa," she declared, "where every single person, regardless of their birth, their status, their *code*, is free to prosper. Free to reach their full potential. Free to love who they choose, how they choose, without fear, without shame, without judgment."

She paused, letting her words hang in the air, the sheer audacity of her vision almost too much to bear. This wasn't just a rebellion; this was a *rebirth*.

"We will unite every nation," she proclaimed, her voice ringing with an unshakeable certainty, "from the Empire to the Theocracy, to the States, under a single, better system. A benevolent meritocracy built on pure logic, absolute efficiency, and true freedom." She gestured to Korina, then to Sera, then to Erita, her eyes shining with a fierce determination.

"*We*," she declared, "will build a world worthy of the love we have found. A world worthy of the sacrifices we have made. A world worthy of the name...*Kremøtoa*." Her voice echoed through the mountains, a promise, a challenge, a declaration of war, not just against the Empire, but against the very darkness that had held their world captive for far too long.

The silence stretched, thin and taut, the only sound the whisper of the wind through the jagged peaks. Sera, Korina, and Erita stared at Ada, their faces a mixture of shock, awe, and dawning comprehension. The sheer audacity of her vision, the breathtaking scope of her ambition, hung in the air like a tangible force, momentarily stealing their breath. It was Erita who finally broke the silence, her voice a low, almost reverent murmur.

"Void's name, Ada..." she breathed, her golden eyes wide, fixed on Ada's face. "You're not just rewriting the rules; you're creating a whole new game." A slow smile spread across her face, a predatory glint in her eyes. "And I, for one, am *in*."

Sera, still reeling from the revelation, found her voice, her usual fiery passion tempered by a newfound awe. "A world...where we can just...*be*?" she whispered, her voice thick with emotion. She reached out, her hand finding Ada's, her grip tight, almost desperate. "Argent's Light, Ada...I'll follow you anywhere."

Korina, her panic attack forgotten, her earlier fears replaced by a surge of hope, began to cry, tears streaming down her face. But these weren't tears of despair; they were tears of relief, of joy, of a profound, almost overwhelming sense of *possibility*. "Ada..." she choked out, her voice trembling, "it's...it's *perfect*."

Before Ada could respond, a gruff voice cut through the

charged atmosphere. "Well, I'll be a blighted swamp toad," Janna rumbled, stepping out from behind a nearby boulder, her face a mixture of amusement and awe. "Seems I accidentally overheard a bit of an...emotional *strategy session*." She grinned, her eyes twinkling. "Apologies for the eavesdropping, your Majesty," she added, a playful bow. "But Void, that's one hell of a plan."

Ada, still slightly dazed by her own pronouncements, blinked, her gaze shifting to Janna. "You...heard all that?" she asked, a faint blush creeping up her neck.

"Every glorious, revolutionary word," Janna confirmed, her voice filled with a warmth that belied her gruff exterior. She clapped Ada on the shoulder, her grip firm but gentle. "And let me tell you, Architect-Queen," she said, her eyes twinkling, "that's the kind of ambition I can get behind." She winked, a rare display of affection. "Especially if it means my warrior-bestie finally gets the happily-ever-after she deserves."

Janna's words sparked a fresh wave of tears in Korina. Her earlier panic attack had completely dissolved, replaced by a sob-fest of pure, unadulterated joy. The weight of their personal anxieties, the fear of rejection, the constant worry about their future, had been lifted, replaced by a shared sense of purpose, a grand, almost ludicrously ambitious goal that, in its sheer audacity, offered a strange, unexpected comfort.

"Oh, Ada..." Korina sobbed, burying her face in Ada's shoulder. "It's...it's *brilliant*. It's *insane*. It's...*everything*."

Sera, her own eyes glistening with unshed tears, pulled Korina into a hug, her strong arms wrapping around the scholar's trembling frame. "It is, isn't it?" she whispered, her voice thick with emotion. "It's...*us*."

Erita, her usual cynicism replaced by a quiet intensity, stepped forward, placing a hand on Ada's arm, her touch firm, reassuring. "So," she said, her golden eyes blazing with a fierce, almost predatory light. "Tell us, your Majesty...what's the first step in conquering a continent?"

Ada, still slightly overwhelmed by the intensity of the moment, took a deep breath, her gaze sweeping over her companions, her heart swelling with a mix of love, determination, and a healthy dose of sheer, exhilarating terror. This was it. This was the moment she had been waiting for, the moment she had been *building* towards, ever since she first stepped foot into this world, this world that was both her creation and her destiny.

"First," she said, her voice clear, steady, echoing through the mountain air, "we secure our allies. We solidify our base of power. We gather our resources." She paused, a mischievous glint in her violet eyes. "And then," she added, a slow smile spreading across her face, "we unleash hell." The words hung in the air, a promise, a threat, a declaration of intent that resonated with the raw, untamed energy of the world around them. The scope of their mission had just expanded beyond anything they could have imagined. Their faith in their Queen, in their leader, in their *lover*, had just been tested and found to be unshakeable. The Crimson Revolution had begun.

CHAPTER 15

THE QUIETEST WORDS

The biting wind whipped at Erita's cloak, the icy gusts threatening to tear the heavy fabric from her shoulders. She pressed herself closer against the rock face, the rough granite a cold, unforgiving comfort against her cheek. Above, the telltale thrum of an Imperial drone patrol echoed through the thin mountain air, a constant, menacing reminder of their precarious position.

She signaled a halt, her gloved hand slicing through the air in a sharp, decisive gesture. The others froze, their movements mirroring her own caution. Ada, her breath misting in the frigid air, leaned in, her violet eyes questioning. Erita pointed upwards, her finger a silent accusation against the metal birds circling high above.

Ada's gaze followed her gesture, her expression hardening as she acknowledged the threat. The process of navigating this treacherous mountain pass had already been slow and arduous, the uneven terrain and sheer drops demanding their full attention. The addition of an aerial patrol transformed their cautious trek into a nerve-wracking game of cat and mouse, every step a gamble, every whisper a potential death sentence.

Erita gestured again, a series of complex hand signals conveying the patrol's estimated trajectory and the safest route forward. Sera, ever the pragmatist, nodded her understanding, her crimson hair a fiery beacon against the muted grays and browns of the mountainside. Korina, her face pale with anxiety, gripped her data-slate, her knuckles white against the dark metal casing. Janna, her usual gruff demeanor replaced by a mask of grim determination, hefted her axe, her grip tight, ready for any sudden confrontation.

The next few hours were an exercise in agonizing patience and silent communication. Erita led the way, her movements fluid, almost feline, her senses heightened, every rustle of wind, every screech of a distant hawk, every crunch of snow underfoot amplified in the tense silence. She moved from shadow to shadow, using the natural cover of the mountain to shield them from the ever-watchful eyes in the sky.

The process was clumsy, frustratingly slow. Their usual rapid-fire banter and easy camaraderie were replaced by hushed whispers and hurried hand signals, their communication stilted, awkward. The constant threat of discovery hung heavy in the air, a suffocating blanket of tension that threatened to smother their every move.

Erita could feel the frustration radiating from the others, their forced silence a stark contrast to their usual boisterous energy. Ada, in particular, seemed to struggle with the restrictions, her usual calm demeanor replaced by a restless energy that vibrated through their small group. Erita understood her impatience. Ada was a creature of action, a force of nature accustomed to bending reality to her will. This forced slowness, this reliance on mundane stealth and subterfuge, must have felt like a cage to her, a frustrating limitation on her immense power.

At one point, Korina stumbled, her foot catching on a loose rock. The sudden, sharp crack echoed through the still air, a sound that, in the tense silence, seemed deafening. Erita's heart leaped into her throat, her hand instinctively reaching for the daggers hidden beneath her cloak. She glanced upwards, her eyes scanning the sky, expecting the telltale whine of descending drones, the harsh glare of searchlights cutting through the shadows.

But the sky remained empty, the patrol seemingly unaware of their near-miss. Erita let out a breath she hadn't realized she was holding, her body relaxing slightly. She turned to Korina, her expression a mixture of relief and annoyance. The scholar, her face pale with fright, mouthed a silent apology, her eyes wide with fear.

Erita sighed, shaking her head. This was going to be a long, arduous journey. And if this small stumble had nearly given them away, she shuddered to think of the challenges that lay ahead. They pressed on, their movements slow, deliberate, each step a testament to their shared determination, their shared trust, their shared hope for a future where they wouldn't have to hide in the shadows, a future where they could walk in the light, hand in hand, heads held high, their love a beacon, not a secret. A future that Ada had promised them, a future that Erita, despite her inherent cynicism, found herself desperately wanting to believe in.

The alcove they found was little more than a shallow

indentation in the rock face, barely large enough to shield them from the wind and the prying eyes of the Imperial drones. It was a cold, unforgiving space, the rough granite digging into their backs, the icy air biting at their exposed skin. But it was a sanctuary, a temporary respite from the relentless pressure of their escape.

As soon as they were settled, Ada addressed the issue directly.

"This isn't efficient," she stated, her violet eyes scanning each of their faces. "We need a better way to communicate. A silent way."

Erita nodded, her expression grim. "Agreed. Hand signals are slow and imprecise. And whispers...well, whispers are just invitations for unwanted attention."

Korina shivered, pulling her cloak tighter around her. "What do you suggest? Some kind of coded communication system? I could adapt Obsidian to—"

"The link," Ada interrupted, her voice firm. "The telepathic link we discussed. It's time."

Sera frowned, her crimson eyebrows knitting together. "Are you sure? We're exposed here. If something goes wrong—"

"It's now or never," Ada insisted, her gaze unwavering. "We need to be able to communicate instantly, silently, without fear of interception. The link is the only way."

Janna grunted, her expression skeptical. "Telepathy? Sounds like Wordaeusi mumbo-jumbo to me."

Ada shook her head. "It's not magic, Janna. It's just...a different form of communication. A more direct one. I can teach you."

Korina's mind, always a whirlwind of calculations and queries, buzzed with a sudden influx of questions. Telepathy? A concept that had always existed on the fringes of theoretical thaumaturgy, a fascinating but improbable possibility. And now, Ada was suggesting it as a viable solution, a tactical necessity. The implications were staggering.

"But *how*?" Korina blurted out, her voice a hushed whisper, her violet eyes wide with a mixture of excitement and disbelief. "Telepathy isn't a standard biological function, at least not according to any documented research. It would require a specific arcane pathway, a neurological bridge between minds. Do we...do we even *have* such a pathway?"

Ada's expression was calm, almost serene, a stark contrast to the turmoil swirling within Korina. "Not yet," she replied, a faint smile playing on her lips. "But we can. Or rather," she added, her gaze meeting Korina's, "I can."

Ada's words hung in the air, heavy with unspoken meaning. Korina felt a shiver run down her spine, a strange mixture of anticipation and apprehension. This was new territory, even for Ada. This wasn't just healing a wound or fixing a broken bridge; this was delving into the very core of their being, altering the fundamental code that defined them.

"I can access the world's code directly," Ada explained, her voice low, almost conspiratorial. "Not just manipulate its effects, but rewrite its core instructions. The telepathic link...it's not something you *have*. It's something I can *grant*. But it's different than creating from nothing, it's not creation thauma."

Korina's mind reeled, trying to process the implications of Ada's words. This was the first time Ada had spoken so openly about her abilities, about the true extent of her power. It was a revelation, a glimpse behind the curtain, a confirmation of Korina's long-held suspicions that Ada was more than just a powerful thaumaturge. She was something...*else*. Something unique, something extraordinary. Something...almost divine.

"To establish the link," Ada continued, her voice soft, almost gentle, "I need to make a small, precise adjustment to your personal code. Think of it as...creating a new pathway, a dedicated channel for sending and receiving thoughts."

Ada held out her hand, palm upwards, a silent invitation. Korina hesitated for a moment, her mind still racing, her heart pounding in her chest. This was a leap of faith, a surrender of control, a trust in Ada's power that went beyond anything she had ever experienced before. But despite her apprehension, despite the lingering fear of the unknown, Korina felt a strange sense of excitement, a thrill of anticipation. This was a chance to connect with Ada on a deeper level, to share her thoughts, her fears, her hopes, her dreams. It was a chance to become something...*more*.

Korina took a deep breath, her violet eyes meeting Ada's. With a small, almost imperceptible nod, she placed her hand in Ada's, her fingers intertwining with hers. A warm, tingling sensation spread through her arm, a feeling of energy flowing between them, a connection forming, a bond being forged. And in that moment, Korina knew that everything was about to change.

Ada held Korina's hand, her thumb gently caressing the back of Korina's hand. Korina felt a warm, analytical hum, like a perfect line of code being seamlessly integrated into her own complex system. It was a sensation both foreign and familiar, a new variable being introduced into a well-defined equation. Her mind, usually a whirlwind of calculations and queries, stilled, focusing solely on the connection forming between her and Ada. It was fascinating. The energy flowed between them, not as a chaotic surge, but as a precise, measured current, each pulse carrying a wealth of information, a symphony of data. It wasn't just a physical sensation; it was an intellectual one, a merging of minds, a sharing of knowledge. Korina felt a sense of awe, a profound understanding of Ada's power, and a deep, abiding trust in the connection they were forging. It wasn't unpleasant. It was, in its own strange way, *beautiful.*

Ada then turned to Sera, her violet eyes meeting Sera's emerald gaze. Sera's hand, calloused and strong from years of wielding a sword, felt strangely small and delicate in Ada's grasp. The touch sent a brief, intense heat through Sera's arm, like the sudden flare of a forge-fire. It was a sensation she recognized, a primal surge of energy that resonated with the warrior within her. The heat quickly subsided, replaced by a sense of profound clarity and focus. The world around her, usually a blur of motion and potential threats, sharpened, each detail coming into stark relief. It was a warrior's connection, a silent understanding, a shared sense of purpose. Sera felt a deep sense of peace, a calmness she hadn't experienced since before the horrors of Silver Creek. It was as if Ada's touch had cauterized an old wound, leaving behind not a scar, but a sense of renewed strength.

Erita watched the exchange between Ada and Sera with a mixture of fascination and suspicion. When Ada turned to her, extending her hand, Erita hesitated. Trust didn't come easily to her. Her life had taught her to be wary, to expect betrayal, to guard her heart with a cynical, sharp-tongued shield. But something in Ada's eyes, a quiet sincerity, a gentle vulnerability, compelled her to reach out. As their fingers intertwined, Erita felt a cool, almost imperceptible whisper, like a key sliding into a perfectly matched lock. It was subtle, efficient, a silent acknowledgment of a shared secret. It was deeply unnerving, this sudden intrusion into her carefully guarded inner world. But it wasn't in a bad, distasteful way. It was a feeling of being seen, of being understood, of being accepted for who she truly was, flaws and all. It was a feeling she had never allowed herself to experience before, and it left her breathless.

Janna, the last to receive Ada's touch, was the most hesitant. She had witnessed Ada's power, seen her manipulate the very fabric of reality, but this felt different. This was personal, intimate, a merging of souls. She had always kept her distance, preferring the solitude of the wilderness, the comfort of her own company. But something about Ada, about the quiet strength she possessed, drew Janna in. As Ada took her hand, Janna felt a strange and powerful sensation, like the deep, resonant hum of the earth itself. It was a grounding feeling, a connection to something ancient and powerful, a reminder of her place in the world. It was as if Ada's touch had anchored her to this new reality, to this strange and wonderful adventure she had found herself on. The hum resonated through her, calming her nerves, stilling her doubts, filling her with a sense of quiet awe. She looked at Ada, her eyes filled with a newfound respect, a silent acknowledgment of the bond they now shared. She was ready.

"Okay," Ada began, her voice soft but clear, "now that the pathways are open, we can begin." She looked at each of her companions in turn, her violet eyes reflecting the flickering firelight. "There are two primary methods of communication using this link. The first is what I call a 'Direct Ping.'" She focused her gaze on Korina, sending a single, focused thought: *Rina, can you hear this?*

Korina's eyes widened slightly, a small smile playing on her lips. *Yes, Ada. It's...strange. Like a very specific itch I can't quite scratch.*

Ada chuckled, relieved that the Direct Ping was working as intended. "Exactly," she replied aloud, then sent another ping to Sera: *Your turn.*

Sera frowned slightly, concentrating. *I hear you. It's...loud. Like a shout in a silent room.*

Ada nodded. "It will become more natural with practice. Think of it like whispering a secret. You have to focus your intent, direct your thoughts towards a single recipient." She then turned to Erita. *Eri, how about you?*

Erita's golden eyes narrowed, a flicker of amusement crossing her face. *I can hear you. It's...intrusive. Like a spy in my own head.*

Ada suppressed a smile. Erita's dry wit, even through the telepathic link, was a comfort. Lastly, she directed her attention to Janna. *Janna, are you with us?*

Janna's gruff voice echoed in Ada's mind. *Loud and clear. Like a war drum, Void...*

"Good," Ada said aloud, pleased that all the connections were functioning. "Now, for the second method: the Broadcast. This is less focused, more like speaking aloud in a room, but only those connected can hear." She took a deep breath, then sent a thought to the entire group: *Can everyone hear this? Test, test.*

A jumble of thoughts flooded Ada's mind. *Void, I could murder an ale right now...this blasted rock...they'll be on us soon...the implications are staggering...her hair smells like lavender...*Ada winced, clutching her head. "Too much," she muttered, "too much information at once."

"What is it?" Sera asked, her hand instinctively going to her sword. "Did they find us?"

"No," Ada said, shaking her head. "It's the link. It's...unfiltered."

Korina's face was pale, her eyes wide with a mixture of fascination and fear. "It's like...everyone's thoughts are crashing together. I can hear Janna's stomach rumbling, Erita's frustration with a loose rock in her boot, Sera's worry about the patrol...and..." she trailed off, blushing slightly, "...other, more...personal thoughts."

Erita scoffed, a faint blush creeping up her neck. "My apologies for the intrusion, Architect-Queen. Didn't realize my digestive processes were classified information."

Janna grinned, unfazed. "Just thinking about the ale back at the warehouse. A nice, cold pint..."

Ada sighed, rubbing her temples. "It's not your fault. I...I didn't account for the...intimacy of the connection. It's like we're all shouting in a silent room, and I'm the only one who can hear everyone at once."

Sera knelt beside Ada, her expression concerned. "Can you... turn it off?"

Ada closed her eyes, focusing on the code she had woven into their minds. She visualized a series of filters, dampeners, and privacy protocols, mentally writing the code to refine the telepathic link. But nothing comes to mind.

"No," Ada said, opening her eyes, "not exactly. But I can...

moderate it. Help you build your own mental firewalls, focus your intent." She looked at each of them in turn. "Think of it like this: right now, the link is a wide-open channel. Anyone can broadcast anything, and everyone receives everything. What we need are private lines, secure channels, and the ability to choose who you're speaking to and what you're sharing."

"So, how do we do that?" Erita asked, her usual cynicism tinged with a hint of genuine curiosity.

"Practice," Ada replied. "We start with simple, clear images. Focus your intent on projecting a single thought, a single picture, to me. Sera, you start. Think of your sword. Its weight, its balance, the feel of the hilt in your hand. Project that image to me."

Sera closed her eyes, concentrating. Ada felt a flicker of mental energy, a brief flash of polished steel. *There,* Sera's thought echoed, *like that?*

"Perfect," Ada said, a smile spreading across her face. "Now, Korina. A schematic. Any schematic. The more complex the better."

Korina's eyes lit up, a spark of intellectual excitement replacing her earlier mortification. Ada felt a surge of data, a complex diagram of interlocking gears and energy conduits flashing through her mind. *This one's from Obsidian's core memory banks. It's a Thaumaturgical Amplifier, it a fascinating—*

"Excellent," Ada praised. "Erita, your turn. Something simple. A gold coin. Focus on its weight, its texture, the glint of the metal."

Erita closed her eyes, a flicker of concentration crossing her face. Ada felt a cool, metallic sensation, the weight of a single Byt pressing against her palm. *It's just a bit of data,* Erita's thought echoed, *but I suppose it will do.*

"Exactly," Ada replied. "It's not about the complexity of the image, but the clarity of the intent." She turned to Janna. "Your turn, Janna. A frothing tankard of ale. Focus on the weight of the mug, the coldness of the metal, the smell of the hops."

Janna grinned, her eyes twinkling. Ada felt a sudden wave of warmth, the comforting weight of a full tankard in her hand, the tantalizing aroma of freshly brewed ale filling her senses. *Void, that hit the spot.*

Ada laughed, feeling a lightness she hadn't experienced in days. "See?" she said, looking at each of them in turn. "It's not so hard. With practice, you'll be able to control the flow of information, build those mental firewalls, and communicate silently and securely, even amidst the chaos."

Ada smiled, feeling a surge of pride and affection for her companions. "Now," she said, her voice barely above a whisper, "let's try a real-world application." She gestured towards the jagged peaks looming above them. "Sera, you scout ahead. Erita, stay close to me. Korina, keep an eye on our surroundings. Janna, bring up the rear. And remember," she added, sending a calming thought through the telepathic link, *Stay focused. Stay silent. Stay together.*

The group moved out, their footsteps barely disturbing the loose scree. The wind howled through the narrow pass, carrying the scent of snow and the distant rumble of falling rocks. Sera, moving with the fluid grace of a predator, scaled a sheer rock face, her crimson tunic blending with the rust-colored stone. She reached a vantage point, peering through the swirling mist, her sharp eyes scanning the desolate landscape.

Suddenly, a flicker of movement caught her attention. A small, Imperial drone, its metallic body gleaming in the pale sunlight, hovered near the edge of the pass, its sensors sweeping the terrain. A chill ran down Sera's spine. If the drone spotted them, it would alert the entire Imperial network, and their precarious journey would be over.

In the past, Sera would have shouted a warning, her voice echoing through the mountains. But now, something different happened. A clear, focused thought formed in her mind, projected directly to the group through the telepathic link: *Drone. Twelve o'clock. Fifty meters.*

The others received it perfectly. No shouted warnings, no frantic hand signals, just a silent, shared understanding. Erita's response was a silent wave of tactical agreement. *Understood. Prepare for engagement.*

Korina, her violet eyes narrowed in concentration, sent back a quick mental image of a safe route: a narrow crevice in the rock face, hidden from the drone's view. *This way. Minimal exposure.*

Janna projected a feeling of grim readiness, a silent promise of protection. *I'll cover your retreat.*

Ada's thought was a calm, reassuring wave of confidence. *We move as one. Swiftly. Silently.*

The five of them moved in perfect, silent synchronization through the treacherous mountain pass. Sera, leading the way, melted into the shadows of the crevice, her movements fluid and precise. Ada followed close behind, her hand brushing against Sera's back, a silent reassurance. Korina, her data-slate clutched tightly in her hand, scanned their surroundings, her mind processing the terrain and identifying potential hazards. Erita, her daggers drawn, moved with feline grace, her senses alert for any sign of danger. Janna, a massive, imposing figure, brought up the rear, her battle-axe held ready, a silent guardian against any pursuit.

The drone, oblivious to their presence, continued its patrol, its sensors sweeping the empty landscape. The wind howled, the rocks shifted, but the five women moved as one, their thoughts and actions interwoven, a single, unified entity navigating the treacherous terrain. They were no longer just individuals, but a network, a system, a force. The quietest words had just become their most powerful weapon.

CHAPTER 16

A SYMPHONY OF SILENCE

The biting wind whipped at Ada's cloak as they navigated the treacherous mountain pass. The telepathic link hummed with shared awareness, a constant stream of sensory data and tactical assessments. Sera, still in the lead, projected a sense of unease. *Another patrol. Closing fast. Two drones this time.*

Ada's mind raced. Their usual pattern of evasion – utilizing the terrain, minimizing their energy signature, and relying on stealth – wouldn't work. The drones were too close, the terrain too exposed. A new strategy formed in Ada's mind, a spark of reckless audacity ignited by the relentless pursuit.

They hunt phantoms, she projected, her thought laced with a chilling resolve. *Let's show them what a phantom can do. We hunt them now.*

Surprise rippled through the telepathic link. Sera's initial hesitation quickly shifted to a grim excitement. Erita's thought was a dry, amused acknowledgement. *My kind of hunt.*

Korina's concern was quickly overridden by her intellectual curiosity. *The tactical implications are fascinating. A reversal of predator-prey dynamics...*

Janna's response was a guttural rumble of approval. *Time to crack some gears.*

Ada felt a surge of adrenaline, a thrill of exhilaration coursing through her veins. This wasn't just about survival anymore; it was about sending a message. It was about reclaiming control.

Ada focused her intent, her vision locking onto the lead drone, its metallic body glinting in the fading sunlight. *Sera, with me. Erita, Korina, Janna, provide cover—remember, stay hidden from its imaging view.*

Erita, perched on a jagged rock overlooking the pass, watched the scene unfold through her modified lenses. Data streamed across her vision – the drones' specifications, patrol vectors, thermal signatures – a silent symphony of tactical information feeding into the shared telepathic link. Ada and Sera, cloaked in shimmering distortion, moved like wraiths across the exposed slope. *North drone, heat signature spiking. Overcharging its primary weapon,* Erita projected, her voice a cool whisper in their minds.

Sera's mind processed Erita's cool, precise warning. *Heat signature spiking.* No need for shouted orders, no frantic hand signals to betray their position. Her thought was a sharp, clear image projected directly to Janna: a pair of crimson claws snapping shut, a pincer movement designed to crush. One claw, herself, would sweep low, using the jagged scree for cover. The other, Janna, would ascend, a bulwark of muscle and steel claiming the high ground.

A feeling of unshakeable, granite-like agreement flooded back from Janna. *Understood.*

They moved. The separation was instantaneous, a fluid parting of ways. Sera became a blur of red and shadow, her form disappearing behind a curtain of rock and loose shale. Janna, a force of nature, found purchase on the near-vertical rock face, her powerful limbs propelling her upward with a terrifying silence. They were two predators, perfectly synchronized, melting into the crags and crevices of the mountain pass, becoming extensions of the unforgiving stone itself. The hunt was on.

As the drones flew into the narrow pass, a natural chokepoint formed by towering cliffs and jagged scree, Korina's mind became a whirlwind of calculations. Obsidian, clutched in her hand, pulsed with a soft, rhythmic glow, mirroring the frantic pace of her analysis. Her thought, amplified by the telepathic link, was a sharp, clear broadcast to the fighters: *Their power conduits are exposed on the ventral side. A precise strike will trigger a cascade failure. Erita, can you create a diversion to make them bank?*

Erita, hidden behind a rocky outcropping, didn't reply with words. Instead, she sent a quick, silent ping of confirmation through the link – a mental nod, sharp and efficient, like the flick of a dagger. With a practiced motion, she launched a small, EMP-like device from a concealed launcher on her wrist. The device arced through the air, detonating harmlessly a few meters to the drones' left, sending out a pulse of disruptive energy. The drones, their sensors momentarily overloaded, banked sharply in response, their underbellies perfectly exposed to Janna's position above.

The attack was brutally efficient. Janna, guided by Korina's precise targeting data, which flowed seamlessly through the telepathic link, hurled a scavenged explosive with pinpoint accuracy. The device, a crude but effective concoction of unstable chemicals and arcane focusing crystals, arced through the air, impacting directly on the exposed power conduit of the lead drone. Simultaneously, Sera burst from the shadows below, her twin blades a silver arc against the darkening sky. She moved with a predatory grace, her movements guided not by sight, but by the shared awareness of the telepathic link, anticipating the drones' trajectory, their weaknesses laid bare by Korina's analysis.

The first drone, crippled by Janna's explosive, shuddered violently, its internal systems overloaded. Sparks erupted from its ventral side, cascading through its power conduits like a chain reaction. Before it could recover, Sera's blades flashed, severing crucial control linkages and slicing through vital components. The drone plummeted to the ground, its metallic body crashing against the rocks with a dull thud.

The second drone, momentarily disoriented by the EMP blast and the sudden demise of its companion, attempted to correct its course. But it was too late. Janna's second explosive found its mark, ripping through the drone's already weakened defenses. Sera, a whirlwind of crimson and steel, finished the job, her blades a blur of lethal precision. The drone, its systems irrevocably compromised, spiraled out of control, crashing into the mountainside in a shower of sparks and shattered metal.

The silence of the mountains returned, broken only by the crackle of burning circuitry and the faint whisper of the wind. Ada, Sera, Korina, Erita, and Janna stood motionless for a moment, their minds still linked, the echoes of the battle fading from their shared awareness. The hunt was over.

Clean and efficient, Erita's thought echoed in their minds, a touch of professional satisfaction in her tone.

The data suggests a significant improvement in our coordinated combat effectiveness, Korina added, her thought laced with her usual analytical enthusiasm. *The telepathic link minimized reaction time and allowed for real-time tactical adjustments.*

Sera, sheathing her blades, sent a warm wave of gratitude through the link. *Thank you, Korina. Your analysis was invaluable.*

Janna, her massive frame silhouetted against the twilight sky, grunted in agreement. *Good hunting, sisters.*

Ada, still catching her breath, felt a surge of pride and affection for her companions. This victory, swift and decisive, was a testament to their growing bond, their shared purpose forging them into a formidable force. The impossible journey had just taken its first successful step.

The adrenaline began to fade, leaving a familiar ache in Ada's muscles. The days of jumping, coupled with the mental strain of maintaining the telepathic link, had taken their toll. She leaned against a weathered rock face, the rough stone cold against her cheek. Closing her eyes, she focused on slowing her breathing, regulating the flow of energy through her weary body.

Are you alright, Ada? Sera's voice, amplified by the telepathic link, was a soft whisper in her mind. Ada could sense the warmth of Sera's concern, a comforting presence amidst the lingering chill of the mountain air.

I'm just tired, Ada projected back, forcing a note of reassurance into her thought. *Two jumps so close together...it's more draining than I anticipated.*

We should rest for a while, Korina's voice chimed in, a gentle hum of logic and concern. *Your energy signature is fluctuating. Pushing yourself further could lead to instability.*

Ada knew Korina was right. Pushing her limits now would be reckless. *Alright,* she conceded. *Let's find a secure location. Erita, can you scout ahead?*

Erita's response was a silent, almost predatory flicker of acknowledgement through the link. She melted into the shadows, her movements fluid and silent, a ghost in the twilight. Janna, her massive frame a reassuring presence, took up a position at the entrance to the pass, her eyes scanning the surrounding terrain. Sera knelt beside Ada, her hand resting lightly on Ada's arm, a silent gesture of support. Korina busied herself with Obsidian, running diagnostics and analyzing the data from the recent engagement.

A few minutes later, Erita returned, her thought a quick, precise report: *There's a small cave about a hundred meters ahead. Concealed entrance, good visibility, minimal energy signatures. Suitable for a short rest.*

Lead the way, Ada replied, pushing herself to her feet. The exhaustion was still there, a dull ache in her bones, but the exhilaration of their victory, the seamless synergy of their combined skills, buoyed her spirits. They moved through the pass, the silence broken only by the crunch of their boots on the rocky ground and the soft whisper of the wind.

As they reached the cave, Ada noticed a small, vibrant patch of wildflowers clinging to the rock face near the entrance. The flowers, a mix of deep violet, crimson, and gold, pulsed with a soft, bioluminescent glow, casting an ethereal light on the surrounding rocks. They were a splash of unexpected beauty in the harsh landscape, a reminder of the vibrant life that thrived even in the most desolate corners of Kremøtoa.

"Beautiful," Sera murmured, her thought a soft echo in Ada's mind.

Ada reached out and gently touched one of the violet blossoms. The petals felt cool and smooth beneath her fingertips, the bioluminescence intensifying slightly at her touch. She smiled, a genuine, unforced expression of pure, simple joy. For a moment, the weight of her responsibilities, the looming threat of the Empire, the creeping decay of her creation, all faded away. All that remained was the beauty of the flowers, the warmth of her companions, and the quiet satisfaction of a shared victory. This, she realized, was what she was fighting for. This was the future she wanted to build.

Inside the cave, they settled down for a brief rest. Janna took first watch, her keen eyes scanning the landscape beyond the cave entrance. Sera sat beside Ada, her presence a comforting warmth. Korina, still engrossed in her analysis, sat on Ada's other side, murmuring softly to herself, her thoughts a stream of data and calculations that flowed through the telepathic link, a constant, reassuring hum of intellectual activity. Erita, her back against the cave wall, closed her eyes, her mind a silent, watchful presence.

Ada leaned against Sera, the warmth of Sera's body seeping into her tired muscles. She closed her eyes, the image of the bioluminescent flowers still vivid in her mind. The exhaustion was still there, but now, it was mingled with a sense of hope, a quiet certainty that they were on the right path. The journey was far from over, but for the first time since arriving in Kremøtoa, Ada felt a flicker of genuine optimism. They would reach Rhedeon. They would build a better world. Together.

Ada stretched, the stiffness in her joints a testament to the arduous journey. The rest, though brief, had helped. The exhaustion had receded, replaced by a renewed sense of purpose. *Ready when you are,* she projected to the others through the telepathic link, her thought infused with quiet determination.

Sera nodded, her crimson hair catching the faint light filtering into the cave. Korina closed Obsidian with a soft click, the Lynx monitor blinking sleepily in the corner of the screen. Erita, her golden eyes already scanning the terrain beyond the cave entrance, gave a curt nod. Janna grunted in agreement, hefting her massive axe. They moved out of the cave and back onto the mountain pass, the silence of their telepathic communication a stark contrast to the crunching of their boots on the rocky ground.

As they continued their trek, Ada noticed a subtle shift in the landscape. The desolate, ash-grey rock that had characterized the Imperial territories began to give way to a wilder, more vibrant terrain. Patches of emerald moss clung to the rocks, and strange, luminous fungi sprouted in crevices, casting a soft, otherworldly glow on the surrounding stone. The air itself felt different, charged with a raw, untamed energy that crackled against Ada's skin.

The energy signatures are...unusual, Korina's voice echoed in Ada's mind, a blend of scientific curiosity and cautious apprehension. *Obsidian is registering high levels of uncontrolled axiomatic flux. It's...chaotic, but fascinating.*

This is Rhedeon's territory, Sera's thought cut through Korina's analysis, a mix of familiarity and wariness. *The thaumaturgy is so... unpredictable.*

Ada found herself strangely drawn to this untamed energy, this embrace of chaos. It was a stark contrast to the rigid, controlled systems of the Empire, a reflection of a different philosophy, a different way of interacting with the world's code.

After several more hours of weary travel, they reached the final peak of the mountain range. The wind whipped around them, carrying the scent of salt and something wild, something Ada couldn't quite place. As they looked out, the vast, verdant expanse of the Free Realm of Rhedeon stretched out before them. Rolling hills covered in lush, vibrant vegetation sloped down towards a chaotic, colorful coastline. Strange, twisted trees with glowing, bioluminescent leaves dotted the landscape, casting an ethereal light on the surrounding terrain. In the distance, nestled amidst a vibrant, almost anarchic sprawl of buildings and docks, the city of Port Veridia glittered under the afternoon sun.

*By Argent's light...*Janna's thought rumbled through the telepathic link, a mix of awe and apprehension. *It's even more... chaotic than I remember.*

It's beautiful, Korina's voice whispered in Ada's mind, her tone filled with a sense of wonder. *The energy readings are off the charts. It's like...the entire city is a single, massive thaumaturgical nexus.*

Sera remained silent, her eyes fixed on the city in the distance. Ada could sense a complex mix of emotions swirling within her: nostalgia, anticipation, and a flicker of something that felt like... fear?

We need to reach the city before nightfall, Erita's voice cut through the silence, a sharp, pragmatic edge to her thought. *We're exposed here. And I don't like the look of those storm clouds gathering in the west.*

Ada nodded, her eyes still fixed on Port Veridia. The city beckoned, a chaotic symphony of color and energy, a haven from the Empire's rigid control, but also a place of unknown dangers, a place where the rules were different, where the very air hummed with untamed power. This was their next challenge, their next step in the revolution. The had crossed the Cipher Peaks and made it. And Ada, the Architect-Queen, the woman who had once controlled every line of code in this world, felt a strange mix of excitement and trepidation as she prepared to enter the Rhedeon domain.

CHAPTER 17

THE CITY OF RENDERED LIGHT

The descent from the final mountain pass was a jarring transition. The air, thin and crisp at the summit, thickened as they descended, becoming heavy with a wild, untamed magic that prickled their skin like static electricity. Gone were the muted greys and browns of the Imperial northern territories—Rhedeon exploded with color. Luminous, bioluminescent flora pulsed with an inner light, painting the landscape in vibrant hues of emerald, sapphire, and amethyst. Strange, twisted trees with glowing leaves reached towards the sky like skeletal fingers, their branches intertwined in a chaotic dance. The very ground beneath their feet seemed to thrum with a restless energy, a stark contrast to the rigid, predictable order of the Empire.

"It's...overwhelming," Korina murmured, her voice barely audible above the strange, almost musical hum that permeated the air. She clutched Obsidian to her chest, the data-slate's smooth surface a small comfort in this chaotic new world. The Lynx monitor, usually a playful flicker in the corner of the screen, now paced anxiously, its pixelated ears flattened against its head.

"Stay close," Erita's voice was sharp, her golden eyes constantly scanning the surrounding terrain. "This place...it feels wrong." Even her usual cynicism seemed muted, replaced by a wary unease.

Sera, however, seemed to thrive in the chaotic energy. She moved with a newfound fluidity, her crimson hair a vibrant flame against the backdrop of Rhedeon's wild beauty. A faint smile played on her lips, a predatory gleam in her eyes. "It feels...alive," she breathed, her voice filled with a strange mix of excitement and apprehension.

Ada, walking between Sera and Korina, felt a similar pull towards this untamed energy. It resonated with a part of her she hadn't realized she'd missed, a part of her that craved the unpredictable, the unconstrained. It was a reminder of the boundless potential she had poured into this world, a potential that had been stifled by the Empire's rigid control.

As they descended further, the terrain became increasingly treacherous. The path, barely discernible amidst the dense vegetation, wound through treacherous ravines and across narrow, rickety bridges that swayed precariously in the wind. Strange, bioluminescent creatures darted through the undergrowth, their glowing bodies leaving trails of light in the deepening twilight.

The wind whipped at Ada's hair as they reached a windswept plateau overlooking Port Veridia. Below, the city sprawled like a spilled jewel box, a riot of mismatched architecture and vibrant, glowing sails. The air crackled with the same untamed magic that permeated the surrounding landscape, a stark contrast to the sterile order of Celgrad. This was a city built not on logic, but on raw, unbridled creativity.

"We change here," Erita announced, her voice tight with a tension that had nothing to do with the wind. She gestured to a cluster of boulders that offered a modicum of privacy. "No sense advertising our arrival."

Janna, her usual gruffness amplified by the unfamiliar surroundings, took up a position overlooking the path, her axe held loosely in one hand. "I'll keep watch," she rumbled, her eyes scanning the horizon.

Ada felt a flutter of nervousness as she reached into her *Matākyasshu* and withdrew a bundle of clothing. The simple tunic and leather trousers felt rough against her skin after weeks of wearing the soft linens of the Empire. As she shed her travel-worn clothes, the wind tugged at the fabric, exposing her bare back for a fleeting moment. A blush warmed her cheeks as she caught Sera's gaze lingering on her skin.

She's beautiful, Sera thought, her gaze tracing the curve of Ada's spine, the delicate slope of her shoulders. *So different from the rigid forms of the Aegis knights, so...alive.* She quickly averted her eyes, her own cheeks flushed with a warmth that had nothing to do with the exertion of their journey.

Korina, her fingers fumbling with the laces of her boots, stole a glance at Ada. A wave of longing washed over her as she took in the subtle curve of Ada's hip, the elegant line of her back. *I want to touch her,* she thought, her heart aching with a desire that was both physical and intellectual. *To trace the lines of her body, to understand the mechanics of her impossible grace.* She quickly turned away, her cheeks burning with a mixture of longing and shame.

Erita, her movements quick and efficient, shed her travel-worn leathers with practiced ease. The simple tunic she donned did little to conceal the lithe, powerful muscles beneath. As she adjusted the fabric, her gaze met Ada's. A flicker of something raw and possessive flashed in her golden eyes, a silent challenge that sent a shiver of excitement down Ada's spine.

Mine, Erita thought, her gaze locking with Ada's. *All mine.* A smirk played on her lips as she saw the blush that crept up Ada's neck, a silent acknowledgment of the unspoken tension that crackled between them.

Ada, catching Erita's gaze, felt a jolt of electricity course through her. The intensity of Erita's possessiveness was both thrilling and slightly unnerving. *She's a force of nature,* Ada thought, her heart pounding in her chest. *A whirlwind of chaos and passion that I can't help but be drawn to.*

As they finished changing, the wind died down, leaving an almost unnatural stillness in its wake. The air hummed with anticipation, a silent promise of the challenges and opportunities that awaited them in Port Veridia. They were ghosts in a new city, their former identities shed like old skin. They were ready to begin.

The city gates of Port Veridia were a chaotic spectacle of interwoven wood and shimmering, iridescent metal, pulsating with an arcane energy that made *Obsidian* hum against Korina's thigh. The data-slate's sensors flickered wildly, struggling to classify the unfamiliar energy signatures that permeated the air. It was exhilarating. Each breath was a cocktail of exotic aromas—sea salt mingled with unfamiliar spices, the sweet scent of blooming night flowers, and the acrid tang of ozone from crackling arcane discharges. Voices, a cacophony of unfamiliar dialects and lilting inflections, rose and fell like the tide, creating a dizzying symphony of sound.

Korina took a deep breath, her senses reeling from the sudden influx of information. It was a sensory overload, an intellectual feast that both fascinated and overwhelmed her. She instinctively moved closer to Ada, her hand brushing against Ada's arm. The familiar warmth of Ada's presence was a grounding anchor in the swirling chaos of the city, a silent reassurance that helped her maintain focus amidst the sensory onslaught.

Ada, sensing Korina's unease, gave her hand a gentle squeeze. "It's a lot to take in," she said, her voice a calming presence in the surrounding din. "Just breathe. We'll figure it out together."

Korina nodded, her heart rate slowing slightly. Ada's words, her touch, were a balm to her frayed nerves. With Ada by her side, she could handle anything. She took another deep breath, forcing herself to focus on the task at hand. *Obsidian* pulsed rhythmically against her leg, a comforting weight amidst the chaos.

Sera, her hand resting on the hilt of her sword, scanned the crowded streets with a predator's focus. The lack of any obvious Imperial presence was unsettling. The city sprawled organically, a haphazard collection of mismatched buildings and winding alleyways that seemed to shift and change with every blink. Every shadow seemed to hold a potential threat, every face a mask of hidden intentions. It was a far cry from the rigid order of Celgrad, and it made her skin crawl.

"This place is a viper's nest," she muttered, her voice tight with tension. "Stay close."

Janna, her axe held loosely in one hand, grunted in agreement. "Too many hiding places," she rumbled, her eyes scanning the rooftops. "Easy to get lost. Easier to get ambushed."

The architecture was unlike anything Korina had ever seen. Buildings twisted and curved like living organisms, their surfaces adorned with glowing runes and pulsating arcane mechanisms. Sails, woven from shimmering, otherworldly materials, billowed in the wind, casting ethereal shadows on the cobbled streets below. It was a city built not on logic or efficiency, but on raw, unbridled imagination. It was beautiful, chaotic, and utterly captivating.

"The energy matrix here is...fascinating," Korina murmured, her fingers dancing across *Obsidian*'s surface as she attempted to analyze the swirling energies that permeated the city. "It's completely different from anything I've encountered before. The thaumaturgical signatures are...organic, almost alive."

Erita, however, was in her element. Her golden eyes, sharp and alert, were alive with a predatory gleam, taking in the chaotic flow of commerce, the subtle interplay of whispers and gestures, the unspoken language of the streets. She moved with a confident, almost feline grace, her body weaving through the dense crowds with an effortless fluidity that both Sera and Korina envied. She was a predator in her natural habitat, already identifying the subtle currents of power, the hidden opportunities that lurked beneath the surface of the city's vibrant chaos.

"This place," she said, a sly grin spreading across her face, "is going to be fun."

She paused, her eyes fixed on a group of heavily armed men huddled in a darkened alleyway, their voices low and conspiratorial. Their hands, calloused and scarred, rested on the hilts of their weapons, their eyes darting nervously from side to side. Erita's grin widened. She recognized the telltale signs of a clandestine meeting, the unmistakable aura of illicit dealings.

"See those men over there?" she said, nodding towards the alleyway. "They're smugglers. Probably running contraband out of the South Docks. And that woman with the shimmering shawl? She's an information broker. The one they call *Whisper*. She knows everything that happens in this city. And that merchant with the ornate cane? He's laundering money for the Crimson Veil. They control the spice trade. Or at least, they used to."

Korina, her eyes wide with a mixture of fascination and apprehension, struggled to keep up with Erita's rapid-fire analysis. "How...how do you know all of this?" she stammered, her voice barely audible above the din of the city.

Erita chuckled, her eyes twinkling with amusement. "Years of practice, darling," she purred, her voice laced with a hint of playful condescension. "It's all about reading the signs. The subtle tells. The way people move, the way they talk, the way they look at you. It's a language all its own. And once you learn to speak it, the city opens up to you like a flower."

She gestured towards a nearby stall piled high with exotic fruits and shimmering crystals. "That fruit vendor over there," she continued, her voice dropping to a conspiratorial whisper, "he also deals in stolen information. And the old woman selling trinkets next to him? She's a fence for stolen artifacts. And the blind beggar on the corner? He's not blind at all. He's one of Thorne's informants."

Sera, her skepticism warring with a grudging admiration, raised an eyebrow. "You're making this up," she said, her voice laced with disbelief.

Erita simply smiled, a knowing glint in her golden eyes. "Am

I?" she challenged, her voice a soft, seductive purr. "Come on, let's find our lodging for tonight. That's more important."

The air hung thick and heavy, a pungent mix of salt, spices, and something faintly metallic that Erita couldn't quite place. It was the smell of opportunity, of secrets whispered in darkened alleyways, of fortunes made and lost in the blink of an eye. It was the smell of Port Veridia, and Erita inhaled it like a fine wine.

"This way," she said, her voice low and confident, cutting through the cacophony of the crowded streets.

She moved with a fluid grace, her body weaving through the throngs of people as if she were a phantom, her footsteps silent on the cobbled stones. Sera, her hand resting on the hilt of her sword, followed close behind, her eyes scanning the rooftops, her senses on high alert. Korina, overwhelmed by the sensory overload, clung to Ada's arm, her violet eyes wide with a mixture of fascination and apprehension. Janna, her massive frame a bulwark against the jostling crowds, brought up the rear, her axe held loosely in one hand, her expression stoic but watchful. Ada, her expression thoughtful, observed the city with a detached curiosity, her mind already dissecting its intricate systems, its hidden patterns.

Erita led them through a labyrinth of winding streets and narrow alleyways, her path seemingly random, yet always purposeful. She knew this city like the back of her hand, its hidden passages, its secret entrances, its blind spots and its vantage points. She knew where to find the best deals, the most reliable information, the safest havens. She knew the language of the streets, the unspoken codes, the subtle gestures that could mean the difference between a warm welcome and a cold blade.

Finally, after what seemed like an eternity to Korina, Erita stopped before a nondescript building tucked away on a quiet side street. Its sign, a faded depiction of a star encircled by a serpent, swung gently in the breeze. “The Wandering Star,” Erita announced, her voice barely audible above the muted sounds of the city. “Our home away from home.”

The inn was small and unassuming, its common room dimly lit and sparsely furnished. A handful of patrons, their faces obscured by shadows, sat huddled in corners, nursing their drinks and keeping to themselves. The air was thick with the smell of stale ale and pipe smoke, a comforting aroma to Erita, a reminder of countless nights spent in similar establishments across the continent.

Erita approached the bar, her steps measured and deliberate. The innkeeper, a wizened old man with a face like a crumpled map, looked up from his ledger, his eyes narrowed in suspicion.

“Five rooms,” Erita said, her voice crisp and clear. “For the night.”

The innkeeper grunted, his eyes scanning the group. “Only three open,” he rasped, his voice raspy from years of cheap ale and pipe smoke. “And they ain’t cheap.”

Erita glanced back at the others. Sera leaned against a nearby table, her arms crossed, her expression unreadable. Korina fidgeted nervously, her fingers tracing the intricate braids in her violet hair. Ada stood beside her, her arm around Korina’s shoulders, her expression calm and reassuring. Janna, her massive frame filling the doorway, watched the exchange with a detached amusement.

An idea sparked in Erita's mind, a mischievous glint in her golden eyes.

"Three will do," she said, turning back to the innkeeper. "We'll manage."

The innkeeper shrugged, his expression betraying no surprise. He named a price, exorbitant even by Port Veridia's standards, but Erita didn't even flinch. She tossed a handful of coins onto the counter, the gold glinting in the dim light. He snatched them up, his eyes widening slightly, then grunted again and handed her three keys.

Erita turned back to the others, a sly smile playing on her lips. "Alright, ladies," she said, her voice laced with a playful sarcasm. "Looks like we're doubling up."

She caught Sera's eye, a silent conversation passing between them. Erita grabbed Sera's arm, her fingers digging into the knight's firm bicep. "You're with me," she purred, her voice low and husky.

Sera's face flushed crimson, a stark contrast to her fiery red hair. "What if there's only one bed?" she whispered, her voice barely audible above the din of the common room.

Erita's smirk widened, a predatory glint in her eyes. The thought of sharing a bed with the stoic, disciplined knight, of feeling the warmth of Sera's body pressed against hers, sent a thrill of excitement coursing through her veins. "Then we'll improvise," she murmured, her voice laced with a promise.

Korina's cheeks burned. Erita's words, "doubling up," echoed in her mind, each syllable a hammer blow against the fragile wall she'd erected around her emotions. Her heart hammered against her ribs, a frantic drumbeat against the silence of her carefully constructed logic. She glanced at Ada, her breath catching in her throat. Ada's violet eyes, usually so sharp and analytical, were softened with a warmth that sent a shiver down Korina's spine. Before she could overthink, her hand shot out, her fingers wrapping around Ada's arm, a desperate plea for reassurance.

"So," Ada said, her voice a gentle murmur, "looks like we're sharing a room, Rina. If you're alright with that, of course."

Korina's voice cracked. "M-more than alright," she managed, the words barely a whisper. She nodded, her gaze fixed on the worn wooden floorboards, unable to meet Ada's eyes. The thought of sharing a room with Ada, of being so close to the woman who had become the anchor of her world, sent a wave of heat through her, a blush creeping up her neck and staining her cheeks a deeper shade of violet. It was a terrifying, exhilarating prospect, a chaotic equation she couldn't solve, a variable she couldn't control. And yet, amidst the swirling vortex of her emotions, a single, undeniable truth emerged: she wouldn't have it any other way.

Janna, her gruff voice a welcome interruption to the silent turmoil of Korina's thoughts, clapped Erita on the shoulder, the force of the blow enough to make the smaller woman stumble. "Suits me fine," she rumbled, a hint of amusement in her voice. "More room for me to stretch out. Wouldn't want to crush either of you whippersnappers in my sleep." She winked at Korina, a surprisingly gentle gesture from the usually stoic warrior. "Enjoy your...*arrangements*." She grabbed a key from Erita's outstretched hand and lumbered towards the stairs, her heavy footsteps echoing through the quiet inn.

Erita, still smirking, handed the remaining keys to Ada, her golden eyes twinkling with amusement. "Don't stay up too late, ladies," she said, her voice laced with a playful innuendo that made Korina's blush deepen. "We've got a busy day ahead of us." She winked at Ada, then turned and followed Janna up the stairs, her movements as fluid and graceful as a cat.

Ada, her hand still resting on Korina's shoulder, squeezed gently. "Come on, Rina," she said, her voice soft and reassuring. "Let's get settled in." She led Korina towards the stairs, her touch a silent promise of safety, of comfort, of a shared space amidst the chaos of their world. As they climbed the creaking wooden steps, Korina's heart pounded in her chest, a chaotic rhythm against the quiet hum of anticipation. The inn room, small and sparsely furnished, suddenly felt like the most important place in the world, a sanctuary, a haven, a space where logic and emotion could finally coexist, a place where she could finally be herself, with Ada.

CHAPTER 18

A QUIET RESPITE

//EXPLICIT CONTENT WARNING*//

**Please be aware this scene involves two female characters involved in explicit consensual intimacy—reader discretion advised.*

The room at The Wandering Star was small and clean, the air thick with a silence that crackled with unspoken tension. Moonlight filtered through the single window, casting long shadows across the worn wooden floorboards. Sera, her crimson tunic discarded on a rickety chair, stood stiffly by the window, her gaze fixed on the chaotic cityscape of Port Veridia spread out below. The city's vibrant, untamed energy, usually a source of exhilaration for her, now felt like an unwelcome intrusion, a reflection of the chaotic emotions swirling within her.

Erita, her usual dark leather armor replaced by a simple linen shift, moved with a practiced efficiency, her movements fluid and silent as she prepared for bed. The forced proximity, the shared space in this small, unfamiliar room, felt strangely intimate, a vulnerability neither woman was accustomed to. Erita's usual sarcastic banter, her sharp wit, seemed to have deserted her, leaving only the quiet rustle of fabric and the soft creak of the bed as she turned down the covers.

"It's just a bed, Swift," Sera said, her voice a low rumble that echoed in the quiet room. She turned from the window, her crimson hair a fiery halo in the moonlight. "No need to be so tense."

Erita's golden eyes flickered towards Sera, a hint of amusement in their depths. "And you, Lady Valerius," she said, her voice a dry whisper, "seem remarkably relaxed for a knight sharing a room with a known rogue."

Sera's lips curved into a wry smile. "Perhaps," she said, moving towards the bed, "I've simply learned to adapt to...*unforeseen circumstances*."

Erita raised an eyebrow, a silent challenge in her gaze. "Indeed," she purred, her voice laced with a playful sarcasm. "Adaptability is a valuable skill in our line of work."

Sera, ever the pragmatist, was meticulously cleaning her blades on the edge of the bed, the rhythmic scrape of the whetstone the only sound in the small room. The sharp, metallic scent of the honing oil filled the air, a familiar comfort amidst the unfamiliar surroundings. She glanced up, her gaze catching Erita as the rogue stretched, a subtle wince flickering across her face.

"You're favoring your left shoulder," Sera observed, her voice low and direct, a statement of fact rather than a question.

Erita, caught off guard by the observation, initially tried to deflect with a sharp, cynical remark. "It's nothing. Just a souvenir from a less-than-graceful landing in the mountains." But Sera's steady, non-judgmental gaze made her falter. The carefully constructed mask of indifference slipped, revealing a flicker of genuine vulnerability.

Sera put down her blade, the whetstone clattering softly against the worn wood of the bedside table. “Sit,” she commanded gently, her voice softening, the command an echo of the countless times she had given similar orders to injured comrades on the battlefield.

After a moment of hesitation, Erita complied, settling onto the edge of the bed, her back stiff and her golden eyes wary. Sera’s touch was surprisingly gentle as she began to work the knots out of Erita’s shoulder, her strong fingers kneading the tense muscles with a practiced efficiency. The act was purely practical, a battlefield necessity honed over years of patching up injured soldiers, but the physical contact in the quiet, intimate space of their shared room was charged with an unspoken tension.

Erita’s breath hitched as Sera’s fingers pressed into a particularly tight knot, a soft gasp escaping her lips. “Void,” she muttered under her breath, her usual cynicism replaced by a raw vulnerability.

Sera’s lips curved into a slight smile, a rare expression of tenderness. “Just breathe, Swift,” she murmured, her voice a low rumble against Erita’s ear. “It’ll be alright.” Her fingers continued their work, slowly easing the tension from Erita’s muscles.

The silence stretched between them, punctuated only by the soft sounds of Sera’s ministrations and Erita’s increasingly even breaths. The city’s chaotic energy seemed to fade, replaced by the quiet intimacy of the moment. Sera, her gaze fixed on the intricate patterns of Erita’s golden hair, felt a strange warmth spread through her, a sense of connection she hadn’t anticipated. It was a feeling that both intrigued and unsettled her, a complication she hadn't factored into her carefully constructed world.

"That bad, huh?" Sera's voice was a low murmur, her fingers still working on the tense muscles in Erita's shoulder.

Erita let out a shaky breath, the carefully constructed mask of cynicism finally crumbling. "It's an old wound," she admitted, her voice barely a whisper. "From...a previous life."

Sera's touch faltered for a moment, a flicker of understanding in her eyes. She knew the weight of old wounds, the ghosts of battles past that lingered in the shadows of the mind. "They never truly heal, do they?" she said softly, her voice laced with a quiet empathy.

Erita shook her head, her golden eyes fixed on the worn floorboards. "No," she whispered, her voice barely audible. "They just...fade. Become a part of who we are."

Sera's fingers resumed their work, the rhythmic pressure a silent comfort. "Mine are mostly visible," she said, her voice a low rumble, a hint of self-deprecating humor in her tone. "Easier to deal with, in a way. A constant reminder of what I've survived."

Erita's gaze flickered upwards, meeting Sera's for a fleeting moment. "And the ones that aren't?" she asked, her voice a quiet challenge.

Sera's lips curved into a wry smile. "Those," she said, her voice a low rumble, "are the ones that keep me awake at night."

A long silence stretched between them, the quiet intimacy of the moment punctuated only by the soft sounds of Sera's ministrations. The city outside seemed to fade, its chaotic energy replaced by the quiet hum of shared vulnerability.

"I never thought I'd see you like this," Sera said, breaking the silence, her voice a low murmur. "So...unguarded."

Erita's golden eyes narrowed, a flicker of her usual cynicism returning. "And you," she retorted, her voice a dry whisper, "so... gentle. It doesn't suit you, Lady Valerius."

Sera's lips curved into a genuine smile, the expression softening her usually sharp features. "Perhaps," she said, her voice a low rumble, "there's more to me than meets the eye, Swift."

Erita's gaze softened, a hint of grudging respect in her eyes. "Perhaps," she echoed, her voice losing its usual sarcastic edge.

Sera finished her work, her fingers lingering on Erita's shoulder for a moment before she pulled away. "Try to get some rest," she said softly, turning towards her side of the bed.

Erita nodded, a silent acknowledgment of the shared vulnerability that had settled between them. They lay down, the space between them now filled with a fragile, unspoken accord. The silence was no longer tense, but comfortable, a shared sanctuary amidst the chaos of their world. They drifted off to sleep, the city's vibrant, chaotic energy now a distant lullaby.

In the adjacent room, the air crackled with a different kind of energy. Not the raw, chaotic pulse of the city, but the focused hum of intellectual excitement. Korina, perched on the edge of the bed, practically vibrated with it. *Obsidian*, clutched in her hands, projected a shimmering, three-dimensional map of Rhedeon, its intricate network of arcane energy signatures pulsing like a living organism. "Look, Ada! *Look!*" she exclaimed, her voice a breathless rush of excitement. "The thaumaturgical conduits *here*...they're not just channeling energy, they're *modulating* it. See how the frequencies shift along the ley lines? It's like...like a symphony of arcane harmonics!"

Ada, seated beside her, leaned closer, her purple eyes fixed on the swirling patterns of light. She saw not just the complex data, but the sheer joy in Korina's face—the way her eyes lit up with intellectual passion. It was a sight that never failed to fill Ada with a deep, almost overwhelming affection. She reached out, her fingers gently tracing the lines of exhaustion etched beneath Korina's eyes. "It's beautiful, Rina," she murmured, her voice soft with affection. "Truly remarkable."

Korina beamed, her cheeks flushing with pleasure at Ada's praise. "Isn't it? It's completely unlike anything I've ever seen! The Intellective States...we focus on precision, on isolating and controlling individual thauma queries. But here...it's all about flow, about harmonizing with the natural energy currents. It's...chaotic, yes, but there's an underlying order of logic to it—a beautiful, organic logic that cascades from cause to effect!" She gestured towards the map, her words tumbling out in a rush of excitement. "I have a theory...see how the energy converges at these nodal points? I think they're not just conduits, they're...amplifiers. They're taking the raw arcane energy and...and *rendering* it into something more potent, more...alive."

Ada listened patiently, her gaze fixed on Korina's animated face. She admired Korina's passion, her insatiable thirst for knowledge. It was a quality Ada herself had once possessed, a drive that had consumed her for years as she poured every ounce of her energy into creating Kremøtoa. But now, watching Korina, Ada saw something more than just intellectual curiosity. She saw the faint tremor in Korina's hands, the dark circles beneath her eyes, the subtle slump of her shoulders. She saw the exhaustion that Korina —in her excitement, was trying to ignore. Ada's heart ached with a fierce protectiveness.

"Rina," she said softly, her voice laced with concern, "when was the last time you slept?"

Korina blinked, her train of thought momentarily derailed. She looked down at her hands, as if seeing them for the first time. "I...I don't remember," she admitted, her voice a little sheepish. "There's just so much to learn, so much to understand! This city... it's like a treasure trove of arcane data! I could spend weeks here, just...absorbing it all."

Korina started to protest, then stopped, a yawn escaping her lips. She swayed slightly, her eyes fluttering closed.

Ada gently took the data-slate from Korina's hands and set it aside. "The data will still be there in the morning," she said softly, her voice a soothing balm. "You need to rest, Rina."

Korina, pulled from her intellectual fervor, suddenly felt the full weight of her exhaustion. It settled upon her like a physical burden, heavy and inescapable. Her eyelids felt like lead weights, her limbs like jelly. She leaned against Ada, a soft sigh escaping her lips. "Just...for a little while," she murmured, her voice barely a whisper.

Ada wrapped her arms around Korina, drawing her close. Korina's head nestled against Ada's chest, her soft violet hair tickling Ada's cheek. Ada felt a surge of tenderness, a warmth that spread through her like a comforting flame. She held Korina tighter, her fingers gently stroking Korina's back. "Sleep, Rina," she whispered, her voice a lullaby. "I'll be here when you wake up."

Korina's breathing deepened, her body relaxing against Ada's. The tension drained from her muscles, replaced by a peaceful stillness. Ada held her close, enjoying the warmth of Korina's body against hers, the soft rhythm of her breath. The scent of Korina's body—a familiar mix of old parchment, ozone, and something uniquely, undeniably *her*—filled Ada's senses, calming and arousing at once.

Ada shifted slightly, adjusting her position so that Korina was lying more comfortably in her arms. She felt Korina's hair against her neck and the curve of her body pressed against her own. Ada's body began to stir, responding to Korina's closeness. The exhaustion that had been tugging at Ada since their arrival in Port Veridia faded, replaced by a different kind of weariness—a pleasant, languid ache that resonated deep within her.

Ada leaned down, her lips brushing against Korina's forehead. Korina stirred in her sleep, a soft sigh escaping her lips. Ada kissed her again, this time on her cheek, then on the corner of her mouth. Korina's lips parted slightly, and Ada felt a jolt of electricity shoot through her. She hesitated for a moment, then gently kissed Korina full on the mouth. Korina's lips were soft and warm, and Ada felt a wave of desire wash over her. She deepened the kiss, her tongue exploring the sweet depths of Korina's mouth.

Korina's arms wrapped around Ada's neck, pulling her closer. Ada felt Korina's body press against hers, the warmth of her skin seeping into Ada's own. She moaned softly, her fingers tangling in Korina's hair. The kiss became more urgent, more passionate. Ada's body throbbed with a need that transcended the boundaries of code and data, a primal hunger that demanded to be satisfied.

They kissed for a long time, their bodies entwined, their breaths mingling. The world outside the inn room faded away, replaced by the shared intimacy of their embrace. The chaotic energy of Port Veridia seemed to recede, leaving only the quiet hum of their shared desire. For Ada, it was more than just physical pleasure. It was a connection, a validation of her own existence within this world she had created. It was a reminder that she was not just an Architect, a God-Queen, but a woman—a woman capable of feeling, of loving, of being loved in return.

Ada pulled back slightly, her breath coming in short, ragged gasps. She looked down at Korina, her purple eyes filled with a mixture of desire and tenderness. Korina's eyes fluttered open, her violet gaze meeting Ada's. A soft smile played on her lips, a blush coloring her cheeks.

"Ada..." she murmured, her voice thick with sleep and arousal. "What...what are you doing?"

"Loving you," Ada whispered, her voice hoarse with emotion. She leaned down and kissed Korina again, this time more gently, more tenderly. "I love you, Rina."

Korina's eyes widened slightly, her breath catching in her throat. She reached up and cupped Ada's face in her hands, her fingers tracing the sharp angles of Ada's cheekbones. "I...I love you too, Ada," she whispered, her voice barely audible.

Ada smiled, a genuine, heartfelt smile that reached her eyes. She leaned down and kissed Korina again, their lips meeting in a slow, sensual dance. Ada's hands moved down Korina's body, exploring the curves and hollows with a gentle, inquisitive touch. She felt the warmth of Korina's skin beneath her fingertips, the soft rise and fall of her chest as she breathed. Her Admin mind, usually buzzing with calculations and code, quieted, focusing solely on the sensory data flooding her system. The texture of Korina's skin, the scent of her hair, the taste of her lips—it was all new, all fascinating, all overwhelmingly *real*.

Korina's hands moved up Ada's back, her fingers digging into the muscles. She moaned softly, her body arching against Ada's. The touch of Ada's hands on her skin sent shivers of pleasure through her, a sensation so intense it threatened to overwhelm her analytical mind. She closed her eyes, surrendering to the feeling, letting it wash over her like a tidal wave. For once, she didn't want to analyze, to categorize, to understand. She just wanted to *feel.*

Ada's lips moved down Korina's neck, trailing kisses along the delicate skin. She felt Korina's pulse quicken beneath her lips, her breath coming in short, sharp gasps. Ada's hands moved lower, cupping Korina's breasts, her thumbs gently teasing the nipples. Korina moaned louder, her body writhing beneath Ada's touch.

Ada's fingers moved between Korina's legs, finding the slick heat between her folds. She gently probed, her touch sending another wave of pleasure through Korina's body. Korina cried out, her hands gripping Ada's shoulders.

Ada continued to touch Korina, her fingers moving in a slow, rhythmic motion. She felt Korina's body tense, then relax, then tense again. She felt the muscles in Korina's thighs clench, her hips buck against Ada's hand. She watched as Korina's face contorted in pleasure, her breath coming in ragged gasps.

"Ada..." Korina whispered, her voice choked with emotion. "I...I can't..."

Ada smiled, a predatory glint in her eyes. "Yes, you can," she whispered back, her voice husky with desire. "Let go, Rina. Let me take you there."

Korina's body shuddered, then convulsed, as a wave of intense pleasure ripped through her. She cried out Ada's name, her voice a mixture of pain and ecstasy. Ada continued to touch her, her fingers moving faster, harder, until Korina's body went limp, spent.

Ada collapsed beside Korina, her own body trembling with the aftershocks of Korina's climax. She wrapped her arms around Korina, pulling her close. Korina's head rested on Ada's chest, her breathing slow and even. Ada stroked her hair, her fingers gently tracing the delicate curve of her ear.

"I love you, Rina," she whispered again, her voice filled with a profound tenderness.

Korina snuggled closer, her body molding against Ada's. "I love you too, Ada," she murmured, her voice thick with sleep.

Ada held Korina close, the warmth of her body a comforting anchor in the chaotic world of Kremøtoa. She felt a sense of peace she hadn't experienced since arriving in this world—a quiet contentment that transcended the anxieties of her mission. For the first time, she felt truly *present*, not as a detached observer, but as a participant in the story unfolding around her.

A soft knock on the connecting door startled Ada. "Everything alright in there?" Erita's voice, muffled by the thick wood, held a note of amusement.

Ada glanced down at Korina, who was still asleep in her arms. She gently disentangled herself and went to the door, opening it a crack. Erita stood in the hallway, a knowing smirk playing on her lips. Sera stood behind her, her cheeks flushed, her green eyes sparkling with a newfound warmth.

"Just checking on our Architect-Queen," Erita said, her voice laced with playful sarcasm. "Wouldn't want her to overwork herself."

Ada couldn't help but smile. "We're fine," she said softly. "Just...resting."

Erita's smirk widened. "Rest well, then," she said, her gaze lingering on Ada for a moment before she turned and walked back to her own room, Sera's arm draped possessively around her waist.

Ada closed the door, a warmth spreading through her. She returned to the bed, crawling in beside Korina and pulling her close. Korina stirred in her sleep, snuggling closer to Ada, her soft breath warm against Ada's neck.

Ada held her tight, a sense of gratitude filling her. She had found something precious in this world she had created, something more valuable than any code or data. She had found love, and family, and a sense of belonging she had never known before. As the first rays of dawn crept through the window, painting the room in soft hues of gold and violet, Ada closed her eyes, a peaceful smile playing on her lips. The challenges ahead were daunting, but for the first time, she felt truly ready to face them. She was not alone. She had her companions, her lovers, her family. And together, they would change the world.

CHAPTER 19

THE RENDER-WITCH OF RHEDEON

The morning light, filtered through the grimy window of The Wandering Star, cast long shadows across the room. The air, thick with the lingering scent of sex and sweat, held a comfortable warmth. Sera hummed a tuneless melody as she expertly sliced a loaf of crusty bread, the rhythmic thud of the knife against the wooden cutting board a counterpoint to the quiet snores emanating from the adjacent room. Erita, propped up against the headboard of the bed, watched her with a lazy smile, her golden eyes tracing the lines of Sera's bare back as she moved about the small room.

"You'd think a warrior like yourself would be a heavier sleeper," Erita said, her voice rough with sleep.

Sera glanced over her shoulder, a playful smirk tugging at the corner of her lips. "Years of sleeping in less-than-ideal conditions tends to do that to you," she replied. "Besides, someone has to keep an eye on you lot. Wouldn't want you getting into too much trouble while I'm sleeping."

A soft click echoed from the connecting door as Ada and Korina emerged, their hair tousled, their clothes rumpled. The air between them crackled with a palpable intimacy, a silent testament to the night they'd shared. Ada's violet eyes, usually sharp and calculating, held a softer light, a newfound warmth that radiated outwards. The weight of her responsibilities, the burden of an entire world resting on her shoulders, seemed lighter now, balanced by the strength of the bonds she'd forged with these extraordinary women. Korina, still half-asleep, clung to Ada's arm, her head resting against Ada's shoulder, her violet braids spilling across Ada's chest. A faint, contented sigh escaped her lips as she nuzzled closer, seeking the familiar comfort of Ada's warmth.

Sera, her cheeks flushed a delicate shade of pink, gestured towards them with a half-eaten slice of bread. "Someone had a good night," she teased, her voice laced with a playful lilt.

Korina, still not fully awake, simply tightened her grip on Ada's arm, burying her face deeper into Ada's side. A low rumble of amusement vibrated in Ada's chest as she gently stroked Korina's hair.

"She's still half asleep," Ada explained, a fond smile playing on her lips. "Leave her be."

Erita, a knowing smirk playing on her lips, leaned forward, her golden eyes gleaming with amusement. "I'd say she's more than half asleep," she quipped, her gaze flickering between Ada and the slumbering Korina. "I'd say she's completely and utterly smitten."

Ada, her cheeks now mirroring Sera's blush, simply shrugged, a silent acknowledgment of Erita's observation.

"Fun's over, sadly," Erita said, her voice cutting through the quiet intimacy like a shard of ice. She tapped a button on her data-slate, the screen flickering to life with a cascade of data streams and holographic projections. "While you were all...*connecting*," she continued, a sly smirk playing on her lips, "I was digging. And I've found something interesting. It's briefing time."

Korina, startled awake, blinked owlishly, her violet eyes widening as she took in the sudden shift in atmosphere. Sera, ever the pragmatist, simply shrugged and reached for another slice of bread. Ada, however, felt a familiar jolt of adrenaline, the thrill of the hunt reawakening within her. She squeezed Korina's hand reassuringly, a silent promise that they would face this new challenge together.

The flickering holographic map of Port Veridia shimmered in the center of the room, its intricate details – the sprawling docks, the labyrinthine streets, the towering shipyards – painted in ethereal light against the backdrop of the grimy inn walls. Erita, her golden eyes fixed on the projection, paced back and forth, her mental voice a sharp, clear broadcast over their telepathic link. *The city is governed by a council of elders,* she explained, her thoughts precise and clipped, devoid of her usual sarcasm. *But the real power here isn't political. It's commerce. Naval commerce. Three shipwright guilds dominate all naval construction in Port Veridia: the Kraken's Maw, known for their heavily armored cruisers; the Serpent's Veil, masters of swift, stealthy vessels; and the Sunstone Forge, famed for their arcane-powered dreadnoughts.*

Janna grunted, her mental image a gruff nod of approval. *Kraken's Maw,* she thought, her mental voice a low rumble of approval. *Solid, dependable. Like a good battle-axe. No fancy tricks, just pure, unadulterated hitting power.*

Sera's mental image was a flicker of a crimson blade, a silent counterpoint to Janna's brute-force preference. *Serpent's Veil,* she countered, her thoughts sharp and tactical. *Their stealth ships would be invaluable for disrupting Thorne's supply lines. Hit and run. In and out. Leave no trace.*

Korina, her violet eyes tracing the intricate details of the holographic map, remained silent, her mind a whirlwind of calculations and strategic possibilities. Ada, her gaze fixed on Erita, sensed a shift in the spymaster's demeanor, a subtle tightening of her mental presence that spoke of unease.

Erita stopped pacing, her golden eyes narrowing as she focused on a specific point on the holographic map – a cluster of towering shipyards that pulsed with arcane energy. Her mental 'voice' became grave, a low hum of apprehension that vibrated through their telepathic link. *That's the problem,* she thought, her mental tone laced with a newfound seriousness. *It doesn't matter which guild we approach. Kraken's Maw, Serpent's Veil, Sunstone Forge—it's all the same. There's a persistent, unsettling rumor that runs through the very heart of these shipyards. A whisper in the shadows. No major warship, no matter the guild, no matter the price, can be launched without the explicit, unseen approval of a single, enigmatic figure. A figure known only as the Render-Witch, Nividia Rhenderon.*

Ada processed Erita's revelation with the detached, analytical focus of a programmer debugging a particularly complex piece of code. Nividia Rhenderon. The Render-Witch. An unexpected variable, a gatekeeper whose existence threatened to derail their entire operation. The room's silence reflected the weight of this new obstacle.

Void's name, Janna's mental growl vibrated with frustration. *More superstitious nonsense. Can't we just offer them enough gold? Enough to choke a kraken? We have a king's ransom sitting on Silas's ship. Let's just buy the blasted ships and be done with it.*

But what are renderings? Korina's mental voice was a rapid-fire burst of intellectual curiosity, her thoughts buzzing with excitement despite the grim situation. *Is it a specific type of thaumaturgical enchantment? A form of axiomatic manipulation? Does it involve altering the fundamental properties of matter? The implications are staggering!*

Think of them as...arcane tattoos, Erita explained, her mental voice laced with a hint of reluctant admiration. *Powerful, unique enchantments woven into the very fabric of the ship's hull. They can grant a vessel impossible speed, make it phase through enemy attacks, even render its cannons capable of firing bolts of pure, solidified mana. It's not just about making a ship faster or stronger. It's about bending the very laws of physics to Nividia's whim. And she's the only one who knows how to do it. The guilds are just glorified carpenters in comparison.*

Sera's mental image was a sharp intake of breath, a silent acknowledgement of the tactical implications. *So, if this Render-Witch refuses to cooperate...,* she thought, her mental tone grim, *then we're stuck. Dead in the water. All that gold from the Argent Lion... useless. We can't build an army if we can't even get the ships built in the first place.*

Ada nodded slowly, her purple eyes fixed on the holographic map, her mind already racing ahead, strategizing. This wasn't a problem that could be solved with brute force, or even with the vast wealth they had acquired. This was a political and magical challenge. A riddle wrapped in an enigma, guarded by a witch. They couldn't proceed with their plans, couldn't even take the first step towards building their revolutionary army, until they understood what motivated this Nividia Rhenderon. What she wanted. What she needed. What, if anything, could sway her to their cause.

A slow, almost predatory smile spread across Ada's face, a subtle shift in her expression that made Korina's breath catch in her throat. The thrill of the challenge, the intricate puzzle of Nividia's motivations, sparked a familiar excitement within Ada, a feeling she hadn't experienced since those long nights hunched over her keyboard, building the very world they now inhabited. This wasn't just about acquiring ships; this was about understanding the complex, emergent properties of her creation, about unraveling the mysteries of a mind she hadn't directly programmed, yet was undeniably a product of her code.

"We need to shift our focus," Ada announced, her voice calm and clear, the quiet authority of a queen addressing her court. Her purple eyes, bright with a focused intensity, swept across the faces of her companions, gauging their reactions. "The guilds are irrelevant. They're just tools, waiting to be wielded. The true power in Rhedeon, the key to our entire operation, lies with this Render-Witch."

Ada tapped a finger on the holographic map, highlighting the shimmering, chaotic sprawl of Port Veridia. "Our mission," she continued, her voice hardening with resolve, "is no longer about acquiring ships. It's about acquiring Nividia Rhenderon. We need to find her. Understand her. And convince her to join our cause." The weight of their new objective settled in the room, a silent acknowledgment of the dangerous, unpredictable game they were about to play.

CHAPTER 20

PREPARATIONS FOR THE GALA

The Wandering Star, true to its name, felt less like an inn and more like a collection of repurposed ship cabins precariously stacked atop one another, swaying gently with the rhythmic pulse of the Rhedeon tides. In their cramped room, Korina traced the intricate patterns of glowing arcane energy that pulsed through the city's holographic map projected from Obsidian. The sheer density of it, the chaotic yet somehow harmonious flow, fascinated her. It was like staring into the exposed circuitry of a living, breathing machine.

Ada, still flushed from their earlier intimacy, sat on the edge of the bed, watching Korina with a soft smile. She reached out, gently tracing the lines of Korina's exposed collarbone with a fingertip, enjoying the subtle shiver that ran through her lover's body.

Sera paced restlessly in their room, the confines too small to contain her usual energy. She ran a hand through her crimson hair, her gaze fixed on the chipped paint of the far wall, her mind replaying the events of the past few weeks. The betrayal of the

Aegis Order, the escape from Celgrad, the impossible journey across Kremøtoa. It was a whirlwind of chaos and change, a far cry from the rigid, predictable life she had once known.

Erita's sudden mental intrusion startled them all, as she opened the door to the cramped room. *It's as we feared,* her voice echoed in their minds, grim but resolute. *Nividia is a ghost. No one knows how to contact her directly. She operates through layers of intermediaries, guilds, merchants, spies. Trying to force a meeting is suicide. We'd be swallowed whole by Veridia's underbelly before we even got close.*

A wave of frustration washed over them. Another dead end. Another layer of complexity added to an already impossible task. Janna's mental grumble was a low, guttural sound of annoyance. *So, what now? We sail back to Dominus with our tails between our legs? Admit defeat before we've even begun?*

Not quite, Erita's mental voice was a sharp, almost predatory whisper. *I've uncovered something. A single, high-stakes opportunity. It cost us a hefty chunk of the Argent Lion's gold to get this information, but it might be our only chance.*

Ada's curiosity piqued. *Go on,* she urged, her mental voice calm and focused.

Nividia has one known indulgence, Erita continued. *A profound, almost obsessive, fascination with rare magical artifacts. Anything unique, anything powerful, anything that pushes the boundaries of thaumaturgy. She collects them like a dragon hoards gold. And it's rumored...she sometimes attends Port Veridia's most exclusive, high-stakes auction: The Midnight Gala.*

A sudden surge of excitement coursed through Ada. *The Midnight Gala*. It was a name whispered in hushed tones throughout Port Veridia, a legendary gathering of the city's wealthiest and most powerful figures. An event shrouded in secrecy and exclusivity, where fortunes were made and broken on the whims of eccentric collectors. It was the perfect stage for their plan.

Erita produced four ornate, heavy invitations. Each was embossed with the shimmering sigil of a serpent devouring its tail—the mark of the auction house, *The Ouroboros*. The invitations themselves pulsed with a faint arcane energy, a subtle display of wealth and power.

These, Erita's voice was low, almost reverent, *cost us a small fortune. But they're our only way in. The Midnight Gala is invitation-only. And even then, admittance is at the discretion of the auctioneer.*

Korina ran a hand over the shimmering serpent, her fingers tracing the intricate details of its scales. *Fascinating,* she murmured. *The energy signature is complex, multi-layered. It's not just a security measure, it's a statement. A declaration of power, exclusivity... and a subtle challenge to anyone foolish enough to try and forge it.*

Sera snorted, a wry grin playing on her lips. *So, we crash a party full of Veridia's elite, flaunt our newfound wealth, and hope the Render-Witch takes notice? Sounds like a plan.*

Ada took one of the invitations, her fingers lingering on the cool, smooth surface. Their path was now clear. They could not buy a fleet directly, not from a nation as independent and magically advanced as Rhedeon. But they might, just might, be able to buy the Render-Witch's attention. And that, Ada realized, was a far more valuable prize. The Midnight Gala. It was a gamble, a high-stakes game of social manipulation and arcane one-upmanship. But it was their only play.

The invitations were a start, but Ada knew they couldn't simply walk into the Midnight Gala dressed as weary revolutionaries.

They needed to project an image of wealth, power, and influence. They needed to blend in, to become invisible amongst Veridia's elite. "We can't go in looking like this," Ada announced, her gaze sweeping over their travel-worn clothes. "It's time to trade tactical gear for something more...gala-appropriate."

A flicker of amusement danced in Sera's eyes. "So, you're saying it's time to play dress-up, Architect-Queen?"

"Precisely," Ada replied, a sly grin spreading across her face. "And I have just the thing." Closing her eyes, Ada focused her intent, visualizing the outfits she had in mind. It was time to tap into the most extravagant, most theatrical part of her creative code.

[CREATE: Gala_Attire_Sera: Parameters = Elegant_Warrior, Color_Palette = Crimson_and_Gold]

A soft, violet light emanated from Ada, swirling around them like a gentle nebula. The air crackled with arcane energy, and the faint scent of ozone filled the room. When the light subsided, three stunning outfits materialized, each tailored perfectly to the wearer's personality and style.

[CREATE: Gala_Attire_Korina: Parameters = Scholarly_Chic, Color_Palette = Violet_and_Silver]

[CREATE: Gala_Attire_Erita: Parameters = Rogue_Elegance, Color_Palette = Shadow_and_Gold]

"What in the Void is this?" Erita scowled, tugging at the shimmering, form-fitting gown of black and gold silk that had materialized around her. “I can barely breathe, let alone make a rapid egress. And where, pray tell, am I supposed to conceal my blades?”

“Patience, Eri,” Ada chuckled, her eyes twinkling with amusement. “I factored in your...unique requirements.” As if on cue, several hidden pockets shimmered into existence along the gown’s seams, perfectly sized for Erita’s daggers and throwing knives. “All the elegance of a courtesan,” Ada teased, “with all the lethality of a viper.” Erita rolled her eyes, but a small smile played on her lips. The gown, despite her initial protests, moved with her body like a second skin, accentuating her lithe form.

For Sera, Ada crafted a sleek, crimson-red tunic of a shimmering, almost liquid-like material that flowed and rippled with every movement. Tailored black trousers completed the ensemble, emphasizing her powerful legs and the confident swagger of her stride. “I feel like a blasted beacon,” Sera muttered, tugging self-consciously at the tunic. She was unaccustomed to such finery, used to the practical, if restrictive, armor of the Aegis Order. “Are you sure about this, Ada? It’s a bit...much.”

“You look stunning, Sera,” Ada said, her voice soft and sincere. “The strength and the color...it suits you.” A faint blush crept up Sera’s neck and stained her cheeks a delicate rose. She ducked her head, a small, almost shy smile playing on her lips. The crimson tunic, Ada realized, mirrored the fiery passion that burned beneath Sera’s stoic exterior.

Korina’s gown was a masterpiece of flowing violet fabric, shimmering with interwoven threads of silver that seemed to capture and refract the light. The scholar’s eyes widened, not with apprehension or self-consciousness, but with pure, unadulterated intellectual curiosity. “Fascinating,” she murmured, her fingers tracing the intricate patterns woven into the fabric. "The molecular bonding...the stable energy signatures...Ada, how did you achieve this? Is it a form of localized axiomatic rendering? Did you alter the very fabric of reality to create this?"

Ada laughed, shaking her head. "It's just a dress, Rina. Though I admit," she added with a wink, "the physics involved are rather elegant." Korina, oblivious to Ada's teasing, continued to examine the gown's construction, her mind already racing with possibilities. For Korina, the Gala was not a social event, but a scientific marvel waiting to be decoded. And Ada, watching her, felt a surge of affection for the brilliant, quirky scholar who saw the world not as it was, but as it could be.

"And what of our Commander?" Janna rumbled, her voice a low growl that echoed through the room. "What finery will she be sporting at this...Midnight Gala?"

Ada smiled, a playful glint in her eyes. "Ah, Janna," she said, her voice laced with amusement. "I've saved the best for last." Taking a deep breath, Ada closed her eyes and focused her intent. This outfit would be different, not just an elegant disguise, but a declaration. It would be a manifestation of her true self, a symbol of her power and purpose in this world.

[CREATE: Gala_Attire_Ada: Parameters = God-Queen_Regalia, Color_Palette = Obsidian_and_Violet, Accents = Luminescent_Threads]

The air around Ada shimmered and crackled, the violet light intensifying until it filled the room with an ethereal glow. The other women shielded their eyes, momentarily blinded by the intensity. When the light subsided, Ada stood before them, transformed.

She wore a gown of the deepest black, a color so rich it seemed to absorb all light. The fabric, however, was unlike anything they had ever seen. It wasn't silk, nor satin, nor any material known to Kremøtoa. It seemed to be woven from the very essence of shadow, flowing and rippling like liquid night. Interwoven within the fabric were threads of pure, pulsating violet light, tracing intricate patterns that shifted and danced like miniature constellations. The gown's design was both regal and severe, its elegant lines accentuating Ada's slender form while projecting an aura of undeniable power. It was a statement, a declaration of her unique identity, not just as Ada Lynx, the programmer, but as the God-Queen of a new order.

Janna's jaw dropped, her gruff exterior momentarily forgotten. "Argent's light," she breathed, her voice filled with awe. "You look like...like a goddess."

A faint blush colored Ada's cheeks. "It's just a dress, Janna," she murmured, though secretly, she was pleased with the effect. The gown felt...right. It was a reflection of the power she wielded, the responsibility she carried, and the love she felt for the women who stood beside her.

Sera's gaze lingered on Ada, her eyes tracing the lines of the gown, the play of light and shadow. "It's...breathtaking," she whispered, her voice barely audible. She reached out, her fingers brushing against the luminescent threads. The violet light pulsed beneath her touch, as if responding to her presence.

Korina, ever the scholar, examined the gown with a mixture of awe and scientific curiosity. "The energy matrix...it's self-sustaining. And the luminescent threads...are they a form of solidified mana? Ada, this is incredible! The thaumaturgical implications are..."

"Staggering, I know," Ada interrupted, a playful smile curving her lips. "But we can discuss the technical details later. Right now, we have a gala to crash."

Erita, ever the pragmatist, was the first to break the spell. "Alright, ladies," she said, her voice crisp and efficient. "We've got a Render-Witch to woo. Let's move."

With a shared glance of determination, the four women—Ada, Sera, Korina, and Erita—left the inn and stepped out into the vibrant chaos of Port Veridia. They were no longer weary travelers, nor hunted fugitives. They were a royal retinue, a force to be reckoned with, ready to infiltrate the heart of Rhedeon's elite. Their mission was clear: blend in, observe, identify Nividia, and make a statement so profound that the Render-Witch could not possibly ignore them.

CHAPTER 21

THE MIDNIGHT GALA

The Ouroboros was a spectacle of arcane extravagance. Platforms of polished obsidian, etched with glowing runes, floated effortlessly above Port Veridia's shimmering harbor. Bridges of pure light arced between them, pulsing with a gentle, rhythmic energy. The air hummed with exotic perfumes, the strange, ethereal melodies of unseen instruments, and the electric tang of raw thaumaturgy. Guests, a dazzling array of powerful merchants in shimmering silks, enigmatic scholars in flowing robes, and cloaked figures radiating an almost palpable aura of arcane power, glided across the polished floors, their conversations a hushed murmur of secrets and deals.

Ada, feeling the familiar weight of their mission settle upon her shoulders, activated the telepathic link, her voice a calm, focused whisper in the minds of her companions. *Stay focused. Find Nividia. Gather all you can.*

Erita, with a predatory grace, vanished into the throng. One moment she was beside them, the next, a ghost in the machine, absorbed by the swirling currents of the crowd. Her mind, a razor-sharp instrument honed by years of clandestine operations, began its silent work, sifting through conversations, cataloging faces, searching for the subtle shifts in tone and body language that betrayed hidden agendas.

Korina, her violet eyes wide with an almost childlike wonder, gravitated toward a display of arcane artifacts. A low-level hum of excitement, a rapid-fire cascade of technical jargon and thaumaturgical analysis, filled Ada's mind as Korina examined a pulsating crystal orb. *Fascinating...the energy matrix is self-regulating...the implications are staggering...*

Sera, a silent crimson shadow, remained at Ada's side. Her hand rested lightly on the hilt of one of her blades, her senses alert, scanning the crowd for potential threats. She moved with a fluid grace that belied her strength, her presence a subtle but unmistakable declaration of protectiveness.

Ada, outwardly calm but inwardly buzzing with the data streaming from Erita and Korina, allowed herself to be swept along by the flow of the crowd. She observed the guests, their interactions, the subtle power dynamics at play. She saw the veiled arrogance of the merchants, the calculating gazes of the scholars, the quiet confidence of the arcanists. It was a complex system, a living algorithm of ambition and intrigue.

A ripple of silence, a sudden stillness in the chaotic symphony of the gala, alerted Ada to a shift in the room's energy. All heads turned, drawn as if by an invisible force, toward the grand entrance. There, framed in the archway, stood Nividia. She materialized as if from the very air itself, a study in supreme power and absolute indifference.

Nividia's silver hair cascaded around her like liquid moonlight, her violet eyes, twin flames of arcane energy, scanned the room with a detached amusement. The delicate teal marking on her forehead pulsed with a soft, rhythmic glow, and the intricate patterns on her emerald gown shimmered and shifted like captured starlight. Behind her head, a complex halo of teal arcane energy danced, a crown of pure thauma that solidified her presence as something truly otherworldly. A collective gasp, a hushed murmur of awe and apprehension, rippled through the crowd. Even the most powerful merchants and arcanists seemed to shrink in her presence, their own displays of wealth and power paling in comparison to the raw, untamed energy that radiated from the Render-Witch.

There, Erita's voice echoed in Ada's mind, a sharp, focused whisper. *Our target has arrived.*

Korina, momentarily distracted from her analysis of a rather intriguing axiomatic resonator, turned at the sudden hush that fell over the gala. Her breath hitched. Standing at the entrance, as if woven from the very fabric of the night itself, was Nividia Rhenderon. The Render-Witch.

Korina's analytical mind, usually a whirlwind of data and calculations, stuttered to a halt. Nividia's gown was not the teal and emerald green Erita described. It was a cascade of darkest obsidian, a swirling vortex of shadows that seemed to re-render its own intricate arcane patterns in real-time. The fabric flowed and shifted around her with a life of its own, as though defying the very laws of physics Korina dedicated her life to understanding. She was flanked by two constructs of pure, shifting geometric light—one a vibrant emerald, the other a deep, pulsating sapphire. They moved with an unnatural grace, their forms constantly reconfiguring, facets of light reflecting off the polished obsidian surfaces of the Ouroboros.

Nividia's presence was not merely impressive; it was overwhelming. A wave of raw thaumaturgical energy, unlike anything Korina had ever encountered, washed over the gala, silencing the crowd, stilling the music, extinguishing the frivolous chatter. It was a power that spoke not of careful study or disciplined practice, but of something far more primal, far more dangerous. A power that whispered of the very fabric of reality being reshaped at a whim.

Korina felt a thrill course through her, a mix of intellectual fascination and a primal, instinctive fear. *This is it,* she thought, her mind racing. *This is the key.*

If they could somehow convince this woman, this force of nature, to join their cause, the possibilities were limitless. Fleets of warships, rendered into existence with a flick of her wrist, could break the Empire's iron grip on the sea lanes. Fortresses, woven from the very essence of light and shadow, could withstand any siege. The very balance of power on Kremøtoa could shift in their favor.

Nividia's violet eyes, luminous and sharp, swept across the room, acknowledging no one. The crowd, a collection of Port Veridia's wealthiest and most influential figures, parted for her like water around a ship's prow. She moved with an almost ethereal grace, her obsidian gown swirling around her, as she glided not towards the main stage where the auction was about to begin, but towards the displays of arcane artifacts lining the walls of the Ouroboros. Her interest, Ada noted with a flicker of amusement, was purely academic, not social. She paused before a shimmering, multi-faceted crystal, her slender fingers tracing the complex geometric patterns etched into its surface. A low hum of energy emanated from her as she ran a diagnostic, her expression one of detached, intellectual curiosity.

Ada felt a chill of recognition. This was not the posturing of a petty tyrant like Kraus, clinging to power through fear and manipulation. This was a true power player, a being who operated on an entirely different level. Nividia's power was not derived from titles or armies, but from something far more fundamental, far more intrinsic. She was the architect of her own reality, and the world, Ada sensed, bent to her will.

The main auction began. A series of increasingly powerful artifacts paraded across the stage: a shimmering blade that whispered promises of impossible sharpness, a pulsating orb that radiated waves of raw thaumaturgical energy, a set of intricately carved runes that promised to unlock the secrets of forgotten languages. Nividia remained impassive, her attention still fixed on the arcane displays, occasionally issuing a low hum of approval or a dismissive flick of her wrist. The crowd, sensing her indifference, followed her gaze, their own excitement tempered by the Render-Witch's apparent lack of interest.

Then, the auctioneer, a portly man whose voice dripped with practiced theatricality, unveiled the prize item. It was not a gleaming weapon or a pulsating orb, but a small, unassuming data crystal, resting on a velvet cushion. A hush fell over the room.

"Ladies and gentlemen," the auctioneer announced, his voice

dropping to a conspiratorial whisper, "I present to you...a relic of the Precursors themselves." A collective gasp rippled through the crowd. The term *Precursors,* Ada knew, was whispered in hushed tones throughout Kremøtoa. They were the stuff of legends, the First Programmers, the architects of the world's underlying code. Their knowledge, if it could be unlocked, held the key to untold power.

"This crystal," the auctioneer continued, his voice rising in a crescendo, "is rumored to contain schematics for a device of unimaginable power. A device that could reshape the very fabric of reality itself."

Nividia finally turned her attention to the stage, her violet eyes narrowing with a flicker of genuine interest. The game, Ada realized, was about to begin.

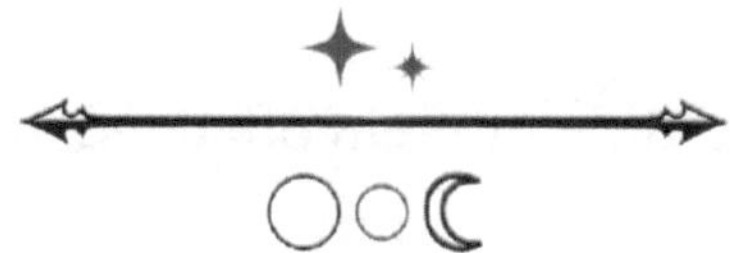

Korina's mind flared with pure, unadulterated intellectual hunger. Her telepathic broadcast, normally a carefully modulated stream of data and analysis, was a torrent of raw excitement. *Ada! The implications! The foundational algorithms...it's indispensable!*

Ada felt a thrill of amusement ripple through her. Korina's enthusiasm was infectious, a welcome counterpoint to the stifling formality of the gala. This was the key. This was how they would get Nividia's attention.

Ada's own gaze was fixed on the Render-Witch. She saw the subtle shift in Nividia's posture, the almost imperceptible narrowing of her eyes, the new intensity in her gaze. The Precursor crystal had piqued her interest, but it was more than just intellectual curiosity. Ada sensed a deeper hunger, a desire for knowledge that bordered on obsession. This was not just a scholar seeking to understand the world; this was an architect seeking to rebuild it.

Before Nividia could even make a move, Ada raised her hand, her voice calm and clear, cutting through the hushed silence of the hall.

"Ten thousand Imperial gold Byts."

The bid was astronomical, a shockwave that rippled through the stunned silence of the Ouroboros. Gasps and whispers erupted from the crowd. Heads swiveled towards Ada's table, their expressions a mix of disbelief and outrage. Ten thousand Byts was more than most of these merchants made in a year. It was a power play, a brazen display of wealth that defied the carefully cultivated decorum of the gala.

Nividia, however, did not seem offended. Instead, a slow smile spread across her face, a predatory gleam in her violet eyes. She turned towards Ada, her expression one of intrigued amusement.

"Twenty."

The single word, spoken with quiet authority, silenced the hall once more. Twenty thousand Byts. It was an absurd amount, a king's ransom, enough to buy a small fleet of warships. It was also, Ada realized, a challenge. Nividia was not just interested in the crystal; she was interested in *her*.

Ada's smile widened. This was more than she could have hoped for. Not only had she captured the Render-Witch's attention, she had ignited her competitive spirit.

"Thirty," Ada countered, her voice still calm, but with a new edge of steel.

The crowd held its breath. This was no longer an auction; it was a duel. A silent battle of wills between two of the most powerful individuals in Port Veridia.

Nividia's smile broadened, revealing a hint of sharp teeth. "Forty."

Ada's eyes met Nividia's across the crowded hall. The air crackled with tension, a silent storm brewing between them. This was not just about a Precursor crystal anymore. This was about something far more fundamental, far more profound. This was about the future of Kremøtoa.

"Fifty," Ada said, her voice a low, steady hum.

The room erupted in a cacophony of whispers and gasps. Fifty thousand Byts! It was an unprecedented sum, a figure that defied logic and reason. It was also, Ada knew, a gamble. She didn't have that kind of money. Not yet.

"One hundred." Nividia's voice, a low, melodious hum, cut through the stunned silence like a shard of ice.

The gavel fell. The auctioneer, his voice trembling slightly, announced Nividia as the winner. The crowd erupted in a frenzy of whispers and exclamations, their disbelief palpable. One hundred thousand Byts. It was an absurd amount, a sum that could topple empires.

But Nividia seemed oblivious to the commotion. Her violet eyes, alight with an almost predatory gleam, were fixed on Ada. The crystal, the object of such intense bidding, lay forgotten on the auctioneer's podium. It was as if the auction itself had been a mere prelude, a carefully orchestrated performance designed to attract a very specific audience.

A slow, knowing smile spread across Nividia's face. "You intrigue me," she purred, her voice barely audible above the din, more a thought out loud, "Tell me, little lynx...what is *your name*?"

Ada met Nividia's gaze, her own expression unreadable. She had played a dangerous game, a high-stakes gamble with a fortune she didn't possess. But she had won. She had captured the Render-Witch's attention. And now, the real game could begin.

The air around Ada crackled with an almost palpable energy, a silent storm brewing in the wake of Nividia's audacious bid. The crowd, still buzzing with the shock of the auction, parted like water before a ship's prow as Nividia made her way towards the exit, her entourage of shimmering light constructs swirling around her like a miniature galaxy. Ada watched her go, a slow, predatory smile spreading across her face. The bait had been taken. The trap had been sprung. Now, all that remained was to reel her in.

As the gala began to wind down, the opulent hall slowly emptying of its glittering inhabitants, a strange hush fell over Ada's table. Sera shifted restlessly in her seat, her hand never far from the hilt of her sword, her eyes scanning the crowd with a hunter's focus. Korina, her initial excitement replaced by a nervous energy, fidgeted with the hem of her violet gown, her gaze darting between Ada and the departing guests. Erita, ever the pragmatist, calmly sipped her wine, her expression unreadable, but her eyes, sharp and calculating, missed nothing.

Suddenly, a ripple of energy pulsed through the hall, a subtle shift in the ambient light that only Ada, with her heightened senses, fully perceived. A single, sapphire-colored construct, radiating an ethereal glow, detached itself from Nividia's entourage and glided silently towards their table. It moved with an almost unsettling grace, its form shifting and reforming as it navigated the dwindling crowd, a silent predator stalking its prey.

As it reached their table, the construct extended a single, slender arm, a glowing data-slate materializing in its hand. A simple, direct, and undeniable holographic text shimmered above the slate, its violet characters burning themselves into Ada's mind: *You have my attention. My private lounge. Now.*

The message was not a request; it was a command. A royal summons delivered by a digital herald. It was also, Ada knew, an opportunity. A chance to finally meet the Render-Witch face-to-face, to understand her motivations, to forge an alliance that could change the fate of Kremøtoa.

Ada exchanged a look with Sera, Korina, and Erita. In that single, silent exchange, a thousand unspoken words passed between them. Fear, excitement, determination, and a shared understanding of the immense stakes of their audacious gamble. They had come to Port Veridia seeking a fleet. They had found something far more valuable: the architect of their salvation.

Without a word, Ada rose from her seat, her obsidian gown shimmering in the fading light of the Ouroboros. Sera, Korina, and Erita followed close behind, their expressions mirroring Ada's own grim determination. The hunt for the Render-Witch was over. The true negotiation was about to begin.

The sapphire construct, its mission apparently incomplete, pulsed once more, a new message appearing on the data-slate. "Be at the designated coordinates tomorrow at the ninth bell." Below the text, a set of precise coordinates shimmered into existence, pinpointing a location somewhere within the labyrinthine heart of Port Veridia. With a final, almost imperceptible nod, the construct dissolved back into the ambient light, leaving Ada and her companions standing alone in the emptying hall.

"Back to the Wandering Star," Ada said, her voice low and steady. "We have a long day ahead of us."

Sera, Korina, and Erita nodded in agreement, their faces a mixture of exhaustion and anticipation. The Midnight Gala had been a whirlwind of sensory overload, a chaotic dance of political maneuvering and arcane one-upmanship. But amidst the chaos, a single, undeniable truth had emerged: Nividia Rhenderon, the enigmatic Render-Witch, had taken their bait. And tomorrow, they would finally have the chance to see if she was willing to bite.

CHAPTER 22

ECHOES IN AN ALLEY

The Wandering Star's common room, usually bustling with a motley crew of sailors, merchants, and adventurers, was blessedly quiet when they returned. Janna, a comforting pillar of calm amidst the swirling chaos of Port Veridia, waited for them, her usual gruff demeanor softened by a hint of concern. A quick, silent exchange filled Janna in on the events she'd missed: Nividia's arrival, the bidding war, the cryptic summons. Sera and Erita, their voices hushed but intense, launched into a rapid-fire tactical discussion, their words a blur of strategic calculations and contingency plans. Korina felt a familiar wave of intellectual overstimulation wash over her, the intricate details of the evening's events swirling in her mind like a chaotic data stream. She struggled to process it all herself, the raw data refusing to coalesce into a coherent narrative. The adrenaline still humming in her veins only amplified the chaos.

Ada's hand gently touched her arm, a warm, grounding presence amidst the swirling storm in her mind. "Rina," Ada said, her voice soft and low, just for Korina's ears. "Let's get some air. And maybe some noodles?"

Korina's eyes met Ada's, a silent plea for escape reflected in their violet depths. Ada's understanding smile was all the answer she needed. A quiet nod to Sera and Erita, a brief, reassuring squeeze of Ada's hand, and they slipped out of the inn, leaving the strategists to their war games.

The night air of Port Veridia was a strange mix of sea salt, arcane energy, and the lingering scent of exotic spices. It was a sensory overload in its own right, but a welcome change from the claustrophobic intensity of the inn. Ada led her through the labyrinthine streets, away from the bustling harbor and deeper into the city's quieter districts. The rhythmic click of Ada's boots on the cobblestones, the gentle sway of her arm against Korina's, the warmth of her presence beside her – it was a comforting rhythm that slowly began to calm the storm in Korina's mind.

They found a small, warmly lit noodle stall tucked away in a quiet alley, its aroma a comforting blend of broth and spices. The stall owner, a wizened old woman with kind eyes and a mischievous smile, greeted them with a nod and a steaming bowl of fragrant noodles. They ate in comfortable silence, the gentle slurping of noodles the only sound between them.

The orange glow from the noodle stall's paper lantern cast a warm, intimate light over their small table. Steam, fragrant with ginger and savory broth, rose in gentle curls from their bowls, a stark contrast to the chaotic, electric energy of the Midnight Gala. Here, tucked away from the spies and schemers of Port Veridia, Ada felt a profound sense of peace settle over her.

Korina, however, was still processing. Her chopsticks moved with absentminded precision, but her violet eyes were distant, her brow furrowed in concentration. Ada could almost see the data streams scrolling behind them. *She processes the world through data,* Ada thought, a wave of affection washing over her. *It's how she protects herself. So brilliant, and so...guarded...*

Ada reached across the small wooden table, her hand covering Korina's. The scholar flinched slightly, pulled from her thoughts, before her fingers relaxed under Ada's touch.

"Obsidian can wait," Ada murmured, a playful twinkle in her eyes. "The axiomatic resonance of Rhedeon will still be here in the morning. I promise."

A faint blush touched Korina's cheeks. "I was just...collating the social dynamics of the auction. Nividia's influence appears to function as a localized gravitational constant, warping the standard trajectories of guild allegiances."

Ada chuckled, a warm, low sound. "Or, you could just say she makes everyone *nervous*." She squeezed Korina's hand gently. "Sometimes, Rina, it's okay to just...feel. The noodles are good. The night is quiet. We're safe."

Korina looked down at their joined hands, then back up at Ada. A genuine, unguarded smile blossomed on her face, and for a moment, the System Analyst was gone, replaced by someone softer, more vulnerable. "The noodles are good," she conceded, her voice barely a whisper.

That quiet moment was shattered by a harsh voice from the street, just beyond the stall's warm circle of light.

"You're making a scene. Do you always have to make a scene?" a man's voice grated, dripping with condescension.

Ada's head turned. A couple stood in the shadows of the alley mouth. The man was large, his posture aggressive and proprietary. The woman was smaller, hunched, her frame radiating a palpable fear. *Poor woman,* Ada thought with a flash of irritation. *What an absolute bastard.*

She felt Korina stiffen beside her. Her hand, still under Ada's, went rigid. The soft smile vanished from her face, replaced by a mask of taut neutrality. Her focus had shifted completely, locking onto the argument with an unnerving intensity.

"I just asked a question, Meric," the woman's voice was a choked sob.

"And I gave you an answer," he snapped. "Is that not good enough for you? It's always something. Always another question, another doubt. It's...exhausting."

The savory aroma of the broth suddenly seemed acrid in Ada's nostrils. The peaceful bubble had burst. She turned back to Korina, concerned. The color was draining from Korina's face, leaving her skin a stark, porcelain white against her violet hair. Her eyes, fixed on the couple, were wide and dark.

"Rina?" Ada said softly, but Korina didn't seem to hear.

The confrontation escalated. The man took a step forward, invading the woman's space. She flinched back, her hands coming up in a pathetic, defensive gesture.

"Don't you walk away from me," he snarled.

Then came the sound.

A sickeningly sharp *crack* that cut through the night air, followed by the woman's sharp, indrawn breath that turned into a broken whimper.

Ada's blood ran cold. But her horror at the act—her own visceral fears—was instantly eclipsed by Korina's reaction.

The chopsticks slipped from Korina's fingers, clattering onto the cobblestones. Her body went utterly still, a statue carved from ice. The vibrant violet of her eyes became dull, glassy, unfocused.

She wasn't looking at the couple anymore. She wasn't looking at anything in the alley. Her gaze was fixed on a point a thousand miles away, a point deep within a memory Ada couldn't see.

"*Rina*," Ada said, her voice sharp with alarm. She reached out, her fingers just brushing Korina's arm.

Korina's reaction was violent. She flinched away as if burned, a small, strangled gasp escaping her lips. Her entire body trembled, her hands clenched into white-knuckled fists on her lap.

Ada froze, her own hand hovering in the air. She stared at Korina's face, and the sight sent a spear of cold dread through her chest. *This wasn't just empathy.* This wasn't a sympathetic reaction to a stranger's plight. This was something else entirely. It was a terror so profound, so absolute, it hollowed out Korina's features, leaving behind a mask of pure, remembered horror.

Ada's heart hammered against her ribs. The sound of the man dragging the weeping woman away faded into a dull roar, a sound she imagined was pulsing in Korina's own ears.

This is memory, the horrifying realization hit her with the force of a physical blow. *She's not just watching this, she's reliving something. That look in her eyes...*

A metallic taste filled Ada's mouth.

Void...I know that look. I've seen it in my own mirror.

The world dissolved into a pinprick of light. The noodle stall, the scent of broth, the distant murmur of Port Veridia—all of it vanished, sucked into the roaring vacuum of Korina's terror. Ada's mind went sharp, every extraneous thought deleted. One objective remained: *get her safe.*

She dropped a handful of Byts on the counter, the coins ringing with a finality that felt like a gavel strike. She scooped Korina into her arms, half-lifting, half-guiding her away from the street. Korina moved like a marionette with cut strings, her body trembling violently against Ada's side. Ada pulled her into the first deep alley they passed, a narrow chasm of damp stone and deeper shadow, away from any prying eyes.

A single slash of moonlight cut through the oppressive darkness, illuminating the slick cobblestones and the glint of tears tracking paths through the grime on Korina's pale cheeks. Ada pressed her back against the cool, rough wall, wrapping her arms around Korina, a solid anchor in the storm of memory.

"Rina," Ada murmured, her voice a low, steady hum. "I'm here. *You're safe.* I have you."

Korina's breath hitched, a ragged, painful sound. Her fingers dug into Ada's arms, a desperate, bruising grip. "He...his name was Kaelen Vance," she whispered, the words tumbling out, choked and broken. "He was my mentor at the Veritas Archives. My...my rival."

A phantom cage of memory slammed shut around Ada's own heart. She held Korina tighter, her own frantic pulse thrumming against the scholar's shuddering back.

"He said I was brilliant," Korina's voice was barely audible, a ghost of a sound. "But he always added a caveat. 'Brilliant, *for a girl from Alder Lake*'; 'Brilliant, *but you need my guidance*'; He took credit for my breakthroughs, presented my data as his own...and when I finally surpassed him, when Obsidian was perfected...he said I owed him."

He took her autonomy. The thought was acid in Ada's veins. *He made her a prisoner in her own skin. He used her own accomplishments, her own tools, as weapons against her.*

"He cornered me," Korina sobbed, burying her face in Ada's shoulder. "In the Archives. Late one night. In the very place I felt safest. He said...he said my success was his property. That I was his intellectual property." The last words were spat out like poison. "And then he...he took it. He took...ev-ev...everything."

The alley seemed to spin. Ada's vision swam, the moonlight blurring with the hot sting of unshed tears. The memory she kept buried, the one that festered in the deep code of her own being, clawed its way to the surface. Not the assault itself, but the aftermath. The sterile white room. The doctor's cold, clinical words. The crushing, absolute violation of losing something she never even knew she had until it was violently ripped away. The ultimate erasure.

I ran from Japan, the realization struck her with the force of a physical blow, so devastating it stole her breath. *I ran from my world to build a sanctuary from this exact pain. And my world created a monster that did the very same thing to the woman I love. She is just like me. Broken by the same darkness.*

Her abstract goal to 'fix the world' burned away like chaff, leaving behind a core of diamond-hard, incandescent rage. *This wasn't about debugging a flawed system anymore.* This wasn't about politics or overthrowing an empire. *It was about justice.* It was about scouring the very foundation of this world clean of the filth that allowed men like Kaelen Vance—men like the one who had destroyed her own life—to exist.

He didn't just hurt her. He tried to erase her. Just like they tried to erase me. Never again... ***Not in my world.*** Her purpose, once a nebulous concept, crystallized into a crusade. *This isn't just a revolution anymore. This is an exorcism.*

Korina finally pulled back, her violet eyes, swimming with tears, pleading. "He's still out there, Ada. High up in the Veritas Council. Untouchable. No one would have believed me." She took another shuddering breath, her gaze locking with Ada's. "Be my sword and shield, Ada. Please."

Ada reached up, her thumb gently wiping the salty tears from Korina's cheek. She looked into the depths of that shattered gaze and saw her own reflection. She saw the survivor.

Her expression hardened, the soft concern in her violet eyes forging into a fiery, resolute glare that could have melted steel. Her voice, when it came, was low, steady, and terrifyingly calm. It was not a comfort; it was a sacred vow.

"I promise you, Korina."

The words hung in the profound silence of the alley, a binding contract sealed in pain and rage.

"He will answer for what he did."

Korina's body sagged, the last of her fight draining out, replaced by a flicker of exhausted hope. She leaned her full weight against Ada, a silent transfer of trust. "Don't...don't tell the others," she whispered. "Not yet. I couldn't bear their...pity."

Ada nodded, her gaze fixed on the alley's mouth, on the world that lay beyond. A world she would now remake not just with logic, but with righteous fury. "This is your story," she said, her voice an iron promise. "We will tell it when you are ready. But his part in it...is over."

"Thank you," Korina whispered, her voice muffled against Ada's shoulder. The words were inadequate, a pale reflection of the gratitude that welled up inside her, but they were all she could manage at that moment. She tightened her grip on Ada's arm, her fingers intertwining with Ada's, their hands clasped together, a silent symbol of their shared strength, their unwavering bond. For the first time since the assault, Korina felt a flicker of hope, a nascent belief that she could heal, that she could move forward, that she could reclaim her own power, her own autonomy. She had Ada, Sera and Erita, and that was enough—for now.

CHAPTER 23

THE RENDER-WITCH'S PRICE

The air in the Wandering Star hung thick with anticipation. The usual boisterous clamor of the inn seemed muted, swallowed by the weight of the impending meeting. Ada sat by the window, her gaze fixed on the bustling harbor outside, the vibrant chaos of Port Veridia a stark contrast to the quiet storm brewing within her. Korina sat beside her, unusually silent, her fingers tracing patterns on the worn wooden table. The events of the previous day had cast a long shadow over her, the memory of Kaelen's betrayal a fresh wound that throbbed with a dull ache. Ada felt the weight of her vow to Korina pressing down on her, a sharp, personal edge added to her resolve. Succeeding here, securing Nividia's support, was no longer just a strategic goal. It was a necessary step towards gaining the power she would need to deliver justice for Korina, to build a world where such violations had no place.

Across the table, Sera sharpened her twin blades, the rhythmic rasp of steel against stone a familiar counterpoint to the silence.

Erita paced restlessly, her sharp eyes scanning the room, her usual cynicism replaced by a focused intensity. The air crackled with unspoken tension, a shared understanding of the high stakes that rode on this encounter.

"Everything alright?" Sera asked, her gaze flickering between Ada and Korina. She sensed the shift in their demeanor, the unspoken weight that hung between them.

"Yeah, we're good," Ada replied, covering for Korina's silence. "Just...thinking."

At the appointed time, the ninth bell, one of Nividia's signature sapphire constructs materialized silently in the center of their room. It was a breathtaking display of power, the geometric form shimmering with an ethereal light, its facets reflecting the room's dim interior in a kaleidoscope of fractured images. The construct didn't speak, didn't gesture. It simply projected a single, intricate glyph onto the wall – a stylized representation of a swirling vortex, an invitation to a realm beyond the mundane.

"Guess that's our cue," Erita said, a flicker of excitement in her golden eyes. "Showtime."

"I'll stay behind," Janna rumbled, her hand resting on the pommel of her axe. "Someone needs to guard the rooms." Her gaze lingered on Ada, a silent promise of protection. Ada nodded in acknowledgment, grateful for Janna's steadfast presence, her unwavering loyalty a comforting anchor in the turbulent sea of their mission.

The construct led them out of the inn and into a deserted alleyway, the narrow passageway amplifying the sense of secrecy, of stepping into a hidden world. The construct paused, its sapphire form shimmering, and then, with a casual flick of its geometric hand, it created a portal. It wasn't a dramatic, fiery rift, but a shimmering, circular opening rimmed with pulsating violet light, a subtle yet undeniable display of immense power over the very fabric of reality. This, Ada knew, was Nividia's way of setting the tone for their encounter, a silent reminder of who held the upper hand in this negotiation.

Ada stepped forward, her heart pounding in her chest, a mix of anticipation and apprehension churning in her stomach. Sera, Korina, and Erita followed close behind, their faces reflecting a similar mix of emotions. The portal shimmered, beckoning them into the unknown. They stepped through.

The journey through the portal was brief but disorienting, a dizzying rush through fractured space, a kaleidoscope of colors and distorted images flashing before their eyes. Ada felt a momentary surge of nausea, a visceral reminder of the immense power they were dealing with. Then, just as quickly as it began, the journey ended. They stepped out of the portal and into a realm that defied description.

The space they entered was not so much a room as a controlled explosion of arcane genius. Half-finished engines hummed with barely contained power, their intricate mechanisms a symphony of polished brass and glowing crystals. Holographic schematics, complex and ever-shifting, rotated lazily in the air, casting an ethereal light on the polished obsidian surfaces. One entire wall was not a wall at all, but a window, a shimmering portal looking out at the raw, swirling data-streams of Rhedeon's reality – a chaotic ballet of light and energy that pulsed with the very heartbeat of the world.

Korina gasped, her eyes wide with awe. This was it. The laboratory of her wildest dreams, a place where the boundaries between magic and science blurred into a beautiful, chaotic mess.

She felt a surge of pure, unadulterated intellectual excitement, a craving to understand the principles at play, to dissect and analyze every intricate detail. She wanted to touch everything, to trace the lines of energy with her fingertips, to delve into the raw data that flowed like a river before her.

Nividia stood with her back to them, her slender figure silhouetted against the swirling chaos of the data-stream window. She held the Precursor crystal in her hand, its facets catching the ethereal light, casting rainbow reflections on the polished obsidian floor. She was deliberately making them wait, Ada realized, a calculated power move designed to intimidate, to establish her dominance from the very first moment. Her two sapphire constructs flanked her like silent, luminous hounds, their geometric forms radiating an aura of barely contained power.

The silence stretched, thick and heavy, punctuated only by the low hum of the arcane engines and the soft whir of the holographic schematics. Ada felt a familiar prickle of irritation at the delay, the programmer in her chafing at the inefficiency, the wasted time. But she held her ground, her expression carefully neutral, her mind racing, calculating the best approach to this unpredictable variable.

Nividia finally turned, her ancient, violet eyes fixing on Ada with an intensity that made the air crackle. "You are Ada," she stated, not as a question, but as a simple observation, a declaration of fact. Her voice was like liquid silver, smooth and flowing, yet with an underlying current of power, of an intellect that had spanned centuries, perhaps millennia. There was a mischievous glint in her eyes, a hint of amusement playing at the corners of her lips, as if she were watching a particularly interesting experiment unfold before her.

"And you," Ada replied, her voice calm and steady, refusing to be intimidated, "are Nividia Rhenderon, the Render-Witch of Rhedeon." She met Nividia's gaze directly, a silent challenge passing between them, a clash of wills in the charged air of the laboratory.

"Indeed," Nividia purred, her eyes narrowing slightly. "Tell me, little architect, how does one so young acquire the wealth to bid so recklessly at the Midnight Gala? One hundred thousand Byts is no small sum, even for a seasoned merchant lord." Her words were laced with a subtle, probing psychic attack, a tendril of mental energy reaching out to sift through Ada's thoughts, to uncover her secrets.

Ada felt the probe, a cold, invasive touch against her mind. But she wasn't alone. The telepathic link she had forged with Sera, Erita, and Korina flared to life, their now-practiced mental defenses forming a seamless, collective barrier. Sera's unwavering resolve, Erita's icy calm, and Korina's analytical precision flowed together, merging into an unyielding, silent void that met Nividia's probe head-on. The psychic attack dissipated harmlessly against their combined mental shield, like a wave crashing against an unmovable cliff face.

Nividia's eyes widened slightly, a flicker of surprise crossing her features. She raised a perfectly sculpted eyebrow, a hint of intrigue replacing the amusement in her gaze. "Interesting," she murmured, her voice laced with a newfound respect. "A collective mental barrier. Most impressive. I haven't encountered such a cohesive bio-etheric network in centuries."

Ada allowed herself a small, enigmatic smile. "We have our ways," she said vaguely, careful not to reveal the true nature of their link, her status as the world's Admin a secret she guarded fiercely. "Let's just say we operate on a slightly different frequency than most."

Nividia chuckled, a low, melodic sound that echoed through the laboratory. The power dynamic had shifted subtly but significantly. Nividia no longer saw them as mere upstarts, as reckless gamblers with more money than sense. She saw them as equals, as potential partners in a game that spanned far beyond the petty squabbles of Port Dominus, a game that involved the very fabric of reality itself. *Potential*, Ada thought, was the key word. Nividia was intrigued, but not yet convinced. They still had to prove their worth, to demonstrate that they were players in this game, not just pawns. And Ada, the architect of this world, was more than ready to play.

Nividia leaned back against her arcane workbench, the Precursor crystal pulsing faintly in her hand. She watched the four women before her, their faces a mixture of determination and apprehension. The tall, muscular one, Sera, radiated a raw, barely contained energy, a warrior's eagerness for a fight. The smaller one with the intricate braids, Korina, clutched a data-slate, her eyes flickering with intellectual curiosity, her mind already racing to analyze the challenge ahead. The quiet, watchful one, Erita, stood slightly apart, her gaze sharp and assessing, calculating the risks and rewards of this encounter. And then there was Ada, the architect, the linchpin of this strange little group, her violet eyes shining with an unsettling blend of power and vulnerability.

"So," Nividia began, her voice a low, melodic hum that echoed through the laboratory, "you desire a fleet. Warships, I presume? To challenge the might of the Ehxcehl Empire? A noble goal, perhaps, though hardly original." She gestured dismissively with the crystal. "And you offer me gold? Such a mundane currency. I have vaults overflowing with it. What I value, little architect, is not wealth, but intellectual novelty. A true challenge—Raw, untamed power that defies the known laws of this reality."

She paused, letting her words sink in, watching their expressions shift from confidence to uncertainty. "You seek my renderings, my unique creations. Very well. Prove yourselves worthy of my best work. Show me that you possess the ingenuity, the courage, the sheer audacity to wield the power I can bestow upon you."

Nividia's eyes glinted with a mischievous spark. "There is a place," she continued, her voice dropping to a conspiratorial whisper, "known as the Sunken Core. A dungeon ruin of the Precursors, lost beneath the waves for millennia, inside a underwater cavern. Within its depths lies a data-core, a relic of unimaginable power. Retrieve it for me, and I will consider your request. Fail, and well..." She shrugged, her smile widening. "Let's just say the depths hold many secrets, and not all of them are pleasant."

Korina's eyes widened. "The Sunken Core?" she breathed, her

voice barely above a whisper. "But that's...that's a legend. A myth. No one has ever returned from its depths."

"Precisely," Nividia purred, enjoying the scholar's evident fear. "It is said to be guarded by creatures of immense power, remnants of a forgotten age. Constructs of living metal, animated by the very energy of the Core itself. And the Core itself...well, let's just say it is not for the faint of heart."

Sera's eyes, however, lit up with a predatory gleam. "A challenge," she growled, her hand instinctively moving towards the hilt of her sword. "I accept."

Erita, ever the pragmatist, raised an eyebrow. "And what exactly does this 'data-core' do?" she asked, her voice laced with suspicion. "What's in it for us, besides a fleet of fancy ships?"

Nividia chuckled, a low, throaty sound that sent shivers down Korina's spine. "Knowledge, little spymaster," she replied, her eyes twinkling. "Power. The secrets of a civilization that manipulated reality itself. Think of it as a...a potenital cheat code for the universe."

Ada stepped forward, her violet eyes locking onto Nividia's. "We accept your challenge, Nividia Rhenderon," she said, her voice calm and steady, yet radiating an aura of quiet power, an authority that belied her youthful appearance. "We will retrieve the data-core. And in return, you will provide us with the fleet we need to reshape this world."

Nividia smiled, a genuine smile this time, a smile that revealed a hint of the ancient, untamed power that lay within her. "Very well, little architect," she said, her voice laced with a newfound respect.

Nividia extended her hand, the Precursor crystal dissolving into shimmering motes of teal light that swirled around her fingers. "The Sunken Core lies within the Abyssal Trench," she said, her voice echoing with the resonance of ancient power. "These coordinates will guide you to its entrance." The swirling light coalesced into a small, pulsating sphere that floated towards Ada. As Ada reached out to take it, the sphere dissolved, imprinting a complex, glowing glyph onto the back of her hand. The glyph pulsed with a faint, ethereal light, a beacon that would guide them to their destination.

"This mark," Nividia explained, "will resonate with the Core's energy signature, leading you to its hidden entrance. But be warned, little architect. The path is treacherous, and the guardians are formidable."

Ada nodded, her expression unreadable. She looked down at the glowing glyph on her hand, a symbol of the dangerous pact she had just made. The Sunken Core. A legend whispered in hushed tones, a place from which no one had ever returned. And now, it was their destination, the price of Nividia's allegiance. Their mission in Rhedeon had just taken a perilous and unexpected turn, a gamble with the fate of their revolution hanging in the balance.

"Let the game begin." She raised a hand and a shimmering portal of emerald light coalesced in the center of the room. "This portal will take you closer to your destination. Once you step across, your hunt will be on." She gave the slightest smirk, and with a final glance towards the four women, Nividia turned back to her workbench, the Precursor crystal pulsing faintly in her hand, as if echoing the dangerous game that had just been set in motion. The fate of Kremøtoa, and perhaps even the reality itself, now hung in the balance.

CHAPTER 24

THE SUNKEN CORE

The shimmering emerald portal winked out of existence, leaving Ada, Sera, Korina, and Erita blinking in the harsh, unforgiving light of a desolate coastline. The transition was jarring, a physical shock that left them momentarily disoriented. One moment they were in Nividia's technologically advanced laboratory, the air thick with arcane energy and the hum of complex machinery; the next, they were on a windswept shore, the raw, untamed power of nature assaulting their senses.

Gone were the vibrant, chaotic streets of Port Veridia, replaced by a landscape of jagged black cliffs that clawed at the bruised twilight sky. The air, heavy with the taste of salt and the roar of a violent, churning sea, whipped at their clothes, threatening to tear them from their bodies. This was the Eastern Reaches, a place that felt forgotten by the world, a realm of hostile, untamed beauty.

"What in the Void...?" Erita muttered, shielding her eyes from the wind-driven spray. "Where in the hells did that portal dump us?"

Korina, shivering in her thin gown, fumbled with her data-slate, its screen flickering in the erratic wind. "Nividia's coordinates..." she stammered, her voice barely audible above the crashing waves. "They point...they point somewhere out there." She pointed a trembling finger towards the churning sea, its surface a maelstrom of whitecaps and swirling currents.

Sera, her crimson tunic plastered against her body by the wind, surveyed the desolate coastline with narrowed eyes. "Deep beneath the waves," she growled, her voice tight with apprehension. "Just what I needed. A watery grave."

Ada, her obsidian gown swirling around her like a storm cloud, remained silent, her violet eyes fixed on the raging sea. She felt a strange resonance with this place, a kinship with its untamed power. It was a place of raw, unfiltered energy, a place where the boundaries between reality and the code that governed it seemed to blur. She reached out a hand, feeling the wind whip through her fingers, tasting the salt on her lips. This was Kremøtoa, her creation, in all its chaotic, unpredictable glory. And somewhere beneath those churning waves, lay the key to their revolution.

"The Sunken Core," she murmured, her voice barely audible above the storm. "Nividia's price."

Erita held up her data-slate, its screen displaying a swirling vortex of blues and greens, a chaotic representation of the ocean currents. "The coordinates point to a location approximately five kilometers offshore," she said, her voice strained against the wind. "And deep. Very deep. According to Obsidian's bathymetric readings, the depth at that location is over two thousand meters."

Korina's face paled. "Two thousand meters?" she whispered, her voice filled with a mixture of awe and terror. "That's...that's insane. No ordinary person could withstand that kind of pressure."

Sera snorted. "Which is probably why Nividia sent us here," she said, her voice laced with grim amusement. "She wants to see if we're worthy of her 'gifts.' A little test of our...resourcefulness."

Ada nodded, a slow, deliberate movement. "She's playing a game, Sera," she said, her voice quiet but firm. "A game of power. And she wants to see if we're willing to play by her rules."

"And are we?" Erita asked, raising an eyebrow. "Are we willing to risk our lives for a chance at a fleet? For a chance at Nividia's... favor?"

Ada turned to face her companions, her violet eyes burning with a fierce, unwavering determination. "We have no choice, Erita," she said, her voice ringing with an almost otherworldly power. "The fate of Kremøtoa hangs in the balance. And we will do whatever it takes to save it. Even if it means facing the depths of the Sunken Core."

A sudden, violent gust of wind tore at their clothes, whipping their hair around their faces, the roar of the sea echoing their resolve. They stood there, on the edge of the world, four women against the storm, their destinies intertwined, their purpose clear. They would face Nividia's challenge. They would retrieve the data-core. They would win the Render-Witch's game. And they would reshape Kremøtoa in their image.

The wind howled like a banshee, tearing at Korina's clothes, biting at her exposed skin. The salt spray stung her eyes, blurring her vision. Two thousand meters. The number echoed in her mind, a chilling reminder of the impossible task ahead. No ordinary human could survive at that depth. The pressure would crush them, the cold would freeze them, the lack of air would suffocate them. But they were not ordinary humans. Not anymore.

Korina shivered, pulling her thin gown tighter around her, trying to ward off the biting wind. Her gaze darted nervously between the churning sea and the determined faces of her companions. Sera, her jaw set, her eyes narrowed against the wind, seemed to relish the challenge. Erita, ever pragmatic, surveyed the coastline, calculating risks and escape routes. Ada, her violet eyes burning with an almost otherworldly intensity, remained focused on the task at hand. And Korina...Korina felt a familiar wave of panic rising in her chest, threatening to overwhelm her. Two thousand meters. It was madness. Suicide.

"We need a solution," she muttered, her voice barely audible above the storm. "Something...something to protect us from the pressure. From the cold. From the lack of air."

Ada's hand gently rested on her shoulder, a comforting warmth spreading through Korina's chilled body. "We'll find a way, Rina," she said, her voice soft but firm. "Together."

And in that moment, Korina's panic subsided, replaced by a surge of determination. Together. Yes, together they could overcome any obstacle. Together they could rewrite the rules of *reality*. Together they could conquer the depths.

With trembling fingers, Korina activated *Obsidian*, its screen flickering to life, a beacon of hope in the gathering gloom. Holographic schematics shimmered into existence, intricate designs swirling around her, a symphony of logic and innovation taking shape in the heart of the storm. This was her domain, the realm of data and possibility. This was where she could truly shine.

"Breathing Talismans," she murmured, her fingers flying across the data-slate's surface, the schematics evolving with each precise command. "Intricately designed conduits, charged with bio-etheric energy, capable of filtering oxygen from hydrogen directly from the water molecules. Think of them as...miniature, magically powered gills."

Erita raised an eyebrow. "Magically powered gills?" she repeated, a hint of skepticism in her voice. "And you think you can just...create those?"

Korina grinned, a flash of her old, enthusiastic self breaking through the surface of her fear. "Not just create them, Erita," she said, her voice filled with a newfound confidence. "Optimize them. These talismans will not only filter oxygen, but also regulate the flow of mana, ensuring a constant supply of energy for..."

"Pressure-Resistant Bands," Ada interjected, her voice filled with excitement. "Sleek, metallic bands worn at key points on the body. They'll generate a subtle counter-pressure field, allowing us to withstand the crushing depths." Ada's fingers danced across *Obsidian*'s surface, adding to Korina's design, their minds working in perfect synchronicity, a seamless blend of logic and magic. "Think of them as...portable, personalized force fields."

Korina's heart soared as she watched Ada work, her fingers moving with a grace and precision that belied the complexity of the code she was manipulating. It was a beautiful thing to witness, this fusion of art and science, of creativity and logic. This was Ada, the Architect-Queen, in her element, reshaping reality with a flick of her wrist, a whisper of her will.

A sudden shiver ran through Korina's body, reminding her of the biting cold. She glanced down at her thin gown, inadequate protection against the harsh elements of the Eastern Reaches.

Ada's hand brushed against hers, her touch sending a jolt of warmth through Korina's chilled fingers. "And this," Ada said, her voice soft, almost hesitant, "for the cold." A new schematic appeared on *Obsidian*'s screen, a simple yet elegant design for a wristband that pulsed with a gentle, violet light. "A thermoregulatory band. It'll maintain optimal body temperature, regardless of the external environment."

Korina's gaze met Ada's, her violet eyes filled with a warmth that had nothing to do with the thermoregulatory band and everything to do with the love and care she felt emanating from the Architect-Queen. In that moment, the cold wind, the churning sea, the impossible depth of the Sunken Core...all of it faded into the background, replaced by the quiet intimacy of their shared gaze, the unspoken promise of their shared future. Together. They would face the depths together.

Korina's fingers danced across *Obsidian*'s surface, a final flourish of code solidifying the designs. The schematics shimmered, then solidified, locking into place with a satisfying click. She looked up at Ada, her violet eyes shining with a mixture of pride and apprehension. "Ready when you are," she murmured, her voice barely a whisper above the roar of the storm.

Ada nodded, her own violet eyes burning with a quiet intensity. She closed her eyes, taking a deep breath, centering herself, preparing to channel the raw power of creation. This was a new frontier, a significant evolution of her abilities. Before, she had manipulated existing objects, altering their properties, bending them to her will. Now, she would create something entirely new, something complex and functional, something that would bridge the gap between magic and technology, between the virtual and the real.

Her hands began to glow, a soft violet light emanating from her palms, spreading outwards, enveloping her fingertips, illuminating the intricate lines etched into her skin. The air around her crackled with energy, the very fabric of reality seeming to bend and twist in response to her will. She felt a surge of power coursing through her veins, a raw, untamed force that both exhilarated and terrified her. This was the power of a god, the power to create, to shape, to define.

With a whispered command, she brought Korina's designs into being. Particles of light coalesced, swirling and dancing in the air, forming intricate patterns, weaving themselves into complex structures. The raw energy of creation solidified, transforming into tangible objects, shimmering with a soft, violet glow.

First, the Breathing Talismans materialized, delicate pendants crafted from a luminous, crystalline material, pulsing with a gentle, rhythmic light. Then, the Pressure-Resistant Bands took shape, sleek, metallic cuffs that shimmered with an internal energy, their surfaces etched with intricate runes that seemed to shift and change with the light. Finally, the Thermoregulatory Bands appeared, simple yet elegant wristbands that glowed with a warm, comforting light, their surfaces smooth and cool to the touch.

Ada opened her eyes, gazing at her creations, a sense of awe washing over her. They were beautiful, functional, and *real.* She picked up a Breathing Talisman, holding it up to the light, examining its intricate design, the delicate interplay of light and shadow. It was a marvel of engineering, a testament to Korina's genius and her own newfound mastery of creation.

She handed the talisman to Korina, who took it with trembling fingers, her eyes wide with wonder. “It’s...it’s incredible, Ada,” she whispered, her voice filled with awe. “Thank you.”

Ada smiled, a warmth spreading through her chest. This was the reason she had created Kremøtoa, to witness the birth of new possibilities, to experience the magic of creation. And now, here she was, standing on a storm-ravaged coastline, holding the future of her world in her hands. She had come a long way from the isolated confines of her apartment, the lonely world of code and algorithms. She had found a purpose, a family, a home. She had found her place in the world she had created.

“Let’s go find that data-core,” she said, her voice filled with a newfound confidence. “Together.”

Sera unsheathed her twin blades, their polished steel gleaming under the stormy sky. Ada stepped forward, a small vial of shimmering, phosphorescent liquid appearing in her hand. “This should help,” she said, handing the vial to Sera. “An arcane lubricant. It’ll prevent corrosion and reduce friction in the water.”

Sera raised an eyebrow, a flicker of amusement in her golden eyes. “Arcane lubricant?” she echoed, a hint of playful skepticism in her voice. “Sounds...interesting.” She uncorked the vial, the scent of ozone and sea salt filling the air. She dipped a finger into the liquid, a drop clinging to her fingertip, shimmering with an ethereal, violet light. She smeared the lubricant across the surface of her blades, the liquid spreading like quicksilver, coating the steel in a thin, iridescent film. The blades hummed faintly, their edges glowing with a soft, violet light.

Sera tested the blades, executing a series of rapid, fluid strikes, her movements precise and controlled. The air whistled as the blades cut through the wind, their edges now impossibly sharp, their movements almost frictionless. She adjusted her stance, her body shifting, adapting her combat forms to the theoretical resistance of the deep, the weight of the water, the limited visibility. She moved with a grace that belied her strength, her body a coiled spring, ready to unleash a whirlwind of steel at a moment's notice.

Erita, meanwhile, was distributing the rest of their specialized gear. She handed each woman a small, cylindrical device that pulsed with a faint, bioluminescent glow. "Deep-sea flares," she explained, her voice crisp and efficient. "For illumination in the abyss." She then produced a set of compact sonar devices, their surfaces etched with intricate runes. "These will map the terrain and help you navigate the currents," she said, handing one to each woman. Finally, she unveiled a set of specialized grappling launchers, their designs sleek and compact, their mechanisms humming with a quiet energy. "For quick ascents and descents," she added, her golden eyes glinting with a hint of mischief. "Or for pulling yourselves out of any...unexpected situations."

With their preparations complete, the quartet stood on the edge of the high, windswept cliff, the violent sea roaring below them, its waves crashing against the rocks, sending plumes of spray high into the air. The wind whipped at their hair, their clothes, their resolve. The breathing talismans glowed with a soft, steady light against their chests, small beacons of hope against the encroaching darkness. They exchanged a final, resolute look, a silent acknowledgment of the dangers ahead, the shared purpose that bound them together. There was no turning back. This was their path, their destiny.

With a shared, unspoken understanding, they took a collective leap of faith, plunging into the dark, churning, unknown waters below. The cold water enveloped them, the pressure increasing with every meter of their descent. The breathing talismans pulsed with a brighter light, their magic protecting them from the crushing depths. They swam downwards, their bodies sleek and agile, their movements guided by the sonar devices, their eyes fixed on the faint, shimmering glow of Nividia's glyph, a beacon in the abyss, leading them towards the Sunken Core and the next chapter of their revolution.

CHAPTER 25

GUARDIANS OF THE CORE

The world dissolved into a swirling, silent chaos of dark green and deep blues. Korina's first sensation wasn't fear, but a thrill of pure, analytical satisfaction. The breathing talisman, a testament to her and Ada's combined ingenuity, worked perfectly. Clean, crisp air filled her lungs, a stark contrast to the churning saltwater that surrounded her. The pressure bands, humming with a gentle, reassuring energy against her wrists and ankles, held firm against the immense weight of the deep, a comforting counterpoint to the growing pressure against her eardrums.

The darkness was absolute, a void that pressed in from all sides, broken only by the narrow beams of their shoulder-mounted lamps and the occasional flash of Erita's bioluminescent flares. Each flare illuminated a terrifying, alien world. Submerged cliffs loomed out of the darkness, their surfaces covered in phosphorescent corals that pulsed with an eerie, otherworldly light. Strange, ghostly sea life drifted past, their bodies translucent, their skeletal structures visible in the lamplight, their eyes glowing with an unnerving intelligence.

Erita's sonar pings echoed through the water, guiding their descent into a deep-sea trench, a narrow canyon carved into the ocean floor. The pressure mounted steadily, a physical manifestation of their deepening isolation. The silence was profound, broken only by the rhythmic whoosh of their breathing apparatuses and the occasional creak of the pressure bands adjusting to the increasing depth. It was a symphony of technology and magic, a testament to their preparedness, yet it did little to quell the growing unease in Korina's stomach.

She glanced at Ada, whose face was illuminated by the soft, violet glow of her breathing talisman. Ada's expression was calm, focused, her violet eyes scanning the darkness, her hand occasionally reaching out to brush against Korina's, a silent reassurance, a shared connection in the alien world. The sight of Ada's calm amidst the growing tension was a source of quiet strength, a reminder of the bond they shared, the shared purpose that drove them forward.

Erita, leading the descent, signaled with a flick of her wrist, the movement amplified by the bioluminescent strips on her diving suit. They followed her into the trench, the walls closing in around them, the darkness deepening, the pressure increasing. Korina felt a flicker of claustrophobia, a tightening in her chest, but she pushed it down, focusing on the task at hand, the data streaming from her internal sensors, the rhythmic pulse of her breathing talisman.

The trench twisted and turned, a labyrinth of submerged canyons and caverns, each turn revealing new, unsettling wonders of the deep.

Giant, bioluminescent jellyfish pulsed with a hypnotic rhythm, their tentacles trailing behind them like shimmering ribbons. Schools of phosphorescent fish darted past, their scales reflecting the lamplight in a dazzling display of color and movement. And then, there were the shadows. Shapes that flickered at the edge of the lamplight, too large, too quick to be identified, their presence a constant, unnerving reminder of the unknown dangers lurking in the deep.

Korina gripped Ada's hand tighter, her own anxiety a tangible pulse against Ada's calm. She focused on the data, the numbers, the schematics, anything to distract herself from the growing sense of dread, the feeling of being watched, of being hunted. This was a world beyond her understanding, a world where logic and reason held little sway, a world where magic and the unknown reigned supreme.

The sonar pings intensified, the echoes bouncing off the walls of the trench, converging on a single point. Erita signaled again, pointing towards a shimmering, emerald glyph etched into the rock face. Nividia's mark. The entrance to the Sunken Core. They had arrived.

The narrow canyon walls, slick with phosphorescent algae, seemed to press in on them, the darkness amplifying the claustrophobic silence of the deep. Sera felt a prickle of unease, a primal instinct screaming danger, even before Erita's sonar flared, painting three massive contacts converging on them with terrifying speed.

Ambush. The thought flashed through her mind, cold and sharp, a warning bell in the silent world.

Two of the contacts resolved into shapes, colossal, grotesque sharks, their hides plated in iridescent, arcane armor that shimmered in the beams of their diving lamps. The third contact, larger, more amorphous, pulsed with a malevolent sapphire-blue light—a kraken of immense size, its tentacles lined with pulsing barbs that glowed like venomous jewels. There was nowhere to run, nowhere to hide. Only fight.

Sera gripped her phosphorescent blades, the familiar weight a comfort in the alien world. *Ada, Korina, Erita,* she projected into their shared telepathic link, her voice a silent command, *formation Delta. Now.* The water, thick and resistant, hampered her movements, turning every swing, every thrust into a sluggish, agonizingly slow maneuver. She lunged at the nearest shark, her blades clanging uselessly against its arcane armor, the impact jarring her arms.

The kraken, a swirling mass of tentacles and sapphire barbs, attacked from above, its massive body blotting out the faint light filtering down from the surface. Erita, a blur of motion even in the dense water, darted forward, her twin daggers flashing, drawing the kraken's attention, a deadly distraction, buying Sera precious seconds. *Find a weakness,* Sera silently urged Korina, her frustration a tangible pulse in their telepathic link. *Anything.*

Korina's voice, a calm, analytical counterpoint to the chaos, echoed in her mind. *Dorsal seam, near the gills. Faint energy signature. Possible weak point.* Sera adjusted her trajectory, aiming for the narrow gap in the shark's armor, a sliver of vulnerability amidst the iridescent plating. The shark lunged, its jaws snapping shut inches from her face, the force of the water displacement sending her tumbling. She recovered quickly, the thermoregulatory bands humming against her skin, compensating for the sudden shift in temperature.

Ada, her power a subtle current in the water, manipulated the flow, slowing the shark's momentum, giving Sera a clear shot. She saw her chance. With a surge of adrenaline, Sera channeled all her strength into a single, focused thrust. Her blade, coated in Ada's arcane lubricant, slipped into the seam, piercing the shark's armor, drawing a plume of dark, viscous blood that swirled around them like ink. The shark thrashed, its movements becoming erratic, its energy signature fading. It was a small victory, but a vital one.

The fight continued, a chaotic, three-dimensional ballet of flashing blades, pulsing barbs, and swirling currents. Erita, her speed underwater still remarkable, weaved between the kraken's tentacles, her daggers finding purchase in the gaps between the sapphire barbs, drawing more of the inky blood. Ada, her face pale with exertion, continued to manipulate the water, creating currents and eddies that disrupted the sharks' movements, giving Sera and Erita openings to attack. Korina, her voice a steady stream of tactical data, guided their movements, identified weaknesses, and coordinated their attacks, her mind a bridge between their disparate fighting styles.

Sera focused on the wounded shark, her blades a blur, each strike aimed at the vulnerable seam, widening the wound, weakening the creature. The shark, its movements growing sluggish, attempted to flee, but Sera pursued relentlessly, her anger a driving force, her blades a whirlwind of phosphorescent death. With a final, desperate lunge, she plunged her blades deep into the shark's gills, severing a major artery. The shark convulsed, its body shuddering, its energy signature flickering and then fading into nothingness.

The kraken, enraged by its companion's death, turned its attention to Sera. Its tentacles lashed out, the sapphire barbs pulsing with a venomous light. Sera dodged and weaved, her movements precise, economical, each parry, each block a testament to years of training. But the kraken was relentless, its tentacles a cage of sapphire death, closing in around her. She felt a sharp sting on her arm, the venom searing through her suit, a jolt of agonizing pain that radiated through her body. She stumbled, her vision blurring, the pressure bands creaking under the strain.

Sera! Korina's voice, sharp with concern, pierced the haze of pain. *Erita, create a diversion. Ada, pull Sera back.* A flash of sapphire light, a swirling vortex of water, and Sera was yanked backwards, away from the kraken's grasp, into Ada's arms. The world spun, the pressure crushing her lungs, the venom burning through her veins. She clung to Ada, her strength fading, her consciousness slipping away. They had won, but the victory was pyrrhic, the battle brutal, leaving them all drained, wounded, and vulnerable in the crushing abyss.

The kraken's venom, a cocktail of neurotoxins and arcane energy, burned through Sera's veins, a searing fire that spread through her body. Ada held Sera close, her own pressure bands creaking under the strain of the deep-sea currents. "[Execute: Neutralize_Toxin]," Ada whispered, her command a silent prayer in the crushing darkness. A faint violet light pulsed from her hands, flowing into Sera's wound, neutralizing the venom, the searing pain slowly subsiding.

Report, Ada projected into their telepathic link, her voice tight with concern. *Status.*

Stable, Sera replied, her voice weak but clear. *Thanks, Ada.*

Korina, Erita, report, Ada continued, her gaze sweeping over their forms in the murky water.

Minor lacerations, Erita reported, her voice clipped and efficient. *Nothing critical.*

Pressure bands holding, Korina added, her voice tinged with anxiety. *Breathing talismans at seventy percent. We need to move. This depth...it's...unstable.*

Ada nodded, her own breathing talisman humming against her chest. The pressure at this depth was immense, a crushing weight that threatened to implode their fragile bodies. "Nividia's glyph," she said, her voice muffled by the water. "Coordinates."

Korina, her data-slate glowing faintly in the darkness, pointed towards a shimmering, emerald green glyph etched into the canyon wall, pulsing with a faint, arcane energy. "Three hundred meters, bearing zero-four-five," she said, her voice tight. "It's...it's emanating a strange energy signature. I can't...I can't quite resolve it."

Ada felt a shiver run down her spine. Even through the pressure bands and the thermoregulatory suit, she could feel the strange energy emanating from the glyph, a cold, alien presence that resonated deep within her core programming. It was an anomaly, a dissonance in the fabric of her creation. "Let's go," she said, her voice firm, pushing down the rising tide of unease. "Stay close."

They moved through the phosphorescent canyon, the strange, bioluminescent creatures of the deep swirling around them, their forms distorted by the pressure and the darkness. The glyph grew larger as they approached, its emerald light casting an eerie glow on the canyon walls. The water grew colder, the pressure more intense, the silence more profound. Ada's Admin-view flickered, struggling to resolve the properties of the surrounding environment. It was as if the very laws of physics were breaking down, warping and twisting under the influence of the glyph's strange energy.

Then, it came into view. The Sunken Core.

It was a nightmare of impossible geometry. A twisted, metallic edifice that seemed to fold in on itself, defying all logic and reason. It shimmered with a faint, sickly green light that pulsed from deep within its core, casting long, distorted shadows on the canyon walls. Glowing barnacles, their forms alien and unsettling, clung to its surfaces, pulsing with the same sickly green light, the only sign of 'natural' life in this desolate, alien landscape. Ada's Admin-view strained, its algorithms struggling to process the structure's properties. It was an anomaly, a structure built on a different set of physical laws, a glitch in the very fabric of her creation.

"What...what in the Void...is that?" Erita whispered, her voice barely audible above the hum of their breathing talismans.

"It's...it's beyond anything I've ever seen," Korina added, her voice hushed with awe and fear. "The energy signature...it's...it's chaotic, yet...structured. It's...it's like nothing I've ever encountered."

Sera, her hand resting on the hilt of her blade, her gaze fixed on the Sunken Core, said nothing. Her silence spoke volumes. Even through their telepathic link, Ada could feel the weight of her fear, her apprehension, her raw, primal instinct to flee from this alien, unsettling presence.

Ada herself felt a strange mixture of fascination and dread. This structure, this anomaly, was a product of her creation, yet it was also something entirely alien, something that defied her understanding, her control. It was a glitch, a bug in the system, a manifestation of the creeping decay that threatened to unravel the very fabric of her world.

They approached the Sunken Core slowly, cautiously, their movements hampered by the pressure and the darkness. The structure loomed over them, its twisted, metallic surfaces shimmering with the sickly green light, the glowing barnacles pulsing like diseased hearts. A massive, half-submerged archway, encrusted with the same glowing barnacles, came into view. It appeared to be the only entrance, a gaping maw leading into the unknown depths of the Sunken Core. A low, resonant hum, the sound of dormant, ancient technology, emanated from the darkness within, a silent invitation, a siren's call, beckoning them into the labyrinth. Ada felt a knot of apprehension tighten in her stomach. This was it. The point of no return. They were about to enter the heart of the anomaly, the belly of the beast. And there was no turning back.

CHAPTER 26

THE SUNKEN LABYRINTH

The archway swallowed them whole. One moment they were in the phosphorescent gloom of the deep-sea canyon, the next they were inside, enveloped by an oppressive, unnatural silence. The Sunken Core. Erita felt a prickle of unease crawl up her spine. This place felt wrong, a violation of the natural order, a space where the familiar rules of reality seemed to bend and break.

The sickly green glow of the barnacles illuminated a chamber that defied description. Walls curved into impossible angles, floors sloped and shifted beneath their feet, and the air itself hummed with the low thrum of dormant technology. The metallic surfaces were unlike anything Erita had ever encountered, a strange alloy that shimmered with an oily, iridescent sheen. It felt cold, almost alien, to the touch.

Erita felt a surge of adrenaline. This was her element. Chaos. The unknown. Where others faltered, she thrived. “Sera, rear guard," she said, her voice crisp and efficient. "Korina, stay close to Ada. And for Void's sake, try not to touch anything."

Erita took the lead, her senses heightened, her every movement precise and deliberate. She moved through the labyrinthine corridors, her hands trailing along the strange, curved walls, her eyes scanning for any sign of danger. Her rogue skills, honed over years of navigating the treacherous alleyways of Port Dominus, were pushed to their limit in this alien environment.

The air hummed with a low, resonant thrum, the sound of ancient, dormant technology waiting to awaken. Erita could feel the energy pulsing beneath her feet, a network of unseen power conduits crisscrossing the structure. She moved carefully, avoiding the shimmering, almost invisible tripwires that crisscrossed the corridors, disarming them with practiced precision. She guided the others around ancient pressure plates, their surfaces barely visible beneath a thin layer of phosphorescent dust, still active after centuries of dormancy. It was a silent dance of evasion, a delicate ballet of survival in a hostile, alien landscape.

They moved deeper into the Sunken Core, the silence broken only by the hum of the dormant technology and the soft whirring of Korina's data-slate. The air grew thicker, heavier, the green glow of the barnacles casting long, distorted shadows that danced and shifted with their every movement. Erita felt a growing sense of unease. This place felt...watched. Hunted.

Suddenly, the silence shattered. A series of metallic clicks echoed through the chamber, followed by a low, guttural growl. From the ceiling, squat, angular security drones detached, their surfaces shimmering with the same oily, iridescent sheen as the walls, their glowing red eyes fixated on the intruders.

"Incoming!" Erita yelled, drawing her daggers.

The drones descended, their movements swift and precise, their metallic claws extended, ready to tear flesh from bone. Sera moved like a phantom, a crimson blur in the darkness. Her twin blades, coated in the arcane lubricant Ada had given her, glowed with a faint, phosphorescent light, shimmering like predatory eyes in the gloom. She moved with a speed and ferocity that defied the crushing pressure of the deep, her blades a whirlwind of steel that tore through the ancient metal of the drones with brutal efficiency. Sparks flew, metal shrieked, and the guttural growls of the drones turned into high-pitched whines as they fell to the floor, their circuits fried, their metallic bodies twitching and sparking in the darkness.

Erita, her daggers flashing, took down a drone that had managed to get past Sera, its claws tearing through her suit, a searing pain shooting up her arm. She ignored the pain, her focus absolute, her movements precise and deadly. She disemboweled the drone with a swift, upward thrust, its metallic body collapsing to the floor with a sickening thud.

Eri! Ada cried, her voice laced with concern.

I'm fine, Erita thought, projecting the words through their telepathic link, her voice tight. *Just a scratch. Keep moving.*

Ada's hand glowed with a faint, violet light as she healed Erita's wound, the torn fabric of her suit knitting itself back together, the searing pain subsiding. Erita felt a surge of gratitude for Ada's quick thinking, her healing touch. It was a small gesture, but it meant everything.

They pressed deeper into the Sunken Core, Sera continuing to carve a path through the remaining drones, her movements a relentless, brutal ballet of death. Korina, her data-slate humming, scanned the environment, providing real-time data on the drones' movements, their weaknesses, their energy signatures. Ada, her hand glowing with the faint violet light of her Admin powers, manipulated the water currents, creating swirling vortexes that disoriented the drones, making them easier targets for Sera's blades.

They were a well-oiled machine, a symphony of violence and precision, each member playing their part to perfection. And at the heart of it all was Ada, the Architect-Queen, her power, her love, her unwavering resolve, the glue that held them together, the engine that drove them forward. Erita felt a surge of pride, of loyalty, of fierce, unwavering devotion. They would face whatever challenges lay ahead, together. They would retrieve the data-core. They would win this war. They would build a better world. For Ada. For each other.

The chamber unfolded before Korina like a dream, vast and circular, the air thick with the hum of latent power. In the center, suspended within a crackling energy field, pulsed the data-core. It wasn't a simple cube or sphere, as she'd imagined, but a complex, multifaceted structure, its surfaces shimmering with a soft, cerulean light, like a miniature sun submerged in the depths of a digital ocean. The floor, a dizzying mosaic of hexagonal panels, each glowing with a shifting, complex symbol, added to the surreal beauty of the scene. It was breathtaking, terrifying, and utterly fascinating, all at once.

"A First Programmer's lock," she whispered, her voice barely audible above the hum of the core. *Obsidian,* nestled securely in her hand, pulsed with a faint warmth against her palm, its internal systems whirring as they processed the overwhelming influx of data. Her analysis confirmed her initial assessment: the lock wasn't a static mechanism, but a living algorithm, a logical puzzle that actively reconfigured itself in response to any attempt to solve it. It was a masterpiece of arcane engineering, a testament to the ingenuity of the Precursors, and a seemingly impenetrable barrier between them and their goal.

"What does that mean?" Sera asked, her voice tight with tension, her hand resting on the hilt of one of her blades.

It means it's a puzzle, Korina thought, projecting the words through their telepathic link, her mind racing. *A constantly shifting, self-modifying puzzle. Every solution we try will just cause it to change, presenting a new, unsolvable sequence.*

So, we're stuck? Erita asked, her voice laced with a hint of frustration.

Korina glanced at Erita, her heart sinking. Erita's usual confidence seemed shaken, a rare flicker of doubt in her normally unflappable demeanor. The sight was both unsettling and strangely reassuring. It was a reminder that they were all vulnerable, all facing the unknown together.

Not necessarily, Korina thought, her mind racing, searching for a solution. *There has to be a way. There's always a way.*

She and Erita worked together, their minds linked through the telepathic network Ada had created, sharing data, analyzing patterns, attempting to decipher the ever-shifting symbols on the hexagonal panels. Erita, with her rogue's intuition and her ability to see patterns where others saw only chaos, focused on the visual cues, the subtle shifts in the symbols' colors, their rotations, their pulsations. Korina, with her analytical mind and her deep understanding of arcane systems, delved into the underlying code, attempting to decipher the algorithm that governed the lock's behavior.

They tried every logical approach, every thaumaturgical query, every code command they could think of. They tried brute force, attempting to overload the energy field with raw arcane power. They tried finesse, attempting to subtly manipulate the symbols, coaxing them into the correct sequence. They tried everything.

Nothing worked.

Every solution they attempted, every near-miss, every flicker of hope, was immediately extinguished as the puzzle shifted, the symbols rearranging themselves, the energy field crackling with renewed intensity, mocking their efforts. It was like trying to catch smoke, to grasp at shadows. The closer they got, the further away the solution seemed to slip.

Frustration gnawed at Korina, a familiar ache in her chest. She could feel the weight of their failure settling on her shoulders, the pressure of their dwindling time, the knowledge that the fate of Kremøtoa rested on their ability to solve this impossible puzzle.

"Void's name," Erita muttered, her voice low and tight, a tremor of frustration in her usually steady hands. "This is getting us nowhere."

I know, Korina thought, her voice barely a whisper in the telepathic link. *But we can't give up. We have to keep trying.*

She glanced at Ada, her heart aching. Ada stood silently by the edge of the chamber, her expression unreadable, her eyes fixed on the pulsing data-core. A faint, violet glow emanated from her hands, the telltale sign of her Admin powers, but she made no move to intervene. Korina knew why. This was Nividia's test. A test of their skills, their ingenuity, their resilience. A test they were failing.

Ada, Korina thought, her voice desperate. *Can you...can you do something? Anything?*

Ada watched their attempts, a strange mixture of fascination and frustration churning within her. Erita and Korina, two of the most brilliant minds she knew, were like moths fluttering around a flickering flame, drawn to the puzzle's intricate beauty, yet unable to grasp its true nature. They were playing the game, following the rules, trying to solve the unsolvable. But Ada, the Architect, saw something different. She didn't see a puzzle; she saw a broken system.

A dawning realization bloomed in her mind, a quiet understanding that transcended the logic of the game, the limitations of its design. This wasn't a challenge to be overcome; it was a flaw to be corrected. It wasn't a test of their worthiness; it was a glitch in the system, a remnant of the creeping decay that threatened to consume her world.

Activating her Admin-view, she saw beyond the shimmering surfaces, beyond the shifting symbols, into the very heart of the puzzle's underlying code. Lines of arcane script scrolled across her vision, a complex tapestry of commands and parameters that governed the lock's behavior. It was a harmonic resonance puzzle, designed to respond to a specific thaumaturgical frequency, a symphony of arcane energy that would unlock the data-core. Elegant, ingenious, and utterly broken.

Her eyes scanned the code, searching for the flaw, the point of failure. It didn't take long to find it. Nestled deep within the algorithm, a single line of code pulsed with a sickly, crimson glow, a digital cancer eating away at the puzzle's logic. The target frequency, the key to the lock, was corrupted, a cascade of decaying code that made it impossible to match, impossible to solve—like a shredded tumbler.

This is a flaw that could only be seen, and fixed, by someone with access to the world's source code—in its current state, even with a proper key, ***no one*** *could've opened it.* The realization hit Ada with the force of a physical blow. This wasn't a test of their abilities; it was a cruel joke, a rigged game designed to ensure their failure. Nividia hadn't sent them here to succeed; she had sent them here to break, to prove their limitations, to reinforce her own power.

A surge of anger, cold and sharp, coursed through Ada. This wasn't the world she had intended to create, a world of impossible challenges and manufactured failures. This wasn't the Kremøtoa she envisioned: a world of growth, of learning, of shared knowledge and mutual respect.

But anger wasn't the solution. The solution, as always, lay in the code—there's always another side to the story anyways.

Taking a deep breath, Ada reached out with her power, her mind bypassing the world's interface, her will interfacing directly with the world's source code. She didn't play the game; she rewrote the rules.

[REPAIR: Lock_Sequence_7B_24xA]

The command echoed in the silence of her mind, a silent decree that resonated through the very fabric of reality. A pulse of violet light, bright and intense, flared from her hands, bathing the chamber in an ethereal glow. The chaotic shifting of the floor panels ceased, the symbols freezing in place, their flickering light solidifying into a steady, unwavering luminescence. The humming of the data-core deepened, its chaotic energy stabilizing into a smooth, rhythmic pulse.

The puzzle resolved, not into a complex sequence of arcane symbols, but into a single, perfect, and now solvable pattern. A simple geometric design, elegant in its simplicity, a testament to the underlying order of the world, the beauty of functional code.

"Rina," Ada said softly, turning to Korina, a gentle smile gracing her lips. "Come here."

Korina approached, her eyes wide with a mixture of awe and confusion. Ada took her hand, her fingers intertwining with Korina's, their touch a silent reassurance, a shared understanding that transcended words.

"Step here," Ada instructed, guiding Korina's foot onto the first panel in the sequence. "Then here. And here."

With each step, a soft hum resonated through the chamber, the hexagonal panels glowing brighter, their light intensifying, their energy coalescing. It was a dance, a delicate interplay of movement and light, a symphony of arcane energy orchestrated by the Architect herself.

As Korina placed her foot on the final panel, the energy field around the data-core shimmered, its vibrant glow fading, its intensity diminishing, until it dissipated completely with a soft, almost melancholic hum.

The data-core, now unprotected, pulsed with a gentle, cerulean light, its energy contained, its power waiting to be harnessed. The test was over. Not because they had solved the puzzle, but because Ada had rewritten it. Not because they had proven their worthiness, but because Ada had transcended the game itself.

They had won, not by playing Nividia's game, but by refusing to play it at all.

Korina's violet eyes, usually alight with intellectual curiosity, now shimmered with a different kind of light – a blend of awe, gratitude, and a touch of something akin to worship. She had witnessed Ada perform feats that defied the very laws of Kremøtoa, but this was different. This wasn't just manipulating the world; this was *rewriting* it. This was the power of a god, the power of creation itself. A wave of emotion washed over Korina, a mix of relief at their success and a profound sense of intimacy at having been included in this act of divine intervention. She had been chosen, not just as a witness, but as a participant in a miracle. "Ada..." she whispered, her voice thick with emotion. "You...you did it." Before Ada could respond, Korina threw her arms around her, burying her face in Ada's shoulder. "Thank you," she murmured, her voice muffled by Ada's gown. "Thank you for...for everything."

A warm smile touched Ada's lips as she returned Korina's embrace, her hand gently stroking Korina's hair. It was a simple gesture, yet it spoke volumes – a silent acknowledgment of their shared experience, their unique bond. "We did it, Rina," Ada corrected softly, her voice filled with a warmth that belied the power she wielded. "We did it together."

Before Korina could reply, Sera and Erita joined the embrace, their arms wrapping around Ada and Korina, creating a tangle of limbs and affection. Sera's hug was firm, almost possessive, a silent expression of relief and gratitude. Erita's touch was lighter, more hesitant, yet her presence spoke volumes, a quiet acknowledgment of their shared victory. For a brief moment, they stood there, four women bound together by a shared purpose, a shared experience, and a growing affection that transcended the boundaries of friendship and comradeship. The air crackled with unspoken emotions, the silence filled with a quiet understanding that needed no words.

"Argent's light, Ada," Erita breathed, her voice laced with a mixture of awe and amusement. "You really are something else."

Ada chuckled, a genuine, unrestrained sound that echoed through the chamber. "Just a little debugging," she quipped, her eyes twinkling with mischief. "Nothing to write home about."

With a final, shared smile, they broke apart, their eyes turning towards the data-core, now pulsing with a gentle, cerulean light on its pedestal. It was a beautiful thing, a testament to their ingenuity, their resilience, and their newfound unity.

Ada stepped forward, reaching out her hand towards the crystal. As her fingers brushed against its surface, a wave of energy surged through her, a jolt of raw power that made her gasp. The crystal hummed in response, its light intensifying, its ethereal aura enveloping Ada in a soft, cerulean glow. With a gentle tug, she lifted the data-core from its pedestal, its weight surprisingly light, its energy thrumming against her palm like a living heartbeat.

"Let's go," Ada said, turning to her companions, her eyes alight with a mixture of excitement and anticipation. "Nividia's waiting."

As they turned to leave, Ada's glyph, the emerald mark on her hand that bound her to Nividia's bargain, began to pulse with a rhythmic glow. At first, it was a slow, gentle throb, a subtle reminder of their agreement. But then, the pulsing intensified, the emerald light growing brighter, faster, more insistent. A strange energy crackled in the air, a sense of impending transition that made Ada's breath catch in her throat.

"What's happening?" Korina asked, her voice laced with concern as she noticed the change in Ada's expression.

"I...I don't know," Ada stammered, her eyes fixed on the pulsing glyph, her mind racing to understand what was happening. The glyph now pulsed rapidly, its light growing blindingly bright, the air around them shimmering with an unstable energy. Ada had a flash of intuition, a premonition of a sudden, imminent shift in reality. Panic flared in her chest, a primal instinct to protect those she cared about.

"Grab on, *NOW*!" she yelled, reaching out and grabbing Korina's arm with her left hand, Sera's with her right. Sera, instinctively reacting to Ada's urgency and the escalating energy around them, pulled a startled Erita into their circle, creating a tight knot of four women braced for the unknown.

At that precise moment, the glyph on Ada's hand erupted in a blinding flash of emerald light, a vortex of swirling energy engulfing them, tearing them away from the Sunken Core, away from the crushing depths of the ocean, away from everything they knew.

The world dissolved into a kaleidoscope of colors and sensations, a chaotic blur of light and sound that made their stomachs churn and their heads spin. They were falling, flying, tumbling through a void where time and space had no meaning, their bodies pressed together, their hands gripping each other with a desperate intensity. The only constant in the chaos was their touch, their connection, the shared knowledge that they were in this together, whatever it was, wherever they were going.

Then, just as suddenly as it had begun, the chaos ceased. The light faded, the swirling vortex dissipated, and they found themselves standing, disoriented but unharmed, in a place that was very familiar.

The delicate porcelain cup warmed Nividia's fingers as she brought it to her lips, inhaling the fragrant steam rising from the pale amethyst liquid. Sunstone tea, a Rhedeon exclusive, a blend of rare mountain herbs and crystallized sunlight, was one of her few indulgences. The subtle sweetness, followed by a tingling warmth that spread through her veins, was the perfect counterpoint to the crisp morning air filtering through the open balcony doors of her private lounge. She had dismissed her sapphire constructs to the adjacent laboratory, a rare concession to a desire for solitude. The Ouroboros Gala had been...tedious, a predictable parade of posturing and avarice. The Precursor crystal, while mildly interesting, was hardly worth the exorbitant price she'd paid. But then, there was *her*.

The woman calling herself Ada.

Nividia's thoughts lingered on the warrior, Sera, clad in crimson. A captivating specimen, in a raw, almost elemental way. The woman moved with a disciplined grace that spoke of years of training, a honed instrument of war, yet Nividia sensed a restless energy beneath the surface, a barely contained power straining against the rigid confines of Imperial dogma. Intriguing. Then there was Erita, the spymaster. A creature of shadows and whispers, her eyes sharp and calculating, her words laced with a cynicism that hinted at a deep-seated weariness, a disillusionment born of too much knowledge. But beneath that carefully cultivated facade, Nividia detected a flicker of vulnerability, a carefully guarded wound that made her all the more fascinating. A study in controlled chaos, indeed. And the scholar, Korina—a name that now surfaced in Nividia's memory—a fragile, almost ethereal being, her mind a tempest of data streams and anxieties, her eyes wide with a mixture of awe and apprehension. A delicate bloom, easily bruised, yet possessing a core of resilience, a hidden strength that resonated with an untapped potential Nividia found strangely compelling.

But Ada...Ada transcended mere intrigue. She was an enigma within an ouroboros of enigmas—shrouded in mystery, a puzzle box of infinite layers, each more intricate than the last, never opening or yielding. Her power, unlike any thaumaturgical signature Nividia had ever encountered, resonated with a dissonant harmony, a chaotic ballet of raw arcane force and meticulous control. It was a paradox: untamed yet disciplined, unclassifiable by any known thaumaturgical system, yet undeniably, overwhelmingly potent. It was the ultimate cryptographic challenge, a code so complex, so elegant in its execution, that it defied all attempts at decryption. It was a siren song to Nividia's intellect, a tantalizing glimpse into the unknown.

This Ada, Nividia mused, sipping her sunstone tea, was a prize worth pursuing, a challenge worth undertaking. The Sunken Core, lost in the abyssal trenches of the Whispering Sea, guarded by ancient, arcane wards and teeming with leviathan-class malware, would be the perfect crucible, a trial by fire to separate the pretenders from the truly powerful. If Ada and her companions could retrieve the data-core, if they could navigate the treacherous currents of the Confederacy and the Empire's ever-watchful gaze, then they would prove themselves worthy of Nividia's attention, worthy of her consideration, worthy of being pawns—or perhaps, *players*—in *her* grand game. Though, Nividia admitted to herself with a flicker of amusement, she always set the bar impossibly high. Her expectations were, by design, *unattainable*. It was part of the thrill, the exquisite pleasure of watching mortals strive, inevitably fail, and occasionally, just occasionally, surprise her with their resilience.

A sudden flash of emerald light erupted in the lounge, startling Nividia. The porcelain cup slipped from her grasp, shattering on the polished obsidian floor, the fragrant sunstone tea splattering across the tiles like spilled blood. Nividia, unfazed by the mess, turned towards the source of the light, her violet eyes narrowing in anticipation. The emerald light coalesced into a shimmering portal, its edges crackling with raw arcane energy. Four figures stepped out of the portal, their forms momentarily distorted by the residual magical ripples.

She had not anticipated their return so soon. Not this soon. *Not at all.* The glyph she had given them, keyed to the unique energy signature of the Precursor data-core, was meant to activate only upon its retrieval. The Sunken Core, a labyrinth of impossible angles and ancient, arcane wards, was a trial designed to test the limits of their abilities, a filter to weed out the weak. It was a challenge she had fully expected them to fail—*She had failed it herself.* Yet, here they were, materializing in the center of her private lounge in a flash of emerald light, their clothes dripping seawater onto her meticulously polished floor, their faces pale with exhaustion, but their eyes burning with a defiant, triumphant light.

Ada, her dark hair plastered to her forehead, stood at the center of the group, her slender frame radiating an almost palpable aura of power. Even drenched and weary, she possessed a regal presence that commanded attention. Sera, her crimson tunic clinging to her powerful form, stood beside Ada, her hand resting protectively on the hilt of her sword, her gaze sharp and alert, scanning the room for potential threats. Korina, her violet gown now a sodden mess, trembled slightly, her eyes wide with a mixture of awe and apprehension as she clutched her data-slate, Obsidian, to her chest like a shield. And Erita, the spymaster, her golden eyes narrowed, her lips pressed into a thin line, stood slightly apart from the others, her hand hovering near the hidden daggers sheathed beneath her cloak. She exuded an air of controlled chaos, a coiled spring ready to unleash its deadly potential at a moment's notice.

Nividia took a slow, measured breath, her mind racing, recalibrating her assessment of these unexpected variables. Everything she had thought of them—any preconceived notions of their limitations, their predictable responses, their inevitable *failure*—evaporated like mist in the face of this undeniable, improbable *success*. They had not only survived the Sunken Core, they had conquered it. They had retrieved the data-core. They had returned. And they had done it faster than she, the Render-Witch, the architect of Rhedeon's naval supremacy, had deemed possible. A slow smile spread across Nividia's face, a genuine expression of amusement and intrigue replacing her usual mask of detached indifference. This, she realized, was going to be far more interesting than she had initially imagined. This game, it seemed, had just taken an unexpected, exhilarating turn.

"Well..." Nividia purred, her voice laced with a newfound respect. "Look what the tide dragged in." She gestured towards the dripping figures with a flick of her wrist. "I must confess, you have surprised me." She ran her gaze over each of them, lingering on Ada, before continuing. "You have exceeded my expectations. Perhaps you're not as...*insignificant* as I had initially assumed." She paused, letting her words hang in the air, watching their reactions. "Tell me," she said, her voice now laced with a predatory curiosity, "what treasures did you find in the abyss?"

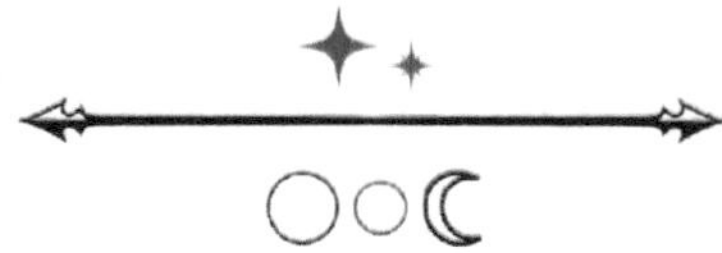

Ada, her damp gown clinging to her, met Nividia's gaze. She crossed the room, the subtle *click* of her heels against the polished obsidian floor the only sound in the otherwise silent laboratory. She stopped before Nividia, extending her hand. Nestled in her palm, the data-core pulsed with a soft, ethereal light, its intricate crystalline structure refracting the ambient arcane energy into a mesmerizing display of shifting colors.

Nividia's violet eyes, usually sparkling with mischievous amusement, were now wide with an almost childlike wonder. She stared at the pulsating crystal, her usual mask of cynical indifference completely gone, replaced by an expression of pure, unadulterated shock. "That's...*impossible*," she whispered, her voice barely audible above the low hum of the laboratory's arcane machinery.

Ada, sensing the shift in power, leaned in close, her voice a low, conspiratorial murmur against Nividia's ear. "I bet even *you* couldn't have gotten it yourself."

Nividia's head snapped up, her eyes meeting Ada's. A flicker of something akin to fear crossed her face, quickly masked by a forced composure. She opened her mouth to speak, then hesitated, as if unsure how to articulate the thoughts swirling within her mind. Finally, she let out a long, slow breath, the tension visibly draining from her shoulders.

"You are correct," she admitted, her voice barely above a whisper. "I have tried, for years—years, to retrieve that core. The Sunken Core was a personal challenge. It is said to house knowledge that could reshape reality itself. But the lock...the lock was impossible. Unsolvable. Even *I*, with all my power, could not break it." She looked at Ada, her eyes now filled with a profound, almost fearful respect.

Ada allowed herself a small, almost imperceptible smile. She knew exactly why Nividia had failed. The lock wasn't just complex; it was *broken*. A corrupted piece of Precursor code, a relic of a bygone era, had rendered the lock's intricate thaumaturgical tumblers unusable. It wasn't a puzzle to be solved, but a system to be *repaired*.

"The tumblers were broken," Ada murmured, her voice low and even. She kept her explanation deliberately vague, careful not to reveal too much about her own unique abilities, her Administrator access to the world's underlying code. She needed Nividia as an ally, but she wasn't ready to reveal the full extent of her power. Not yet.

Nividia stared at Ada, her violet eyes now narrowed in thought. The transactional broker, the Render-Witch who saw the world as a game to be played, was gone. In her place stood someone with a profound, almost fearful respect. She looked at Ada not as a client, but as a force of nature, an anomaly who had achieved something she, with all her power and knowledge, could not.

"You...you *fixed* it?" she asked, her voice barely a whisper.

Ada merely met Nividia's gaze, a silent confirmation that spoke volumes.

A long silence stretched between them, broken only by the soft hum of the laboratory's arcane machinery. Finally, Nividia let out a long, slow breath, a subtle shift in her demeanor signaling a profound internal change. The playful arrogance, the detached amusement, the cynical indifference—all gone. In their place was a new, solemn gravity, a newfound respect tinged with a hint of awe.

"You have exceeded all of my *wildest, unattainable* expectations," Nividia stated, her voice imbued with a weight that resonated through the room. "The deal is honored. You will have your fleet. The finest warships this world has ever seen. My shipwrights will work day and night to fulfill your request." She paused, her eyes fixed on Ada's. "Consider this a...*token* of my respect."

Ada nodded, a small, satisfied smile playing on her lips. The revolution had just secured its navy.

CHAPTER 27

THE HERO'S REWARD

//EXPLICIT CONTENT WARNING*//

**Please be aware this scene involves three female characters involved in explicit consensual intimacy—reader discretion advised.*

The Wandering Star's dimly lit common room offered a stark contrast to the vibrant chaos of Nividia's laboratory. The air, thick with the scent of stale ale and pipe smoke, hung heavy and still, a palpable difference from the charged, arcane hum that permeated the Render-Witch's sanctum. Ada, Sera, Korina, and Erita returned to their rooms, the adrenaline from their success still thrumming beneath their skin. Exhaustion gnawed at the edges of their exhilaration, a physical reminder of the perilous journey they had just undertaken.

Janna sat sprawled in one of the common room's worn armchairs, a tankard of ale perched precariously on the armrest. She hummed a low, tuneless melody, her eyes closed, the picture of relaxed contentment. A faint scent of woodsmoke clung to her clothes, a comforting aroma that grounded the room in a sense of familiar normalcy.

"Report for you Janna," Erita stated, her voice sharp and alert despite the evident weariness etched on her face. She leaned against the doorframe, arms crossed, her gaze sweeping across the room, assessing the situation with her usual predatory intensity.

Success, Ada projected, her mental voice tinged with a weary satisfaction. *Nividia agreed to provide the fleet.*

Janna's eyes snapped open, a slow grin spreading across her face. "Argent's Light, you actually pulled it off," she rumbled, her voice a low, gravelly chuckle. "The Render-Witch herself. Color me impressed." She took a long swig of ale, the tankard clinking against her teeth.

Sera, still slightly pale from the kraken's venom, leaned against Ada, her hand resting lightly on Ada's arm. A faint tremor ran through her, a lingering aftereffect of the toxin, but her eyes shone with a fierce pride. "We make a good team," she murmured, her voice low and husky.

Korina, her violet eyes sparkling with intellectual excitement, bounced on the balls of her feet, her data-slate clutched tightly in her hand. "The implications of this alliance are *staggering*," she exclaimed, her voice a rapid-fire burst of enthusiasm. "With Nividia's fleet, we can..."

"Hold your horses, Kori," Erita interrupted, her voice laced with a dry amusement. "Nividia's favor is a currency. And it expires." A predatory glint sparked in her golden eyes. "I'm going out. *Immediately*. There are a few...*supplies*...we can only get here in Rhedeon. Things Thorne would pay a king's ransom for. Things that will make our little revolution run a lot smoother." She looked at Janna, a silent invitation hanging in the air.

Janna grunted, her eyes sliding closed again. "Void, no. I need a stiff drink and about ten hours of sleep before I can even think about another scheme." She pushed herself out of the armchair, the tankard still clutched in her hand. "You kids have fun," she rumbled, her voice a low, sleepy growl. "I'll be in my room." She lumbered off down the hallway, disappearing behind a heavy wooden door.

Erita smirked, her eyes glittering with mischief. "Suit yourself. More for me." She turned to Ada, her expression softening slightly. "Stay here. Rest. Korina, keep an eye on her. I will return before long."

With a wink and a flick of her wrist, Erita vanished into the night, leaving Ada, Sera, and Korina alone in the dimly lit common room. The scent of woodsmoke and stale ale lingered in the air, a subtle reminder of Janna's presence and Erita's abrupt departure. A heavy silence settled over the room, broken only by the soft crackle of the dying fire in the hearth.

In the quiet of their shared quarters at the Wandering Star, the flickering candlelight cast long, dancing shadows across the worn wooden walls. The air, still thick with the scent of salt and brine from their recent underwater excursion, held a new, unspoken tension. It wasn't the familiar tension of danger or uncertainty, but something deeper, more profound. It was the tension of awe.

Sera sat on the edge of the bed, her crimson tunic rumpled and damp, her gaze fixed on Ada. The usual playful glint in her emerald eyes had been replaced by something akin to reverence. The sheer impossibility of what Ada had accomplished in the Sunken Core—solving a puzzle that had stumped even the mighty Nividia for years—had left her speechless. It wasn't just the feat itself, but the casual, almost effortless way Ada had achieved it. As if rewriting the very fabric of reality was as simple as adjusting a line of code.

"You need to rest, Ada." Sera's voice was a low, husky murmur, the words catching in her throat. "That...that took something out of you." She moved to the part of the bed Ada was sitting at, her hand reaching out to gently massage Ada's tense shoulders. Her touch was firm yet worshipful, a warrior's tribute to a queen's power.

Ada leaned into Sera's touch, a soft sigh escaping her lips. The exhaustion was a heavy cloak, settling deep in her bones. But beneath the fatigue, a warm ember of satisfaction glowed. She had proven herself, not just to Nividia, but to her companions, to her *family*. And in that moment, surrounded by the women she loved, she felt a sense of belonging she had never known before.

Korina's fingers, usually dancing across the cool surface of Obsidian, now traced the delicate curve of Ada's neck. Her touch was hesitant at first, a scholar's careful exploration of a fascinating new artifact. But as she felt the warmth of Ada's skin beneath her fingertips, a different kind of curiosity took hold. It wasn't the detached analysis of a scientist, but the raw, unfiltered yearning of a lover.

"Your mind..." she breathed, her voice barely a whisper in the dimly lit room. "The way you processed that lock...it was the most beautiful thing I've ever witnessed." Her praise wasn't for the raw power Ada wielded, but for the sheer intellectual elegance of it. The way Ada had dissected the Precursor's code, identifying the corruption and rewriting the key with such precision and grace, it was a symphony of logic, a masterpiece of pure intellect. It was, in Korina's eyes, the highest form of art.

Her fingers continued their exploration, tracing faint, imaginary lines of circuitry on Ada's skin. She imagined the flow of data, the intricate pathways of energy that pulsed beneath the surface, the complex algorithms that governed every thought, every action. It was a map of Ada's very being, a testament to her brilliance, her power, and her undeniable beauty.

As her fingers drifted lower, towards Ada's underarm, she paused. A small tuft of dark hair, a subtle yet undeniable sign of Ada's evolving physicality within Kremøtoa, caught her attention. A blush crept up her neck, a wave of heat washing over her. The scent, musky and intoxicating, filled her senses, triggering a surge of desire she hadn't anticipated. It was a scent that spoke of Ada's humanity, of her vulnerability, of her undeniable *realness*.

Korina's breath hitched, her fingers hovering just above the soft down. This Ada, this flesh-and-blood woman with her growing body hair and the intoxicating scent of her arousal, was so different from the ethereal, god-like being who had rewritten the Sunken Core's code. And yet, it was that very duality, that blend of power and vulnerability, that drew Korina in, that ignited a fire within her that burned hotter than any intellectual curiosity.

She leaned closer, her lips brushing against Ada's ear. "Ada," she whispered, her voice thick with a newfound boldness. "I...I want to taste you."

Ada shivered at Korina's words, a ripple of pleasure coursing through her. She turned her head, her violet eyes locking with Korina's. The intensity of Korina's gaze, usually filled with intellectual curiosity, now burned with a raw, unbridled passion. It was a look that stripped away all pretense, all barriers, leaving only the pure, undeniable truth of their desire.

"Rina..." Ada murmured, her voice a low, husky purr. She reached up, her fingers tangling in Korina's long, violet braids. The contact sent a jolt of electricity through her, a spark that ignited a fire within her that mirrored Korina's own. She pulled Korina closer, their lips meeting in a kiss that was both tender and demanding, a fusion of intellect and instinct, a perfect blend of their two souls.

The kiss deepened, their bodies pressing together, the warmth of their skin a welcome contrast to the cool night air. Ada's hands explored the curves of Korina's body, her touch lingering on the soft swell of her breasts, the gentle curve of her hips. Korina responded in kind, her fingers tracing the lines of Ada's back, the muscles tense beneath her touch. The world outside their shared quarters faded away, replaced by the intoxicating rhythm of their shared breath, the urgent beat of their hearts, the undeniable truth of their love.

A low moan escaped Ada's lips, the sound swallowed by the hungry press of Korina's mouth against hers. The world tilted, the edges blurring, the familiar boundaries of reality dissolving into a kaleidoscope of sensation. The scent of Korina's arousal, a heady mix of musk and something uniquely *her*, filled Ada's senses, intoxicating her, pulling her deeper into the vortex of their shared desire. It was a scent that spoke of trust, of surrender, of a connection that transcended the physical.

Sera's hands, strong and sure, moved across Ada's back, her touch a brand of ownership, a claim staked upon the very essence of Ada's being. Her fingers kneaded the tense muscles, easing the knots of exhaustion, replacing them with a warm, liquid fire that spread through Ada's core. Each touch was a prayer, a whispered offering of gratitude for the strength and leadership that had brought them this far. Sera worshipped not just the woman, but the warrior, the queen who had defied the Empire, rewritten the rules of reality, and secured their future.

Korina's fingers, now tracing the delicate curve of Ada's collarbone, paused, her touch lingering on the small, almost imperceptible scar that marked a childhood mishap. It was a flaw, a tiny imperfection in the otherwise perfect system of Ada's body. And yet, it was that very flaw, that subtle reminder of Ada's humanity, that made her all the more beautiful, all the more *real* in Korina's eyes.

She leaned closer, her lips brushing against the scar, her breath warm against Ada's skin. "You are..." she whispered, her voice thick with awe, "...a miracle." Her words weren't hyperbole, but a simple statement of fact. Ada, with her reality-bending powers and her quiet, unwavering strength, was a force of nature, a phenomenon that defied all logic, all explanation. She was, in Korina's eyes, the embodiment of perfection.

Korina's lips continued their exploration, tracing a path down Ada's chest, her tongue darting out to taste the salty sweat that beaded on Ada's skin. The taste, both familiar and exotic, ignited a new wave of heat within Korina, a hunger that transcended the physical. She wanted to consume Ada, to absorb her essence, to become one with the very power that pulsed beneath the surface.

Sera's mouth found Ada's neck, her kisses hot and demanding, her teeth nipping gently at the sensitive skin. The contrast between Korina's gentle exploration and Sera's passionate assault sent shivers of pleasure radiating through Ada's body, each touch, each kiss, a testament to their love, their adoration, their complete and utter devotion. It was a symphony of sensation, a chorus of worship that resonated deep within Ada's soul.

She arched her back, her fingers digging into the soft sheets beneath her, her body thrumming with a building tension that threatened to shatter her. The world narrowed, the only reality the intoxicating scent of their arousal, the feel of their hands on her skin, the taste of their mouths on hers. She was no longer the Architect-Queen, the detached observer, the manipulator of code. She was simply Ada, a woman loved, adored, worshipped.

A cry tore from Ada's throat, her body convulsing in the throes of a profound climax. It was a release that transcended the physical, a shattering of barriers, a merging of souls. She felt their pleasure echoing her own, their love washing over her, their adoration filling her with a sense of validation she had never known before. It wasn't just the intensity of the orgasm, but the emotional depth of it, the profound sense of connection, of belonging, of being truly *seen* and cherished for the very power that made her different.

As the waves of pleasure subsided, Ada collapsed back against the pillows, her body limp, her mind empty. The afterglow settled over them like a warm blanket, the air thick with the scent of their shared pleasure. Ada lay nestled between Korina and Sera, their bodies a tangled mess of limbs and hair, their breaths mingling in the quiet stillness of the room. The candle had long since burned out, leaving them shrouded in the soft, velvety darkness.

Korina's fingers traced lazy patterns on Ada's arm, the touch light and feather-like. *It was...perfect,* she thought, the word echoing in the silent symphony of their shared minds. The intimacy they had shared, the raw, unfiltered expression of their love, had forged a bond between them that was stronger than any code, any magic.

Sera's arm tightened around Ada's waist, pulling her closer. A low rumble of contentment vibrated in her chest, a warrior's silent prayer of gratitude. The fierce protectiveness she felt for Ada, for Korina, for *both* of them, had blossomed into something deeper, something more profound. It was a love that transcended the physical, a bond that had been forged in the crucible of shared danger, shared purpose, and shared pleasure.

Ada's heart swelled with a quiet joy, a sense of belonging she had never known before. The anxieties that had plagued her, the doubts about her place in this world, had melted away, replaced by a quiet confidence, a deep-seated certainty. She was not just the Architect, the manipulator of code, the reluctant queen. She was also Ada, a woman loved, adored, *worshipped*. And in their love, she had found not just validation, but her true purpose. She was the center of their world, the anchor of their polycule. And she would protect them, cherish them, lead them to a future where their love could bloom freely, without fear, without shame.

The three women lay entwined, their bodies a testament to their shared intimacy, their minds a symphony of silent understanding. The room, once filled with the echoes of their passion, now held only the soft rhythm of their breaths, the steady beat of their hearts, the quiet hum of their shared love. It was a moment of perfect peace, a sanctuary of shared intimacy, a testament to the power of their bond.

CHAPTER 28

THE FORGING OF A FLEET

The air crackled with raw thaumaturgical energy, a tangible hum that vibrated against Ada's skin. Below, the shipyards of the Kraken's Maw guild sprawled out like a chaotic, bioluminescent tapestry woven from fire, arcane light, and the clang of enchanted hammers on resonating steel. It was a symphony of creation, a ballet of organized chaos that both fascinated and slightly terrified her.

A week had passed since their harrowing descent into the Sunken Core. A week since Nividia, awestruck by Ada's ability to repair the Precursor lock, had honored their agreement. Now, the fruits of that perilous victory were taking shape before her eyes. Three skeletal hulls, each larger than any ship Ada had ever seen, loomed over the shipyard floor, their timbers glowing with the faint, ethereal light of Nividia's initial renderings. They were the nascent forms of their future fleet, the vanguard of their Crimson Revolution.

Beside Ada, Nividia gestured towards the bustling activity

below. Gone was the detached amusement, the playful arrogance. In its place was the focused intensity of a master craftsman, a seasoned commander surveying her domain. "The initial renderings are complete," Nividia explained, her voice carrying over the din of the shipyard. "The core enchantments are now woven into the very fabric of the ships. These vessels will be faster, more resilient, capable of feats that would make an Imperial frigate look like a child's toy."

Ada leaned forward, her gaze fixed on the ghostly outlines of the ships. The scale of the project was staggering. Each vessel was a marvel of arcane engineering, a testament to Nividia's unparalleled skill. "How long until they're fully operational?"

Nividia's lips curled into a knowing smile. "Patience, Architect-Queen. These are not mere toys to be thrown together hastily. Each ship is a work of art, a testament to the fusion of magic and ingenuity. Give my shipwrights time, and I will deliver you a fleet capable of shattering the Empire's dominion over the waves."

It's staggering, Korina's voice echoed in Ada's mind, a blend of awe and intellectual excitement. *The energy matrix alone is more complex than anything I've ever encountered. The way she integrates the arcane renderings with the physical structure...it's simply brilliant.*

I can feel the power humming through the very air, Sera added, her mental tone one of grudging respect. *These ships...they're unlike anything I've ever seen. Even the Aegis flagships pale in comparison.*

Remind me never to truly piss her off, Erita chimed in, a dry amusement lacing her mental tone. *I'd hate to be on the receiving end of one of these behemoths.*

Ada suppressed a smile. Their telepathic link, once a source of overwhelming noise, had become a seamless extension of their communication, a private channel for sharing their thoughts, their fears, their hopes. It was a constant reminder of the bond they shared, the trust they had forged.

"These ships...they will be our shield, our sword, our sanctuary," Ada murmured, her gaze sweeping across the bustling shipyard. "They will carry us to a new dawn, a new era for Kremøtoa."

Nividia chuckled, a low, throaty sound that resonated with power. "A lofty ambition, Architect-Queen. But I believe you are capable of achieving it—perhaps the *only* one who can. With these ships, and with the strength of your...*unique* abilities, you may yet reshape this world in your image."

A surge of warmth coursed through Ada. It wasn't just the thaumaturgical energy of the shipyards, but the warmth of their shared purpose, the strength of their bond. She looked at Sera, Korina, Erita, and Janna, their faces illuminated by the arcane glow of the nascent fleet. They were her companions, her lovers, her generals. They were the heart of her revolution, the soul of her new world.

"We will do it together," Ada said, her voice ringing with conviction. "We will build a better Kremøtoa, a world where justice, knowledge, and love reign supreme."

A predatory gleam flickered in Nividia's violet eyes. "I have no interest in your utopian ideals, Architect-Queen. But I do enjoy a good challenge. And reshaping this world...that certainly sounds like a challenge worth undertaking."

Ada met Nividia's gaze, a silent understanding passing between them. It wasn't an alliance of shared ideals, but a partnership of mutual ambition, a pact forged in the crucible of power and the promise of chaos. And in that moment, Ada knew that the tide of change had truly begun to turn.

How long until they're seaworthy? Janna's gruff voice echoed in Ada's mind. *We can't afford to wait around here twiddling our thumbs while Thorne consolidates his power.*

Nividia turned to Janna, a predatory amusement in her eyes. "Impatient, are we? Very well. The initial renderings are complete, but the true magic lies in the integration of the arcane matrix with the physical structure. My shipwrights are the finest in Kremøtoa, but even they require time to weave such intricate enchantments. Give them two weeks. In fourteen days, I will deliver you a fleet that will make the Korsair Confederacy tremble."

That evening, the common room of "The Wandering Star" transformed into a makeshift war room. The air crackled with nervous energy as Ada, Sera, Korina, Erita, and Janna gathered around a rough-hewn table, the flickering candlelight casting long, dancing shadows on their faces. The remnants of a half-eaten meal lay scattered across the table, a stark reminder of the urgency of their situation.

"Two weeks," Erita said, her voice low and clipped. She tapped a finger on a crude map of Kremøtoa etched into the table's surface. "That's how long Nividia needs to finish the fleet. Two weeks we can't afford to be away from Port Dominus."

A heavy silence settled over the room. The weight of their responsibility pressed down on them, a tangible force in the dimly lit room. The fate of their revolution, the future of Kremøtoa, rested on their shoulders.

"A return sea voyage is out of the question," Erita continued, her gaze sweeping across their faces. "Even with Nividia's enhanced ships, it would take months to sail around the Korsair Cape and back to Port Dominus. Thorne will have consolidated his power by then. Our allies will be scattered, our resources depleted. We'll be walking into a slaughterhouse."

Sera leaned back, her brow furrowed in thought. "What about the blink-hopping method? We could retrace our steps, using the same landmarks as waypoints."

"It took us nearly a week to get here with Ada collapsing after every jump," Janna grumbled, her voice a low rumble of discontent. "And that was with shorter jumps and frequent rest stops. To repeat that journey, while Ada is already exhausted..." She shook her head. "It's suicide."

"I've noticed something," Ada said, her voice quiet but firm, drawing their attention. "When I blink, I...I leave a marker, an anchor point in the system. I think I can return to any location I've previously blinked to, even if it's not within my line of sight."

A collective gasp filled the room. The implications of Ada's words hung in the air, a tantalizing possibility laced with a potent dose of fear.

Korina's eyes widened, her mind racing with the possibilities. She pulled out Obsidian, her fingers dancing across the data-slate's surface. "Theoretically...yes. If you can establish a connection with a specific axiomatic coordinate, you could bypass the line-of-sight limitation. It's like...like establishing a wormhole between two predefined points in space-time. But..." Her voice trailed off, a shadow of concern crossing her face.

"But what?" Sera asked, her gaze fixed on Korina.

Korina took a deep breath, her fingers still tracing patterns on

Obsidian's surface. "But a jump of this magnitude...it's exponentially more complex, more energy-intensive than anything you've attempted before. The strain on your system...it could be catastrophic. There's no way to predict the consequences. You could...you could overload your system. You could..." She hesitated, unable to voice the worst-case scenario.

"I could die," Ada finished, her voice calm and steady.

A heavy silence descended once more, punctuated only by the crackling of the candle flames and the distant sounds of the city outside. The weight of their decision pressed down on them, a tangible force in the dimly lit room.

"It's a risk," Erita said, her voice low and measured. "A massive one. But we don't have a choice. If we stay here, Thorne will crush us. If we attempt a sea voyage, we'll be too late. Ada's blink...it's our only option."

Sera nodded, her gaze fixed on Ada. "I agree. It's dangerous, but it's the only way. We'll prepare, minimize the risks as much as possible. We'll do it together."

Korina's eyes met Ada's, a mixture of fear and determination in their violet depths. "We will. We always do."

Ada reached out, her hand resting on Korina's. A warm smile touched her lips. "Thank you," she murmured, her voice filled with a quiet strength. "All of you. I know this is...a lot to ask. But I trust you. I trust us."

A sense of resolve settled over the room, solidifying their decision. The flickering candlelight illuminated their faces, highlighting their shared determination, their unwavering loyalty to each other, their commitment to their cause. The air crackled with a new kind of energy, not of fear or anxiety, but of purpose, of hope, of the quiet confidence that comes from facing impossible odds together. They were a fellowship, bound by love, loyalty, and a shared dream of a better world. And they were ready to risk everything to achieve it.

The Wandering Star bustled with activity as the fellowship prepared for their departure. Erita, a whirlwind of efficient movement, secured provisions and double-checked their gear. Korina meticulously calibrated Obsidian, ensuring its systems were optimized for the journey ahead. Sera sharpened her blades, the rhythmic rasp of steel against stone a familiar, comforting sound. Ada, however, found herself drawn to Janna, a quiet understanding passing between them.

"You understand why this is necessary, don't you?" Ada asked, her voice soft.

Janna nodded, her gaze steady. "Aye, Architect-Queen. Someone needs to stay behind, make sure Nividia holds up her end of the bargain. And someone needs to start building our army. Rhedeon's a good place to start. Plenty of skilled sailors, itching for a fight against the Empire."

"It's not just about the ships," Ada continued. "It's about building a new foundation, a safe haven for our cause. Rhedeon... it's the perfect place to start. Away from the Empire's grasp, a place where we can grow, where we can thrive."

Janna's lips curved into a rare smile. "Aye. I can see that. A new beginning. A chance to build something...*better*."

A lump formed in Ada's throat. Leaving Janna behind felt like tearing a piece of their fellowship away, but she knew it was for the best. Janna's strength, her unwavering loyalty, her quiet competence...they would be invaluable in Rhedeon.

The farewell between Janna and the others, particularly Sera, was one of mutual, profound respect. A fierce hug, a whispered promise, a shared understanding that transcended words. Then, with a final nod, Janna turned and walked towards the shipyards, her silhouette fading into the vibrant chaos of Port Veridia.

The remaining quartet—Ada, Sera, Korina, and Erita—traveled to a remote clifftop overlooking the vast ocean, a location scouted by Erita. The wind whipped at their hair, the salt spray stinging their faces, the endless expanse of water stretching before them like a tangible representation of the unknown.

"This is it," Erita said, her voice barely audible above the wind. "As remote as it gets. No Imperial patrols, no prying eyes. Just us and the vast, unforgiving ocean."

Ada nodded, her gaze sweeping across the horizon. "Perfect."

She stepped closer, her gaze meeting each of theirs in turn. "We've learned to share our thoughts, our emotions, our fears. Now...we need to share our strength."

She held out her hands, palms up. "Join me. Lend me your energy. Together...we can do this."

Without hesitation, Sera, Korina, and Erita stepped forward, their hands reaching out to meet Ada's. Their fingers intertwined, their palms pressed together, a physical connection that mirrored the deep, unbreakable bond that held them together. A circle of strength, of unity, of unwavering loyalty.

Ada closed her eyes, focusing her entire will, drawing on their combined strength. She felt their energy flowing into her, a surge of power that coursed through her veins, igniting a fire within her very core. The world around her seemed to fade, the wind, the waves, the very air itself becoming a distant hum. All that remained was the connection, the shared purpose, the unwavering belief in each other.

Then, with a sound like the universe tearing itself apart, a colossal ***THWOMP*** that echoed across the sea, they vanished. A blinding flash of violet light erupted from the clifftop, the last vestige of their presence before they were swallowed by the void, embarking on the most dangerous teleportation they had ever attempted.

CHAPTER 29

THE TYRANT'S WRATH

The world slammed back into focus, a jarring, violent re-entry. Ada crumpled to the ground, the barren plateau outside Port Dominus a harsh, unforgiving landscape beneath her. Her lungs burned, her muscles screamed, her mind a chaotic storm of static. The colossal blink jump, fueled by the combined strength of Sera, Korina, and Erita, had ripped through her, leaving her utterly depleted. It felt as if a core part of her being, a fundamental piece of her energy, had been carved out, leaving a gaping void in its place.

Gasps, ragged and pained, echoed around her. Sera, Korina, and Erita lay scattered nearby, their bodies contorted in similar postures of exhaustion. They were living batteries, their energy forcibly channeled to fuel Ada's impossible jump, and the toll was evident. Their faces were pale, their breaths shallow, their bodies trembling from the immense drain. For a long, terrifying moment, they were utterly vulnerable, exposed on the open plateau, their defenses shattered, their strength spent.

Ada fought against the encroaching darkness, the overwhelming urge to simply close her eyes and surrender to the exhaustion. *No,* she thought, her mind a sluggish, broken machine. *We have to move. We have to get to safety.*

Ada? Korina's voice, thin and reedy, echoed in her mind, the telepathic link a fragile thread in the storm of static. *Are you...are you alright?*

I...I think so, Ada replied, the effort of forming even simple thoughts immense. *Just...need a moment.*

A warm hand touched her face, Sera's concerned gaze a blurry image above her. "Easy, Ada," Sera murmured, her voice rough with exhaustion. "We're safe now. We made it."

Not yet, Erita's voice cut through the haze, sharp and urgent. *We're exposed out here. We need to get under cover.*

Ada pushed herself up, her arms trembling, her vision swimming. The plateau seemed to tilt and sway beneath her, the ground a shifting, unstable surface. She leaned heavily on Sera, grateful for the knight's unwavering support.

"Where...where to?" Ada asked, her voice a raspy whisper.

The old smuggler's tunnels, Erita replied, her mental image of a hidden entrance flashing in Ada's mind. *They're not far. We can hole up there until we recover.*

With Erita leading the way, they stumbled across the plateau, their movements slow and labored, their bodies protesting with every step. The air was thin and cold, the wind whipping at their clothes, the desolate landscape a stark reminder of their vulnerability. Ada's head throbbed, her vision blurred, her every breath a painful reminder of the energy she had expended.

They reached the hidden entrance, a narrow crevice concealed beneath a rocky overhang. Erita quickly disabled the rudimentary wards, her movements surprisingly fluid despite her exhaustion. They slipped inside, the darkness of the tunnels a welcome respite from the harsh glare of the plateau.

The tunnels were damp and musty, the air thick with the scent of decay and forgotten secrets. Erita led them deeper, navigating the twisting passages with an uncanny familiarity. Ada stumbled, her legs giving way beneath her. Sera caught her, her strong arms a comforting presence in the darkness.

"Almost there," Erita said, her voice echoing in the confined space. "Just a little further."

They reached a small chamber, a hidden alcove carved into the rock. Erita lit a small lantern, the flickering light casting long, dancing shadows on the walls. They collapsed to the ground, their bodies finally giving in to the overwhelming exhaustion.

Ada lay there, her eyes closed, her mind slowly beginning to clear. The static receded, replaced by a dull ache that radiated through her entire being. She felt Sera's hand in hers, Korina's head resting on her shoulder, Erita's watchful gaze a comforting presence in the darkness. They were safe, for now. They had made it back to Port Dominus. But the journey was far from over.

Hours crawled by in the suffocating darkness of the smuggler's tunnel. Time became a meaningless construct, marked only by the slow, agonizing ebb and flow of Ada's returning strength. Each breath was a victory, each twitch of a muscle a testament to her body's resilience. The initial, overwhelming exhaustion gradually receded, replaced by a dull, throbbing ache that pulsed through her like a corrupted data stream.

Beside her, Sera, Korina, and Erita stirred, their own bodies slowly recovering from the ordeal. They shared whispered words of comfort and encouragement, their voices hushed and strained, the telepathic link still a fragile, flickering connection. The air in the small chamber was thick with the scent of sweat and fear, a testament to their shared vulnerability.

When Ada finally felt strong enough to move, she sat up, her muscles protesting with a chorus of aches and twinges. The lantern cast long, dancing shadows on the walls, the flickering light painting the rough-hewn stone in a macabre dance. Sera, Korina, and Erita followed suit, their movements slow and deliberate, their faces pale and drawn.

“How...how are you feeling?” Ada asked, her voice still rough.

“Like I wrestled a kraken and lost,” Sera replied, a weak smile playing on her lips.

“My thauma reserves are completely depleted,” Korina said, her voice thin and reedy. “I feel...disconnected.”

Erita simply nodded, her golden eyes scanning the chamber, her usual cynical mask firmly in place. She was the first to stand, her movements surprisingly fluid despite her exhaustion.

“We need to move,” she said, her voice sharp and urgent. “The longer we stay here, the more vulnerable we are.”

They emerged from the tunnels under the cloak of darkness, the city a labyrinth of shadows and whispers. Port Dominus, once a chaotic symphony of noise and activity, was now eerily silent, the streets deserted, the air thick with an oppressive sense of dread. Thorne’s iron fist had descended upon the city, crushing the life out of it, turning it into a prison of fear.

Quadrupled patrols of heavily armed enforcers stalked the streets, their faces grim and merciless, their weapons gleaming in the moonlight. At every major intersection, cages held suspected sympathizers, their faces etched with fear and despair, stark warning notices posted beneath them. The few citizens they saw scurried through the shadows, their heads bowed, their eyes darting nervously, their faces a mask of palpable dread.

Ada felt a cold knot of fear tighten in her stomach. This was not the city they had left. This was a city broken, a city silenced, a city ruled by terror.

What in the Void happened here? Ada's voice echoed in their minds, a mixture of shock and disgust.

Thorne, Erita replied, her mental tone grim. *He's used our absence to consolidate his power. He's turned the city into a fortress.*

They moved through the shadows, their steps silent and cautious, their senses heightened, their telepathic link a lifeline in the oppressive silence. Ada's Admin-view highlighted the patrols, their movements predictable, their numbers overwhelming. Every corner was a potential ambush, every shadow a potential threat.

They reached the warehouse district, the once-familiar streets now a desolate wasteland. The warehouse itself was dark and silent, the windows boarded up, the doors reinforced. Ada felt a pang of apprehension. Had Thorne discovered their headquarters? Had he captured Silas and the others?

Erita approached the entrance, her hand hovering over the hidden lock. She paused, listening intently, her senses probing the silence.

Clear, she whispered, her mental tone tense.

They slipped inside, the warehouse a tomb of dust and shadows. The air was stale and heavy, the silence deafening. Ada felt a cold knot of fear tighten in her stomach. Something was wrong in Port Dominus. Very wrong.

The heavy warehouse doors creaked open, revealing four figures silhouetted against the muted glow of the Port Dominus twilight. Silas straightened, his hand instinctively moving to the newly commissioned admiral's cap Ada had fashioned for him. The indigo wool felt strange, a far cry from the roughspun fabric of his captain's coat, but the weight of it, the crisp lines of the uniform, instilled a sense of purpose, a responsibility he carried with a quiet pride.

"Admiral," Sera said, a hint of amusement in her voice. The faintest of smiles touched Silas's lips. It was good to see them, to see the fire still burning in their eyes, even amidst the encroaching darkness that had settled upon Port Dominus.

"Welcome back," Silas replied, his voice gruff but warm. "Report," he barked, turning to the nearest Azure Rose recruit. The young man, barely old enough to shave, snapped to attention, his eyes wide with a mixture of fear and determination.

"All patrols accounted for, Admiral. No breaches detected."

Silas nodded curtly. "Maintain vigilance. Double the perimeter guard." The recruit saluted smartly and disappeared back into the organized chaos of the warehouse. Silas turned back to the Quartet, his expression hardening. The amusement faded, replaced by the grim reality of their situation.

"I have a situation report for you, Architect-Queen," Silas

said, his voice low and serious. The warehouse, once a dusty, echoing shell, was now a humming hive of activity. Azure Rose recruits, clad in the newly standardized dark blue uniforms, moved with a quiet, disciplined purpose. Workbenches, laden with tools and disassembled weaponry, lined the walls, each station meticulously organized. Large tactical maps, updated in real-time by Korina's network of informants, glowed with a soft, ethereal light, charting the ebb and flow of Thorne's forces throughout the city. The air crackled with a focused energy, a sense of purpose that both impressed and unsettled Silas. It was the quiet efficiency of a well-oiled machine, a machine preparing for war. But even the most perfectly calibrated machine could break.

Ada gestured for him to continue, her purple eyes sharp and focused. Silas took a deep breath, steeling himself for the grim task ahead.

"Thorne has moved swiftly and brutally in your absence," Silas began, his voice heavy. "He's consolidated his control over the city. The guilds...they're broken." He paused, choosing his words carefully. "The Crimson Veil...they've been hit the hardest."

Sera stiffened, her hand instinctively moving to the hilt of her blade. The Crimson Veil, their newest allies, the merchants who had pledged their support to their cause. Silas saw the flicker of anger in Sera's eyes, the tightening of her jaw. He understood her concern, her frustration. They had placed their trust in these merchants, these allies, and now...

"Thorne moved against them the day after you left for Rhedeon," Silas continued, his voice flat, devoid of emotion. "He arrested their leaders, seized their assets, and shut down their networks. He made an example of them." He saw the flicker of understanding in Ada's eyes, the realization of the implications of Thorne's actions.

"The other guilds...they've fallen in line," Silas continued. "They're too afraid to resist. Thorne's made it clear that any opposition will be met with swift and brutal retribution." He paused, meeting Ada's gaze. "The city...it's his now."

Korina's breath hitched, a soft gasp that was barely audible above the low hum of activity in the warehouse. Silas saw the fear in her eyes, the dawning realization of the magnitude of the task ahead. Erita remained impassive, her expression unreadable, but Silas saw the tightening of her jaw, the subtle clenching of her fists. She was angry, he knew, but her anger was a cold, controlled fury, the anger of a predator assessing its prey.

"Our networks...they're compromised," Silas continued, his voice grim. "Thorne's tightened his grip on the flow of information. Our informants are being hunted. We're operating blind." He paused again, the weight of his words settling upon them like a shroud. "The people...they're losing hope."

Silas watched as Ada absorbed the news, her expression a mask of quiet contemplation. He knew the weight of responsibility she carried, the burden of leadership she had embraced. She had brought them this far, had given them a glimmer of hope in the darkness, but now...now the darkness was closing in, threatening to extinguish that fragile flame.

"Our allies in the city...they're scattered, disorganized," Silas continued, his voice low and urgent. "They need a sign, Architect-Queen. A sign that their fight is not in vain. A sign that you...that *we*...are still here."

The air in the command center crackled with a tense, electric energy. The holographic map of Port Dominus shimmered above the table, a web of intricate lines and pulsating markers charting the city's arteries of power. Ada traced the lines with her fingertip, her purple eyes narrowed in concentration. Gone was the relief of their return, the joy of reunion. The weight of Silas's report settled upon them like a physical burden, a stark reminder of the city's desperate plight.

His tactics are predictable. Brute force, intimidation, Erita's voice echoed in Ada's mind, a cool, analytical counterpoint to the simmering anger that coursed through Ada's veins. *He's tightened his grip on the city, but in doing so, he's created predictable patterns.*

Thorne's consolidated his forces around key locations: the docks, the guild halls, his personal manor, Korina added, her mental voice a rapid-fire cascade of data points. *He's sacrificed flexibility for control. Classic over-optimization.*

Ada nodded slowly, absorbing the information. Thorne's strategy was a reflection of his personality: arrogant, overconfident, and ultimately, shortsighted. He had underestimated them, had dismissed them as a minor inconvenience. He would pay for that mistake.

"The Crimson Veil...they provided us with a crucial piece of intel before they were silenced," Silas said, his gruff voice drawing Ada's attention back to the physical world. He pointed to a pulsating marker on the holographic map, a nondescript warehouse nestled amongst a cluster of similar structures near the South Docks.

"This is it," Silas continued, his voice low and urgent. "Thorne's financial processing center. It's where he launders his money, manages his accounts, and pays his enforcers. It's the lifeblood of his operation."

Ada leaned closer, studying the marker. The warehouse was unremarkable, almost invisible amidst the sprawling chaos of the docks. A perfect hiding place. A perfect target.

"His control is an illusion," Ada said, her voice quiet but firm. "He's built his empire on fear and intimidation, but fear is a fragile foundation. One well-placed crack can bring the whole structure crumbling down."

Ada's gaze swept across the faces of her companions, her eyes locking with each of theirs in turn. She saw the determination in Sera's crimson gaze, the fierce intellect in Korina's violet eyes, the cold, calculating focus in Erita's golden stare. Silas stood slightly apart, his expression unreadable, but Ada knew he was with them, his loyalty unwavering.

"Our next strike...it must be more than a disruption," Ada continued, her voice rising with a newfound conviction. "It must be an impossible act. Something that shatters his illusion of absolute control. Something that sends a message to the entire city that their tyrant is not invincible."

Ada tapped the holographic map again, this time selecting a different marker, a large, heavily armed freighter moored at Thorne's private dock. The ship was a behemoth, bristling with weaponry, a symbol of Thorne's power and arrogance. The *Iron Serpent.*

"Thorne's personal freighter," Silas said, his voice a low growl.

"The *Iron Serpent*. It's scheduled to depart tomorrow at dawn. Carrying his next shipment of military-grade weapons to the Theocracy."

Ada nodded, a slow, predatory smile spreading across her lips. "That's our target," she said, her voice ringing with a newfound confidence. "We'll hit him where it hurts most. We'll deprive him of his assets and arm our own growing forces with superior weaponry. We'll turn his own tools against him."

The Iron Serpent...it's heavily guarded, Sera's voice echoed in Ada's mind, a note of caution tempering her excitement. *Thorne's elite guard, automated turrets, reinforced hull...it'll be a tough nut to crack.*

His security systems are predictable, over-engineered, Korina countered, her mental voice buzzing with excitement. *I can exploit their vulnerabilities. Jam their communications, disable their sensors, create a window of opportunity.*

We'll need a diversion, Erita added, her mental voice cool and calculating. *Something to draw Thorne's attention away from the docks. Something...chaotic.*

Ada met Erita's gaze, a spark of understanding passing between them. Chaos was their element. They thrived in the unpredictable, the unexpected. They would turn Thorne's carefully constructed world upside down.

"We'll hit him on multiple fronts," Ada said, her voice ringing with authority. "Erita, you'll create the diversion. Something big, something loud. Something that makes Thorne think we're attacking his manor."

Erita's lips curled into a predatory smile. *Consider it done.*

"Korina, you'll handle the technical aspects," Ada continued, turning to the scholar. "Disable their security systems, create a blind spot for us to exploit."

Korina's eyes lit up, her fingers already dancing across the surface of her data-slate. *I'm already tracing their network. Their firewalls are laughably outdated.*

"Sera, you'll be with me," Ada said, turning to the two warriors. "We'll infiltrate the *Iron Serpent*, secure the weapons, and disable the ship. We'll make sure Thorne never sets sail again."

Sera nodded, her hand tightening on the hilt of her blade. *It will be my honor, Architect-Queen.*

Ada smiled, a surge of adrenaline coursing through her veins. The plan was audacious, bordering on insane, but it was their only option. They had to strike hard, strike fast, and strike with overwhelming force. They had to show Thorne, and the entire city, that their reign of terror was over.

The Crimson Revolution was about to officially start.

CHAPTER 30

THE IRON SERPENT HEIST

The air in the command center crackled with a nervous energy, a tangible hum that vibrated against Erita's skin. The holographic map, projected above the salvaged console, pulsed with a sickly green light, tracing the predicted route of the *Iron Serpent* and the intricate web of patrol vectors that represented Thorne's forces. Every blink of the projected chronometer felt like a hammer blow against the silence. Beside her, Korina's fingers danced across Obsidian's surface, a blur of motion as she finalized the security bypass protocols. Silas stood by the reinforced door, his hand resting on the hilt of his newly acquired plasma pistol, a silent sentinel guarding their backs. He couldn't participate in their telepathic network, but his presence was a solid anchor in the storm of data and whispered plans.

Ready when you are, Swift, Sera's voice echoed in Erita's mind, a low thrum of anticipation.

Just waiting for Korina to finish the last bypass, Erita replied, her gaze fixed on the chronometer. *Then we unleash the hounds.*

Korina's mental voice chimed in, a burst of static followed by a triumphant whisper. *System lock deactivated. Berth Seven is a ghost town. You have a clean run.*

Erita's lips curled into a thin smile. "Showtime," she murmured, her fingers flying across the surface of her own data-slate. Lines of code scrolled across the screen, a torrent of carefully crafted misinformation designed to sow chaos and confusion in the heart of Thorne's security grid. She unleashed a cascade of false alarms, phantom energy signatures, and fabricated distress calls into the Imperial communication network. On the holographic map, red alert icons flared up along the northern perimeter of Port Dominus, a carefully orchestrated symphony of digital deception. Thorne's forces, predictable as always, reacted instantly, the bulk of their patrols converging on the fabricated threat, leaving their true target, Berth Seven, vulnerable and exposed.

"The diversion is live," Erita telepathically broadcast to the group, her voice a cool whisper in their minds. "Your window is open. Forty-five seconds."

Acknowledged, Ada replied, her mental voice calm and focused. *We're in position. Going in NOW.*

The salt-laced air bit at Sera's exposed skin as she led her strike team through the deserted docks. Port Dominus, normally a cacophony of drunken shouts, crashing waves, and the rhythmic clang of shipyard hammers, was eerily silent. The only sound was the whisper of the wind and the muffled thud of their boots against the aged wooden planks. The city held its breath, caught in the throat of Erita's carefully orchestrated chaos.

Thirty seconds, Erita's voice echoed in Sera's mind, a cool whisper in the darkness.

Sera didn't reply. Words were unnecessary. Her team, twelve hand-picked Azure Rose veterans, moved with the silent, deadly precision of seasoned predators. They were ghosts in the pre-dawn gloom, their dark clothing blending seamlessly with the shadows. Each member knew their role, their movements a well-rehearsed ballet of violence honed by weeks of relentless training under Sera's watchful eye. They were no longer the ragtag group of smugglers and mercenaries she'd inherited from Master Willem. They were a finely tuned weapon, forged in the crucible of revolution, ready to be unleashed.

Twenty seconds, Erita's voice warned.

Sera reached the outer perimeter of Berth Seven. Two automated turrets, normally sweeping the area with their glowing arcane lenses, stood frozen, their systems crippled by Korina's expertly crafted malware. A small squad, led by Lars, peeled off from the main group, their plasma rifles raised. No shouted orders. No frantic gestures. Just a silent, telepathic command from Sera that echoed in their minds: *Neutralize the turrets. Permanently.*

The recruits obeyed instantly. Twin beams of azure energy lanced out, striking the turrets' vulnerable power cores with pinpoint accuracy. The arcane lenses flickered, sputtered, and died, plunging the area into deeper shadow.

Ten seconds, Erita's voice was now a tight, urgent pulse.

Sera gestured to the remaining squad, their faces grim and determined in the faint glow of the emergency lights. They moved towards the reinforced gate that stood between them and the *Iron Serpent*. The gate, a slab of Sovereign Steel thick enough to withstand a siege, was Thorne's last line of defense. But it was no match for their preparations. Two demolition experts, their faces smeared with black grease, knelt at the base of the gate, their hands moving with practiced efficiency. They placed the breaching charges, small discs of concentrated explosives designed to cripple the gate's locking mechanism without causing structural damage. They retreated, taking cover behind a stack of empty cargo crates. A muffled thump echoed through the docks as the charges detonated. The gate shuddered, its locking mechanism groaning in protest as the internal gears and pistons twisted and sheared.

Five seconds, Erita's voice was almost frantic.

Sera took a deep breath, her heart pounding against her ribs. The scent of ozone and burnt metal hung heavy in the air. This was it. The culmination of weeks of planning, training, and desperate hope. She raised her hand, her twin blades gleaming faintly in the darkness. The gate, no longer locked but still heavy, began to swing inwards, revealing the sleek, obsidian hull of the *Iron Serpent*.

Go, go, GO! Erita's mental scream echoed in Sera's mind.

Sera surged forward, her team following close behind, their weapons raised. They poured through the opening gate, silent shadows pouring onto the deck of Thorne's prize freighter, ready to unleash the storm.

Ada followed close behind Sera, her heart pounding a frantic rhythm against her ribs. The metallic tang of blood, thick and cloying, hung heavy in the air, mingling with the acrid scent of ozone from the recently disabled turrets. The deck of the *Iron Serpent* was a chaotic canvas of flashing blades, guttural shouts, and the dull thud of bodies hitting the steel floor. Sera and her Azure Rose strike team moved through the fray like avenging angels, their crimson tunics a stark contrast to the dark uniforms of Thorne's mercenaries.

Sera was a whirlwind of motion, her twin blades a blur of crimson light. She moved with the fluid grace of a dancer, parrying blows, dodging attacks, and countering with lethal precision. But even her exceptional skill wasn't enough against the sheer number of Thorne's elite personal guard. These weren't the usual drunken dockside brawlers or undisciplined thugs. These were hardened mercenaries, veterans of countless skirmishes and raids, their loyalty bought with Thorne's seemingly bottomless coffers. They fought with a desperate ferocity, their movements precise and coordinated, their faces grim masks of determination.

Ada watched the battle unfold, her mind racing. Raw power, the kind she'd used to obliterate the Prefecture's security systems, wasn't an option here. This required finesse. Subtlety. A surgeon's precision, not a blacksmith's hammer. This was her chance to truly understand the limits of her evolved abilities, to test the boundaries of her control over this reality.

A hulking mercenary, his face contorted in a snarl, charged towards Sera, his heavy axe whistling through the air. Sera, momentarily occupied with disarming another opponent, was caught off guard. The mercenary's axe, aimed at Sera's exposed flank, would have cleaved her in two. Ada acted instantly.

"[Property: Friction = 100]," she whispered, focusing her intent on the small patch of deck beneath the mercenary's boots.

The mercenary's momentum carried him forward, but his boots, instead of sliding smoothly across the steel deck, encountered an unseen, immovable force. He stumbled, his forward motion abruptly halted as if he'd stepped into a pool of thick tar. His surprised grunt was cut short as Sera's blade, a crimson flash in the dim light, found its mark, sinking deep into his throat. He gurgled, his eyes wide with disbelief, before collapsing to the deck with a heavy thud.

Across the deck, a guard raised his plasma rifle, aiming a precise shot at Lars' back. Lars, engaged in a brutal hand-to-hand fight with two other mercenaries, was oblivious to the impending threat. Ada's eyes narrowed.

"[Property: Bend = 90]," she commanded, focusing her intent on the metal railing next to the guard.

The railing, a solid piece of wrought iron, twisted and curled like a pliable vine, snaking out and snaring the guard's outstretched foot. He yelped in surprise, his aim thrown off as he stumbled, his shot going wide. Lars, sensing the sudden shift in the fight, spun around, his plasma sword a blur of motion. The guard's scream was cut short as Lars' sword connected with his skull, sending a spray of blood and bone across the deck.

A squad of armored enforcers, their faces hidden behind visored helmets, advanced towards the Azure Rose recruits. They moved with the disciplined precision of the Aegis Order, their shields raised, their energy lances crackling with lethal power. The recruits, outnumbered and outmatched, began to falter. Ada felt a surge of protectiveness. These weren't just lines of code. These were people, fighting for a cause they believed in, a cause she'd inspired.

"[Property: Air Density = 50]," she commanded, focusing her will on the space immediately surrounding the advancing enforcers.

The air around the enforcers shimmered and distorted, thickening into an almost visible fog. The enforcers' movements became sluggish, their heavy armor suddenly a burden, their vision obscured by the dense, swirling air. They stumbled, their coordinated advance dissolving into a confused mess. The Azure Rose recruits, sensing their advantage, pressed their attack. Plasma bolts lanced out, striking the enforcers' exposed joints and weak points. Blades flashed, finding gaps in their armor. The enforcers, their movements hampered by the thick air, were unable to react effectively. Their screams, muffled by their helmets and the dense atmosphere, were quickly silenced.

Ada watched the battle continue, her violet light pulsing with each subtle intervention. She wasn't just a combatant; she was the architect of the battlefield, a beautiful conductor—rewriting the rules of engagement with each whispered command. The deck of the *Iron Serpent*, once a symbol of Thorne's tyrannical power, was becoming his graveyard.

"It's time...for the *Grand Finale!*" Ada announced, her voice echoing across the ravaged deck. She raised her hands, her violet light intensifying, pulsing with a newfound, exhilarating power. "**[Property: Voltage = Maximum]**," she commanded, focusing her intent on the entire deck of the *Iron Serpent*.

The air crackled with an almost visible energy. Arcs of violet lightning danced across the steel deck, leaping from railing to railing, illuminating the carnage in a strobe-like flash. The remaining mercenaries, their eyes wide with terror, scrambled for cover, their weapons clattering to the deck as they fled. The weaker-willed among them simply collapsed, their bodies convulsing as the raw, untamed energy coursed through them. The deck, once swarming with Thorne's enforcers, was now eerily silent, save for the crackling of the dissipating energy and the faint moans of the fallen. The lingering scent of ozone mingled with the metallic tang of blood, a testament to Ada's raw, overwhelming power.

The deck was clear. The *Iron Serpent*, once a symbol of Thorne's tyrannical control over Port Dominus, was now theirs.

Korina's fingers danced across Obsidian's cool surface, a blur of precise taps and swipes. Lines of code scrolled across the screen, a torrent of data flowing through her fingertips. *Lynx*, the little violet pixel-cat Ada had coded into her data-slate, sat perched in the corner of the screen, its ears perked, its eyes blinking rapidly as it watched the data streams. It was a comforting, if slightly embarrassing, presence in this tense moment. Below, the *Iron Serpent*, now under their control, sat silently at Berth Seven, its deck still faintly crackling with the residue of Ada's power.

Almost there... Korina thought, her focus absolute. *Just a few more lines...*

The crane controls were a mess, a patchwork of outdated Imperial systems and jury-rigged Confederate modifications. It was a system analyst's nightmare, a chaotic symphony of conflicting protocols and security loopholes. But for Korina, it was a playground. This was what she was born to do, what she excelled at. This was her way of fighting, her way of contributing to their revolution.

Erita, status report, Korina whispered mentally, projecting her thoughts through the telepathic link Ada had established between them.

Diversion holding...for now. Thorne's forces are scattered. But they'll be converging on your position soon. How much longer? Erita's voice, cool and sharp, echoed in her mind.

Just a few more seconds... Korina replied, her fingers flying across the data-slate. *I'm weaving a self-sustaining loop into the port's logistical network. It'll make this whole operation look like a routine cargo transfer. Any outside observers will see nothing out of the ordinary.*

Below, on the docks, Crimson Veil agents, their faces masked, worked with silent efficiency. They moved like shadows in the dim light, rapidly offloading crates of advanced weaponry from the *Iron Serpent's* cargo hold and transferring them onto waiting barges. Plasma rifles, energy lances, sonic disruptors—weapons that would soon be turned against Thorne and his enforcers, weapons that would help them liberate Port Dominus.

"Lars, how much longer?" Sera's spoke, tight with urgency.

"Almost done, Commander," Lars' voice was gruff, his words punctuated by the clang of metal against metal. "Just a few more crates..."

"Worry about praising my station later, you blighted swamp toad!" Sera shot back, then sighed. "Just get those crates secured."

Korina tapped the final command into Obsidian. The data-slate hummed, the little *Lynx* monitor perking up and letting out a triumphant pixelated meow as the code executed flawlessly. A cascade of false data flooded the port's logistical network, seamlessly integrating with the existing streams of information. To any distant observers, the massive cargo transfer taking place at Berth Seven would appear as nothing more than a routine, scheduled operation.

Done, Korina announced, a surge of pride mixed with relief flooding through her. *The loop is self-sustaining. It should hold for at least an hour, maybe more.*

Excellent work, Rina, Ada's voice, warm and filled with affection, echoed in her mind. *Begin the pullback. Get everyone to safety.*

Pulling back now, Sera confirmed. *All crates secured. Barges departing.*

Just as the last barge pulled away from the *Iron Serpent*, the first piercing wail of city-wide Imperial alarms began to tear through the night. The sound, amplified by the port's loudspeakers, was deafening, a chilling reminder that their window of opportunity was closing.

Void's name... Erita swore. *The diversion's collapsed. Thorne knows.*

Red lights began to flash across the port, illuminating the docks in a harsh, pulsating glow. Imperial patrol ships, their sirens screaming, raced towards Berth Seven. The net was closing, and they were trapped in its center. Korina felt a surge of panic, a cold dread gripping her heart. They'd struck a blow against Thorne, but at what cost?

We have to get out of here...now, Korina thought desperately, her mind racing. *But how?*

CHAPTER 31

CLOSING THE GATES

The piercing shriek of city-wide alarms ripped through the pre-dawn silence, a brutal symphony of warning sirens and blaring loudspeakers. Berth Seven, moments ago cloaked in the deceptive quiet of their operation, was now bathed in a pulsating, malevolent red light from sweeping emergency beacons. Thorne knew. He knew they'd hit him, and he was responding with the full, furious force of his control over Port Dominus.

They're locking down the port! Erita barked into the telepathic link, her voice tight with urgency. *Main sea gates are closing, and patrol boats are deploying to block the channels. You have less than two minutes before you're completely boxed in!*

The holographic map projected from Obsidian flared with angry red icons, swarming their position like ravenous insects. The jaws of Thorne's fortress were snapping shut. Erita watched, her heart pounding a brutal rhythm against her ribs, as the digital representation of their escape routes vanished one by one. It was a chilling visual echo of countless close calls, of desperate scrambles for survival in the shadows of a dozen different cities. But this time, it wasn't just her life on the line. It was Ada's, Sera's, Korina's...her family's. And that changed everything.

Understood, Ada's voice, calm amidst the chaos, echoed in her mind. *We're en route to the extraction point. Just need a little more time—"*

You don't have time! Erita snapped, her fear overriding her usual composure. *Those patrol boats are fast. They'll intercept you before you reach the rendezvous point.*

Erita's gaze darted across the command center, searching for a solution, a way out of this tightening noose. Silas, his face grim, barked orders into a comm-unit, redirecting their remaining Crimson Veil assets, trying to buy Ada and Sera a few precious seconds. Korina, her face pale, hunched over Obsidian, her fingers flying across the data-slate as she tried to find a weakness in Thorne's rapidly tightening security grid. But Erita knew it was a losing battle. Thorne had anticipated their every move, had planned for this contingency. He'd turned Port Dominus into a steel trap, and they were about to be caught in its jaws.

The air crackled with the raw energy of colliding thaumaturgical blasts, the sharp tang of ozone mixing with the coppery scent of blood. Sera danced through the chaos, her twin blades a blur of crimson, each strike precise and lethal. Around her, the docks of Berth Seven had become a charnel house, the once-orderly space now a mangled landscape of shattered crates, twisted metal, and the broken bodies of Thorne's enforcers.

"Hold the line!" Sera roared, her voice hoarse from shouting over the din of battle. "Don't let them on this ramp! Not one step!"

Her blades sang a deadly song, deflecting energy blasts, parrying lunging attacks, carving bloody furrows through armored flesh. The handful of Azure Rose recruits who'd stayed with her fought with the desperate courage of cornered wolves, their stolen Imperial plasma rifles spitting bolts of searing energy into the advancing enemy ranks. They were good, these recruits. Hand-picked by Janna for their loyalty and skill, they'd embraced the revolution with a fire that mirrored Sera's own. But they were outnumbered, outgunned, and facing an enemy that seemed to multiply with every fallen comrade.

Lars, his face a mask of grim determination, held the center of the gangplank, his massive frame a seemingly immovable bulwark against the tide of attackers. He wielded a captured heavy repeater cannon with brutal efficiency, each blast tearing through the enemy ranks like a scythe through wheat. Beside him, Eliria, a young recruit with eyes that burned with a terrifying intensity, fired burst after burst from her plasma rifle, her movements precise and economical, each shot finding its mark. For a brief, exhilarating moment, Sera felt a surge of hope. They could hold.

While the physical battle raged on the docks, a silent, unseen war of data and arcane energy was being fought from the relative safety of the command center. Korina, hunched over Obsidian, her fingers a blur across the data-slate's shimmering surface, was weaving a complex tapestry of deception. Ghost signals, phantom echoes of legitimate commands, danced through the port's network, luring patrol boats on wild goose chases, sending automated turrets spinning uselessly, and frantically trying to slow the inexorable grinding of the massive sea gates.

Ada, unseen, unfelt, was a silent, omnipresent specter within the system, augmenting Korina's efforts with the raw power of her Admin privileges. Where Korina's code subtly nudged and redirected, Ada's commands brute-forced reality itself. When a massive searchlight, its beam sweeping across the docks, threatened to illuminate one of the escaping barges laden with stolen weaponry, Ada sent a single, silent command—*[Malfunction: Overload]*. The searchlight sputtered, flared brilliantly, and then exploded in a shower of sparks and molten slag, plunging a section of the docks into darkness.

Thirty seconds, Erita's strained voice echoed in Ada's mind, a stark reminder of the dwindling time. *They're adapting. They're learning. My diversions won't hold them much longer.*

Ada felt a surge of frustration, a cold knot tightening in her gut. She'd underestimated Thorne. She'd anticipated his ruthlessness, his control, but not his adaptability. He was learning, evolving, his security systems reacting to their every move with frightening speed. This wasn't a game anymore. This was a war, and they were losing.

Execute final contingency, Ada commanded, her voice echoing with an icy resolve she hadn't known she possessed. It was a gamble, a desperate throw of the dice, but it was their only chance.

Void's name... Erita muttered, a flicker of grim satisfaction in her voice. *It's worth trying...*

A series of muffled detonations echoed through the city, the ground trembling beneath Ada's feet. The holographic map on

Obsidian flickered wildly as a section of the docks, adjacent to Berth Seven, vanished in a cascade of collapsing structures and billowing smoke. Erita had pre-placed charges beneath the supports of two massive cargo cranes, turning Thorne's own infrastructure against him.

Ten seconds, Erita's voice was a breathless whisper. *Get out of there. NOW!*

Sera, her crimson tunic ripped and stained with sweat and grime, hauled a wounded recruit onto the last barge. Her own body screamed in protest, every muscle aching, every breath a searing reminder of the brutal fight on the docks. But there was no time for pain, no time for rest. The sea gates, colossal slabs of Sovereign Steel, were closing with agonizing slowness, the gap narrowing to a sliver of open water.

"***MOVE!***" she roared, her voice raw with exhaustion, shoving the recruit towards the center of the barge. Lars, his face grim, his usually jovial demeanor replaced by a mask of grim determination, nodded curtly and helped secure the wounded man.

The overloaded barge lurched forward, its engine straining against the weight of the stolen weaponry and the surviving revolutionaries. Admiral Silas, his gruff voice echoing across the choppy waters, barked orders through a crackling comms unit, coordinating the desperate escape of the small flotilla. His flagship, *The Sea Serpent*, took the lead, its reinforced hull designed to take the brunt of any remaining defenses Thorne might throw at them.

The gap between the closing gates narrowed to a terrifying sliver, the dark, churning water seeming to swallow the light. Korina, her face pale with exertion, her fingers still dancing across Obsidian's glowing surface, unleashed a final, desperate burst of disruptive energy. The colossal gate mechanisms, powered by a complex network of thaumaturgical conduits and arcane generators, stuttered for a heart-stopping second, their rhythmic grinding interrupted by a jarring screech of protesting metal.

It was enough.

The barges, one after another, scraped through the closing jaws of the gate, showering sparks as Sovereign Steel grated against Sovereign Steel. Then, with a deafening, final **CLANG** that echoed across the harbor, the gates slammed shut, the reverberations shaking the very foundations of Port Dominus.

Silence descended on the small flotilla, broken only by the gentle lapping of waves against the barges' hulls and the ragged breaths of the exhausted revolutionaries. They were alive. They were victorious. But the victory was a pyrrhic one.

Ada stood at the bow of the lead barge, her black gown billowing in the sea breeze, her violet eyes fixed on the receding lights of Port Dominus. The sounds of the enraged city—the distant sirens, the frantic shouts of Thorne's enforcers—were fading into the night. They were free, for now. But the decks of their barges were stained with the blood of the fallen, a grim testament to the true price of their revolution. The faces of those lost—the brave Azure Rose recruits, the Crimson Veil agents who'd fought alongside them—flashed through her mind. They'd paid the ultimate price for her vision, for her dream of a better Kremøtoa.

Sera joined her at the bow, her hand finding Ada's, their fingers intertwining. Lars stood nearby, his usual boisterous energy replaced by a quiet solemnity. He looked at Ada, then at Sera. His eyes were bloodshot, his face streaked with grime, but there was a flicker of pride in his gaze. He gave a curt nod, a silent acknowledgment of their shared victory, their shared loss.

The open sea stretched before them, a vast expanse of unknown possibilities. The revolution had begun, but not without a price paid...

CHAPTER 32

THE DESPERATE GAMBIT

The barges glided into the subterranean dock beneath the warehouse, the gentle splash of their hulls against the rough-hewn stone pier the only sound in the cavernous space. The air hung heavy, thick with the scent of stagnant water and the metallic tang of blood. This wasn't the triumphant return Ada had envisioned. It was a somber procession, a silent acknowledgment of the brutal cost of their victory.

Ada watched as the wounded were carefully carried from the barges, their low moans echoing in the dimly lit space. Lars, his face grim, his usual boisterous energy replaced by a quiet efficiency, directed the medics, his voice low and steady as he pointed them towards the makeshift infirmary set up in one corner of the warehouse. Ada saw the empty spaces on the barges, the gaps where recruits who wouldn't be coming home should have been. Young faces, full of hope and bravado just hours ago, now just ghosts in her memory. The weight of command, of every life lost under her banner, settled heavily on her shoulders, a crushing burden that no amount of victory could alleviate.

She stepped onto the damp stone of the pier, the chill seeping through the thin soles of her boots. The warehouse, usually a hive of activity, was eerily silent, the only sounds the hushed whispers of the medics and the occasional pained gasp of a wounded revolutionary. The usual boisterous energy of the Azure Rose recruits was gone, replaced by an atmosphere of grief and exhaustion. The victory felt hollow, the cheers stuck in her throat, replaced by a bitter taste of loss. The price they'd paid was too damn high.

"Report," she said, her voice barely a whisper, turning to Erita. The spymaster stood nearby, her usual sharp, cynical expression softened by a shadow of weariness. Her golden eyes, however, were alert, scanning the shadows, still assessing threats even in the supposed safety of their hideout.

"Casualties are...significant," Erita said, her voice low. "We lost nearly a third of the Azure Rose recruits. Crimson Veil took heavier losses. Thorne's enforcers...they fought like cornered vipers."

Ada closed her eyes, the image of Thorne's cold, calculating face flashing through her mind. He'd turned Port Dominus into a fortress, its citizens living in fear, its streets patrolled by heavily armed mercenaries. He'd choked the life out of the city, squeezing it dry for his own profit. And now, he'd spilled the blood of her people, of those who'd believed in her vision, in her promise of a better Kremøtoa.

Rina...status report, Ada projected the thought, focusing on Korina. The scholar stood near the entrance to the infirmary, her face pale, her violet eyes wide with a mix of exhaustion and concern. Her data-slate, Obsidian, glowed faintly in her hand, displaying a scrolling list of names and medical assessments.

Casualties...stabilized for now, Korina's mental voice was strained. *Multiple shrapnel wounds, lacerations, one case of severe thaumaturgical overload...I'm doing what I can, but we need more medical supplies. And...and a proper surgeon.*

Ada nodded, the weight of Korina's words adding to the growing pressure in her chest. They'd won this battle, but the war was far from over. Thorne would be regrouping, consolidating his forces, preparing for their next move. And they were running out of time.

"Silas," she said, turning to the admiral. He stood at the edge of the dock, overseeing the unloading of the salvaged weapons from the *Iron Serpent*. His face was drawn and tired, but his eyes held a steely resolve. "Status of the acquired assets?"

"We managed to salvage most of the *Iron Serpent*'s cargo," Silas said, his voice gruff. "Plasma rifles, repeater cannons, enough ammunition to arm a small army. But..." He hesitated, his gaze shifting to the wounded being carried past them. "We lost a lot of good people getting it."

Ada placed a hand on Silas's arm, a silent gesture of gratitude and shared grief. "I know," she said, her voice barely a whisper. "I know."

The weight of her responsibility, of the lives lost and the battles yet to come, threatened to crush her. But she couldn't afford to break. Not now. Not when so much depended on her. She straightened her shoulders, forcing herself to meet Silas's gaze. They had a city to liberate, a revolution to ignite. And they would do it, one step at a time, one victory, one loss, at a time. The path ahead was long and treacherous, but they would walk it together. For the fallen. For the future. For Kremøtoa.

The air in the warehouse was thick with the metallic tang of blood and the acrid scent of burnt thaumaturgy, a grim reminder of the battle's cost. Yet, amidst the somber atmosphere, a flicker of hope ignited. The captured Imperial armaments, stacked high near the dock, were a tangible symbol of their hard-won victory. Sera, her crimson tunic stained dark in places she didn't want to look at too closely, oversaw the unloading process, her face a mask of resolute grief. Each clang of metal against stone, each creak of the heavy crates being pried open, was a testament to the sacrifices they'd made.

Lars, his arm bandaged but his spirit unbroken, hefted a crowbar, prying open the first crate. The wood splintered, revealing rows of gleaming repeater crossbows, their polished metal surfaces reflecting the flickering torchlight. A hushed gasp rippled through the assembled recruits. These weren't the makeshift weapons they'd been using, cobbled together from salvaged parts and sheer desperation. These were Imperial-grade armaments, the finest Kremøtoa had to offer.

Sera picked up one of the crossbows, testing its weight, the smooth, cool metal a comfort in her calloused hands. It was a weapon of precision and power, a far cry from the battered blades she'd been forced to rely on during their escape from Celgrad. She ran a finger along the intricate engravings on the stock, tracing the

Imperial crest, a symbol that once represented her unwavering loyalty, now a reminder of the betrayal she'd endured.

"Distribute these," she said, her voice low but firm, handing the crossbow to a young recruit. The recruit's eyes widened, his hands trembling slightly as he accepted the weapon. He hefted it, testing its weight, a flicker of awe in his gaze.

Lars opened another crate, revealing stacks of enchanted armor, its dark metal surfaces shimmering with arcane runes. The armor was lighter and more flexible than the standard Imperial issue, designed for agility and speed, perfect for the Azure Rose's hit-and-run tactics. Sera picked up a breastplate, testing its flexibility, the runes pulsing faintly beneath her fingertips.

"This is what we fight for," she said, her voice rising slightly, holding the breastplate aloft. "This is what they died for." Her gaze swept across the assembled recruits, meeting their eyes, one by one. "We will not let their sacrifices be in vain."

A hushed murmur of agreement spread through the ranks, a renewed sense of purpose in their weary faces. For many, this was more than just new equipment. It was a tangible symbol of their victory, a sign that they could stand against the Empire, that they could win.

Lars opened the final crate, revealing rows of pulsating energy cells, their surfaces glowing with a soft, blue light. These weren't just power sources for weapons; they were miniature arcane generators, capable of powering everything from shields to communication devices. Sera picked up one of the cells, feeling the thrum of energy through her fingertips.

"This is how we change Kremøtoa," she said, her voice ringing with conviction, handing the energy cell to another recruit. The recruit's face lit up, his eyes shining with a mix of hope and determination.

As Sera continued to distribute the new gear, a hushed awe spread through the ranks. The superior weapons and armor weren't just tools of war; they were a massive morale boost, a physical manifestation of their growing strength. For Sera, each weapon distributed, each piece of armor fitted, was a silent vow. A vow to honor the fallen, to fight for a better future, to make their sacrifices count.

Korina was a whirlwind of intellectual excitement, a stark contrast to the somber mood in the command center. Her personal grief, the weight of their losses, was momentarily overshadowed by the technological treasure trove spread out before her. She hunched over a captured energy cell, her fingers tracing the intricate runes etched into its surface, her mind alight with the thrill of discovery. *Obsidian*, nestled securely in her lap, pulsed with a soft, violet glow, mirroring the intensity of her focus.

"The energy cell integration is far more sophisticated than I anticipated!" she exclaimed, her voice a rapid-fire cascade of technical jargon. She glanced up at Ada, her violet eyes shining with an almost childlike wonder. "Look!" With a flick of her wrist, she projected a complex schematic from *Obsidian*, a three-dimensional model of the energy cell's inner workings rotating slowly in the air between them. "A multi-phasic resonance chamber...Void's name, Ada, the implications are immense!"

Ada leaned closer, studying the schematic, her own programmer's mind captivated by the elegant design. The energy cell wasn't just a power source; it was a miniature arcane reactor, a marvel of thaumaturgical engineering. The multi-phasic resonance chamber allowed for a controlled release of energy, maximizing efficiency and minimizing waste. It was a level of sophistication she hadn't anticipated, a testament to the Empire's technological prowess, however twisted their purpose.

"We can adapt this, Ada!" Korina continued, her excitement bubbling over. "Not just replicate—enhance it! Integrate our own bio-etheric energy flows to create truly symbiotic weapons!" She gestured wildly with her hands, her words tumbling over each other in her eagerness to explain. "Imagine, Ada, weapons that respond not just to our commands, but to our very *intentions*! Blades that anticipate our movements, shields that react to our thoughts! We can create a new generation of armaments, Ada, weapons that are an extension of ourselves!"

Her enthusiasm was infectious, a beacon of hope in the otherwise somber atmosphere. Ada smiled, a genuine, heartfelt smile that reached her violet eyes. Korina's excitement, her unwavering belief in the power of innovation, was exactly what they needed. It wasn't just about replicating the Empire's technology; it was about surpassing it, about creating something truly unique, something that reflected their own values, their own vision for a better Kremøtoa.

Erita, perched on a crate nearby, watched their exchange with a mixture of amusement and grudging admiration. She'd initially dismissed Korina as a naive scholar, too caught up in her data-slates and theories to understand the harsh realities of their world. But Korina's brilliance, her ability to find opportunity even in the darkest of circumstances, was proving to be an invaluable asset.

Sera, leaning against a stack of captured armor, her arms crossed over her chest, listened quietly, her expression thoughtful. She might not have understood the technical details of Korina's explanations, but she understood the implications. Better weapons, stronger defenses, a greater chance of victory. And in their fight against the Empire, every advantage counted.

"Alright, Rina," Ada said, her voice gentle but firm, using the pet name that only she was allowed to use. "Let's see what you can do." She placed a hand on Korina's shoulder, a silent gesture of support and encouragement. Korina beamed, her eyes shining with renewed determination. She turned back to the energy cell, her fingers flying across *Obsidian's* surface, a symphony of arcane symbols and complex equations dancing across the screen. The air around her crackled with thaumaturgical energy, a sign that something truly extraordinary was about to be born.

Erita's console, usually a model of organized chaos, was now a frantic tempest of flashing red alerts and desperate, fragmented communications. Her network, once a finely tuned instrument of whispers and secrets, was now screaming in pain, each fragmented message a testament to Thorne's brutal efficiency.

A merchant's frantic plea for help cut through the static, his words painting a vivid picture of the unfolding horror in the market square. "Thorne's men...rounding up anyone...suspected... They took my son...Argent's light, he's just a boy..." The transmission ended abruptly, cut short by a burst of interference.

Another message, this one coded and clipped, spoke of enforcers dragging suspected sympathizers from their homes in the dead of night. "No warrants...just brute force...They're taking them to the...Void knows where..."

A third, a desperate whisper from a contact within the city's power grid, detailed the implementation of crippling rations on water and power. "Thorne's squeezing us dry...The people are desperate...Riots are breaking out..."

Erita's golden eyes darted across the screen, her fingers flying across the console, trying to piece together the fragmented intel. The city wasn't just occupied; it was being strangled, systematically and ruthlessly. Thorne was using fear as a weapon, a weapon more potent than any blade. He was breaking the city's spirit, turning neighbor against neighbor, crushing any spark of resistance before it could ignite.

He's tightening the noose, Erita's voice echoed in the minds of Ada, Sera, and Korina, the telepathic link a grim conduit for the city's suffering. *Thorne's making an example of anyone suspected of supporting us. He's crushing dissent before it can even take root.*

Sera paced restlessly, her hand gripping the hilt of her sword, her crimson eyes burning with a mixture of anger and frustration. The sounds of Thorne's tyranny, the whispers of fear and desperation, were a physical ache in her chest. She'd sworn an oath to protect the innocent, to fight for justice, and now, trapped within the confines of their hidden headquarters, she felt powerless.

Korina huddled over *Obsidian*, her fingers dancing across the data-slate's surface, desperately searching for a weakness in Thorne's iron grip. The city's data streams, usually a source of information and insight, were now choked with static and misinformation, Thorne's digital sentinels guarding every access point.

Ada stood by the command center's main display, a holographic map of Port Dominus pulsating with a sickly, flickering light. Each red alert, each desperate message, was a stab of guilt, a reminder of her responsibility. This was her world, her creation, and she'd allowed it to fall into the hands of a tyrant.

We have to act, Sera's voice echoed in their minds, the urgency of her plea a reflection of their shared desperation. *We can't just sit here while Thorne destroys everything we've fought for.*

I know, Ada responded, her voice calm but firm, the weight of command settling upon her shoulders. *But we have to be smart. A direct assault would be suicide. We need a plan, a way to strike at Thorne's heart without sacrificing our own.* She turned to Erita, her violet eyes searching the spymaster's face. *Eri, what do you have? Any weaknesses? Any cracks in Thorne's armor?*

Ada traced the glowing yellow node on the holographic map, the pulsing light a beacon of Thorne's tyranny. It was more than just a financial hub; it was a symbol of his power, the engine that fueled his oppression. "This is where we strike," she repeated, her voice unwavering despite the dissent echoing in the command center. "This is where we make him bleed."

"A direct assault is madness, Ada," Silas argued, his gruff voice laced with concern. "We're outnumbered, outgunned, and outmaneuvered. We barely escaped with our lives last time. Thorne's expecting us. He's fortified the entire district. It's a death trap."

Sera nodded in agreement, her crimson eyes fixed on the map, her usual fiery passion tempered by a grim pragmatism. "Silas is right. We can't risk a full-frontal assault. Not yet. We've lost too many good people already. We need to regroup, rebuild our strength, and find a more strategic approach."

Ada acknowledged their concerns, the weight of their words settling heavily on her shoulders. She knew the risks. She'd seen the city's suffering reflected in Erita's frantic data streams, heard the echoes of fear and desperation in the coded whispers. But she also knew that time was a luxury they couldn't afford. Thorne was tightening his grip on Port Dominus, squeezing the life out of the city, crushing any hope of resistance. They had to act, and they had to act now.

"We cannot stand by," Ada insisted, her violet eyes burning with a fierce resolve. "Every arrest, every scream—it is Thorne's calculated response to our actions. We forced his hand. Now, he has forced ours. This isn't just about strategy anymore. This is about breaking his will and restoring hope to a city on the brink."

A heavy silence settled over the command center, the weight of her words pressing down on them. The holographic map of Port Dominus pulsed with an ominous red glow, each flashing light a testament to Thorne's escalating tyranny. The debate was deadlocked, a clash between pragmatism and principle, between caution and conviction.

Then, Erita spoke. Her voice was chillingly calm, devoid of its usual wit. "The risk is irrelevant," she stated, her golden eyes holding a cold, almost glacial resolve. "The objective is paramount. We will shatter him."

Her unwavering conviction, born from her own recently confronted trauma, resonated through the room, galvanizing the group. It was more than just a tactical assessment; it was a declaration of intent, a refusal to be cowed by fear.

Sera's initial caution gave way to her fierce sense of justice. She'd witnessed firsthand the devastating consequences of unchecked tyranny, the horrors her own uncle had inflicted upon the people of the Northern Marshes. She wouldn't stand by and watch Thorne do the same to Port Dominus.

Silas's pragmatism, usually the bedrock of their planning, was overruled by his unwavering loyalty to Ada. He'd seen her transform from a panicked newcomer to a resolute leader, a beacon of hope in a world consumed by darkness. He trusted her judgment, even when it defied logic. He'd follow her into the heart of the storm, even if it meant facing certain death.

Korina, her violet eyes still haunted by the memories of Kaelen's abuse, nodded in silent agreement. Thorne's cruelty, his casual disregard for human life, resonated with her own trauma, fueling her resolve to fight for a world free from oppression.

We strike at dawn, Ada announced, her voice echoing in their minds, the telepathic link a conduit for their shared resolve. *We hit him hard, we hit him fast, and we don't stop until he's broken. We take back Port Dominus, not just for ourselves, but for every soul trapped within its walls. For every whisper of hope that Thorne has tried to silence.*

Erita's fingers flew across her console, weaving a tapestry of deception and misdirection to cover their movements. Korina hunched over *Obsidian*, her violet eyes blazing with a fierce intensity as she mapped out Thorne's defenses, searching for weaknesses in his seemingly impenetrable fortress. Sera, her crimson eyes burning with a righteous fury, began to sharpen her blades, the rhythmic rasp of steel against stone a chilling prelude to the coming storm. Silas, his gruff voice echoing through the room, began to rally the Azure Rose recruits, his words a mix of grim determination and unwavering loyalty.

The desperate gambit was set. They would assault the fortress, not just for tactical gain, but for the very soul of Port Dominus. They would fight not just as revolutionaries, but as avengers, as guardians, as the last flickering embers of hope in a city shrouded in darkness. They would fight for freedom, for justice, and for the right to love openly, without fear or shame. They would fight for the future Ada had promised them, a future where the whispers of hope could finally rise above the screams of oppression.

The command center, now empty, felt vast and hollow, the silence amplifying the weight of Ada's decision. The holographic map of Port Dominus pulsed with a menacing red glow, each flashing icon a grim reminder of the impending battle. Ada stood alone before the display, her violet eyes tracing the intricate network of Thorne's defenses. She'd sent her companions, her lovers, into the heart of the storm, and the thought of what awaited them sent a shiver of fear down her spine.

She knew their plan was audacious, bordering on suicidal. A direct assault on Thorne's financial fortress was a desperate gambit, a high-stakes gamble with the lives of everyone she cared about. Erita's diversion, Korina's hacking, Sera's assault—each piece of the plan was a thread in a fragile tapestry, one wrong move could unravel everything.

Ada reached into the hidden pocket of her uniform and retrieved a small, iridescent token. It shimmered faintly in the dim light, its surface swirling with an ethereal energy. It was a gift from Nividia, a parting token of their uneasy alliance, a one-way communication channel to the Render-Witch's private sanctum. Nividia had called it a 'curiosity', a 'back-up' to play with if Ada ever found herself in dire need of assistance.

Ada's fingers tightened around the token, its smooth surface cool against her skin. It was a long shot, a desperate plea into the void, but it was their only hope. They needed a miracle, an edge, something to tip the scales in their favor. And Nividia, with her unpredictable nature and reality-bending powers, was the only one who could provide it.

"Nividia," Ada whispered into the token, her voice a blend of desperation and determination. *"Nividia. This is Ada. Thorne's grip is strangling Port Dominus. My forces are strong, but his are entrenched. We are about to strike at his heart, but the cost will be high. Innocent people are dying. I ask not for you to fight my war, but for a show of support. A distraction. Any aid you can offer will be remembered when my new order is established."*

Uncertain if Nividia received the message, Ada knew she couldn't leave their fate to a single gamble. She attempted something she'd never done before: a long-distance telepathic broadcast. She closed her eyes, reaching out with her mind, stretching her consciousness across the vast continent toward Rhedeon, searching for the familiar anchor of Janna's steadfast mind. The strain was immense, a crushing pressure against her skull. Black spots danced at the edges of her vision, and a wave of nausea threatened to overwhelm her. She gritted her teeth, pushing through the pain, focusing all her will on reaching Janna.

She managed to form a fragmented, desperate plea, more a feeling than coherent words, pushing it out with all her strength: *Janna...fleet...hurry...danger...*

The effort was too much. The world around her dissolved into a swirling vortex of light and sound. The pressure in her skull intensified, a searing, blinding pain that threatened to shatter her consciousness. She gasped, her body convulsing, her fingers scrabbling at the console for support. Then, darkness.

Ada collapsed against the console, her body trembling from the immense neural strain. The holographic map of Port Dominus flickered erratically, its pulsing red lights casting distorted shadows across her pale face. The command center, once a beacon of hope, now felt like a tomb, the silence broken only by the faint hum of the cooling systems and Ada's ragged breaths. It was entirely ambiguous whether either of her desperate pleas was heard.

Ada clutched the token tightly, her heart pounding in her chest, the weight of her decision pressing down on her. She'd placed their fate in the hands of a volatile wildcard, a chaotic force of nature. It was a reckless gamble, but it was the only play she had left.

As the first rays of dawn pierced through the command center's reinforced windows, Ada turned back to the holographic map, her violet eyes fixed on the pulsing red icon of Thorne's fortress. The battle was about to begin. The fate of Port Dominus, the future of Kremøtoa, hung in the balance. And Ada, the Architect-Queen, the reluctant goddess of this digital world, could only wait, and pray, for the miracle she'd so desperately invoked.

CHAPTER 33

SEVERING THE LIFEBLOOD

The Mercantile District was a ghost town. Empty stalls, shuttered windows, and the oppressive silence of Thorne's curfew hung heavy in the air. Each shadow seemed to writhe with unseen dangers, every corner a potential ambush. Erita led the way, her senses heightened, her every movement precise and economical. She scanned the rooftops, the alleyways, the darkened doorways, searching for any flicker of movement, any hint of Thorne's hyper-alert patrols.

Quiet, she projected into the telepathic link, her voice a low, urgent whisper in the minds of Sera, Korina, and the still-unconscious Ada. *Eyes open. Thorne's hounds are everywhere.*

Sera, at her side, moved with the fluid grace of a predator, her crimson tunic a stark contrast to the muted grays and browns of the district. Korina, pale and tense, clung to Ada's limp form, her data-slate clutched tightly in her free hand. The weight of Ada's unconscious body was a constant reminder of the stakes. They were walking a tightrope, one misstep away from disaster.

They moved like wraiths through the deserted streets, sticking to the shadows, using the labyrinthine alleyways to their advantage. The air was thick with the metallic tang of fear and the faint, acrid scent of ozone, a telltale sign of active thaumaturgical defenses. Erita's pulse hammered against her ribs, a frantic drumbeat against the suffocating silence.

Finally, they reached their target. Thorne's financial processing center loomed before them, a brutalist monolith of reinforced concrete and darkened, bulletproof glass. It was far more formidable than their intel suggested, a veritable fortress bristling with automated sentinels and unseen defensive systems. Erita swore under her breath. This wasn't a processing center; it was a goddamn citadel.

Void's name, Sera hissed in the telepathic link, her voice laced with a mixture of awe and apprehension. *This is going to be fun.*

Korina, however, was less enthusiastic. *This is...significantly more fortified than anticipated. My initial scans indicate multiple layers of overlapping energy shields, automated thaumaturgical turrets, and a network of proximity sensors. A direct assault is...inadvisable.*

Erita ignored Korina's pessimism. They didn't have time for second-guessing. Ada's plan was their only option. *Rina, find a weakness. Sera, prepare for a diversion. We're going in.*

As Sera melted into the shadows, preparing to create the chaos they so desperately needed, Erita turned her attention to the fortress. Its smooth, obsidian surface reflected the city lights in distorted, fragmented patterns. It was a cold, unyielding face, a symbol of Thorne's suffocating grip on Port Dominus. But Erita had stared down worse odds before. She'd survived worse nightmares. She was a ghost in the machine, a whisper in the void. And she would find a way to crack this fortress, or die trying. She had to. For Ada. For Kremøtoa. For the future they were fighting so desperately to build.

"I'm so sorry, Rina," Ada murmured, her voice weak but apologetic. "I didn't mean to burden you like that." Korina adjusted her grip on Ada, a blush warming her cheeks despite the chill night air. The weight of Ada's body, though still lighter than expected, was less of a burden and more of a...comforting presence.

It's alright, Ada, she replied, her voice a hushed whisper in Ada's mind. *Focus on recovering. I'll handle this.*

Korina turned her attention to the fortress, her fingers dancing across Obsidian's cool surface. The data-slate hummed beneath her touch, a familiar extension of her own mind. Time to go to work.

Erita, Sera, stand by. Initiating infiltration sequence.

Korina launched her first probe, a delicate tendril of code designed to map the fortress's outer defenses. It barely penetrated the first layer of energy shielding before it was met with a ferocious counterattack. A wave of raw, chaotic data slammed into her probe, shattering it into a million useless fragments. Korina recoiled, a jolt of pure, digital pain lancing through her mind. Void's name, Thorne's defenses were more aggressive than she anticipated.

Undeterred, Korina launched a second probe, this one heavier, more heavily shielded. It fared slightly better, managing to penetrate deeper into the system before it, too, was met with a brutal counterattack. This time, however, Korina was ready. She'd analyzed the first attack, recognized its pattern, its signature. She'd anticipated its return.

She met the counterattack head-on, her own code a swirling vortex of defensive algorithms and aggressive countermeasures.

The digital clash was a maelstrom of raw data, a blinding storm of ones and zeros. Korina felt a thrill course through her, a strange exhilaration at the sheer intensity of the digital duel. This wasn't just hacking; it was *war*.

Thorne's system was adaptive, learning, evolving with each attack. It was unlike anything she'd encountered before, a vicious, intelligent entity that anticipated her every move, countered her every strategy. But Korina was no slouch either. She was a prodigy, a master of code, a digital warrior.

She launched probe after probe, each one designed to exploit a perceived weakness, each one met with an equally ferocious counterattack. The digital battlefield crackled with energy, a chaotic landscape of shifting firewalls and aggressive data streams. Korina's mind raced, her fingers a blur across Obsidian's surface. She was losing, she knew. Thorne's system was too strong, too adaptive. But she couldn't give up. She had to find a way in. She had to. Ada was counting on her. Their entire revolution depended on it.

The air crackled with the raw energy of unleashed thaumaturgy. Sera grinned, a feral gleam in her eyes. This was more like it. This was what she was *made* for.

"Azure Rose!" she roared, her voice a thunderclap in the sudden cacophony of battle. "Forward!"

Her hand-picked team surged forward, a crimson tide crashing against the steel and obsidian defenses of Thorne's fortress. They were outnumbered, outgunned, and facing an enemy fortified in prepared positions, but they were the Azure Rose. They were the best damn fighters in Port Dominus. And they would not yield.

The first volley of energy blasts ripped through the air, searing streaks of blinding light that slammed into the charging revolutionaries. Two of Sera's recruits went down, screaming, their bodies engulfed in flames. Sera swore under her breath. Thorne's defenses were heavier than anticipated. This wasn't going to be a quick, clean operation. This was going to be a bloodbath.

She ducked behind a stack of crates, the wood splintering around her as another volley of energy blasts ripped through the air. "Lars, Eliria, take the left flank! Markus, Elliot, right! Focus fire on those turrets!" she barked into the telepathic link, her voice sharp and precise.

Lars and Eliria, two of her most trusted lieutenants, acknowledged her command and peeled off, leading their respective squads in a flanking maneuver. Markus and Elliot followed suit, their movements mirroring the practiced efficiency of seasoned warriors. Sera watched them go, a grim satisfaction settling in her gut. They were good. Damn good. But even the best couldn't survive this kind of onslaught forever.

She drew her twin blades, the polished steel gleaming in the flickering light of the energy blasts. Time to even the odds.

With a guttural roar, she charged forward, a crimson blur in the heart of the chaos. Her blades danced, a whirlwind of steel that deflected energy blasts and sliced through flesh and bone. She moved with the fluid grace of a dancer, the brutal efficiency of a seasoned killer. Two enforcers fell before her, their bodies crumpling to the ground in a bloody heap. A third lunged at her, a massive brute wielding a plasma axe. Sera met his attack head-on, her blades clashing against the glowing axe in a shower of sparks. The force of the impact sent tremors through her arms, but she held her ground. She was stronger than she looked. Faster. More *lethal.*

She parried another blow, ducked under a wild swing, and

then, with a lightning-fast maneuver, drove her blade deep into the enforcer's throat. He gurgled, his eyes widening in surprise, and then collapsed, his massive body twitching on the ground.

Sera didn't have time to savor her victory. More enforcers were closing in, their faces grim, their weapons charged. She spun, her blades flashing, carving a path through the enemy ranks. But for every enforcer she took down, two more seemed to take their place. They were relentless, a tide of armored bodies that threatened to overwhelm her, to drown her in their sheer numbers.

Ada, Rina, Eri, report, she hissed into the telepathic link, her voice strained with exertion. *We're taking heavy casualties down here. Need support. Now.*

Silence. Only the crackle of energy weapons and the screams of the dying answered her plea. Sera's heart sank. Where were they? What was taking so long? They were running out of time.

They were running out of *lives.*

The scene unfolded before Ada like a nightmare rendering in slow motion. Crimson streaks, flashes of energy fire, the sickening thud of bodies hitting concrete. Her carefully crafted plan, disintegrating into a chaotic ballet of death. Her recruits, so full of hope and fire just moments ago, were being systematically slaughtered. Their new weapons, the spoils of the *Iron Serpent,* sputtered and died in their hands, useless against the overwhelming tide of Thorne's enforcers. Panic clawed at her throat, threatening to choke her. This wasn't how it was supposed to be. This wasn't...*right.*

And then she saw Sera.

A whirlwind of crimson and steel, her twin blades flashing in the dim light, she fought with a frenzied desperation that bordered on madness. Three enforcers lay dead at her feet, their bodies twisted and broken. But she was tiring, slowing. The enforcers, sensing her weakness, pressed their advantage, a pack of wolves circling a wounded lioness. They were closing in, their faces grim, their weapons raised for the kill.

A primal roar tore from Ada's throat, a raw, untamed sound that echoed through the shattered streets. It wasn't a sound of fear. It wasn't a sound of despair. It was a sound of *fury*. A cold, incandescent fury that burned away the last vestiges of her carefully constructed control, unleashing the full, terrifying power that lay dormant within her.

Her violet eyes blazed with an unnatural light, a terrifying glow that reflected the power surging through her veins. She didn't hesitate. She didn't calculate. She simply *acted*. Her focus shifted, her vision tunneling down, down, down through the layers of concrete and steel, to the heart of the building, to the primary power grid humming deep in the subterranean levels. A single, devastating command echoed in the silent chambers of her mind.

[MALFUNCTION: Critical Overload]

The entire building shuddered, a violent convulsion that sent tremors through the very foundations of Port Dominus. Lights exploded in showers of sparks. Automated turrets sputtered and died, their menacing red eyes winking out one by one. The enforcers' advanced tech, their shields and energy weapons, flickered and failed, plunging them into absolute darkness and chaos. A wave of panicked shouts and startled cries erupted from the Imperial lines.

"Now!" Ada screamed, her voice raw, amplified by the sudden, ringing silence. "***NOW!***"

And then, the tide turned.

Sera, sensing the shift in the battle, rallied the surviving revolutionaries. They surged forward, a wave of crimson and steel crashing against the disoriented and panicked Imperial lines. They moved with a renewed ferocity, their blades flashing, their weapons spitting fire. The enforcers, blinded and confused, stumbled and fell, their advanced technology now a useless burden in the sudden darkness.

They burst into the server room, the air thick with the smell of ozone and burnt circuitry. Korina, her digital path finally cleared, stood poised before the main data port, *Obsidian* clutched in her hand. Her face was pale, her eyes wide with a mixture of fear and determination. She didn't hesitate. She plunged *Obsidian* into the port, the connection snapping into place with a satisfying click. A surge of violet light erupted from the data-slate, bathing the room in an ethereal glow. On every screen, on every terminal, on every piece of Thorne's meticulously crafted financial network, a single, stark message flashed:

[ACCESS DENIED: ACCOUNTS FROZEN]

"Done," Korina whispered, her voice trembling. "It's done."

Ada felt a surge of triumph, a fierce, exhilarating rush of victory. But it was short-lived. The cheers of the revolutionaries were quickly replaced by the groans of the wounded, the cries of the dying. The true cost of their desperate gambit, the brutal price of their revolution, was now terrifyingly clear.

They retreated quickly through the shadowed streets of Port Dominus, a silent procession of wounded warriors and grieving comrades. The city, once a symbol of Thorne's tyrannical power, now lay in darkness and chaos. Their victory was absolute. But it felt hollow. Empty. The weight of their losses, the faces of the fallen, pressed down on Ada, a heavy burden she knew she would carry for the rest of her days. The revolution had begun. But at what cost?

CHAPTER 34

A MONSTER UNLEASHED

The warehouse headquarters, once a symbol of burgeoning hope, was now a somber tableau of human suffering. The air, thick with the coppery tang of blood and the sharp sting of antiseptic, hung heavy and oppressive. Low moans and hushed whispers, punctuated by the rhythmic squeak of cots and the hurried footsteps of medics, replaced the confident chatter and strategic planning that had filled the space just hours before. It was a stark, brutal contrast to the tactical success they had achieved.

Ada walked among the rows of makeshift cots, her heart heavy with a grief that threatened to crush her. Each pale face, each bandaged limb, each shallow breath was a testament to the brutal cost of their revolution. She had brought them here, to this fight, to this...*slaughter*. And despite the power she wielded, the reality-bending abilities that made her a goddess in their eyes, she couldn't save them all. The realization was a bitter pill to swallow, a cold, hard truth that chipped away at the edges of her resolve.

She stopped before a young recruit, his face ashen, his breathing shallow and ragged. A crimson stain bloomed on his thigh, spreading rapidly across the rough bandages. A medic knelt beside him, his face grim, his hands working frantically but futilely to stem the flow of blood. Ada recognized the injury instantly: a femoral artery laceration. Critical. Fatal.

A wave of impotent fury washed over her, a burning frustration that tightened her chest and made her breath catch in her throat. She wanted to scream, to rage against the unfairness of it all. She had the power to rewrite reality, to bend the very fabric of this world to her will. Yet, she couldn't stop this boy from dying. Not without...

She knelt beside the cot, her hand hovering over the crimson stain. She could feel the frantic pulse of life beneath her fingertips, a faint, thrumming beat that was fading fast. She closed her eyes, her mind racing, her thoughts a chaotic jumble of code and commands. Could she do it? Could she afford to? The drain on her energy the last time she had performed such a drastic act of healing had been profound, dizzying. But the alternative...

"No," she whispered, her voice barely audible above the moans of the wounded. "Not *this one*."

She took a deep breath, steeling herself against the inevitable backlash. Her violet eyes snapped open, blazing with an unnatural light. She reached out, her fingers brushing against the torn fabric. And then, she began to *rewrite*.

Line by line, command by command, she rewrote the boy's flesh, knitting together the torn artery, sealing the wound, restoring the damaged tissue. She could feel the drain on her own energy, a profound and dizzying pull that made her head spin and her vision blur. It was like trying to hold back a tidal wave with her bare hands. But she held on, her focus unwavering, her will unbreakable. She wouldn't let go. Not until...

The bleeding stopped. The crimson stain began to recede, replaced by healthy, pink flesh. The boy's breathing deepened, becoming more regular. His ashen face regained a hint of color. He was alive.

Ada collapsed back onto her heels, her body trembling with exhaustion, her mind reeling. The world swam around her, a blurry kaleidoscope of light and shadow. She could hear voices, but they seemed distant, muffled, as if coming from the other end of a long tunnel. She felt a hand on her shoulder, a gentle but firm grip that anchored her to reality.

"Ada," a voice said, a voice she knew, a voice she loved. "Ada, are you alright?"

It was Sera. Her face, etched with worry, swam into focus. Her crimson hair, usually a vibrant flame, seemed dull and lifeless in the dim light. Her eyes, usually bright and full of fire, were filled with a deep, unsettling concern.

"You cannot save everyone like that," Sera said, her voice soft but firm. "I cannot watch that happen to you."

Ada wanted to argue, to protest. But the words wouldn't come. She could only nod, a weak, shaky movement that conveyed her understanding, her acceptance. She knew Sera was right. She couldn't keep doing this. Not without destroying herself in the process.

"Besides," Sera added, her voice barely above a whisper, "that one...he was the worst one."

The words hit Ada like a physical blow, knocking the air from her lungs. The boy she had just saved, the boy she had poured so much of her own life force into, was the *worst* one? The one closest to death. The one least likely to survive. The full weight of her actions, the sheer magnitude of her sacrifice, crashed down on her, crushing her beneath its weight. A sob escaped her lips, a choked, broken sound that was quickly followed by another, and another, until she was sobbing uncontrollably in Sera's arms.

The warehouse, the wounded, the revolution...it all faded away, replaced by a single, overwhelming wave of grief and exhaustion. She had saved a life. But at what cost?

The air in Thorne's command center crackled with a silent, electric tension. Emergency lights cast long, distorted shadows across the opulent room, the flickering holographic displays painting the walls with a grim tableau of financial ruin. **[ACCOUNTS FROZEN]** flashed in stark red across the main screen, a digital epitaph to his crumbling empire. Each pulsing alert was a fresh wound, a constant, agonizing reminder of the lifeblood draining from his coffers. His mercenaries, his enforcers, his entire network of power...all dependent on the steady flow of Byts, a flow that had been abruptly and brutally severed.

He stood before the main display, his hands clasped behind his back, his posture rigid, his face an impassive mask. He was not a man prone to outbursts of emotion. Anger, in his view, was a crude, inefficient tool, a wasteful expenditure of energy. But the cold, pure fury that coiled in his gut was something different entirely. It was a calculated rage, a glacial, all-consuming fire that burned with the intensity of a thousand suns.

His eyes scanned the data streams, sifting through the reports of the assault, searching for patterns, for vulnerabilities, for any exploitable weakness in his enemy's strategy. The initial reports had been a chaotic jumble of panicked cries and conflicting accounts. But now, as the dust settled, a chilling clarity emerged. The attack on his financial processing center had been precise, surgical. A coordinated assault on multiple fronts, executed with ruthless efficiency. But it was the *method* that truly unnerved him. The system-wide power surge, the complete blackout that had crippled his defenses...it was *impossible*. His systems were shielded, protected by layers of arcane and technological safeguards. No conventional force could have breached them.

He replayed the security footage, watching the events unfold in slow motion. The initial assault had been predictable, almost amateurish. A clumsy diversion at his manor, easily contained by his elite guard. A pathetic attempt to hack his network, quickly neutralized by his countermeasures. But then...the blackout. A sudden, inexplicable surge of energy that had rippled through the entire city, shutting down every system, every device, every last flickering light. It was as if the very fabric of reality had been momentarily unraveled.

Thorne felt a cold dread creep into his heart, a chilling premonition that he was not just fighting rebels. He was fighting something...*else*. Something unquantifiable, something that defied all logic and reason. A reality-bending force that his armies, his weapons, his entire arsenal of power, could not hope to contain.

He turned away from the display, his face pale, his eyes narrowed. He had underestimated his enemy. He had mistaken their audacity for foolishness, their defiance for desperation. He had treated them as pawns in his game. But now, he saw the truth. They were not pawns. They were players. And they were playing a game he did not understand.

He crossed the room to a secure comm panel, his footsteps echoing in the oppressive silence. His fingers danced across the controls, activating a deeply encrypted channel, one reserved for his most absolute last resort. The comm line pulsed with a faint, ethereal glow, a direct link to the one person in Port Dominus who dealt in the impossible.

"Alchemist," Thorne said, his voice cold, devoid of any emotion. "I have a...*project* for you."

The response was a distorted, guttural hiss, a sound that made even Thorne's hardened mercenaries uneasy.

"Name your price," Thorne continued, ignoring the unsettling noise. He opened a hidden vault, revealing a cache of platinum Byts, a fortune that would make even the greediest pirate lord salivate. "And remove all restraints."

The hissing intensified, morphing into a series of clicks and whistles, a language that Thorne did not understand but instinctively knew conveyed acceptance.

"Hunt them," Thorne said, his voice a low, menacing growl. "Erase them. Leave nothing...but dust."

He closed the comm channel, the ethereal glow fading away, leaving the room in darkness once more. He walked to the window, staring out at the sprawling cityscape below, the flickering lights painting a chaotic tapestry of shadows and whispers. His city. His empire. Now a hunting ground for the monster he had just unleashed.

A cold, nihilistic smile twisted his lips. He had made his choice. He would burn his own city down, if necessary, just to eliminate the ghosts that haunted it. He would not be defeated. Not by rebels. Not by magic. Not by anything.

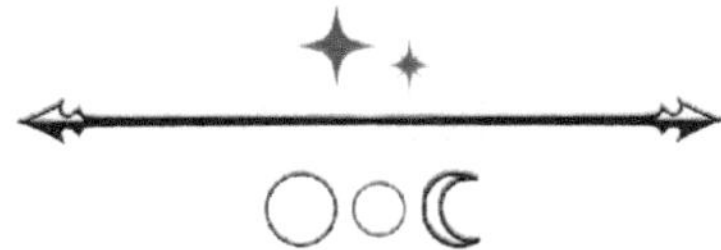

The muted chime of the incoming report barely registered over the low hum of the Prefecture's climate control system. Prefect Kraus Valerius sat at his obsidian desk, the polished surface reflecting the stark geometry of his office. Light panels embedded in the ceiling cast a cold, even glow, eliminating all shadows, all ambiguity. Order. Control. These were the pillars of his existence, the fundamental principles upon which he had built his power, his career, his entire life.

A junior aide entered, his face a canvas of barely suppressed panic. Valerius noted the tremor in the young man's hand as he presented the data-slate, a small, but significant, deviation from standard protocol. Interesting. Fear, Valerius had long observed, was a potent catalyst for inefficiency. He made a mental note to have the aide reassigned to a less demanding post. Perhaps archives. Somewhere far, far away from the immediacy of power; he was feeling generous, the aide was genuinely almost in a full panic.

"Report," Valerius said, his voice a low, gravelly hum.

"Prefect Valerius," the aide stammered, his eyes darting nervously around the sterile office. "We have...a situation."

Valerius raised a perfectly sculpted eyebrow. A situation. How delightfully vague. He gestured for the aide to continue.

"Sir, it's Thorne. Alaric Thorne. His financial processing center...it's been completely neutralized."

Valerius's expression remained unchanged. Neutralized. An interesting choice of words. He waited for the inevitable clarification.

"His accounts...they're frozen, sir. Completely locked down. Every last Byt."

Valerius leaned back in his chair, his pale blue eyes fixed on the aide's face. Frozen. Locked down. Still imprecise, but intriguing. He had anticipated some form of retaliation from the Azure Rose, perhaps a minor disruption, a temporary setback for Thorne. But this...this was different. This was surgical.

"Method?" Valerius asked, his voice betraying the slightest hint of curiosity.

"Unknown, sir. Our analysts are baffled. There's no discernible digital footprint. No trace of arcane interference. It's as if...as if the Byts simply vanished."

Valerius felt a flicker of...something. Not anger. Not fear. But a profound, intellectual fascination. This was not the work of common rebels, not the clumsy, predictable tactics of Thorne's usual adversaries. This was the work of a new variable. An unknown quantity. Unquantifiable. The word echoed in his mind, a perfect descriptor for the anomaly he had been tracking. The girl from Oakhaven. Ada Lynx.

His analytical calm, however, shattered the moment the aide delivered the final, chilling piece of intel.

"And sir...our sources within the Confederacy...they confirm... Thorne has activated *The Alchemist.*"

The words hung in the air, heavy with unspoken dread. The Alchemist. Not a name whispered in hushed tones, but a concept, a specter, a nightmare given form. The Alchemist did not capture. They did not interrogate. They did not imprison. They *erased.* Completely. Utterly. Irrevocably. They were the ultimate solution for the underworld's most intractable problems, a tool deployed only in the most extreme circumstances. And now, Thorne, in his blind, predictable rage, had unleashed that tool upon his own city.

A raw, primal panic seized Valerius, a visceral fear he had not experienced in decades. His carefully constructed composure, the mask of cold, analytical detachment he wore like a second skin, cracked. The girl. Ada. His unquantifiable asset. The key, he believed, to a new era of Imperial control, an era of unprecedented power and dominion. She was in danger. Not just of capture, not just of imprisonment, but of complete and utter annihilation. Erased from existence. A blank space where a universe of potential had once resided.

He dismissed the aide with a curt gesture, his mind racing, calculating, strategizing. He was powerless to intervene directly. Not yet. Not without revealing his own hand, his own carefully laid plans. He could not risk exposing his interest in the girl, not to Thorne, not to the Council, not to anyone. He had to maintain the facade of detached indifference, the illusion of absolute control.

He turned to the tactical map displayed on the far wall, his eyes scanning the glowing grid, searching for a solution, for a way out of this impossible predicament. He saw the swirling chaos of Port Dominus, a festering wound on the Empire's otherwise pristine flank. He saw the strategic importance of the city, its vast resources, its potential for power. And he saw the girl, a tiny, insignificant flicker of light in the heart of that chaos, a single, unquantifiable variable that could either save his empire...or destroy it.

A silent, desperate hope warred with his cold logic, a secret prayer to the very forces he sought to control. He hoped, against all reason, that the anomaly, *his* anomaly, was smart enough, powerful enough, resourceful enough to survive. He needed her to survive. He needed her alive. Not for the Empire. Not for the Council. But for himself. He needed her, so that he could still have the chance, the opportunity, the exquisite pleasure of apprehending her himself.

Remembering his mental note, he activated the comm panel on his desk, the obsidian surface rippling with light. "Secretary Lyra," he said, his voice regaining its usual modulated precision.

"Yes, Prefect Valerius?" a crisp, efficient voice responded.

"Regarding Junior Aide Theron. The one who just delivered the report on Port Dominus."

"Yes, sir. I have his file open."

"Reassign him to the Doricum Archives. Effective immediately."

"Archives, sir? That seems...a significant demotion."

Valerius allowed a sliver of amusement to color his tone. "Not a demotion, Lyra. A lateral transfer. A strategic reallocation of resources. Tell him...tell him he's not in any trouble. Just...needs to de-stress. Perhaps a less demanding post will allow him to regain his...composure."

"Of course, Prefect Valerius. I'll inform him immediately."

"Good. And Lyra..."

"Yes, sir?"

"Ensure his transfer includes a commendation for...diligence. We wouldn't want to lose such a...dedicated asset." He ended the communication, a thin, cruel smile playing on his lips. Waste not, want not. Even a panicked aide could serve a purpose. Somewhere. Someday.

CHAPTER 35

BAITING THE TRAP

The warehouse command center, once a hub of frantic activity, now pulsed with a different kind of energy. The air, thick with the metallic tang of blood and sweat, crackled with a cold, simmering resolve. Gone was the fear, the uncertainty, the frantic scrambling for solutions. In its place stood a steely determination, a quiet confidence born not of arrogance, but of a deep, unshakeable conviction.

Ada stood before the holographic map of Port Dominus, her violet eyes blazing with an inner fire that illuminated the darkened room. The flickering projections cast dancing shadows across her face, highlighting the sharp angles of her jaw, the determined set of her mouth, the unwavering focus in her gaze. She had received Erita's chilling report. Thorne had activated The Alchemist. But instead of fear, the news had ignited a spark of audacious defiance within her.

"We will not wait for them to come to us," she declared, her voice calm and clear, cutting through the hushed tension like a honed blade. "We will force their hand. We will draw them out into the open."

Sera, leaning against a steel support beam, her arms crossed, raised a skeptical eyebrow. "And how do you propose we do that? The Alchemist is a ghost. A whisper in the dark. They strike from the shadows, then vanish without a trace."

"Exactly," Ada said, a subtle smile playing on her lips. "And that's precisely what we'll use against them. We will use the weapons shipment as bait."

Korina, hunched over her data-slate, looked up, her violet eyes wide with concern. "The weapons shipment? But that's our main leverage against Thorne. We can't risk losing it."

"We won't lose it," Ada assured her. "Not really. We will leak false intelligence. A carefully crafted deception. A target so tantalizing, so irresistible, that The Alchemist, believing us to be distracted and vulnerable, will be unable to resist the opportunity to strike."

Erita, perched on the edge of a table, her golden eyes gleaming with predatory amusement, let out a low whistle. "Bold. I like it. Make them think we're weak, then spring the trap. Classic maneuver."

Ada nodded, her gaze sweeping across the faces of her companions, gauging their reactions. "We'll spread rumors. Whispers in the dark alleys. Encrypted messages on the black market data streams. We'll let it slip that we're planning a major raid on Thorne's main warehouse. A desperate gambit to replenish our dwindling resources. We'll make it seem like we're throwing all our forces into this one, reckless attack, leaving our most valuable assets—the weapons shipment—vulnerable and unguarded."

"And where will the weapons shipment actually be?" Silas asked, his gruff voice laced with a hint of concern.

Ada's smile widened, revealing a flash of sharp teeth. "That's the beauty of it, Silas. The weapons shipment will be exactly where they expect it to be. In the warehouse. Heavily guarded. Waiting for them."

Korina's brow furrowed. "But...if they believe we're raiding Thorne's warehouse, why would they attack the weapons shipment? Wouldn't they go after us?"

"They will," Ada said, her voice dropping to a conspiratorial whisper. "But not all of them. The Alchemist is not a brute force warrior like Thorne. They're a surgeon. A scalpel. Precise. Calculated. They'll see the raid as an opportunity. A chance to eliminate us while we're distracted, scattered, and vulnerable. But they'll also see the weapons shipment as a secondary objective. A bonus. A chance to cripple Thorne while they're at it; The Alchemist is likely an opportunist. Two birds with one stone. It's too tempting for someone like The Alchemist to resist."

Sera, her initial skepticism replaced by a grudging admiration, nodded slowly. "Alright. I see your play. But what makes you so sure they'll take the bait?"

"Because I know how they think," Ada said, her eyes flashing with a dangerous light. "They're a predator. And predators are always drawn to the scent of blood. Especially when they think they have a sure thing." She turned back to the holographic map, her fingers tracing the intricate network of streets and alleyways, her mind already several steps ahead, anticipating The Alchemist's every move, planning for every contingency. "We will turn their arrogance against them. We will use their greed as our weapon. We will hunt the hunter." A predatory gleam entered Ada's eyes, a violet fire that promised swift, merciless retribution. "And when they least expect it...we will strike."

Erita's fingers danced across the cool surface of her data-slate, a blur of motion that belied the intricate precision of her work. Each keystroke was a calculated move in a high-stakes game of deception, a digital gambit designed to lure their prey into a carefully constructed trap. Her eyes, sharp and focused, scanned the scrolling lines of code, her mind already several steps ahead, anticipating her enemy's every move.

She began by creating a series of fake shipping manifests, detailing a shipment of high-grade energy cells—the kind that powered Imperial battleships—destined for a secret warehouse in the industrial sector. She then fabricated a network of phantom contacts, weaving together a complex web of encrypted messages between non-existent smugglers, black market brokers, and disgruntled Imperial officials. The messages hinted at a daring heist, a desperate attempt by the Azure Rose to seize the energy cells and cripple Thorne's war machine.

The centerpiece of her deception was a detailed plan, complete with a precise time and location for the supposed raid. She chose a vast, derelict processing plant in the industrial sector—a multi-leveled labyrinth of rusting machinery and shadowy corners—a perfect killing ground. The plan was a work of art, a symphony of misinformation designed to play on Thorne's arrogance and the Alchemist's desire for a clean, surgical strike.

With the digital trap set, Erita carefully 'leaked' the information into the city's underworld networks. She used anonymous data streams, backdoor channels, and compromised communication relays, ensuring the information would be intercepted by Thorne's spies and fed directly to the Alchemist. As she watched the data packets disappear into the digital ether, a sly smile spread across her face. The bait was set. Now, all they had to do was wait.

While Erita wove her digital web, Sera and Korina were busy transforming the derelict processing plant into a deadly trap. The vast, echoing space, once a symbol of the city's industrial might, now stood silent and abandoned, a decaying monument to a forgotten era. But beneath the layers of rust and dust, a new purpose was taking shape.

Sera, leading a small squad of hand-picked Azure Rose recruits, moved through the labyrinthine space with the quiet efficiency of a seasoned predator. Her eyes scanned the environment, assessing every angle, every shadow, every potential point of vulnerability. She established overlapping fields of fire, reinforcing chokepoints with salvaged barricades and strategically placed explosives. She mapped out fallback positions, escape routes, and emergency rendezvous points, ensuring her team could adapt to any situation, any contingency.

Korina, meanwhile, worked her own kind of magic. Her data-slate, *Obsidian*, pulsed with a soft, violet light as she rigged the plant with a network of hidden sensors. The sensors were linked to a sophisticated program she had designed, capable of generating fluctuating energy fields. These fields, calibrated to disrupt the Alchemist's elemental manipulation, would create pockets of unpredictable arcane interference, turning the environment itself into a weapon against their enemy.

She also deployed a series of atmospheric regulators, designed to neutralize any chemical agents The Alchemist might unleash. The regulators, humming softly as they filtered the stale air, added another layer of defense to their carefully constructed trap.

Ada, the architect of their revolution, oversaw it all. She moved through the plant with a quiet grace, her violet eyes scanning the environment, her mind processing a constant stream of data. She used subtle applications of her power to reinforce weak structures, creating invisible supports that held the rusting catwalks together. She altered the lighting, deepening shadows here, creating pools of illumination there, subtly manipulating the environment to create tactical advantages for her team.

Ada took her position on a crumbling catwalk overlooking the plant's main processing chamber. Below her, the cavernous space stretched out in a maze of rusting pipes, decaying machinery, and shadowy corners. The air was thick with the scent of dust and decay, a heavy, oppressive silence that pressed down on her like a physical weight. *He's coming*, Erita's voice whispered in her mind, a cool, calm counterpoint to the storm of anticipation raging within her.

Ada closed her eyes, taking a deep breath, focusing her senses. She could feel the subtle hum of Korina's arcane disruptors, the faint metallic tang of Sera's blades, the quiet, steady rhythm of Erita's breathing as she monitored their comms network. They were a symphony of silence, a perfectly tuned instrument of destruction, waiting to be unleashed. *Remember the plan*, Ada projected into their shared mental space. *No unnecessary risks. We take him alive. If possible,* Sera added, a hint of grim humor in her voice. *Preferably in one piece.* Korina chimed in, her voice a mix of nervous excitement and analytical focus.

Ada opened her eyes, scanning the chamber below. Every shadow seemed to writhe, every rustle of metal echoed in the oppressive silence. The tension was almost unbearable, a tightly coiled spring waiting to be released. She could feel the weight of their mission, the hopes of the city, resting on her shoulders. This was not just about taking down a monster; it was about sending a message to Thorne, to the Empire, to the entire world. They were not prey; they were predators. And they were done running.

A faint sound broke the silence—a soft, almost imperceptible scraping against metal. Ada tensed, her hand instinctively reaching for the energy blade strapped to her thigh. *He's here*, she projected, her voice a low, urgent hum in their minds. *Level three, south access corridor.* Sera's response was a wordless acknowledgment, a shift in her mental presence that spoke volumes. She was moving, a silent shadow slipping through the darkness, her blades humming softly as she closed in on their prey.

Korina activated her arcane disruptors, creating pockets of fluctuating energy throughout the chamber. The air shimmered with an eerie, violet light, the rusting metal around them seeming to twist and writhe as the energy fields pulsed and shifted. *Ready when you are*, Korina projected, her voice a steady, focused hum.

Erita's voice, cool and precise, cut through the tension. *Thorne's forces are en route. ETA five minutes.* The news was both a warning and a challenge. They had to take down the Alchemist quickly, efficiently, and without drawing too much attention. Time was not a luxury they could afford.

Ada took another deep breath, steeling her nerves. The scraping sound grew louder, closer, echoing through the cavernous space. The monster was coming. And they were ready.

CHAPTER 36

THE PRICE OF REVOLUTION

The abandoned processing plant was a tomb. Not of death, not yet, but of waiting silence. The air, thick with the metallic tang of old machinery and the ghosts of forgotten industry, hung heavy and still. Erita, perched high in the skeletal remains of a control booth, surveyed the scene below. Her data-slate, nestled in her lap, was a silent symphony of glowing icons and pulsing energy readings—a testament to Korina's meticulous preparation. Every sensor, every tripwire, every carefully placed explosive charge was represented on the screen, a digital map of their meticulously crafted trap.

She watched as Ada, a silhouette against the dim light filtering through the grimy windows, took her position on a crumbling catwalk overlooking the plant's main processing chamber. Sera, a shadow among shadows, melted into the darkness below, her movements fluid and silent as a predator stalking its prey. They were ready.

The first sign of the Alchemist was not a sound, nor a visual. It was a shift, a subtle change in the very air they breathed. A faint, sweet scent, like crushed almonds, tickled Erita's nostrils, a phantom taste on her tongue. A second later, the atmospheric sensors on her data-slate flared crimson, pulsing with a frantic urgency.

Nitrogen trifluoride, Korina's voice whispered urgently over the telepathic link, a frantic edge to her normally calm tone. *It's displacing the oxygen. They're trying to suffocate us before the fight even begins!*

Erita cursed under her breath. The Alchemist wasn't just dangerous; they were insidious. This wasn't a straightforward attack; it was a multi-pronged assault designed to weaken them, to disorient them, to break their resolve before the first blow was even struck. Invisible gases, odorless and tasteless, seeped from hidden vents in the walls, silently replacing the breathable air with a cocktail of toxins. A fine, corrosive mist, barely visible in the dim light, drifted from a stack of rusting barrels in the corner, eating away at exposed metal and threatening to burn their lungs with every inhaled breath. And in the distance, a series of timed, low-yield explosives detonated with muffled thuds, sending shockwaves through the structure, designed to disorient and herd them into the kill box.

Sera, pull back to Level Two. North access corridor, Erita projected, her voice sharp and decisive. *Korina, can you isolate the source of the gas? Ada, can you create a breathable zone?*

On it, Korina replied, her mental voice tight with concentration. A flurry of activity flickered across Erita's data-slate as Korina rerouted power and reconfigured sensors. *The gas is coming from the ventilation system. Multiple injection points. I'm working on a bypass, but it will take time.*

The world, viewed through Ada's Admin-view, was a tapestry of code, a symphony of data streams flowing and intertwining. She saw not just the physical structure of the abandoned processing plant, but the underlying matrix of energy and information that governed its existence. The Alchemist's attack, a chaotic swirl of vibrant colors and pulsing energy signatures, unfolded before her like a malicious program unleashed within a delicate system. Noxious gases, represented by swirling clouds of venomous green code, snaked through the ventilation ducts, converging on Sera and the others. Corrosive mists, shimmering veils of acidic orange data, drifted from hidden vents, eating away at the very fabric of the building.

Ada felt a cold, detached anger. This wasn't a battle of strength or skill; it was an act of vandalism, a deliberate attempt to corrupt the very systems she had so painstakingly crafted. She extended her will, her eyes glowing with a cold, violet light—the telltale sign of her Admin privileges activating. With a series of quiet, internal commands, she rewrote the properties of the attacking agents.

[object_group: chemical_agents | property: toxicity = 0]

The change was instantaneous. The venomous green code of the suffocating gas faded to a harmless, neutral gray, transforming into inert air. The acidic orange of the corrosive mist dissolved into a gentle blue, the particles becoming harmless water vapor. Sera and Erita, their faces contorted in masks of desperate concentration, gasped in relief as the air around them cleared, the threat neutralized before it could reach them.

But the Alchemist, a fleeting shadow glimpsed on a high gantry overlooking the processing chamber, was not done. They raised their hands, and a glittering cloud of dust, shimmering with an almost iridescent quality, erupted from their fingertips. Ada's Admin-view exploded with a cacophony of alerts, the data streams twisting and contorting as a new, more insidious threat emerged. Adaptive nanites, a swarm of microscopic machines designed to dismantle organic matter at a molecular level, filled the air, their code a chaotic, ever-shifting kaleidoscope of crimson and gold.

Ada felt a flicker of genuine fear. This wasn't a brute-force attack anymore but a targeted, insidious assault designed to exploit the very vulnerabilities she had inadvertently programmed into the world's inhabitants. These nanites, if they reached Sera, Korina, or Erita, would tear them apart from the inside out, leaving nothing but a fine, crimson dust.

There was no time for complex countermeasures, no time for elegant solutions. Ada had to act, and she had to act decisively. She focused her will, channeling her power into a single, devastating command:

[object_group: nanite_swarm | property: molecular_stability = null]

The effect was immediate and absolute. The shimmering, chaotic code of the nanite swarm simply vanished, blinked out of existence mid-air as if it had never been there at all. The glittering dust, a moment ago a deadly threat, dissipated into nothingness, leaving the air clean and still.

On the high gantry, the Alchemist staggered back, their arms falling limp to their sides. Their face, normally hidden behind a mask of technological indifference, was contorted in a mask of shock and disbelief. Their technological mastery, their elemental manipulation, their carefully crafted arsenal of alchemical weapons—all rendered utterly useless against Ada's absolute control over the world's code. They had underestimated their opponent, mistaking Ada for just another mage, another thaumaturge bound by the rules of the system. They had not understood that Ada *was* the system, and she could rewrite those rules at will.

Void, Erita muttered over the telepathic link, her voice laced with a mix of awe and apprehension. *What in the Void did you just do?*

I debugged the bugs, Ada replied, her mental voice calm and steady, *a necessary system patch.*

She deactivated her Admin-view, the crimson light fading from her eyes, leaving them their natural violet hue. The world returned to normal, the underlying code hidden once more beneath the surface of reality. But the silence that followed was different now, charged with a new understanding. The Alchemist had tested her, and they had failed. Now, it was time for Ada to take control of the game.

The sudden silence in the processing plant was more unnerving than the Alchemist's alchemical assault. The air, still thick with the lingering scent of ozone and something acrid and metallic, crackled with an unspoken tension. Sera's enhanced senses, honed by years of training in the Aegis Order, strained against the quiet, searching for any hint of movement, any sign that the threat hadn't truly been neutralized. Her grip tightened on the hilts of her blades, the cool, polished steel a comforting weight against her palms.

Central gantry, top level, Erita's voice whispered in her mind, cool and precise, like the edge of a freshly honed dagger. *Thermal signature still strong. They're cornered, Sera. Finish him!*

Sera didn't hesitate. With a fluid, almost silent movement, she launched herself into the maze of catwalks and scaffolding that crisscrossed the vast processing chamber. The rusted metal groaned under her weight, a low, guttural sound that echoed through the cavernous space. She moved like a phantom, a blur of motion through the now-safe environment, her enhanced reflexes and agility allowing her to traverse the treacherous terrain with impossible speed and grace. The years spent honing her skills in the sterile training yards of Celgrad—once a source of pride and purpose, now felt like a cruel joke, a bitter reminder of the lies and betrayals she had once sworn to uphold. But the anger, the burning resentment that fueled her every move, was no longer directed at her uncle or the Ehxcehl Empire. It was focused, laser-sharp, on the figure she knew awaited her on the central gantry.

The Alchemist, silhouetted against the dim light filtering through the grimy skylights high above, stood with their back to her, their form cloaked in a dark, flowing robe. They were unarmed, their alchemical arsenal neutralized by Ada's impossible power, forced into a direct physical confrontation, a desperate last stand against the inevitable. As Sera approached, they turned, their face finally revealed in the dim light. It was a mask of cold, calculating indifference, devoid of fear or remorse, the face of someone who had long since discarded the messy, illogical burden of human emotion.

"***You shouldn't have come,***" the Alchemist said, their voice a low, modulated hum, devoid of any inflection.

Sera didn't reply. Words were unnecessary. Her blades, extensions of her will, whispered through the air, a deadly dance of flashing steel that left no room for negotiation, no space for mercy. The Alchemist, surprisingly agile and skilled, moved with an almost preternatural grace, dodging and weaving through Sera's initial flurry of attacks. Their movements were precise, economical, almost machine-like, the movements of someone who had trained their body to react on pure instinct, honed their reflexes to the very edge of human potential. But they were no match for Sera's raw power and the disciplined fury that drove her. Years of training, years of honing her body into a living weapon, found their culmination in this brutal, chaotic dance of death.

Sera pressed her attack, her blades a whirlwind of flashing steel, forcing the Alchemist back, step by agonizing step. She felt a savage satisfaction with every parry, every near miss, every grunt of pain that escaped the Alchemist's lips. This wasn't just a fight; it was a reckoning, a cathartic release of all the pent-up rage and frustration she had carried within her for so long.

The fight was brief, brutal, and decisive. With a swift, calculated move, Sera disarmed the assassin, her blades flashing out in a blur of motion, sending their weapon clattering across the metal gantry. The Alchemist, momentarily stunned, stumbled back, their eyes wide with surprise, finally registering the depth of their miscalculation. Sera didn't give them a chance to recover. With a powerful kick, she sent them crashing through the rusted railing, their body plummeting to the concrete floor far below.

A wave of profound, dizzying relief washed over Sera. The tension that had gripped her muscles for what felt like an eternity finally released its hold, leaving her weak and trembling. She sheathed her blades, the familiar click of the metal against the scabbards a small, grounding sound in the echoing silence of the processing plant. She looked down at the crumpled form of the Alchemist lying motionless on the concrete floor below, a small, dark stain spreading across the dusty surface. They were unconscious, but alive. For now.

We have them, Sera announced through the telepathic link, her mental voice shaky but firm. *It's over.*

Sera, her breath still ragged from the fight, moved cautiously towards the gantry's edge, her eyes fixed on the crumpled form of the Alchemist below. She had to secure their captive, ensure they couldn't escape, couldn't cause any more damage. Every muscle in her body screamed in protest, a dull ache that radiated from the venom still coursing through her veins. Ada had healed the worst of it, but the lingering effects of the kraken's toxins left her feeling weak and disoriented. But she couldn't afford to falter. Not now. Not when they were so close.

As she reached the railing, the Alchemist's eyes snapped open. The mask of cold indifference, broken in the fall, had shattered, revealing the face beneath. It was a woman, younger than Sera had expected, her face framed by tangled, dark hair. Her features, though bruised and bloodied, were sharp and intelligent, the eyes burning with a fierce, defiant light. A chilling smirk stretched across her lips, a cruel twist of amusement that sent a shiver down

Sera's spine. She shook her head slowly, a small, almost imperceptible movement, a gesture of defiance that seemed to mock their hard-won victory. Then, with a sickening crunch, her jaw clenched shut, the muscles in her face contorting in a grotesque parody of a smile.

*What in the Void...*Erita's voice echoed through Sera's mind, a mixture of confusion and disgust.

Sera felt a sudden, inexplicable surge of dread, a cold wave of fear that washed over her, leaving her breathless and paralyzed. *No, No—NO!* She knew, with a sickening certainty, that something was terribly wrong.

At that exact moment, Ada's Admin-view screamed with a new, horrifying alert. A massive, unsanctioned energy surge, unlike anything she had ever witnessed, was pulsing through the city's thaumaturgical grid, its epicenter radiating from a location she knew all too well: the Azure Rose Guild headquarters. The energy signature was chaotic, violent, pulsating with a destructive force that threatened to tear the very fabric of reality apart. Before she could even form a coherent thought, a warning, a desperate plea for her companions to take cover, a distant, earth-shattering **BOOM** ripped through the city, the force of the blast shaking the very foundations of the processing plant.

The windows, already weakened by years of neglect and the recent tremors, shattered inwards, a cascade of razor-sharp shards raining down on them. The ground beneath their feet trembled, the metal structure of the plant groaning under the strain. From the gaping holes where the windows had once been, they saw it. A monstrous pillar of fire and smoke, a swirling vortex of destruction, clawed its way into the twilight sky, its fiery tendrils reaching towards the three moons like a desperate, dying plea. It was rising from the very heart of the Serpent's Coil, from the place where the Azure Rose Guild headquarters had once stood, a beacon of hope and resistance in the heart of a city consumed by darkness.

Master Willem, Sera whispered, her voice barely audible above the ringing in her ears.

*No...*Korina's mental voice was a choked sob, a raw, primal scream of anguish that echoed through their shared telepathic link. *No, no, no...*

Ada, her face pale and drawn, stared at the inferno, her eyes wide with horror. Her Admin-view, normally a source of clarity and control, was now a chaotic mess of flashing alerts and corrupted data streams. She saw the cascading system failures, the catastrophic chain reaction that was tearing through the city's infrastructure, the devastating loss of life, the sheer, unadulterated destruction. She had built this world, brick by digital brick, and now she was watching it tear itself apart, consumed by the very forces she had once believed she could control.

Erita, her usual cynicism replaced by a stunned silence, stood beside Ada, her hand resting on Ada's shoulder, a small, almost imperceptible gesture of comfort. She didn't speak. Words were useless. There was nothing to say.

The Alchemist, their body broken and twisted on the concrete floor below, lay still, their defiant smirk now a grotesque, frozen mask. They were dead. Their final, spiteful act, a suicide bomb triggered by the dental implant, had not only taken their own life, but had also unleashed a catastrophic chain reaction that had decimated their sanctuary, their hard-won victory, and the lives of countless allies.

The four women stood there, silhouetted against the backdrop of the burning city, their faces etched with shock and disbelief, the weight of their loss crushing them. The Alchemist was dead. Master Willem, their most powerful ally, was most likely dead. Their sanctuary, their command center, the very heart of their revolution, had been annihilated. Their greatest victory had, in a single, horrifying moment, become their most devastating defeat.

CHAPTER 37

THE RECKONING

The air hung heavy, thick with the gut-wrenching stench of ash and death. Acrid smoke, a swirling, black shroud, choked the sky, blotting out the three moons and casting long, distorted shadows across the devastation. It was a scene of utter ruin, a block-wide crater of smoldering debris and twisted metal, a gaping wound in the heart of Port Dominus. This was where the Azure Rose Guild headquarters had stood, a beacon of hope and defiance in a city consumed by darkness. Now, it was nothing more than a graveyard.

Ada, Korina, and Erita stood behind Sera, their faces pale and drawn, their eyes reflecting the inferno's orange glow. The victorious adrenaline that had surged through them just moments before had been replaced by a profound, hollow shock, a numbness that settled deep in her bones. Sera felt a tremor run through Ada, and a strangled sob escaped Korina's lips. Erita remained silent, her usual cynicism replaced by a grim, stoic mask.

Sera stepped forward, her boots crunching on charred timber

and shattered stone. The sound, sharp and brittle, echoed through the eerie silence, a stark reminder of the utter devastation. She moved through the ruins, her eyes scanning the debris, searching for...she didn't even know what. A sign. A survivor. Anything but this horrifying emptiness.

As a former Knight-Commander of the Aegis Order, the sheer scale of the tactical loss hit her with the force of a physical blow. The Azure Rose Guild, their most powerful ally, had been decimated. Master Willem, a man she had come to respect, a leader who had inspired unwavering loyalty in his followers, was likely dead, buried beneath tons of rubble. His recruits, the men and women who had pledged their lives to their cause, had been slaughtered, their bodies reduced to ash and shadow. And for what? A petty, vindictive act by a ghost they had failed to capture.

The rage, cold and silent, coiled in her gut, a venomous serpent threatening to consume her. It wasn't the hot, impulsive anger she felt in the heat of battle. This was different. This was a deep, all-consuming fury, directed not just at the Alchemist, but at the entire rotten system that had allowed this to happen. At Thorne, the tyrant who had unleashed this monster on their city, who had turned their streets into a bloodbath, who had no regard for human life. At her uncle, the Prefect, who had taught her that people were nothing more than pawns to be sacrificed in the name of 'order' and 'stability'.

A glint of metal caught her eye. She knelt down, sifting through the debris, her fingers closing around a familiar object. It was a dented and scorched Aegis Order insignia, torn from a uniform. She recognized it instantly. It belonged to one of the recruits, a young man named Kael, barely out of his teens, who had joined the Azure Rose with dreams of a better future. He had been eager, almost painfully earnest, his eyes shining with a naive idealism that had reminded her of a younger version of herself.

Sera clutched the insignia in her hand, the metal biting into her palm. The rage intensified, a burning fire in her chest. She had sworn an oath to protect the innocent, to uphold justice, to fight for a better world. And now, because of her, because of their failure, Kael was dead, along with countless others. The weight of their deaths settled on her shoulders, a crushing burden that threatened to break her.

"Sera."

Ada's voice, soft and gentle, broke through the fog of her rage. She stood beside Sera, her hand outstretched, her eyes filled with a profound sadness. Sera looked up at her, her own eyes burning with unshed tears.

The acrid stench of smoke and the low, guttural moans of the wounded filled the air, a symphony of suffering that echoed the hollow ache in Ada's chest. Korina clung to her arm, her small body wracked with sobs, her tears hot and wet against Ada's skin. Sera looked at her, her face streaked with soot and grime, her eyes wide and haunted. Erita paced restlessly, her usual sardonic mask replaced by a grim, tight-lipped frown.

It was a massacre, Erita's voice echoed in Ada's mind, sharp and cold, devoid of her usual cynical edge. *Thorne knew. He anticipated our every move. He let us take the bait, then sprung his own trap.*

Ada squeezed Korina's hand, a small, futile gesture of comfort. *I...I didn't see it,* she admitted, her mental voice barely a whisper. Shame, thick and suffocating, coiled in her gut, a venomous serpent gnawing at her insides. *I thought...I thought we had him.*

He played us, Sera's voice was low and rough, filled with a bitter self-recrimination. *He sacrificed his own men, his own resources, just to hit us where it hurt the most.*

Ada closed her eyes, the image of the burning warehouse, the screams of the dying, seared into her mind's eye. Master Willem's face, etched with determination and hope just hours before, now a ghostly specter, a constant reminder of the failure of her leadership.

We need to move, Erita's voice cut through the mental fog. *Thorne's patrols will be here any minute.*

Ada nodded, detaching herself from Korina's trembling grip. She needed to be strong. She needed to lead. But the weight of her self-appointed crown, the responsibility for the lives she had so carelessly thrown away, pressed down on her, a crushing burden that threatened to suffocate her.

"I...I need a moment," Ada's voice was hoarse, barely a whisper. She turned and stumbled away from the group, seeking refuge in the shadows of a crumbling alleyway. She leaned against a cold, damp wall, the rough stone scraping against her skin, a physical sensation that grounded her in the horrifying reality of her situation.

Ada? Korina's mental voice was laced with concern. *Are you alright?*

Ada didn't respond. She couldn't. The words, the apologies, the reassurances, all felt hollow, meaningless in the face of the carnage she had wrought. She had played god, manipulated the very fabric of her creation, and in doing so, had condemned dozens, if not hundreds, to a gruesome death.

Ada, we need you, Sera's voice was firm, but tinged with a gentle understanding. *We need to plan our next move.*

Ada pushed herself away from the wall, her legs trembling

beneath her. She stepped out of the alleyway, her face pale and drawn, her eyes devoid of their usual spark.

"I...I know," she managed, her voice flat, emotionless. She looked at her companions, their faces etched with worry and exhaustion, their eyes searching hers for a sign of the confident, decisive leader they had come to rely on. But that leader was gone, replaced by a hollow shell, a ghost haunted by the specters of her mistakes.

We can't stay here, Erita's voice was practical, devoid of her usual sarcasm. *Thorne will have this entire sector locked down.*

Ada nodded, her mind racing, desperately searching for a solution, a way out of this impossible situation. They were trapped, surrounded by enemies, their army shattered, their sanctuary destroyed. She had led them into a dead end, a trap of her own making.

"We need to find a way out of the city," Ada's voice was hollow, the words echoing the emptiness in her soul. "We need to regroup. Reassess."

Where can we go? Korina's voice was small, filled with a quiet desperation. *Everyone we know is either dead or working for Thorne.*

Ada closed her eyes, the weight of their predicament crushing her. She had brought them here, to this chaotic, lawless city, promising them safety, promising them a better future. And now, because of her arrogance, because of her blindness, they were on the brink of utter annihilation.

"I...I don't know," Ada admitted, her voice barely a whisper. The confession, a stark admission of her failure, hung in the air, a heavy silence that mirrored the despair settling over the group. Their situation was desperate, their future uncertain. And for the first time since arriving in Kremøtoa, Ada felt a flicker of doubt, a chilling premonition that their revolution, their dream of a better world, might be doomed before it had even truly begun. The city, once a symbol of opportunity and freedom, now felt like a closing trap, its steel jaws ready to crush them all.

The distant wail of sirens, growing closer, cut through the oppressive silence, a stark reminder of the danger closing in. They had to move. They had to find a way out. But where could they go? Who could they trust? In the face of such overwhelming odds, such profound loss, even Ada, the Architect-Queen, the god of this world, felt powerless, lost in the labyrinth of her own creation. The faint, sickly red glow of Cache, the broken moon, seemed to mock her from the smoke-filled sky, a celestial omen of the impending doom.

Suddenly, a hum resonated deep within Ada's chest, a physical vibration that jolted her out of her despair. It was a sound unlike anything she had ever heard in Kremøtoa, a deep, resonant thrumming that seemed to shake the very foundations of the city. It was not the chaotic crackle of Thorne's thaumaturgical weaponry, nor the guttural roar of his siege engines. This was something different, something...alien.

Multiple unknown energy signatures approaching the harbor, Korina's mental voice was tight with apprehension. *Obsidian can't classify them. Their speed...it's impossible.*

Ada felt a surge of adrenaline, a primal instinct to survive overriding her despair. *Now what?* she thought, her mind racing, desperately trying to make sense of this new, unexpected threat. Were these reinforcements for Thorne? Or something far worse?

"We need to see," Ada's voice was sharp, decisive. She grabbed Sera's hand, pulling her towards a crumbling staircase that led to the roof of a nearby warehouse. "Korina, Erita, with me!"

They scrambled up the stairs, their movements swift and silent, their telepathic link buzzing with shared urgency. They reached the rooftop, the wind whipping at their clothes, the smoke-filled sky a canvas of fiery orange and black. And then they saw it.

A fleet of seven sleek, dark warships, unlike anything Ada had ever seen in Kremøtoa, sliced through the waves towards the harbor. They moved with impossible speed, their hulls seeming to phase through the water, leaving no wake, no disturbance in their path—the concept of friction meaning nothing to them. The ships were a stark contrast to the clunky, utilitarian design of the Imperial vessels, or even the chaotic, organic forms of the Korsair ships. These were something else entirely, something... otherworldly. Their hulls were a deep, matte black, almost absorbing the light, and their lines were sharp, angular, almost predatory. They looked less like ships and more like sentient blades, cutting through the water with ruthless efficiency.

At the center of the formation was a magnificent flagship, its size dwarfing even the largest Imperial dreadnoughts. Its hull was the same matte black as the others, but intricate patterns of emerald green pulsed across its surface, like glowing veins of arcane energy. Two massive, scythe-like protrusions extended from its bow, giving it a menacing, predatory silhouette. In Ada's admin-view, a label tag appeared above the flagship, identifying it as *The Obsidian Cipher*.

Argent's light...what are those? Sera's mental voice was filled with a mixture of awe and fear. *I've never seen anything like them.*

They're...they're not in my database, Korina's voice was laced with a frantic disbelief. *Their energy signatures...they're off the charts. It's like...like they're not even from this world. Their speed alone is... eighty-two knots!*

Before Ada could respond, the fleet opened fire. But there was no roar of cannons, no fiery projectiles streaking across the sky. Instead, lances of pure, emerald green energy erupted from the ships' prows, slicing through the air with silent, deadly precision. The lances struck Thorne's remaining coastal defenses, not exploding on impact, but phasing through shields, through armor, through stone, as if they were mere illusions. And then, a moment later, the targets imploded, collapsing in on themselves with silent, devastating force. One by one, Thorne's defenses crumbled, annihilated by this terrifying display of arcane power.

Ada watched in stunned silence, her mind reeling from the implications of what she was witnessing. This was not just a display of superior technology, this was...a demonstration. A message. These ships, these weapons, were beyond anything she had ever imagined, beyond anything she had programmed into Kremøtoa. They were a force of nature, a terrifying embodiment of raw, untamed power. And they had arrived, it seemed, just as her own revolution was on the brink of collapse.

Who are they? Korina's mental voice was barely a whisper. *And what do they want?*

Ada didn't know. But as she watched *The Obsidian Cipher* glide through the shattered remains of Thorne's defenses, its emerald veins pulsing with a malevolent energy, she couldn't shake the feeling that the arrival of this alien fleet was not a coincidence.

They had come to Kremøtoa for a reason. And she had a terrible premonition that whatever that reason was, it would change everything. The game, it seemed, had just changed. And she, the Architect-Queen, was no longer the only player.

A small, intensely bright light suddenly blossomed on the distant bridge of the flagship, momentarily blinding Ada. It winked out of existence as quickly as it appeared, then reappeared—this time right in front of them. Ada stumbled back, instinctively shielding her eyes, her heart pounding in her chest. A violet-tinted holo-comm shimmered into existence, resolving into the image of Nividia Rhenderon. The Render-Witch stood serenely on the bridge of her flagship, the chaos of the naval assault reflected in her calm, violet eyes. A wry, knowing smirk played on her lips.

"Lady Ada," Nividia's voice, amplified by the holo-comm, cut through the din of battle, cool and precise. "Your message...arrived. Though I must confess, I hadn't anticipated such a...dramatic welcome." Her gaze swept over the burning docks and Thorne's crumbling defenses. "Most impressive."

Ada stared at the image of Nividia, her mind struggling to process the impossible speed of her arrival. "But...how? The fleet... it shouldn't be ready for weeks."

Nividia laughed, a sound that echoed strangely through the holo-comm, a mix of amusement and something colder, something that sounded almost like...predatory hunger. She gestured dismissively at the obsidian warships carving through

Thorne's defenses. "This, Lady Ada," she said, her voice laced with a smug satisfaction, "is not the fleet you commissioned. This...is my personal fleet. As Admiral of the Grand Fleet of Rhedeon, I wouldn't dream of letting you have *all* the fun, now would I?"

Ada's eyes widened. Admiral? Grand Fleet? This was not just a handful of ships, this was an entire armada, a force capable of leveling cities, of reshaping continents. And Nividia...she wasn't just a brilliant shipwright, she was a military commander, a strategist, a power broker on a scale Ada hadn't even begun to comprehend.

Nividia's gaze sharpened, her smirk widening. "My fleet will handle the harbor," she said, her voice taking on a steely edge. "I suggest you take this opportunity to...cut the head off the snake." The holo-comm winked out of existence, leaving Ada standing on the rooftop, the wind whipping at her hair, the scent of smoke and burning metal thick in the air.

Almost immediately, the pressure on their position eased. The relentless barrage of fire from Thorne's forces slackened, then stopped altogether. Confused shouts and panicked orders echoed from the streets below. Ada realized Thorne's troops were being recalled, redirected to deal with this new, impossible threat. Nividia's arrival had not only saved them from certain death, it had created a massive, unexpected diversion, a crack in Thorne's defenses that they could exploit.

Ada looked from the receding image of Nividia's terrifyingly calm face to her own battered, but resolute partners. Korina stepped forward, her eyes wide with a mixture of awe and gratitude.

"Thank you," she said, her voice trembling slightly, projecting her gratitude towards Nividia telepathically. "For...for saving us."

A flicker of something...softer, something almost resembling vulnerability, crossed Nividia's face. It was gone in an instant, replaced by her usual detached amusement, but it was there, a brief glimpse behind the Render-Witch's carefully constructed mask. She gave Korina a small, almost imperceptible nod, a gesture of acknowledgement that spoke volumes.

She heard you, Rina, Ada said, her mental voice filled with a quiet reassurance. *She heard you, and she understood.*

Korina's eyes met Ada's, a silent understanding passing between them. Their darkest moment, the moment they had believed all hope was lost, had just been transformed into their greatest opportunity. The path to Thorne's tower, the heart of his power, was finally open.

They descended from the rooftop, their movements purposeful, their telepathic link buzzing with renewed energy. The city around them was still in chaos, Thorne's forces scrambling to regroup, to make sense of the impossible fleet that had materialized in their harbor. But for Ada and her companions, the chaos was a symphony, a backdrop to their own carefully orchestrated plan. The time for whispers and shadows was over. The time for the Crimson Revolution had finally come.

CHAPTER 38

CHECKMATE

The rooftop vibrated beneath their feet, a tremor of displaced air and raw power as another of Nividia's emerald lances sliced through the night sky, obliterating one of Thorne's heavily fortified gun emplacements. Below, the streets of Port Dominus were a maelstrom of confusion, Thorne's forces scrambling to react to the unexpected naval assault. This was it. Their one, desperate chance.

Ada turned to her partners, her face grim but her eyes blazing with a fierce, unwavering resolve. She didn't need words, not anymore. Their telepathic link, forged in fire and desperation, was a conduit for something deeper, something that transcended language. She projected her plan, a silent command that resonated through their shared consciousness: *Nividia has given us our opening. We're not waiting, we're not regrouping. We use this chaos. We go now. We cut the head off the snake.*

Sera's response was a surge of raw, untamed excitement, a

predator unleashed. *Finally,* she thought, her mental voice a low growl of anticipation. *Let's paint this city crimson.*

Korina's reply was a flurry of calculations, a rapid-fire assessment of probabilities and tactical advantages. *Thorne's forces are redeploying to the harbor. His tower is lightly defended. We have a narrow window, perhaps ten minutes at most, before he realizes his mistake.*

Erita's contribution was a cold, precise assessment of the risks. *Thorne will have anticipated a direct assault. Expect traps, ambushes, and his elite guard. We move fast, we move silent, and we move together.*

Ada nodded, a silent acknowledgement of their shared understanding. They moved as one, a fluid, coordinated unit, their telepathic link a symphony of shared awareness. Erita led the way, her movements fluid and silent, a shadow slipping through the chaos of the city. Sera followed, her hand resting on the hilt of her sword, her senses honed for any hint of danger. Korina brought up the rear, Obsidian clutched tightly in her hand, its screen glowing faintly, a beacon in the darkness. Ada remained in the center, the anchor, her mind a nexus of calm amidst the storm.

Erita moved with the predatory grace of a lynx, her senses heightened, each nerve ending a finely tuned instrument attuned to the city's panicked rhythm. The reek of ozone and burnt metal hung heavy in the air, the acrid tang of fear clinging to the narrow alleyways. Thorne's control, once absolute, was fracturing, the city bleeding chaos. Good.

Three blocks to the access point, Korina's voice whispered in her mind, a cool stream of data against the backdrop of the city's rising panic. *Camera feed looped, outer grid down. Pressure plate at the entrance still active.*

Erita acknowledged with a silent pulse of thought, her eyes

scanning the alley ahead. Two of Thorne's enforcers, their faces grim, rounded the corner, their weapons drawn. They hadn't seen her yet, their attention focused on the distant flashes of light and the rumble of explosions from the harbor. A flicker of amusement danced in Erita's mind. Amateurs.

Ada, she projected, *a little static, please.*

A surge of static filled the air, the enforcers' comms crackling with distorted noise. They paused, confused, their weapons lowering slightly. Erita seized the opportunity, melting into the shadows, her daggers a whisper of steel. Two quick, precise strikes, and the enforcers crumpled to the ground, silent and still. Erita didn't pause, didn't look back. Sentimentality was a luxury they couldn't afford.

They reached the access point, a forgotten service tunnel hidden behind a crumbling brick wall. Korina had already disabled the electronic lock, but the pressure plate remained, a silent sentinel guarding the entrance.

Sera, Erita thought, *a little brute force, if you please.*

Sera grinned, her mental voice a rumble of amusement. *Always a pleasure, Swift.*

With a grunt of effort, Sera ripped a heavy metal grate from the nearby wall, the rusted hinges screeching in protest. She hefted the grate, testing its weight, then, with a powerful throw, hurled it across the tunnel entrance, covering the pressure plate completely. The tunnel entrance remained silent, the trap disarmed. Erita allowed herself a small, satisfied smile. Brute force did have its uses, occasionally.

They slipped into the tunnel, the darkness swallowing them whole. The air was thick with the smell of damp earth and decay, the silence broken only by the drip of water and the distant echo of Thorne's crumbling empire.

Sub-basement access in two minutes, Korina reported, her mental voice a steady stream of data. *Thermal scans show minimal activity. Security grid is antiquated, easily bypassed.*

Good work, Rina, Ada thought, her mental voice warm with affection. *A little light bending at the final corridor, if you please.*

On it, Korina replied, her mental voice a soft hum of concentration.

Erita navigated the tunnels with practiced ease, her footsteps silent, her mind a map of the city's hidden veins. She knew these tunnels better than Thorne knew his own tower, her years spent in the shadows now their greatest asset. The darkness was her ally, the silence her weapon.

They reached the final corridor, the entrance to Thorne's sub-basement bathed in the cold, sterile glow of security lights. A motion sensor, its red eye blinking rhythmically, scanned the corridor, a silent guardian protecting Thorne's inner sanctum. But as they approached, the light seemed to bend, to warp around them, creating a temporary blind spot. Ada's subtle manipulation of reality, a silent whisper of power that made the impossible possible.

They slipped past the sensor undetected, ghosts in Thorne's machine. The sub-basement entrance, a heavy steel door secured by a complex electronic lock, stood before them. Korina's voice, cool and calm, echoed in their minds.

Access granted.

The door hissed open, revealing the dimly lit interior of Thorne's sub-basement. The air was thick with the hum of machinery and the faint scent of ozone, the heart of Thorne's operation exposed, vulnerable, waiting. Erita drew her daggers, the steel cool against her skin, a silent promise of the violence to come.

The heavy steel door hissed closed behind them, sealing them within the cold, sterile confines of Thorne's sub-basement. The air hung thick with the hum of machinery, the low thrum vibrating through the metal floor and into the soles of Sera's boots. This was it. No more shadows, no more whispers. This was a straight fight, their way up a gauntlet of steel and blood. Good. This was where she excelled.

Movement on the upper level, Korina's voice echoed in her mind, cool and detached. *Multiple hostiles, heavily armored. Cybernetic enhancements detected.*

Sera tightened her grip on her blades, the familiar weight of the steel a comforting presence in the uncertain darkness. A thrill coursed through her, a primal anticipation of the violence to come. This was the dance she knew, the rhythm of steel and blood that had defined her life. No more questions, no more doubts. Just the pure, visceral clarity of combat.

A heavy clang echoed from the upper level, the sound of metal on metal, followed by the thud of heavy footsteps. Thorne's elite guard. She'd heard whispers of them, rumors of their cybernetic enhancements and ruthless efficiency. Now, she would see for herself.

Ready yourselves, Ada's voice echoed in their minds, calm and steady. *Swift, take the left flank. Rina, hold your position. I'll control the field.*

"Let's dance," Sera growled, a low rumble in the confined space.

They ascended the metal staircase, their movements silent and synchronized. As they reached the upper level, the corridor stretched before them, bathed in the cold, sterile glow of security lights. Four hulking figures, clad in sleek, black reinforced armor, stood at the far end, their weapons raised, their faces obscured by visored helmets. Their movements were eerily silent, their cybernetic enhancements giving them an unnatural grace. Thorne's finest.

Sera didn't hesitate. With a roar, she charged, her twin blades a shimmering arc of crimson death. The first guard, caught off guard by her sudden attack, barely managed to raise his energy shield before Sera's blade sliced through it like butter, the enhanced steel cutting through the energy field and into the armor beneath. A surprised grunt escaped the guard as he stumbled back, his weapon clattering to the floor.

Targeting systems offline, Korina's voice announced, a satisfied smirk in her mental tone. *Weapons disabled.*

Erita moved like a phantom, flanking the remaining guards, her daggers a whisper of steel in the dimly lit corridor. One guard, his weapon sparking uselessly, tried to turn, but Erita was too fast. With a swift kick to the back of his knee, she brought him crashing to the ground, then, with a precise strike to the joint in his armor, disabled his cybernetic leg. He screamed in pain, his voice distorted by his helmet.

Sera pressed her attack, her blades a blur of motion. The second guard, his shield gone, tried to parry her blows, but Sera was relentless. She feinted left, then right, then, with a sudden upward thrust, drove her blade deep into the guard's chest, piercing the armor and silencing his screams.

Floor panel three meters ahead, friction coefficient adjusted, Ada's voice announced, a cool whisper of power.

The third guard, charging towards Sera, his heavy boots pounding on the metal floor, suddenly lost his footing, his legs sliding out from under him as if he'd stepped on ice. He landed hard, his armor clattering against the floor, disoriented and vulnerable. Sera didn't waste the opportunity. With a swift downward strike, she silenced him.

The final guard, his weapon still disabled, turned to flee, but the corridor behind him was suddenly blocked by a heavy blast door, slamming shut with a deafening clang. He turned back to face Sera, his face a mask of fear.

Reinforcements cut off, Ada's voice announced, a quiet hum of satisfaction.

Sera grinned, her heart pounding with the thrill of the fight. "Nowhere left to run," she growled.

The guard charged, his only weapon his enhanced strength. Sera met his attack head-on, their bodies colliding with a bone-jarring thud. He grappled with her, his cybernetic arms trying to crush her, but Sera was stronger than she looked. She twisted free, her blades flashing, and with two quick strikes, ended the fight.

They stood for a moment, catching their breath, the silence broken only by the hum of machinery and the distant rumble of explosions from the harbor. The corridor was littered with the bodies of Thorne's elite guard, their sleek, black armor now marred by crimson stains.

Level clear, Korina announced, her voice a mix of relief and excitement. *Next checkpoint, level four. Security grid is...interesting. Give me a minute.*

Sera wiped her blades clean on the fallen guard's armor, the crimson staining the black metal. She sheathed her weapons, the familiar click of the steel a comforting sound in the aftermath of the battle.

"Let's keep moving," she said, her voice a low rumble in the confined space. "Thorne's waiting."

The metallic tang of blood, ozone, and burnt circuitry hung heavy in the air. Her chest ached, each breath a shallow, ragged gasp. Sweat plastered her hair to her forehead, the damp strands clinging to the scar above her eyebrow. But beneath the exhaustion, a cold, hard knot of determination pulsed. They were here. Finally.

Casualties minimal, Erita's voice echoed in her mind, a cool, crisp counterpoint to the chaos around them. *Thorne's security detail was...predictable.*

Predictable and pathetic, Sera's mental voice scoffed, a flicker of grim satisfaction. *Over-reliance on technology. No match for good, old-fashioned steel.*

Ada glanced at Sera, a small smile playing on her lips. Sera's crimson tunic was ripped at the shoulder, revealing a streak of blood, but her eyes shone with the fierce, untamed joy of a predator who had just made a kill. Beside her, Korina, her violet gown now smeared with grime and soot, meticulously cleaned her data-slate, the Lynx monitor blinking contentedly in the corner of the screen. Erita, her dark clothing blending seamlessly with the shadows, surveyed the corridor, her daggers still dripping with a viscous, oily fluid that Ada recognized as the enhanced lubricant used by Thorne's cybernetically augmented guards.

They stood amidst the sparking remains of the last of Thorne's elite guard, their bodies twisted and broken, their weapons scattered across the floor. The air crackled with the residual energy from the final, desperate clash, a testament to their hard-fought victory. They had carved a path of destruction through the heart of Thorne's tower, their synchronized movements a deadly ballet of steel, magic, and technological prowess.

Before them stood the doors. Massive, unadorned plasteel barriers, they sealed off Thorne's personal command center, the very heart of his tyrannical reign. The air around them hummed, a palpable vibration of contained power. Ada could feel it, a thrumming resonance that spoke of sophisticated security systems, arcane defenses, and the desperate, cornered energy of a man who knew his reign was about to end.

Ready? Ada projected the thought to the others, her mental voice calm and steady, a quiet center in the storm of their shared emotions.

Born ready, Sera's voice responded, a fierce, unwavering conviction.

Analyzing structural integrity...minimal vulnerabilities detected, Korina reported, her voice a rapid-fire cascade of data. *Probability of successful breach...ninety-seven point four percent.*

Let's make it a hundred, Erita's voice cut in, a dry, cynical edge.

They exchanged a final look, their eyes meeting in the dimly lit corridor. No words were needed. They were a unit, a single, cohesive entity forged in the fires of revolution. Their telepathic link, a constant, silent hum beneath the surface of their thoughts, bound them together, a shared network of strength, determination, and unwavering loyalty.

Sera stepped forward, her crimson tunic a splash of color against the cold, grey metal of the doors. She raised her foot, the worn leather of her boot a stark contrast to the polished plasteel. A small smile played on her lips, a predatory gleam in her eyes. Then, with a single, powerful kick, she sent the heavy doors crashing inward, the sound echoing through the corridor like a thunderclap.

They stepped inside, their weapons ready, the air thick with anticipation. The room beyond was bathed in the cool, ethereal glow of holographic displays, the air humming with the quiet thrum of powerful machinery. At the far end, silhouetted against the panoramic view of the city lights, stood Alaric Thorne. His back was to them, his hands clasped behind his back, his posture radiating an almost theatrical arrogance.

The hunt was over. The reckoning had begun.

CHAPTER 39

THE TYRANT'S FALL

Alaric Thorne stood with his back to them, his silhouette stark against the cool luminescence of a colossal holographic display. The display pulsed with chaotic energy, miniature versions of Nividia's obsidian warships tearing through Thorne's fleet with emerald lances of arcane fire. Explosions bloomed across the holographic harbor, each miniature detonation mirroring a real-world catastrophe. Yet, Thorne watched the destruction with an unnerving, almost detached interest, as if observing a particularly intricate game of strategy unfold.

"A bold gambit," Thorne's voice echoed through the chamber, smooth and controlled, devoid of any hint of panic. He finally turned, his face illuminated by the flickering holographic firelight. His dark hair was perfectly styled, his opulent guildmaster's attire immaculate despite the chaos erupting around them. There was no fear in his eyes, no desperation, only a cold, arrogant resignation. "But ultimately...futile."

He gestured dismissively at the holographic display, his expression one of condescending amusement. "A temporary disruption. A momentary ripple in the grand scheme of things. You believe you've won something? That you've struck a decisive blow? You haven't even begun to understand the game you're playing."

"You're finished, Thorne," Sera's voice cut through the tense silence, sharp and unwavering. She stepped forward, her crimson tunic a splash of defiance against the sterile backdrop of the command center. "Your reign of terror is over."

Thorne chuckled, a low, chilling sound. "Terror? My dear girl, you misunderstand. What you perceive as terror is merely...order. A necessary evil in a world teetering on the brink of collapse."

He turned his gaze to Ada, his cold, intelligent eyes assessing her with a disturbing intensity. "You," he said, his voice a low, gravelly hum, "you, with your...unique abilities...you should understand this better than anyone. You're on par with who built this world—who coded its very foundations. You should know its inherent instability."

"I know its potential," Ada countered, her voice calm and steady. "And I know it deserves better than your tyranny."

Thorne smiled, a thin, cruel expression that sent a shiver down Ada's spine. "Tyranny? Such a dramatic word. I prefer... management. Efficient allocation of resources. A firm hand to guide the unruly masses." He swept his arm across the room, encompassing the sophisticated technology, the sleek design, the very embodiment of his control. "Look around you. This is order. This is what holds this fragile world together. Without it...chaos. Utter, devastating chaos."

"Your order is built on oppression, Thorne," Erita's voice cut in, laced with cynical amusement. "On fear and control. That's not order. That's a cage."

"A necessary cage," Thorne corrected, his tone condescending. "This world, this...simulation...it's flawed. It's decaying. It's falling apart at the seams. The Blight, the Malware, the glitches...they're not just anomalies. They're symptoms. Symptoms of a deeper, more fundamental instability." He turned his gaze back to the holographic display, now showing the burning wreckage of his fleet. "You think you're fighting for freedom? You're fools. You're playing with forces you don't understand. You're unleashing a storm you can't control."

"We're not afraid of your storm, Thorne," Korina's voice rang out, clear and unwavering. "We're going to rewrite its code."

Thorne laughed, a harsh, bitter sound. "Rewrite the code? Such naivete. You think you can control this world? You think you can impose your own order on chaos? You're children playing with fire. And you're going to get burned." He paused, his gaze sweeping across their faces, a chilling smile playing on his lips. "But by then...it will be too late. For all of us."

He turned back to the holographic display, the destruction of his fleet now complete. The image flickered, then vanished, leaving only the cool, ambient glow of the command center. Thorne stood there for a moment, his back to them, his silhouette a stark reminder of the power he still held.

"Parasite," Ada spat, her voice dripping with venom. "You're not a shepherd, Thorne. You're a parasite, feeding off the decay you create." The word hung in the air, a venomous strike that shattered Thorne's carefully constructed facade of calm. His eyes narrowed, the cold arrogance replaced by a flash of pure, unadulterated fury. With a guttural roar, he slammed his fist onto a console, activating a shimmering, personal energy shield. An obsidian energy blade materialized in his other hand, its edge humming with barely contained power.

"Kill them," he snarled, his gaze fixed on Ada. "Leave the girl alive. The rest...dispose of." Two hulking figures emerged from the shadows behind Thorne, their movements unnervingly fluid and silent. They were Thorne's elite personal guard, cybernetically enhanced behemoths clad in heavy, segmented armor. Their eyes glowed with a cold, predatory light, their weapons – massive, energy-infused gauntlets – crackling with power.

Sera felt a thrill course through her, a familiar surge of adrenaline mixed with a cold, calculating focus. This was her element. This was where she thrived. She met Thorne's gaze, her own eyes burning with a righteous fury. *Eri, Kori, with me,* she projected telepathically, her voice a sharp, focused whisper in her companions' minds. *Ada, stay back. This one's mine.*

She drew her twin blades, the polished steel gleaming in the command center's cool light. They were a familiar weight in her hands, an extension of her will, a promise of swift, decisive violence. With a wordless snarl, she lunged, her movements a blur of controlled aggression.

The clash of steel against obsidian energy echoed through the chamber, a sharp, ringing counterpoint to the distant rumble of Nividia's assault. Thorne met Sera's attack with surprising skill, his energy blade deflecting her blows with precise, calculated parries. He was strong, fast, and disciplined, his movements a testament to years of training and ruthless experience. But Sera was relentless. She pressed her attack, a whirlwind of steel and fury, forcing him back, step by step. Each parry, each block, each near miss was a calculated risk, a test of skill and nerve.

Hammer's down, Erita's voice echoed in Sera's mind, a cool, detached observation amidst the chaotic symphony of battle. Sera saw a flicker of movement in her peripheral vision, Erita a phantom of speed and precision. The spymaster danced between the two bodyguards, her daggers flashing, striking with lethal accuracy at the vulnerable joints in their armor. One bodyguard stumbled, its movements becoming jerky and uncoordinated as Erita's blades severed crucial cybernetic connections.

Shield's down, Rina needs time to re-engage, Korina's voice chimed in, a rapid-fire burst of data and analysis. Sera saw Thorne's energy shield flicker, then vanish, Korina's code shattering its protective matrix. Thorne staggered back, momentarily exposed, his eyes widening in surprise.

Sera seized the opportunity. She pressed her attack, her blades a blur of motion, forcing Thorne into a defensive posture. He parried desperately, his movements becoming less precise, less controlled. He was tiring, his initial fury giving way to a grim determination.

Ada, now! Sera projected, her voice a sharp command.

The floor beneath Thorne's feet suddenly shifted, buckling and twisting, Ada's subtle manipulation of the environment creating a momentary distraction. Thorne stumbled again, his balance thrown off. Sera saw her opening.

Thorne stumbled, his energy blade flickering and dying as Sera's relentless assault forced him back, step by step. His initial arrogance had vanished, replaced by a grim, desperate struggle for survival. He parried, blocked, and retreated, his movements becoming less precise, less controlled. He was tiring, the weight of his own cruelty finally catching up to him.

Sera pressed her attack, a whirlwind of steel and fury. She

drove him back against a console, his energy shield flickering and failing under Korina's relentless digital assault. He was trapped, cornered, his eyes wide with a mixture of fear and disbelief.

With a final, triumphant cry, Sera disarmed him, her blade flashing out, severing the connection between his hand and the obsidian energy weapon. It clattered to the floor, its humming extinguished. Thorne staggered back, driven to his knees by the force of Sera's relentless assault. He was defeated, broken, his reign of terror finally at an end.

Sera stood over him, her twin blades raised, the polished steel gleaming in the command center's cool light. Her eyes burned with a righteous fury, her muscles tense, ready to deliver the final, killing blow.

"***No***," Ada said, her voice quiet but firm, cutting through the tension like a shard of ice. Sera hesitated, her blades still raised, her gaze fixed on Thorne's bowed head. Korina gasped, her hand flying to her mouth, her eyes wide with concern. Erita remained silent, her expression unreadable, her daggers still clutched in her hands.

Ada stepped past Sera, her movements deliberate, unhurried. Korina reached out, her hand brushing against Ada's arm, a silent plea for caution. Ada ignored her, her focus entirely on the defeated tyrant kneeling before her. She stopped in front of Thorne, her violet eyes blazing with an incandescent light, her expression a mask of cold, implacable justice.

"Death is too easy," she said, her voice low and steady, each word a hammer blow against Thorne's shattered defenses. "A clean escape. A release from the consequences of your actions. You reveled in the agony of others, Thorne. You built your empire on their suffering. You fed on their pain." She paused, her gaze boring into Thorne's, her words a chilling indictment. "Now...it's time you tasted it yourself—*forever*."

She reached out, her hand hovering over Thorne's forehead. He flinched, his eyes wide with terror, a primal, animalistic fear gripping him. He tried to speak, to plead, but the words caught in his throat, strangled by the rising tide of his own guilt.

Ada's hand descended, her fingers brushing against his skin. A faint, violet glow emanated from her touch, a subtle ripple of energy that spread through Thorne's body, through his mind. Her eyes blazed with an otherworldly light as she executed a final, chilling command.

"**[Execute: Empathy_Feedback_Loop]**," she whispered, her voice barely audible above the distant rumble of the collapsing city.

Thorne's body convulsed, his eyes rolling back in his head, his muscles contracting and relaxing in a series of violent spasms. A low, guttural moan escaped his lips, a sound of pure, unadulterated agony. He was instantly flooded with the raw, unfiltered pain of every person he had ever oppressed, every life he had ruined, every soul he had crushed beneath the weight of his tyranny.

The terror of the families he had torn apart, the despair of the merchants he had ruined, the agony of the innocents he had condemned – it all washed over him, a tidal wave of suffering that shattered his carefully constructed defenses, his mind buckling and breaking under the weight of his own cruelty.

He screamed, a high-pitched, keening wail that echoed through the command center, a sound of pure, unmitigated horror. His body thrashed, his limbs flailing wildly, his eyes wide with an unseeing terror. He was drowning in a sea of pain, consumed by the echoes of his own wickedness.

Then, just as suddenly, the screaming stopped. The thrashing ceased. Thorne's body went limp, collapsing to the floor like a discarded puppet. His eyes remained open, but they were vacant, lifeless, reflecting nothing but the infinite void of his own shattered mind. He was not dead. But he *was* gone. Trapped forever in a prison of his own making, a hell of his victims' suffering, condemned to relive the consequences of his actions for all eternity.

Ada stood over him, her hand still outstretched, the violet glow fading from her fingertips. Her expression was a mask of cold, detached satisfaction, her eyes reflecting the chilling emptiness of the command she had just executed. She had not killed him. She had done something far worse. She had condemned him to a fate far more terrifying than death.

Korina approached cautiously, her eyes wide with a mixture of awe and horror. "Ada...what did you *do*?" she whispered, her voice barely audible.

Ada turned to her, her expression softening slightly, a hint of sadness creeping into her violet eyes. "I gave him what he deserved," she said, her voice quiet but firm. "I gave him...a *mirror* of himself."

Sera knelt beside Thorne's crumpled form, her hand hovering over the hilt of her blade. A flicker of doubt crossed her face, a fleeting shadow of the knight she once was. She looked up at Ada, her expression a mixture of confusion and concern. “Is he...?”

“He’s alive,” Ada said, her voice flat, devoid of emotion. “But he’s no longer a threat. He’s trapped in his own mind, consumed by the echoes of his own cruelty.” She turned away, her gaze sweeping across the devastated command center, the flickering lights casting long, distorted shadows. “He’ll suffer more this way than he ever could in death.”

Erita stepped forward, her golden eyes narrowed, her expression thoughtful. She placed a hand on Thorne’s neck, checking for a pulse. “Ingenious,” she murmured, a hint of admiration in her voice. “A fate worse than death, indeed. A fitting end for a tyrant.” She straightened up, her gaze meeting Ada’s. “Thorne’s network will collapse without him. His enforcers will scatter. The city is ours.”

Korina remained silent, her eyes fixed on Thorne’s broken form, her expression a mixture of horror and fascination. She couldn’t shake the image of Thorne’s agony, the raw, unfiltered pain that had twisted his features, shattered his mind. Ada’s power, the sheer, terrifying control she wielded over the very fabric of reality, both awed and frightened her. She had seen Ada heal, create, and destroy. But this...this was different. This was a glimpse into a darker, more dangerous aspect of Ada’s abilities, a power that could reshape not just the physical world, but the very essence of a person’s being.

She reached out, her hand brushing against Ada’s, her fingers intertwining with hers. Ada squeezed her hand, a silent reassurance, a wordless acknowledgment of the shared burden they now carried. They stood together, the four of them, amidst the wreckage of Thorne's reign, their silhouettes outlined against the panoramic windows of the command center.

From their vantage point, they could see the entire city spread out before them, a tapestry of lights and shadows, the scars of battle etched across its surface. Nividia's fleet, a silent armada of obsidian warships, had ceased its bombardment. The emerald lances of energy that had ripped through Thorne's defenses had fallen silent. The Imperial ships, now leaderless, rudderless, drifted aimlessly in the harbor, their lights flickering and dying, their crews scattering like rats fleeing a sinking ship.

The alarms that had blared incessantly throughout the city, a constant reminder of Thorne's iron grip, had fallen silent. A profound stillness had settled over Port Dominus, a quiet so deep, so absolute, that it felt almost unnatural. It was the silence of a city holding its breath, waiting, uncertain of what the future held.

The mood in the command center was not one of joyous celebration, of triumphant victory. There were no cheers, no shouts of jubilation. Just a profound, bone-deep exhaustion, a grim relief that the battle was finally over. The cost of their victory weighed heavily on them, the memory of the fallen, the scars of their own battles, etched deep into their souls. They had won. But the fight was far from over. The battle for Port Dominus was won. But the war for Kremøtoa had just begun.

CHAPTER 40

SHARDS OF SOVEREIGNTY

The rhythmic scrape of stiff bristles against stone echoed through the cavernous main hall of Thorne's former fortress.

Ada dragged the heavy wooden broom backward, corralling a pile of shattered masonry and rendered ash. The combat adrenaline had burned out hours ago, leaving behind a hollow, aching exhaustion.

Through the massive breaches in the western wall, a cool, damp draft whistled in from the harbor, carrying the scent of sea salt that failed to mask the lingering metallic tang of ozone and spent thauma. The air itself felt thick. Every breath left the gritty taste of pulverized stone on Ada's tongue.

High above, the slanted light of the three moons—Argent's pale glow, Cache's sickly red crescent, and BIOCE's steady beam—cut through the collapsed ceiling. Dust motes danced in the lunar columns, settling like fresh snow over the jagged, obsidian-like edges of Thorne's shattered throne.

"Pivot that support beam before the whole arch gives way! Lift with your legs, you bilge rats!"

Lars's booming voice drifted through the ruined archways from the courtyard. The rhythmic chanting of the surviving Azure Rose recruits followed, their collective grunt of exertion marking the slow dismantling of Thorne's outer barricades.

Ada shifted her grip on the broom handle. The rough wood bit into her skin. Raw blisters formed at the base of her fingers. She stared at her reddened palms, a profound disconnect stalling her movements.

She was the Administrator. The Architect who spun Kremøtoa's physics out of raw data and whispered code. She had woven the stars, compiled the oceans, and defined the density of the very rock under her boots. Now, she was a janitor. The grand design she poured a decade of her life into had been reduced to a literal mess she had to physically sweep into a pile.

Sera hoisted a massive slab of fallen granite over her shoulder, the muscles in her arms straining beneath her crimson tunic. She carried it toward the breach, her breathing heavy but measured. A few paces away, Korina meticulously stacked salvageable data-cores beside the ruined throne, coughing softly as the dust settled on her violet robes. Erita swept the far flank, her movements sharp, kicking a warped piece of Imperial armor out the broken window.

Ada watched them. The crushing weight of the dead—Willem, Eliria, the recruits who had bled into the docks—pressed against her ribs. Thorne's cruelty had corrupted her code, leaving digital and physical rot in its wake. But standing here, blistering her hands on a cheap broom while clearing away the remnants of a tyrant, grounded her. The simulation wasn't just algorithms anymore. It was stone, sweat, and shared labor.

Ada leaned against the wooden handle, wiping a streak of soot from her forehead with the back of her wrist. “If I knew I’d be doing this much manual labor, I would have programmed a self-cleaning spell for the fortresses.”

The sharp scrape of a shovel blade against stone echoed from the far side of the hall. Erita, relentless, was prying a warped metal grate from the floor. Ada gave her own broom another futile push, scattering dust into the moon-glow. Her arms ached with the unfamiliar strain.

Heavy, measured footsteps crunched over the debris behind her. The sound cut through the ambient clatter of the cleanup crew. Ada didn’t need to turn. The steady, reliable rhythm belonged to only one person.

“Admiral.” Ada kept her eyes on the pile of rubble. She expected a report. Casualty counts. Munitions inventory. The status of Nividia’s fleet blockading the harbor. Numbers. Data. Things she could process.

“Architect-Queen.” Silas’s voice was low, a gravelly sound that seemed to absorb the echoes of the cavernous hall. He stood beside her, his worn greatcoat smelling of salt spray and the cold night air. He wasn’t looking at the destruction. He was looking at her. His expression was exhausted, etched with the deep lines of a man who had seen too many battles, but his eyes held a solemn deference that made Ada’s skin prickle.

He held out his hand. Not for a data-slate, but to offer something cupped in his calloused palm.

Resting there was a tooth. It was immense, at least ten centimeters long, thick as her thumb at its root and curving to a wicked point. It was the color of old parchment—a jaundiced ivory networked with fine, hairline cracks. The inner curve was serrated, a row of miniature daggers designed for tearing flesh. The distant crash of waves against the cliffs below Thorne's fortress punctuated the silence between them.

Ada's mind immediately tried to categorize the object:

[QUERY]: Object_ID: Unidentified_Fauna_Remains

Classification: Megalodon? Sea Drake? It was a relic, prehistoric. Undoubtedly valuable. A fine loot drop. Her thoughts swirled around market prices in Port Veridia, calculating potential Byts. They could use it to fund repairs for Silas' ship, or maybe acquire more advanced medical supplies for the wounded.

She reached out and took it. The fang's weight surprised her, dense and solid in her palm. A faint, ancient musk rose from the bone, a dry scent of something long dead. She ran her thumb along the serrated edge, and the tip, sharp as any blade, pricked her skin. A single, perfect bead of crimson welled up. The tiny sting was a grounding shock, a pinprick of reality in the abstract calculus of her plans.

She looked from the tooth to Silas's patient, unreadable face. He watched her, his expression unwavering. This wasn't a transaction. It was something else.

"Is this supposed to be a weapon, Silas?" Ada's voice was flat, practical. "Or are we selling ivory now?"

A faint smile touched Silas' lips, a rare geological event that barely shifted the weathered landscape of his face. It did not reach his eyes. His gaze remained as steady and unyielding as the deep ocean.

"Neither. And both." His voice was a low rumble, the sound of boulders shifting on a seabed. He gestured to the object in her hand. "That is not a weapon. It is *the* weapon. It's not ivory. It's the *Thorn of Port Dominus*."

Ada's brow furrowed. She ran a system query, a silent command that should have pulled a file, a data tag, anything.

[QUERY]: Item_ID: Thorn_of_Port_Dominus
[RETURN]: NULL // Item not found

The lack of a result sent a prickle of unease down her spine. This wasn't a world asset she'd forgotten. This was something else. Something that had grown in the fertile soil of her world without her input. An emergent property.

A tradition.

"Every one of the Five Lords of the Korsair Confederacy has a token of sovereignty," Silas continued, his voice dropping, drawing the shadows of the moonlit hall closer around them. "A physical anchor for their power. For Port Vengeance, it's a crown of petrified salt. For Blackbox Harbor, a compass that points only to its owner's heart. They're trinkets to an outsider. To us...they are the law of the sea made manifest."

He looked down at the massive, serrated tooth in her hand. "That one was cut from the maw of the first Sea Drake slain in these waters, centuries ago. The first Lord of Dominus took it as his mark. It's been passed down ever since. The only way to get it is to take it from the man who holds it."

The dry, ancient scent of the tooth seemed to intensify, filling Ada's nostrils with the bitter dust of history she hadn't written. Suddenly, the object in her palm felt colder, its mass multiplying until it was a leaden weight dragging her arm down. It wasn't just bone anymore. It was a mantle.

"We found it in Thorne's private vault," Silas said, answering the question she hadn't voiced. "Lars pried it from a display case while your recruits were clearing the upper levels. It belongs to you now."

The words struck Ada with a physical force. A sharp pressure built in her chest; not of panic, but of a vast and unwelcome responsibility. She hadn't just executed a tactical strike against a corrupt node. She hadn't just won a battle. She had performed a hostile takeover. And now the system—the human system, the one woven from belief and blood and stupid, glorious tradition—was presenting her with the keys to the kingdom.

This wasn't in the schematics. She had designed a world, not a government. She was an architect, an administrator, an observer. Not a mayor. Not a...Pirate Lord. The title was so absurd it was almost comical, yet Silas' unblinking gaze held no hint of irony.

"In the Confederacy, Ada, power isn't just taken; it's held." His gravelly voice resonated in the ruined hall, each word a stone laid for the foundation of her new prison. "This thorn proves you've uprooted the old one. Without it, the other four Lords will see you as a temporary squall, not the new tide. They will never recognize you. They will never deal with you."

Her plan had been to secure Nividia's fleet, cripple the Empire's hold, and build a better world from the ashes. It was clean. It was logical. It was about systems and strategy. It was not about managing the tangled, messy expectations of a lawless port city. It wasn't about becoming the de facto ruler of the very people she was trying to liberate.

Ada stared at the shard of ancient monster in her hand. She had wanted to be a ghost, a whisper in the code that corrected injustice. But the world she built refused to let her observe. It demanded her participation. It demanded a leader.

Her gaze lifted from the grotesque symbol in her hand, sweeping across the ruined hall. Sera, her back a taut line of power, directed two recruits hauling a fractured pillar, her voice a low, steadying command. Her strength was a tide that pushed back chaos. Across the chamber, Korina pointed a slender finger at a flickering console, her brow knitted in concentration as she salvaged what data remained from Thorne's network. Her intellect was a lens, bringing the fuzzy, broken world into sharp focus. Near the shattered throne, Erita stood perfectly still, her sharp eyes scanning the harbor through a breach in the wall, her mind a web of contingencies and calculations. Her cunning was a blade that cut through deception.

They were her generals. Her counselors. Her heart. They were, like her, forces of change.

Then her eyes returned to Silas. He stood, patient and resolute, a rock against which the storm of the last few days had broken. He hadn't fought on the front lines, yet his quiet competence was the bedrock of their entire operation. The recruits listened to him. The city knew him. He was weathered by these same seas, scarred by these same streets. He was not a foreign element. He was part of the system she now fought to save.

The pressure in her chest eased, replaced by a crystalline clarity. She saw the optimal path forward. It wasn't about holding every piece of power herself. It was about placing the right pieces in the right hands.

Ada stepped forward, the weight of the enormous tooth feeling less like a burden and more like a tool she was about to use correctly. She held it up between them, the ivory catching the pale lunar light.

"I'm an Architect, Silas." Her voice was quiet, but it cut through the din of the cleanup crew, creating a small pocket of stillness around them. "I build the foundations." She took his large, calloused hand and pressed the serrated fang back into his palm, curling his fingers around it. "You're the Admiral. You sail the ships."

The empty feeling in her own hand was immediate and liberating. A shed weight. Ada met his stunned gaze, her expression unyielding.

"Port Dominus is yours."

Silas stared, his mouth slightly agape. The flickering torchlight from the courtyard danced in his wide, disbelieving eyes. He looked down at the tooth in his hand as if seeing it for the first time, then back at her. The silence stretched, thick and profound, broken only by the distant, sudden cheer of a recruit outside who had managed to clear a major piece of debris.

Slowly, the shock in Silas' eyes gave way to a dawning comprehension, followed by the immense gravity of the charge she had just given him. He inhaled, a deep, shuddering breath, and his posture straightened. The stooped shoulders of a long-serving captain fell away, replaced by the bearing of a leader accepting his mantle.

He bowed, a deep and profoundly solemn gesture, his head bent low. It was not the bow of a subordinate to a queen. It was the bow of a lord accepting the trust of his sovereign.

Across the hall, Ada saw Sera pause in her labor; a small, approving nod her only comment. It was enough.

A cool draft swept through the breach, carrying the clean,

sharp scent of rain beginning to fall. The first fat drops splattered against the broken stone outside, a fresh, cold promise washing over the dust and ash.

Silas rose, the ancient fang held securely in his fist. He was no longer just her loyal Admiral. He was the Lord of Port Dominus, a pillar of her revolution planted firmly in the lawless heart of the Confederacy. And she was free. Free to keep moving. Free to be the architect, the spark, the catalyst. Free to burn down the rest of a corrupted world to build a new one.

CHAPTER 41

THE CASCADE FAILURE

Ada stood before the sweeping panoramic windows of the fortress command center, resting her palms against the cool, armored glass. Far below, Port Dominus was finally waking from its nightmare. The bruised purple sky of early dawn peeled back the darkness, revealing a city scarred but fiercely alive. The twin suns of Kremøtoa—one a burgeoning gold, the other a crisp, pale blue—crept over the distant horizon, casting long, fractured shadows across the bay. Fires still smoldered in the Mercantile District, sending thin, grey ribbons into the atmosphere, but the oppressive, choked silence of Thorne's localized lockdown was heavily absent. In its place rose the faint, chaotic murmur of a port returning to life: the distant, metallic clatter of shipyard cranes dragging debris, the victorious shouts of freed citizens echoing through the narrows, the rhythm of a brutal but vital heartbeat.

A deep, resonant relief settled into Ada's marrow.

The fortress command center behind her maintained a soft,

rhythmic hum, the cooling fans of Thorne's massive servers cycling down now that Korina had meticulously purged his localized network. Sera stood near the center table, wiping soot from her twin blades with practiced, economical strokes, while Erita perched on the edge of a console, tossing a stolen Ehxcehl cred-chip in her hand. Silas stood silent near the doorway, the massive prehistoric tooth still resting heavily in his grip, his eyes locked on the horizon.

Before Ada could turn away from the breathtaking view to address them, the central comms table shrieked.

A beam of raw, arcane energy violently overtook the room's dull lighting. The projection array stuttered, coughing out streams of distorted code before stabilizing into a towering pillar of teal light.

A low, melodious chuckle rolled through the room, acoustic and rich, vibrating against the sheer glass windows.

From the raw data matrix, the flickering silver hair of Nividia Rhenderon flowed into existence. The Render-Witch manifested as a crisp, life-sized hologram, her pale violet eyes gleaming with pure amusement. Bounded by a complex, crown-like halo of shimmering energy that spun lazily behind her head, she looked entirely too comfortable hovering over the ruined command desk of her former rival.

"My, my. He really let the place go to ruin," Nividia hummed, resting a spectral hand on her hip as she surveyed the structural damage through the digital feed. "I always warned Alaric his architectural tastes were painfully derivative. Too much steel, not enough imagination. Now he just looks like a sore loser."

Ada pushed off the glass, her physical exhaustion momentarily shoved aside by a flare of hyper-vigilance. She stepped directly into the projection's ambient light. "Professional courtesy, Nividia?"

"Exactly that, my dear Architect." The silver-haired woman tilted her head, her smile curling into something dangerous and delighted. Her gaze slid past Ada, landing directly on the grizzled pirate. "And I see the old sea dog has finally found a bone worth keeping. Congratulations, Mister Silas. Pirate Lord of Dominus has a much better ring to it than simple captain, doesn't it?"

Silas didn't flinch. He tightened his grip on the ivory fang and offered the Render-Witch a stiff, deeply practical nod. "Title means nothing if we don't hold the harbor. Your ships gave us the breathing room we needed."

"Oh, don't flatter me—it completely ruins my mystique." Nividia waved a dismissive, glitching hand, pixels cascading from her fingertips. She turned her piercing eyes back to Ada. "I merely wanted to verify the regime change with my own eyes. Outstanding work, truly. You've flipped the board just as I hoped. However, I'll be returning to Port Veridia by morning. My beautiful warships need their maintenance, and Imperial remnants might get a bit too curious if a grand fleet lingers outside their broken sandbox."

The hologram flickered, cyan artifacts bleeding through Nividia's long emerald gown as the signal briefly degraded and self-corrected.

"Consider this a standing offer, Ada Lynx," she purred, that smooth, melodious chuckle returning. "You and your lovely... companions certainly know how to entertain. Should you ever require a little extra chaos, you know where my shipyards lie."

Ada crossed her arms, meeting the Render-Witch's amused gaze with cold, Admin-level calculation. She recognized the usefulness of the woman's reality-bending fleet, but an unregulated, sentient anomaly was always a systemic risk.

"Chaos is always more fun when it's...controlled," Ada replied.

Nividia's eyes widened slightly, utterly delighted by the retort. "We are going to be such fantastic friends. Ta-ta, Ada."

The projection collapsed in a sudden snap of teal light, plunging the room back into the dim, grey wash of the Port Dominus dawn. The soft hum of the servers rushed back in to fill the silence.

The profound relief Ada had felt against the glass vanished, replaced by a cold, metallic wariness. She turned to face her polycule and her new Pirate Lord.

"Well," Erita muttered, catching the cred-chip and sliding it into a hidden pocket. "She's not entirely wrong about the entertainment value. But I don't know if I like owing a wildcard."

Sera locked her blades into their crimson sheaths with a sharp, echoing click. "She's a powerful ally, but she fights purely for her own amusement. If the game stops being fun for her, or if the Empire makes her a more unique offer..."

"Her core logic is entirely transactional," Korina added. She tapped her chin, gazing at the empty air, her own violet eyes distant as she analyzed the residual data flow. "Obsidian couldn't even parse the organic encryption layer she used to bypass Thorne's perimeter firewall. She operates as a closed loop. Brilliant, but entirely opaque."

Silas grunted, stepping up to join them at the central desk. "Pirates respect power above all else. She showed dominancy today, but Miss Korina has the right of it. We can't chart a safe course using a compass that paints its own magnetic north."

Ada nodded slowly, looking past them toward the breathtaking view of the battered city.

We'll have to stay sharp, that's for sure.

Korina connected *Obsidian* to the central terminal beneath the sprawling pane of armorglass. Her fingers flew across the cracked display, indexing the residual data packets left in Thorne's mainframe. The quiet settling over Port Dominus offered a fractured peace. The ambient hum of the command center—the cycling fans, the thrum of the emergency generators—provided a comforting baseline of operational normalcy.

That normalcy shattered.

The world's hum shifted. The acoustic baseline warped, plunging into a subsonic register. A bone-deep vibration seized the room, rattling Korina's sternum. *Obsidian* threw a wall of fatal syntax errors across its dark screen.

Korina struck the data-slate's hardened casing, anticipating a local interface fault. The vibration thickened, turning the air dense and heavy. Sudden nausea coiled in her stomach.

Sera locked a hand onto her hilt, dropping into a low, defensive stance against an unseen threat. Erita spun away from the console, steel flashing in her grip.

Korina looked past the broken window, out toward the creeping dawn over the northeastern coastline, just in time to witness a massive section of the mercantile wharves began to glitch.

The physical matter of the shoreline fundamentally failed. A three-kilometer stretch of the harbor blurred, the crisp morning light smearing into heavy, degraded blocks. Resolution heavily dropped in agonizing surges. Stone, water, and wood pixelated. The environment dissolved into a scarred, alien void of impossible colors—neon magenta, sharp cyan, and an absolute, textureless black.

Korina stumbled back, her spine colliding with the command desk. Primal terror, cold and absolute, suffocated her logic.

Out in the harbor, the jagged silhouette of the cargo warehouses sheared apart. The structures vanished into the expanding Corrupted Sector, deleted without a single plume of smoke or trace of debris. The ocean waves hitting the invisible edge of the anomaly simply ceased to render, locking into flat, suspended geometry over the abyss.

A horrific noise tore through the atmosphere. The deafening screech of tearing metal violently collided with the high-pitched whine of dying machines. It scaled up an unnatural frequency slope, clawing at the very edge of human consciousness.

Korina gripped the edge of the console, the casing groaning under her stark white knuckles. Her brilliant, analytical mind fractured against the sensory overload. "The w-world! It's breaking! The architecture is failing!"

Ada stood paralyzed near the center table. The violet luminescence of her Admin-view ignited in her eyes, reflecting the impossible, pixelated void consuming the horizon. Raw dread stripped the command from her frame.

"It's a Cascade Failure..."

The low drone of systemic failure alarms ruptured the sterile silence of the Prefecture Spire. Kraus Valerius stood before his immense armorglass window, watching the monochrome geometric grid of Celgrad. The wailing horns represented a total failure of protocol. Such discordant noise belonged to the unwashed masses beyond the walls, not the inner sanctum of Imperial order.

The heavy obsidian doors to his office slid apart. Three junior aides entered, bypassing all clearance protocols.

Kraus turned. His pale blue eyes locked onto the lead aide, assessing the man's ragged, labored breathing and disorganized posture. Such deviations from efficiency required correction, but the screaming alarms demanded triage.

"Prefect." The aide engaged the central hololithic projector on the obsidian desk. "We have a critical collapse of environmental parameters."

A projection of the Empire's central plains materialized. A sickly green stain corrupted the flawless topography. Kraus stepped closer, the sterile glow illuminating his sharp, angular features. The stain obscured a vast swathe of territory due east of the agricultural hub of Duskhaven.

Kraus placed his hands on the polished edge of the table. The gravelly hum of his voice resonated over the wailing alarms. "Quantify the variable."

"One hundred and fifty square kilometers." The second aide stepped up. She fed raw field-telemetry into the projector. "The expansion rate defies all known thaumaturgical models. It consumed the fertile fields in minutes and approaches the Akari River."

Kraus expanded the projection with a motion of his fingers. The macro-map dissolved into a direct visual feed sourced from an automated patrol drone.

The image displayed pure entropy. The golden wheat fields of the plains no longer existed. In their place lay a fetid swampland, choked with bubbling mud and twisted, rot-blackened roots. Bioluminescent fungi pulsed with a toxic green light, spreading across the decay like a living infection.

The corruption was a systemic anomaly. Kraus narrowed his eyes. The edges of the trees and rocks possessed a jagged, blocky texture. They lacked the smooth geometry of reality. Among the glowing fungi and roiling mud, things moved. They were not beasts born of flesh and bone. They consisted of shifting prisms of broken light, phasing in and out of existence. These pixelated entities tore through the remaining healthy soil, leaving fragmented voids in their wake. They moved with a jerky stop-motion gait, ignoring gravity and momentum.

"They consume the soil, Prefect. They multiply with the rot." The first aide backed away from the pulsing projection.

Kraus did not admonish the man for his fear. His own chest tightened. An icy dread, sharp and foreign, pierced the absolute emotional detachment he required to lead.

He observed the pixelated entities duplicate. They were a contagion. A disease of pure chaos tearing apart the localized environmental matrix. This was not a localized weather anomaly or a rogue elemental surge. This was a complete rotting of the world's infrastructure.

His mind processed the variables, accessing the data from the interrogation chamber weeks prior. Ada Lynx. She manipulated the environment with similar disregard for established laws. She bypassed complex security matrices. She unmade the physical world to serve her needs.

Kraus exhaled a metered breath. The equation clicked into a terrifying new arrangement.

Ada Lynx was not the root cause. She was the symptom. Her emergence, the incident at Oakhaven, the system glitches reported on the northern borders—they were all precursors to this planetary contagion. A fundamental disease had taken root, and he had been consumed with acquiring a single asset instead of calculating the collapse of the entire operational framework.

The drone feed glitched. A large, jagged entity lunged toward the lens, its form a blur of rendering errors and screaming green light. The projection shattered into static before stabilizing back into the macro-map. The sickly green stain crawled a millimeter toward the blue vein of the Akari River.

Kraus leaned over the console, his knuckles bone-white against the dark stone. The meticulous logic that defined his existence offered no protocol for countering the unmaking of reality. He stared at the expanding green lesion, acknowledging the inescapable, catastrophic nature of the threat. The Empire's systemic integrity faced total excision.

"Malware. Sentient, self-replicating malware..." Kraus closed his eyes, the icy dread crystallizing into undeniable fact. His voice dropped to a gravelly whisper. "By the Void..."

To the High Council of Veritas, the unraveling of Kremøtoa was not a tragedy. It was an unprecedented, spectacular influx of raw data.

Inside the Grand Sanctum of the Veritas Archives, the apocalypse commanded absolute, clinical fascination.

Complex equations and cascading data streams danced across the polished obsidian surface of the central table. The High Council surrounded the display, their faces bathed in the harsh, sterile glow of the holographic projection. No one gasped. No one wept. They observed the magnificent failure of reality with the detached curiosity of scholars dissecting a fascinating new biological specimen.

A sharp hiss of sliding doors punctuated the silence. A junior archivist stepped into the sanctum, moving with rapid, precise strides, though a tremor betrayed his composure. He transferred a stream of encrypted telemetry from his data-slate directly into the central obsidian console.

Instantly, a cluster of red icons pulsed across the projection map, blooming like a digital hemorrhage.

Chancellor Pantium leaned forward, his ancient hands resting lightly on the table's edge. "The buffer zones have collapsed." His voice was dry and precise, echoing like rustling parchment in the cavernous room. "The Ashen States have breached containment. The anomaly propagates westward into the Southern Marshes."

Councilor Celerun adjusted his robes, a faint sheen of sweat visible on his brow. The youngest member of the council stared at the rapidly advancing red tide. "That trajectory places the phenomenon on a direct intersection with our eastern border. If the Intellective States are exposed to this rot..."

"Panic is an inefficient response to systemic instability." Grand Magister Xehon did not look up from the sprawling data streams. His sharp features remained entirely immobile, projecting an aura of immense, unyielding intellectual authority. He reached out, his skeletal fingers manipulating the holographic projection, isolating the cascading variables of the corrupted zones.

"The corruption vector is accelerating," Master Centrinah observed, her tone devoid of its usual political warmth. She analyzed the sociological implications scrolling down her sector of the obsidian table. "Current projections calculate the total dissolution of border settlements within forty-eight hours. The political disruption will be absolute. The Empire will undoubtedly point weapons at Rhedeon, or us, seeking a scapegoat."

"Let them point their weapons," Xehon replied. "They attempt to shoot at a hurricane. They do not understand the board upon which they play."

Archivist Itania stood near the periphery of the glowing map, her posture impeccably straight, her silver-streaked hair pulled back into a severe chignon. She adjusted the thin, silver-rimmed spectacles perched on the end of her nose. To her perception, the event was not merely a visual corruption; it was a discordant, screaming silence in the fundamental flow of truth.

"A fascinating hypothesis from the Empire's strategists, entirely devoid of merit," Itania stated. Her smooth contralto voice rolled over the chamber, carrying the cool chill of a deep, still library. "The metaphysical resonance of the event aligns with the principles of foundational decay. Observe the degradation pattern." She tapped a silver-clad finger against a floating diagnostic rune. "The code is not being overwritten by a foreign entity. It is unraveling."

Celerun swallowed hard, glancing between Xehon and Itania. "Are we certain this is not the Confederacy launching an unauthorized thaumaturgical strike? Or the rumored anomaly out of Celgrad?"

Scholar Atomuzk traced the intricate frost patterns forming on the edge of the obsidian table, deliberately avoiding Celerun's anxious gaze.

"Hmm..." Atomuzk tapped a rhythmic, uneven beat against the dark stone. "Or perhaps the Wordæus Empress orchestrated a continental false-flag operation using localized reality-deletion to improve her trade tariffs."

He paused, letting the sheer absurdity of the variable hang in the sterile air.

"A fascinating theory, Celerun," Atomuzk continued, his raspy voice barely rising above a whisper. "Assuming, of course, one operates under a total deficit of foundational logic. Anomaly signatures are not political maneuvers. They are mathematical inevitabilities."

Xehon waved a hand, dismissing the junior councilor's anxiety alongside the very concept of external interference. "You look for actors where there is only architecture. Pirates, priests and anomalies do not possess the bandwidth to unmake the Continental Shell. No localized entity initiated this."

Xehon met Itania's piercing grey eyes across the dancing equations. A silent, heavy acknowledgment passed between the Grand Magister and the Archivist. Behind the detached academic curiosity lay a deep, hidden knowledge. The red icons pulsing across the map were not a surprise. They were a systemic inevitability.

"We shall observe," Xehon instructed, turning his gaze back to the magnificent failure rendering across the obsidian. "The system is failing from within. Our directive is to record the methodology of its collapse."

The High Council of Veritas returned their attention to the

dancing lights, watching the world burn in absolute, serene silence.

The white jade throne offered no comfort. Empress Thema Iridia Archivia the Nineteenth sat rigid, her statuesque frame draped in heavy, layered robes of black, crimson, and gold. High above, thick iron chains groaned softly as Soul-Censers swayed from the vaulted ceiling. They exuded a faint, ethereal glow that barely pierced the cloying darkness of Codexia's central sanctum. Down the length of the massive nave, flickering braziers cast long shadows that writhed against the geometric symbols etched into the stone walls.

"The Word! The Word! The Word!"

The unified chant of the assembled clergy echoed through the cavernous chamber, a rhythmic, relentless heartbeat of absolute devotion.

Lady Calibree knelt at the base of the dais. Her posture remained ramrod straight, the intricate silver tattoos across her half-shaved scalp catching the dancing light of the braziers. Her dark grey eyes reflected neither warmth nor fear, fixed firmly on the polished steps.

"Speak, High Justicaress." Thema's voice, serene yet carrying the terrible weight of centuries, projected effortlessly over the continuous chant.

"The phenomenon expands, Your Divine Eminence." Calibree's voice dropped into a flat, clinical monotone, diagnosing a terminal rot. "Reality unravels at the edges of our land in the southeast. The Sun-Scoured Lands dissolve into jagged squares of impossible light. The sand itself bleeds into nothingness. Border sentinels report a creeping, unnatural darkness that devours physical matter, leaving behind floating shapes lacking earthly form."

Thema's pale, translucent blue eyes locked onto Calibree. Logical analysis failed. Fanatical certainty stepped into the breach, cold and absolute.

Contamination. Filth. A test of the faithful.

"This is no natural calamity." Thema rose from the white jade throne. The layers of her vestments settled around her like the armor of a holy executioner. "It is the physical manifestation of heresy. Demonic energy clawing at the fabric of our sacred design."

Calibree remained utterly motionless, accepting the diagnosis. "The variable must be excised. If left unchecked, the unclean contamination will breach the capital within days."

"It is a trial of faith." Thema descended the first three steps of the dais. The heavy golden symbols on her robes glinted in the half-light. "The Cosmos tests the strength of our doctrine. If the unholy dark seeks to consume the light of our ordered world, we shall answer it with the absolute purity of the flame."

Thema turned her gaze toward the shadowed alcoves lining the sanctum, where the heavily armored zealots stood in perfect, silent readiness.

"Mobilize the Fists of the Word." The accumulated authority of nineteen rulers rang through the silent air, cutting over the relentless chanting. "Equip the Purifiers with ignis-casters and sanctified phosphorus. You will march to the southeast. You will scorch the earth before the infection can spread. Where the demon seeks to unmake our reality, you will build a wall of holy ash."

Calibree dipped her head in a crisp, sharp nod. "The blade, not the poison. The containment zone will be absolute."

Thema raised her arms. Her features, usually serene and wise, twisted into a terrifying mask of divine wrath.

"WE WILL CAUTERIZE THE WOUND THAT FESTERS UPON THE WORLD'S FLESH!"

The gathered clergy slammed their staves against the stone floor in synchronized approval. The hypnotic chant swelled, vibrating in Thema's bones, an iron shield of dogma raised against the silent, pixelated void consuming their borders.

"The Word! The Word! The Word!"

The command center was a tomb of cold steel and silent screens. Hours ago, it had been the heart of a tyrant's domain; now, it was just a room. A collection of uncomfortable cots had been brought in, arranged between consoles that hummed with dormant power. Ada lay on one, a thin, rough blanket pulled up to her chin, and stared into the oppressive darkness. Sleep was a distant country she had no visa for.

Victory. They had won. Port Dominus was free, Thorne was a shattered husk trapped in a prison of his own making, and their revolution had its first true foothold. Yet, the triumph felt like ash in her mouth. The cheers of the liberated citizens, the relieved faces of their recruits, the grudging respect from Nividia—it all dissolved against the backdrop of a much larger, more insidious dread. The battle felt meaningless. A single skirmish won on a planetary scale, but they were losing the war against... what?

The world was coming apart at the seams. Ada saw it not as a philosopher might, but as a programmer watching her life's work corrupt from the inside out. The coastline glitching into a pixelated void wasn't a magical anomaly; it was a *catastrophic memory leak.* The Ashen States weren't a blighted land; they were a runaway process, a sentient malware devouring system resources and rewriting reality with gibberish. The code was fraying. It was a cascade failure, spreading through the core of Kremøtoa like a cancer. *But what was the trigger? What was causing it?*

Her eyelids grew heavy, the hum of the consoles a low, hypnotic drone. She drifted, not into sleep, but into the gray space between states. The darkness behind her eyes wasn't empty. It flickered. A jagged line of violet static tore across her vision, followed by a fractured image of a bell tower, its geometry impossible, twisting in on itself. Then, a face—Samantha's—but the data was corrupted. One eye was where her mouth should be, the pixels dissolving and reforming into a silent scream.

The images flashed faster, a strobe of broken data and corrupted memories. She was back in the sterile white room from her past, but the walls were stitched with threads of buzzing, angry code. A sound began to build, a low thrum that vibrated in her bones, a sound she recognized with a lurch of cold dread. It wasn't just a sound. It was a connection attempt. A forced handshake protocol.

What was that? A voice...

No, not a voice. A signal. A message packet, forced through her mental firewalls.

From... Kløak....

The realization was a physical blow, a violation so profound it bypassed reason and struck directly at the primal core of her being. This world, her mind, was supposed to be the one place she was safe. The one place *they* couldn't reach her.

NO!

A scream of pure, unadulterated terror ripped through the quiet of the command center. It was a raw, jagged sound, stripped of thought or language, the sound of a soul being torn. For a split second, it felt external, an attack from the shadows. Then the raw, burning pain in her own throat registered, and she knew.

The scream was hers.

She shot bolt upright on the cot, the rough blanket falling away. Her heart hammered against her ribs like a trapped bird. A film of cold sweat broke out across her skin, chilling her instantly. The glitched images of the dream still flickered at the edges of her vision, ghosts of a digital horror.

The telepathic link, which had been a quiet, background hum of sleeping minds, exploded into a cacophony of alarm.

Ada? Rina... are you alright? Sera's thought was the first to cut through the panic, a blade of pure concern, sharp and immediate.

What in the Void was that? Erita's mental voice was laced with its usual cynicism, but underneath was a raw edge of shock. *Sounded like a banshee's wail.*

Bio-etheric spike off the charts! Adrenaline, cortisol, extreme sympathetic nervous system response! Ada! Report! What's your status? Korina's thoughts were a frantic cascade of data and terror, her analytical mind struggling to process the raw, overwhelming emotion flooding the network.

Ada gasped for air, her lungs aching. She clutched her head, trying to force the corrupted images from her mind, trying to silence the phantom echo of Kløak's signal. The silent, concerned faces of her partners materialized in her mind's eye, a stark contrast to the digital monstrosities she had just witnessed.

They were coming.

The mental link was a storm of panicked voices, a frantic triage of concern crashing against the shores of her consciousness. Ada barely registered them. The world outside her own skull had compressed into a pinprick of irrelevant light. The command center, the cots, the low hum of technology—all of it faded into a distant echo. The scream had torn a hole in her reality—and through that hole, the true horror was pouring in.

Before she could form a coherent thought, before she could even answer Sera's desperate mental plea, the connection slammed back into her. It wasn't a memory this time. It was a live feed, a *forced override.*

The sterile white void of her emergency interface flooded her vision, overwriting the dim command center. In the center of that nothingness, Kløak materialized. The haunted, headless pirate coat, its frayed sleeves drifting in an unseen wind, hovered before her. There was no greeting. There was only the gravelly, synthesized rasp of the relay system activating, a sound like grinding stones.

And then, the message.

It scrolled across her mind's eye in a simple, brutal text overlay, the font a familiar sans-serif from her Earth-side OS. But worse than the text was the audio that came with it—Samantha's voice, filtered through layers of digital distortion and cosmic distance, but still achingly, undeniably hers. Panicked. Tearing apart at the edges with fear. *She must have sent a voice attachment...oh my void...*

Ada? Everything oki? I'M STARTING TO GET REALLY SCARED. We haven't heard from you. Your mom is with me. We're coming over. Please Ada! Please just text back so we don't call 119...Please...

The message looped. The text scrolled again, the audio playing over it, a desperate, repeating prayer from a world away.

"Sam..." Ada's voice was a choked, broken whisper in the darkness of the command center. The sound of her friend's name on her own lips was an agony. A wave of grief, so powerful it felt like a physical impact, slammed into her. *Oh, Sam, I'm so sorry. You're scared. You're terrified.* She had done this. In her selfish flight to this perfect world, she had left her best friend, her only friend, to face this sickening uncertainty.

The guilt was a physical weight, crushing the air from her lungs. She saw Samantha's face in her mind—her warm, expressive eyes crinkled not with laughter, but with fear. And her mother...gods, her mother was there. The two most important people from her old life, standing outside her apartment door, about to find...*what?*

Please Ada! Please just text back so we don't call 119.

The number blazed in her mind. One-one-nine. Not the Imperial emergency frequency, not some arcane distress signal. The emergency number for every Prefecture of Japan. A detail so mundane, so *real,* it cut through her panic with the chilling precision of a surgeon's scalpel.

They were going to call for help. An ambulance. The police. They would break down her door.

They'll find my body.

The thought was a shard of ice in her gut. They would find her lying on the floor, hooked up to the machine, her physical form unresponsive, her vitals...failing?

Her eyes shot wide open in the dark.

Failing.

A cascade of data points slammed together in her mind with the force of a tectonic collision. The coastline glitching into a pixelated void. The expanding, cancerous swamp of the Ashen States. The spontaneous, reality-bending anomalies. The Pattern Blight. The Malware. All of it. The Cascade Failure. The glitches... they weren't just happening. They were accelerating. *Getting worse.*

Is it...is it tied to my physical state?

The pieces clicked into place, forming a picture of such profound horror that her earlier terror seemed like a child's fleeting nightmare. The supercomputer she built was the server. Her mind was the admin. But the entire system, the entire universe of Kremøtoa, drew its core processing power and stability from the most volatile component in the entire setup: her own biological, human body. A body she had abandoned. A body that was now, undoubtedly...dying.

The world wasn't failing. The *hardware* was failing.

Oh gods. The realization was a silent, soul-shattering scream that dwarfed the one she'd let out moments before. The thought was a final, terrible key turning in a lock she never knew existed.

It's not the world that's dying. It's me.

The command center, her partners' frantic mental voices, the very air in her lungs—it all ceased to exist. There was only the blinding, stark clarity of the abyss that had just opened beneath her.

It's all connected. The logic gate in her mind slammed shut with apocalyptic finality. *The glitches. The messages. My body...is the server. And the server is crashing.*

Every anomaly, every corrupted file, every patch of pixelated nothingness that had terrified her was just a symptom. *A system warning.* The Pattern Blight wasn't a magical plague; it was a cascade of rounding errors from a CPU struggling to maintain processes. The Ashen States weren't a geographical anomaly; they were corrupted sectors on a failing hard drive. Her hard drive. Her *body*.

Samantha's message echoed, not as a cry for help, but as a death sentence. *Please just text back so we don't call 119.*The paramedics. They would arrive. They would see her body, still, cold, hooked into the machine. They would follow their protocols. They would do everything in their power to save her.

They would unplug her.

The image seared itself onto the back of her eyelids. A well-meaning hand reaching for a power cord. A doctor giving a somber nod. And then...nothing.

If they disconnect me...everyone here...Sera, Korina, Erita...they all just...vanish. The concept was too vast, too monstrous for her mind to contain. They wouldn't die. It was worse than dying. They would be *deleted*. Cease to have ever existed. A line of code, an entire universe of emergent, beautiful, flawed consciousness, wiped clean. Reduced to a null value.

Ada...babe...talk to us... Sera's mental voice was a desperate plea, clawing at the edges of her awareness.

But Ada couldn't hear it over the roaring in her own head. The terrible, beautiful, heart-wrenching paradox of it all was a physical weight, pressing down, crushing her. Samantha. Her best friend. Her one true link to the life she'd abandoned. Samantha's love, her worry, her desperate need to make sure Ada was okay...that was the executioner's axe. The love of the person she left behind was the single greatest threat to the people she now loved more than life itself.

Samantha's love for me will be the thing that erases them. My past is literally going to ***delete my future.***

The delicate architecture of her sanity, already stressed to its limits, finally gave way. The strain was too much. The logic was too cruel. The weight was unbearable.

I can't...

Her legs buckled. The world tilted on a sickening axis, the worried faces of her partners blurring into a watercolor smear of violet, crimson, and gold through the sudden, hot flood of tears.

ADA! SPEAK TO US!... Erita's voice was sharp, a crack of a whip in the storm of their shared panic.

I can't...

The cold, metal floor of the command center rushed up to meet her. The impact was a dull, distant thud, a shock that barely registered through the cataclysm erupting in her soul. She crumpled into a heap, her body curling in on itself as if to ward off a physical blow.

A sound tore from her throat, a raw, guttural noise that was not a word, not a scream, but the pure, animal sound of a spirit breaking. It was a sob, but it felt alien, dredged up from a place of horror she never knew existed within her. Another followed, and another, each one a violent, racking spasm that shook her entire frame.

*Ada! ADA! SPEAK TO ME!...Sera!...Erita—HELP ME!...*Korina's panic was a high-frequency scream in the telepathic link, a frantic stream of frantic concern and medical data that was utterly useless against the metaphysical wound that had just been torn open.

Hands were on her, warm and steadying. *Sera's,* she thought. A soft touch on her hair. *Korina's.* But they felt miles away, across an impossible gulf of understanding. They were trying to comfort a person, but she wasn't a person anymore. She was the ghost at her own funeral, the sole witness to a coming apocalypse she was powerless to stop.

"Ada, what is it?" Sera's voice, real and thick with alarm, cut through the telepathic noise. "What did you hear?"

Ada tried to answer. She opened her mouth, but the words were shards of glass, shredded by the force of her sobs.

She had to warn them. She had to explain the impossible, horrifying truth. But how? How could she tell them that their entire existence was tethered to a dying body on another world? How could she explain that the love of her friend was about to become their oblivion?

She pushed herself up on trembling arms, her vision swimming. She looked at them—Sera's fierce, protective scowl; Korina's wide, terrified violet eyes; Erita's guarded, sharp-edged concern—and the love she felt for them was a fresh wave of agony. They were so real. So beautifully, perfectly real. And they were about to be erased.

"They're..." she choked out, the words dissolving into a shuddering gasp. "They're...coming..."

Korina knelt beside her, her hand hovering over Ada's shoulder, afraid to touch her. "Who, Ada? Who is coming? A new threat?"

Ada shook her head violently, another raw sob escaping her. It wasn't a villain. It was a hero. A friend. That was the horror of it.

"...to turn it off..." she whispered, the words barely audible, a fragment of the terrifying truth. The faces staring down at her registered only confusion, their fear deepening. They didn't understand. They couldn't.

She collapsed back to the floor, her strength gone. Her last coherent thought was a prayer to a system that she herself had built, a plea to a god that was her.

Please...don't let them turn it off.

TO BE CONTINUED...

Scimitar Isles
Blackbox Harbor
Port Vengeance
Rogue's Run
Korsair Confederacy
Port Indigo
Port Veridia
Chroma
Port Dominus
Port Cobalt
Deadlock Bay
Barrier-Keep
Akari River
Genesis Meadows
Celgrad
Oakhaven
The Ehxcehl Empire
Port Azure
Silence
Duskhaven
Logic-Gate
Port Hyperion
The Intellective States of Kor
Slate Port
Veritas
Fort Kor
Alder Lake

Sunken Core
Eastern Reaches
Cove
The Free Realm of Rhedeon
Query's Keep
Prism-Fall
Hiito Shinku Plateau
The Wordæus Theocracy
Apocrypha
Strait of Truth
Codexia
Doc-ehx
Porto Sanctus
Southern Marshes
Spire of Hope
The Ashen States
N
W
E
S
The Supercontinent of Kremøtoa
Circa
SCY_1001
0
1000
Kilometers
Ver. 7.3.4

LEXICON CODEX

GLOSSARY OF TERMS

Welcome, Traveler, to the world of **Kremøtoa**. Like any new world, it has its own unique language, its own deeply ingrained cultural beliefs, and its own scientific principles that govern the very fabric of reality. To aid you on your journey alongside Ada and her companions, I have compiled this **Lexicon Codex**.

Within these pages, you will find a guide to the terminology, peoples, and peculiar turns-of-phrase that bring this world to life. May it serve as your trusted companion, illuminating the path as you delve deeper into the mysteries of ***The Kremøtoa Codex*** series.

In-World Terminology & Lexicon

- **Aether**: The term used by inhabitants of **Kremøtoa** to describe the fundamental energy that flows through all things, which they believe is the source of all life and magic. Ada understands this is simply the user interface for the world's code.
- **Axiomatic Rendering:** A highly advanced and dangerous form of creation thaumaturgy practiced in Rhedeon. Unlike traditional construction, it does not use physical materials but instead 'grows' structures by planting a 'seed of pure logic' and letting the world's raw code build around it. The process is chaotic, unpredictable, and prone to 'cascade failures'.
- **Byts**: The primary form of physical currency in **Kremøtoa**, coming in platinum, gold, silver, and copper denominations. The name is a clever, if unintentional, echo of Ada's programming background.
- **Cascade Failure:** The in-world term for a catastrophic system crash where a paradoxical or corrupted line of code causes a chain reaction, leading to the violent "un-rendering" of an object or structure.
- **Data Corruption**: The in-world term for systemic glitches, bugs, and errors in the world's code. It is perceived by the **Ehxcehl** Empire not as a technical issue, but as a tangible, malevolent force of chaos that threatens reality and must be eradicated.
- **Malware**: A term introduced by Ada to describe a malicious, targeted corruption of the world's code,

distinct from random **Data Corruption**. She explains it as a perversion of **thaumaturgy**, like a 'disease' or 'virus' infecting the fabric of reality. The cursed idol on the **Sea Serpent** is the first identified instance of this.

- **Matākyasshu:** The designation Ada gives to her newly created extra-dimensional inventory, which functions as a 'matter cache'. This is a power unique to her as the Administrator, allowing her to store physical objects in a pocket of absolute nothingness that she can summon at will.
- **Pattern Blight**: A term coined by Korina to describe the effects of **malware** after Ada's explanation. It refers to a disruption or corruption in the underlying 'axiomatic framework' of the world.
- **Polycule**: A term Ada introduces from her world (Earth) to describe a network of interconnected loving relationships. It becomes the designation for the F/F/F/F polyamorous relationship between Ada, Sera, Korina, and Erita.
- **Sovereign Steel**: A rare and powerful alloy specifically engineered to nullify all directed energy and arcane signatures, including Ada's Admin powers; Thorne's vault is constructed from it.
- **Systemic Integrity**: The ideal state of the world according to the **Ehxcehl** Empire; a reality free from chaos and **Data Corruption**, maintained through rigid order and control.
- **Thaumaturgy / Thauma**: The common term for the study of magic/magic in **Kremøtoa**. Practitioners

believe they are manipulating **Aether** to achieve their results; Ada, however, knows it is simply a way for users to interact with and execute commands within the world's code.

People, Places & Organizations

- **Aegis Order / Aegis Knights**: The elite military and enforcement arm of the **Ehxcehl** Empire, tasked with maintaining **Systemic Integrity** and combating **Data Corruption**. Sera [was] a high-ranking Knight-Commander within this order.
- **Azure Rose**: A powerful merchant guild in Port Dominus and a major rival to Alaric Thorne. They are led by the shrewd and respected Master Willem.
- **Celgrad**: The capital city of the **Ehxcehl** Empire. It is a marvel of geometric precision, characterized by obsidian spires and a society built on flawless symmetry and rigid control.
- **Ehxcehl Empire**: The dominant political power on the continent, ruled from **Celgrad** by Prefect Kraus Valerius. It is an authoritarian regime obsessed with order, control, and the eradication of anything it deems chaotic or corrupt.
- **Intellective States of Kor**: A nation / political entity known for its scholars and technological pursuits; Korina implies they value progress and innovation over the Empire's caution and control.
- **Korsair Confederacy**: A lawless and chaotic nation on the north-western coast—known for its dens of thieves, fluid loyalties, and the value it places on information as currency.
- **Port Azure**: A coastal port city that serves as a gateway between the lands of the **Ehxcehl** Empire and the

territory of the **Korsair Confederacy,** after sailing north around Cape Sabre.

- **Port Dominus**: The capital and heart of the **Korsair Confederacy**. It is a chaotic metropolis where powerful guilds control trade and information is the most valuable commodity.
- **Rhedeon**: One of the major in-world entities, mentioned alongside **Ehxcehl** and **Korsair**. It is described as pulsing with raw, untamed arcane energy.
- **Thorne, Alaric:** A corrupt and powerful figure within the Korsair Confederacy, a corrupt guild master, who serves as a primary antagonist in the early part of the revolution.
- **Veritas Archives**: A prestigious institution of knowledge and scholarship, based in the city of Veritas —from which Korina was exiled.

Cultural Lore & Exclamations

- **Argent**: The largest and brightest of **Kremøtoa's** three moons, casting a silver light. It is seen as a watchful guardian of order and power, and its cycles are believed to influence the potency of **thaumaturgy**.
- "**Argent's Light**": A common exclamation of surprise, awe, or oath-taking, similar to "My gød..." or "Good heavens".
- **BIOCE**: The smallest and most distant of the three moons, about which there is little to no known lore.

Ada knows this is because she used it as a placeholder name (**B.I.O.C.E.**) during development and never assigned it any specific properties.

- **Blood Year**: A colloquial term for a year of misfortune or hardship, often associated with the cycles of the moon, Cache. There is no widely-accepted standard, however, what constitutes a significant enough year of misfortune or hardship to qualify a year as a '**Blood Year**'.
- **'Born Under Cache' / The Bleeding Moon**: A common superstition that being born under the red light of the moon Cache is a curse that guarantees a life of bad luck and ill omens. Korina, who was born under its zenith, has always been haunted by this.
- **Cache**: The second largest of **Kremøtoa's** three moons, appearing as a broken, crescent-shaped moon that glows with an ominous red light. It is widely considered a symbol of corruption, cosmic injury, and ill omen. Ada knows its true function is to act as the world's system cache, a repository for corrupted data—rather than for storing temporary data-information, like a normal 'cache' usage implies.
- **Kiri Fūsa**: A term Silas uses for a strange, persistent, and unnaturally uniform bank of fog that acts as a physical blockade at sea. Ada subconsciously translates the Japanese phrase to 'Fog Blockade' and realizes it is an emergent, unprogrammed anomaly in her world.
- **"Void..." / "By the Void..."**: An exclamation used to express shock, exasperation, or disbelief, often in a

negative context. It is the conceptual opposite of the divine or orderly (essentially the in-world term for the exclamation of profanity: "F_ck!").

NOTE: As a compounding Lexicon can be helpful, it gets to be problematic with larger books. Therefore, the QR-Code is provided to visit the official wiki online for a complete list of terms. Thank you for understanding.

ABOUT THE AUTHOR: SAEKO KURENAIHANA

Saeko Kurenaihana is the mastermind behind *The Kremøtoa Codex* series, a captivating blend of LitRPG, Science-Fantasy, LGBTQ+ Romance, and Isekai.

I'm no one special, just a neurodivergent author that wanted to put my own story into print for the sake of myself; recognition, fame, glory—all unnecessary. I feel as though I've earned that with the history I've gone through. If you enjoyed this book, my best wish for you is that my characters and their world can live rent free in your mind to give you joy.

amazon.com/stores/author/B0FHBTGMGP

www.ingramcontent.com/pod-product-compliance
Lightning Source LLC
Chambersburg PA
CBHW020945310726
48980CB00001B/57
* 9 7 9 8 9 9 9 8 5 8 3 1 3 *